The Bend of the River

Book Two in the Tenochtitlan Trilogy

Edward Rickford

ISBN: 978-1-7351319-1-7

Table of Contents

Mexico 1519

KEY:

☁	Cholula	∩	Quiahuiztlan	⚓	San Juan de Ulua
🐾	Tlaxcala	◄	Villa Rica de la Veracruz	✳	Pontochan
⚔	Tenochtitlan	○	Cempoala		

Gulf of Mexico

Iztaccihuatl Matlalcueitl

Popocatepetl   Citlaltepetl

Pacific Ocean

Central Mexico 1519

KEY:

☁	Cholula	⬧	Xaltocan	◡	Chalco
🐾	Tlaxcala	○	Tetzcoco	∩	Otompan
⚔	Tenochtitlan	🦗	Iztapalapa		
🐾	Tepeaca	◖	Tlacopan		

Iztaccihuatl   Matlalcueitl

Popocatepetl

Glossary

Mexica: the most powerful people in pre-Hispanic Mexico. Also known as the Aztec, an erroneous demonym popularized by 19th century historians.

Great Speaker: term that refers to the highest-ranking political figure in the Mexica Confederacy.

Totonacs: disgruntled vassals of the Mexica.

Tlaxcala: an independent nation in the basin of Mexico. Avowed enemies of the Mexica.

Motecuhzoma: leader of the Mexica Confederacy. The Anglicized version of his name is Montezuma and the Hispanicized version of his name is Moctezuma.

Spanish League: about 3 miles. Similar in length to a long-run, a Mexica unit of length.

Malintze/Doña Marina: indigenous woman who translates for the Spanish. Enslaved for most of her childhood, she speaks Nahuatl, Yoko Ochoko, and Spanish.

Teteo: Nahuatl term that roughly translates, in English, to powerful, mystical people. Singular of this word is *teotl*.

Pronunciation key

In Nahuatl, x is pronounced the same way that English speakers pronounce sh in shell.

In Nahuatl, tz in pronounced the same way that English speakers pronounce tz in ritzy.

In Nahuatl, i is pronounced the same way that English speakers pronounce ee in seep.

Synopsis for The Serpent and the Eagle, Book One in The Tenochtitlan Trilogy:

In early 1519, Hernando Cortés sails for the New World with a Spanish army as factious as it is rapacious. They arrive in the Yucatan Peninsula expecting to be welcomed by friendly Indians—only to discover the local war chiefs are keen on battle.

Shortly after landing, the weary explorers must decide if they will abide by a distasteful ultimatum or if they will engage a numerically superior foe. The Spaniards choose the latter and crush the local forces. Chastened by defeat, the war chiefs bend the knee and inform Cortés of a mysterious people far to the north that live in magnificent cities far grander than any in Europe. These people are known as the Mexica, some today call them Aztec, and they have amassed a fortune of Biblical proportions though trade and battle.

To march upon their cities will invite conflict with a fearsome monarch who commands a military machine unrivaled both in power and brutality. Undeterred by the prospect of war, Cortés leads the Spaniards northward.

The Spaniards reach Mexica lands in short time, but the sheer might of the Mexica polity deters them from launching an immediate attack. Instead, they begin dialoguing with local envoys. The Mexica strive to be generous hosts and the Spaniards are quite pleased to be greeted with lavish presents rather than a hostile army. Their hosts, however, are far from pleased by Cortés' persistent entreaties for a personal audience with the Mexica monarch. Hoping to put an end to such impetuous talk, the Mexica terminate all trading relations with the "pale people" and the Spaniards are forced to fend for themselves in a harsh, alien environment.

Many Spaniards clamor to return home as disease takes its toll. Desperate to save the expedition, Cortés enters into an alliance with aggrieved Mexica vassals. His would-be allies soon prove they are not above treachery or deceit, but Cortés insists they play a vital role in the prospective march on the Mexica capital. His fellow countrymen harbor serious reservations about the fledgling alliance; some fear the Mexica cannot be defeated. Battling mutiny and desertion, Cortés sinks the ships that could be used to escape the mainland. With no option of retreat, the Spaniards must commit to a grueling campaign that could lead to unimaginable wealth or gruesome death.

Part One
The March
August-December, 1519.

Totonac Province

Tetzcoco Province

Chapter 1

Malintze hugged her legs close as a cold blast of wind tore through the mountain pass, prompting a bout of howling and cursing from the *teteo*. Their loud protests warmed her about as much as her thin woolen hose, but it did provide some validation. During the first few hours of the march, the *teteo* had been merry as children and spent practically every minute extolling the beauty of the land. They marveled over giant felines that could tread water like a dog, dragonflies that zipped by with the speed of arrows, four-legged river animals with plated skin, trees that reached thrice as high as any mast... but that was in the lowlands.

Thereafter, the route gave way to highlands dominated by an enormous rocky mountain range stretching all the way to the horizon and beyond. During the first day of the ascent, the *teteo* refused to give voice to their pain, and Malintze might have forgotten their presence altogether had it not been for their continuous grunting and panting.

Come evening, the army encamped on a large plateau, but none of her traveling companions made mention of the stunning view. The lowlands were visible in every direction for countless long-runs, as well as the beach where Fort Veracruz had been erected and the bay where Cortés scuttled the fleet. Nevertheless, the weary marchers appeared to only be concerned with the monstrously steep trail that seemed to ascend all the way to that place the *teteo* called Heaven.

Come morning, the marching began anew, and she joined the long procession of *teteo*, Totonacs, soldiers, and slaves moving up the trail. A suffocating silence hung over the group, and there were few sounds other than labored breathing and muttered curses. She had grown used to the *teteo* blurting out every little thing that came to mind—Malintze now knew exactly how much a feline pelt would fetch back in Spain and how long it would take to convert a copse of pine trees to lumber—so their failure to remark on the rigors of the march was jarring. Surely they also noticed the sharp rocks that stabbed through leather soles, the miserable chill brought on by the thin air that gave her such terrible headaches.

The temperature had to be the worst aspect of the climb. Never in all her life had she been so cold. She wrapped herself in every layer she could find but that was not enough to keep the shivers away. Judging by the dreary expressions of the porters and the slaves, they were just as ill-prepared for the drop in temperature. Even the *teteo* were struggling with the cold, despite their thick cotton armor and their familiarity with that strange season called winter, a time when lakes froze over and the skies rained ice. Not so long ago, those stories about winter seemed ridiculous. Now she wondered if she might see some of those wonders for herself.

Malintze buried her chin in her chest and rubbed her frozen arms. Tired as she was, she hoped the march would soon resume. Stillness brought on a cold that no amount of layering could protect her from. As much as her back ached from marching, she knew she could not stay seated more than a few minutes.

I would give anything for some hot pepper soup. A soup so hot it could warm not only her mouth, not only her face, but her entire body. She looked for ingredients but saw only rocks, shrubs, and trees. She shook her head and bit her lip in frustration.

A *teotl* sat down next to her and offered his canteen. Armor covered so much of his body that it took her a

2

moment to recognize the figure as Cortés. Malintze wrapped her layers tighter rather than reaching for the canteen. "Too cold... to take out arms," she said in Spanish.

Cortés nodded. "Tilt your head back so I can pour." She did as commanded but watched with some trepidation as he clicked open the container. "You do not have to drink it, but it will warm you."

She nodded. Cortés brought the canteen to her lips, slowly tipping it upwards so she could drink at her own leisure. The taste—first sweet, then sour—was so startling she almost spat it out. A combination of exhaustion and thirst was all that stopped her.

When Cortés pulled the canteen away, she was tempted to ask for more. Then the effects became more pronounced, and she decided against it. She suppressed a burp, and her eyes widened in a mixture of surprise and embarrassment.

"What was that?" she asked in an awed voice.

"We call it wine." Cortés leaned back, looking very pleased. He propped himself up on an elbow and stroked his chin. His stubby fingernails disappeared into the dark curls of his beard. What would happen if he stopped shaving altogether? His sharp chin and his pale cheeks would probably disappear from view completely, followed afterward by his creased, vellum-thin lips.

Malintze cleared her throat. "Your wine does the same as our *octli*—but the taste. It is as if it..."

"Came from a different world?"

She nodded half-heartedly and wiped her mouth on the blanket, surprised but grateful the droplets had not frozen to her lips.

"Still adjusting to the cold?"

She nodded again and flashed him a small smile.

"Such a pretty smile," Cortés said. "But hidden behind so much pain."

3

Malintze gazed at the ground. A strand of hair dangled in front of her face, still damp from the morning fog, and she blew it aside with a small gust of air.

"The Totonacs say our march will take us to places even colder," Cortés continued. "I know not to trust all the Totonacs, the Fat Chief promised me an army of thousands and delivered me a sorry lot of half a thousand instead, but I think they are telling the truth this time."

Malintze tried wiggling her toes. It felt as if she were trying to shift stone. "This cold causes me unpleasantness. I hope we start marching soon."

Cortés chuckled under his breath. "What is the name of that mountain?" He pointed southwest to a massive protrusion of rock that stabbed into the sky like a white-tipped spearhead.

"Citlaltepetl," Malintze answered.

Cortés looked at her expectantly.

"It means Star-Mountain."

Cortés arched his brow.

"Sometimes the mountain becomes angry and throws boulders all the way to the stars," she explained.

He turned his gaze back toward Citlaltepetl. "We have star-mountains in the Old World also. We call them volcanoes there. But we do not have anything half as big as *that* in my country."

Malintze nodded and rocked back and forth for warmth. She wondered if she would ever see his country, if she even wanted to see his country. She honestly did not know, just as she did not know how to feel about Cortés. She admired his tenacity and ambition, but they caused her no small amount of angst and alarm.

"That mountain is very pretty, like you," he said. "I would refer to that mountain by your namesake, but certain men would take offense. A shame that beauty must always stir up strife."

Malintze rubbed her arms and tried to stop her teeth from chattering.

"God as my witness, that is the most magnificent mountain I have ever seen," he added. "However, I would be none surprised if we came across greater beauties during our march. This land never ceases to amaze."

"What do you mean namesake?" Malintze asked.

Cortés stared at her with a blank expression.

"You said you would refer to mountain by my namesake—"

"I would name the mountain after you," he said.

Malintze blinked and took a moment to gather her thoughts. "It is not yours to name," she said.

"Why not?"

"It already has a name."

"And this means I cannot give it a new name? Caesar and Alexander would beg to differ. I suspect that some great man probably looked at this mountain and gave it the name you know. Long ago there may have been a different name in a different tongue for this very same mountain."

Malintze furrowed her brow. "I do not know of Caesar and Alexander."

"They are great men who conquered vast territories and won many vassals."

Malintze nodded. She wondered if there were any places in the world where men were not idolized for wreaking destruction, a place where women did not have to form a bond with cutthroats to rise above bondage. "They are like Ahuitzotl and Motecuhzoma then," she replied. "When Caesar and Alexander conquered, did they not leave territory the same?"

"Heavens no. They named nearly everything they saw after themselves. Or those dear to them."

Malintze's chest tightened. "The mountain already has name." She drew her legs in to conserve warmth.

5

"Remember, the Mexica are the conquerors of the One World."

Cortés smiled. "For now."

~ ~ ~

Tezoc did his best to ignore the pungent perfumes of the cliffside bath and studied Cacama with the learned eye of a warrior. Even in repose, the leader of Tetzcoco struck an imposing figure. His thick limbs were marked by scars, proof of his piety and his combat experience, and he stood a head taller than most. Despite losing half his domain to his brother no less than four years ago, Cacama's cheerful face bore no sign of anxiety or shame. Then again, *pilli* did not need much to be happy. So long as they had servants and dignitaries to wait on them, men like Cacama would always find cause for joy.

Tezoc cleared his throat. Cacama lifted his arm from the bath's stone rim and opened his eyes. He looked up at Tezoc and grinned. "Enjoying the view?"

Cacama's attendants snickered.

"Of course," Tezoc said. "The view of Lake Tetzcoco from this precipice is most splendid. The lake sparkles like a thousand jade stones when it catches the light."

Cacama nodded. "On this we agree. Tenochtitlan appears small from a distance, does it not?"

Tezoc stared out at the horizon from the rocky ledge. The canals and pyramids of Tenochtitlan were hardly visible from their vantage point, but the verdant Valley of Mexico—home to tens of thousands and the origin of foodstuffs traded all throughout the One World—stretched out in almost every direction for countless long-runs.

It was a sight both stunning and humbling, and he imagined that his son, Tlalli, would have enjoyed the view. Just when his son might get the chance to enjoy such a view was an open question since Tezoc's foolishness would prevent Tlalli from ever serving in the

6

military. He cleared those dark thoughts from his head to focus on the task at hand.

"Appearances can be deceptive," Tezoc replied. "Peering out from this aerie, Tetzcoco appears as one, not a divided domain."

Cacama's smile vanished. "Why did Motecuhzoma send you here?"

"We must know how many warriors you can field in a battle against the pale people."

Cacama arched his brow. "I thought Motecuhzoma decreed it improper to attack."

"Improper or not, the pale people intend to march an army into the Valley of Mexico."

Cacama frowned. "I thought that army was invited into the valley by Motecuhzoma."

"The invitation was a ploy to cleave the pale people from the bosom of the Totonacs."

"So battle is a certainty?" Cacama asked.

"Not yet. But we must prepare for every outcome."

Cacama grunted. "Has a location been chosen for battle?"

Tezoc hesitated. He did not trust Cacama with important information, but he would inevitably play a key role in Motecuhzoma's coalition. "If Motecuhzoma decides on war, we will attack the pale people as they enter the Valley of Mexico," Tezoc said. Cacama's guards did not bother to hide their shock. "The march to reach our valley will drain their strength, and we will fall upon them as soon as they enter the lowlands."

"If we think they have sinister designs, why let them march into our valley? We can attack them before they reach our farms and settlements."

"Because we can quickly field a large army if we fight them in the valley." Tezoc pointed to the mountains in the east. "If we have to march our warriors beyond those mountains, and the mountain range after that, we will be marching with a reduced number and extending our supply lines needlessly. The rains have not abated yet so we must be mindful of logistical matters."

Cacama nodded. "I can rally five thousand within a moon. However, I am sure I can rally an even larger number if my subjects knew my usurping brother would soon be removed from power. Tetzcoco ought to be united, no?"

Tezoc pursed his lips. He was not surprised Cacama would condition great support upon a great favor. Politics infected even the most noble endeavors, and no responsible statesmen would ever let a crisis go to waste. But if every Speaker did the same as Cacama, it would be impossible to cobble together an effective coalition. "The pale people take priority over dynastic disputes. We may have to raise a sizable force to defeat them. The Speaker that contributes the most can call upon Motecuhzoma for many favors."

Cacama's attendants muttered amongst each other but quieted when Cacama shot them a sharp glare. "Where are the pale people now?"

"They are nearing Xocotlan."

Cacama cocked his head toward the distant mountains. "It seems we have succeeded in drawing the pale people out from Totonac refuge then." A dark look passed over Cacama's face. "Xocotlan is not far from Tlaxcala. How do we prevent the *teteo* from seeking out the teat of the Tlaxcalteca?"

For a moment, Tezoc was caught off guard. He assumed Cacama's political interests did not extend beyond Tetzcoco so the interest in Tlaxcala took him by surprise. "It is possible the pale people will seek out Tlaxcala for succor," Tezoc said. "But the Tlaxcalteca will not be in any rush to receive them. We have urged them to receive the pale people as honored guests of Tenochtitlan."

Cacama chuckled. "I suspect the Tlaxcalteca would be quite happy to give our honored guests Flowery Deaths."

"If we are truly fortunate, the Tlaxcalteca and the pale people will destroy each other in battle, and we will never have to worry about either in the future."

Cacama's grin faltered. "Fortune can be a whimsical mistress." He stared into the cloudy water and rubbed his throat. "Some have suggested that Motecuhzoma has too much talent for diplomacy and not enough appetite for war. If Motecuhzoma had not been so eager to broker a truce with my treacherous brother, the domains of my great father would be commanded by one, not two. And now with the pale people, Motecuhzoma opts for diplomacy. We could be making a terrible mistake by letting them pass through the mountains unharried."

Tezoc bit the inside of his lip. Cacama was blinded by his own interests. Many of the *pilli* in Tetzcoco were happy to lend their support to his usurping brother, Ixtli. Motecuhzoma's willingness to broker a truce between the northern and southern domains of Tetzcoco had prevented civil war. But it would be impolitic to remind him, just as it would be impolitic to let Cacama know that he also worried Motecuhzoma was not confronting the pale people aggressively enough. If Tezoc had his way, the Mexica would have marched on the pale people while they were still in Totonac territory.

"We have already deployed a contingent of three thousand warriors to Xocotlan," Tezoc said. "Motecuhzoma will be keeping a close eye on the *teteo* as they travel to Tenochtitlan."

Xocotlan

Tlaxcala

Chapter 2

Cortés, mounted atop Arriero, ambled alongside rank and file to study the appearance of his men. Their pinched expressions spoke volumes about the rigors of the past ten days. The ascent had been most trying—the bitter cold brought on by night made restful sleep near impossible—but Cortés assumed that would be the worst part of the march. The descent, however, offered little in the way of respite and there was hardly a moment when they were not tormented by fierce winds or raging tempests. One storm had pelted them with rain, sleet, and hail so mercilessly that three of the porters from Cuba took sick and died.

The terrain did not become much kinder once they left the mountain pass. Thereafter, the army had to trek through a barren desert devoid of freshwater, shade, and game. They were not even halfway to Tenochtitlan, but the land had grown noticeably harsher as they journeyed deeper into Mexica territory, like some kind of warning.

Cortés sat up in his saddle. They had been on the move for over a week, but it felt like ages. He knew little about the region and relied entirely upon the local guides and scouting reports. He would have traded half his *encomienda* for a good map.

Even more frustrating than his ignorance of the terrain was the army's vulnerability. Locals had flocked to his banner, fifteen hundred Totonac warriors had joined the march, giving him a fighting force of almost two thousand. It wasn't enough. Motecuhzoma had the ability to field tens of thousands of warriors; many of his officers feared that Motecuhzoma's offer to host them in

Tenochtitlan was an elaborate ruse to lure them from safety.

Cortés wiped sweat from his brow. The blazing sun, the dry wind, the cloudless sky; it was all too much, and his head ached as if he had been hit with a club. He had never done battle with a foe like the desert and had severely underestimated his enemy. Worse yet, he had overestimated the strength of his men.

The heat had driven certain men mad. When the expedition passed by a lagoon a few days prior, some of his men tried to slake their thirst with foul salt water. The sound of their retching had been like pins in his ears, and he prayed they found some solace in their final hours.

Cortés focused his attention on the village that would be responsible for providing succor. The village, known as Xocotlan, had only a few hundred people, and his army had easily encircled it. So long as the locals provided them with lodging and sustenance, no harm would come to them.

A scout shouted, "Movement ahead."

Cortés brought his horse to a standstill and shaded his eyes. What with the bright glare of the sun, it took a few seconds to spot the litter-bearing retinue heading their way. Cortés ordered his men to assume a defensive formation and called for Doña Marina. Within moments, his soldiers had shields and arms ready, and the speedy transformation of his men from ragtag ruffians to organized squadron made his heart flutter.

"I am here," Doña Marina said. He turned her way as she stepped out of the crowd of soldiers. Her sunken eyes and sallow skin made him catch his breath. *I have failed to provide for you—I will do better in the future.* He stifled a cough and said, "Translate for us."

Doña Marina nodded, and Cortés turned toward the retinue. The attendants had lowered the massive litter to the ground and kneeled to carry out a dirt-kissing ceremony. Cortés had lost count of all the times he had seen Indians perform the same rite and suspected that his soldiers, unsteady on their feet and weary from marching, had little desire to watch a drawn-out ceremony. If he told the men to sack Xocotlan for food and water, he knew none of them would protest the command.

Perhaps sensing their impatience, the Indians soon finished with their ritual. Attendants stepped forward to brush back the curtain, revealing a startlingly obese man with more chins than hands.

Cortés' stomach rumbled. How pleasing it would be to run a spear through the man's rotund belly, to simply take all the food in Xocotlan and spare himself conversation with some lackey of Motecuhzoma.

He pushed the thought from his head and said, "My name is Hernando Cortés, and I wish to know who I will be speaking with."

The glutton whispered to an attendant who then yelled something in an Indian tongue. "He urges us to call him Olintetl and wants us to know he is the leader of this town," Doña Marina said.

"Ask Olintetl if he is a vassal to Motecuhzoma."

Doña Marina said, "Olintetl answers with question. He asks: who is there that is not vassal of Motecuhzoma?"

Cortés chuckled drily. "Tell him we are most certainly not vassals of Motecuhzoma, that we serve the great and powerful king Don Carlos and that Don Carlos heaps many favors upon his subjects. Don Carlos recognizes Jesus as his savior and will receive eternal salvation; Don Carlos understands there is no need to sacrifice enemy people to make the sun rise, and strives to always protect his subjects from corrupting, dangerous influences. His subjects are very well-provided for, whether new or old."

Cortés studied Olintetl's porcine face as Doña Marina translated. Xocotlan was a small town, but Olintetl did not seem to lack for material comforts. If he could be

13

persuaded to share his riches, to lend warriors to Cortés' cause, it would surely be a boon to the mission. But instead of bending the knee, Olintetl laughed and shook his head once he heard the full translation.

"Olintetl says no ruler is more powerful than Motecuhzoma," Doña Marina said. "He says his domains stretch all the way from the waters in the east to the waters in the west, that he rules thirty *altepetl* with more than a hundred thousand warriors each, that he lives in a beautiful city that has never been taken by force and sacrifices countless enemy people to the gods every year."

Cortés forced a smile in response to his outrageous claims. He could believe that the city had never been taken by force, but to believe that Motecuhzoma ruled thirty different *altepetl* with more than a hundred thousand warriors each beggared belief.

"I come from a land far away to the east and know Motecuhzoma to be very generous," Cortés said. "He did us a great honor by inviting us to Tenochtitlan, and we have traveled very far to be in his company. We have great need for food and water so it comforts us to know that a loyal vassal of Motecuhzoma would not refuse a friend of Motecuhzoma."

Olintetl's face darkened. He whispered something to his attendants, but none of them gave Doña Marina a statement to translate. Instead, a small cadre of Olintetl's men rushed back to the town of Xocotlan. Cortés shot a quick glance at his nearby officers. He was heartened to see they had their weapons ready. They were too hungry, too thirsty, and too tired to tolerate any treachery.

"Doña Marina, ask Olintetl what he is doing."

Doña Marina obeyed without question and, judging by her tone, she feared for their safety also. Her eyes lit up when Olintetl gave her an answer. "Olintetl says he

14

has told his attendants to bring out food and water for Motecuhzoma's friends."

The men that overheard Doña Marina broke out in excited chattering. Soon it seemed every man in the company knew that respite was finally within reach. Cortés held up a hand to quiet the chattering. "Your generosity reflects well upon Xocotlan and is a credit to Motecuhzoma. Has Motecuhzoma been so generous as to gift you gold?"

Doña Marina pursed her lips at the mention of gold but translated his statement anyway. "Olintetl says Motecuhzoma has gifted him gold, along with more valuable riches."

Cortés huffed. The dismissive attitude of the Indians toward gold, as compared to green jade or Quetzal feathers, was not something he would ever fathom. "Motecuhzoma is such a generous host that I am sure he will gift me great quantities of gold when I visit him in Tenochtitlan," Cortés said. "Surely a vassal of Motecuhzoma can share some gold samples so we can learn more about the bounties of this land."

Olintetl scoffed. "He says he could share a great deal of gold with you, but says he must receive permission from Motecuhzoma first."

Cortés arched his brow. A part of him admired the audacity of Olintetl. To admit that he had gold but would not share it with the army that surrounded his town was bold. But Olintetl did not strike him as bold, and Cortés suspected Olintetl was withholding important information. Men nearby muttered they should seize Olintetl and torture him until he gave them all his riches. He could only pick up on certain words—strappado, hot irons, rack—but their unity of purpose heartened him immensely. It had been days since the company enjoyed a proper meal, but it comforted him to know they had not lost their fighting spirit.

"Motecuhzoma must be powerful indeed to command the loyalty of a vassal such as yourself."

An unmistakable smirk split Olintetl's face when he heard the translation. "When you see Tenochtitlan, you will learn for yourself the power that Motecuhzoma commands. The Mexica are so industrious, so resourceful they have created a home for themselves in a lake so vast it could be mistaken for the sea. But you need not wait until your arrival in Tenochtitlan to see proof of his power. A Mexica battalion will arrive here in five days, and they will be quite willing to educate you on Motecuhzoma's military might."

The torture chatter stopped at the mention of the Mexica battalion. Cortés wanted to put more questions to Olintetl—to ask exactly how many, to ask their intent—but now was not the time. To take a great interest in the battalion would be a public admission of fear, and he could not afford to look weak. As much as Cortés wanted to wipe the smug expression off Olintetl's face, to educate him so thoroughly on the might of Spain he would never again assert that Motecuhzoma wielded more power than Don Carlos, he had to reckon with the threat posed by the Mexica.

He thought upon his campaign against the Potons. They had vastly outnumbered his own forces, but that had not stopped the cavalry and the infantry from routing them. Perhaps his meager force could prevail against the Mexica, perhaps they could win a grand victory that would inspire disgruntled vassals to flock to his banner in the thousands.

Or maybe they would win a Pyrrhic victory instead, and the local forces would desert them afterward. A simple stalemate would be equally disastrous, if not more. No, he needed to avoid battle for now. Victory would only be feasible once he won new allies.

Cortés licked his chapped lips and shouted, "Men, prepare to make camp. The townspeople will provide us food and water during our stay, but we must not tarry while gold awaits us in Tenochtitlan. We depart at dawn, three days from now."

Within a few moments, the neat rows of soldiers disintegrated into self-organized units concerned only with pitching tents and setting up fire pits.

While the men busied themselves with making camp, Cortés leaned forward to whisper to Doña Marina. "Tell Olintetl that I owe him a great debt. I am glad to make his acquaintance."

Olintetl's smile brightened immensely once he heard the translation. "Olintetl says he has enjoyed speaking with you. He hopes you visit the townsquare of Xocotlan so you can see firsthand what fate befalls enemies of the Mexica," Doña Marina said. "He feels you will be very impressed by the *tzompantli*."

Cortés narrowed his eyes. "And what does *tzompantli* mean?"

Doña Marina turned his way. There was no mistaking the grave expression on her face. "It means skull rack."

~ ~ ~

Xicotencatl the Younger studied the Totonac envoys that had just arrived in Tlaxcala. Four total and none appeared to be warriors. Nonetheless, they had all traveled from Xocotlan to speak on behalf of the mysterious *teteo*. Judging by the hungry look in their drawn faces, it had been a while since any of the Totonacs had a proper meal. Nonetheless, not one envoy touched any of the delicacies laid out on the low table.

Xicotencatl breathed in the heady aroma of freshly cooked food. Two bowls of *chilocuil*, marinated in a rich stew of green tomatoes and yellow peppers, were being served with warm corn cakes and slices of avocado, but it was the *tzoalli*, topped with diced cherries and fresh *pitahaya,* that held his gaze. *Tzoalli* had always been one of his favorite treats, and he welcomed the chance to mix it with the foods he had come to appreciate later in life.

The envoys, on the other hand, seemed far more interested in the *chilocuil.* Xicotencatl allowed himself a small smile. Hungry men always focused on meat and *chilocuil* were difficult to find outside of Tlaxcala. One of the envoys made a furtive feint toward a nearby plate of roasted fowl stuffed with herbs, *nohpalli,* and mushrooms. The envoy sitting to his right stopped him with a none-too-subtle slap and Xicotencatl wondered if they were friends or kin. They did share some features—thin lips, prominent cheek bones—and he would not have been surprised if they were cousins. The other two envoys did not appear to be related at all. One looked thin and reedy and donned all kinds of jewelry, while the other was stout and short and wore no jewelry whatsoever.

A loud rumbling grabbed his attention. Xicotencatl thought at first he had picked up on distant thunder, but he belatedly realized the sound had a more gastronomic origin.

"My house is your house," Xicotencatl said. "Please, try some of the foods we have laid out for you." He stared at the one who had tried to sneak food. "You must try the *chilocuil.* They came early this year and will not be around much longer. We will have plenty of time to talk about the pale people once you have eaten."

He watched as the men who had been trying so hard to restrain themselves finally gave in to their hunger. Xicotencatl gestured to an attendant to bring him a plate and ordered another to bring hot chocolate.

Giddy smiles crossed the faces of all the envoys at the mention of hot chocolate. Xicotencatl lifted the cup to drinking level and took a deep sniff. The potent mix of bitter chocolate and heady spices inspired no small amount of salivation, but he took only a sip before setting the piping hot drink back down. The short envoy proved unable to exercise similar restraint and downed the beverage in the flutter of an eyelid.

Xicotencatl bit into a corn cake topped with *chilocuil* and avocado. The creamy avocado made for a nice complement to the crunchy *chilocuil*, and he reached for another one.

After a moment, Xicotencatl spoke again. "I trust you enjoyed your meal."

The thin one nodded his head enthusiastically. "It was most delicious."

"My heart turns white to hear that. Food can be so difficult to procure here in Tlaxcala. Our cooks will be pleased to know you enjoyed the meal. Has food been hard to come by during your march?"

The cousins exchanged a quick glance, but it was the thin one who spoke again. "We have experienced some shortages as of late so your munificence moves us greatly. Truly, there must be no people kinder than the Tlaxcalteca. We will sing praise of Xicotencatl the Younger for many years to come."

Xicotencatl scratched his cheek. "Your lands are not so far away from our lands. Why has food been so hard to come by? Are you traveling with a very large party to Tlaxcala?"

"We are passing through dangerous lands. Moving with a large group is usually safer—"

"How many do you travel with exactly?" Xicotencatl asked.

Silence settled over the room like a sudden rainstorm.

"We are one hundred times twenty, not including the porters and servants," the thin envoy said.

Xicotencatl rubbed his arm rest. "It seems you are traveling with many warriors. Do you mean to tell me you are marching with an army to Tlaxcala?"

19

The thin envoy bit into the *tzoalli* wafer. "One could call it an army. But we come bearing words of peace. The *teteo* wish to make an alliance, and we are here as their intermediaries."

Xicotencatl nodded. "Why would the pale people wish to make an alliance with us? We know nothing about them, and they know nothing about us. And why are the Totonacs acting as intermediaries? Twenty and fifteen years I have lived, but I cannot recall the Totonacs ever taking a great interest in the affairs of the Tlaxcala."

The thin envoy straightened. "Times are changing. The *teteo* march for Tenochtitlan and hope Tlaxcalteca forces will join them on their journey."

Xicotencatl laughed. "I fear the charms of Tenochtitlan might be lost on me. I find the smell of ordure most unpleasant and have little love for the Mexica. I think I will be staying in Tlaxcala. With my warriors." Xicotencatl waited so the envoys could count all the warriors present in the room. The envoys had been outnumbered by a factor of five to one ever since they entered the room, and no amount of food would give them the strength to overcome those odds. "I must apologize I could not offer salt with the *chilocuil*," Xicotencatl added. "Motecuhzoma, in his infinite wisdom, has levied many sanctions against the nation of Tlaxcala. Former allies refuse to trade with us because of their Mexica overlords so we must do without salt and cloth. Tell me, why would I wish to travel to Tenochtitlan?"

"How else will you let Motecuhzoma know of your grievances?" the thin envoy asked.

Xicotencatl laughed and rapped his fingers on the armrest. A simple wave of his hand and his guards would kill all the Totonac envoys. Better to get information first, though. Xicotencatl scratched his cheek and leaned forward. "Not long before you arrived, Mexica delegates instructed us to show every kindness to the pale people as they travel through Tlaxcala. We have been informed they are honored guests of Motecuhzoma. Would you suggest we do as the Mexica command?"

The thin envoy conferred with the others before answering. "The *teteo* are very powerful—"

Xicotencatl slammed his hand down on the table in front of him. "So are the Tlaxcalteca."

The thin envoy sighed. "Not like the *teteo*. They have weapons that can fell a copse of trees in the flutter of an eyelid and ride giant, hornless stags that can trample grown men like stalks of corn. The Totonacs have already lent many warriors to the *teteo* army. If the Tlaxcalteca were to join our forces, no army could stand before us."

Xicotencatl narrowed his eyes. If the envoy was telling the truth, battle with the *teteo* would be no simple affair. Their weapons, however, sounded most desirable. Perhaps his own men could learn how to use them.

"The Mexica can summon quite the army," Xicotencatl said. "Reports indicate a contingent of four hundred times eight have taken to the field. No reports have come in to indicate this contingent has done anything to harass the *teteo* army. Instead, we hear that Mexica warriors trail behind the *teteo* army, like some type of supporting force. It is very suspicious. Some of us wonder if the *teteo*, the Mexica, and the Totonacs have reached some kind of agreement regarding Tlaxcala."

The envoys gaped at him in shock, and the thin envoy stood. "We are in league with the Mexica no more than the Tlaxcalteca are. But if we are not welcome here, we will leave."

Xicotencatl shook his head. "No, you will not. But you will tell me more about the pale people and their weapons. Otherwise, no morsel of food will ever pass through your lips again. I trust you enjoyed this decadent meal, but surely you do not want it to be your last." The nearby Tlaxcalteca warriors nocked arrows and readied

21

clubs. Xicotencatl leaned back in his seat, a familiar excitement stealing over him. Diplomacy was a game for old blind men like his father—nothing made Xicotencatl's blood pump like the prospect of battle. "I want to hear more about these animals you call hornless stags," Xicotencatl added. "We are very interested in learning how to kill them."

Tlaxcala Province

Chapter 3

Diego tore his eyes away from the stone fortifications of Tlaxcala to glance at his trembling hand. A bead of sweat trickled down his palm, and he wiped his hand dry with the saddle horn. He always got clammy before a battle, but it was hard to know if it was because of fear or excitement.

There hadn't been a real battle since Potonchan and nearly six moons had passed since then. Was that enough time to lose his edge? He hoped not. Otherwise, riding for Tlaxcala with the scouting party could prove a terrible mistake.

There was a chance that Tlaxcala would receive them peaceably, but the recent omens—a ghost woman wandering through camp and a flock of three-eyed birds—made it difficult to discount the possibility of battle. Even those who did not believe in such signs were wary considering the Totonac envoys had not returned from Tlaxcala.

Judging by the massive stone wall that stood as tall as two grown men and stretched more than a league in each direction, the Tlaxcalteca were not the welcoming type. The dry stone wall was low enough that Diego had been able to see over it a half-league out, craggy hills and scraggly trees dominated Tlaxcala territory, and he worried that hostile could hide near the entrance.

As far as he could tell, the entrance lacked a gate, but it was so narrow he estimated that no more than five horsemen could enter abreast. Moreover, owing to the sharp corner design, rushing through would not be possible.

Despite the danger, Cortés insisted upon leading the exploratory party. Six horsemen, Diego included, would also assist with scouting, but the vast majority would stay close to the infantry. Diego sat up straighter in his saddle. His father used to tell him the more danger, the more honor. When his family learned of his exploits, Diego knew they would be proud. He couldn't wait to tell them about the New World! Indian armies as big as the ocean crashing into them, savages running at them with nothing more than clubs... he could already see the look of wonder on their faces.

"Two rows, everybody. First with four, second with three," Cortés ordered. The process was messy, but the riders slowly took on Cortés' formation. The captain-general took a place in the front row and so did Diego.

They were forty paces from the wall, and Diego marveled at the impressive dimensions of the Tlaxcalteca defenses. The wall stretched across the whole length of the valley, curving and bending like a river, and the base seemed wide as a house. But for some strange reason, not one sentry walked the ramparts and not one person guarded the entrance.

Cortés brought the riders to a stop. Diego looked around; things felt too quiet, too peaceful, and the overcast sky only added to his unease. He stared into the entrance, only twenty paces away, and wished he could see beyond the turn. Nonetheless, his wishing did nothing to change the corner design. He had to accept that hostile forces could be waiting on the side of the wall, just waiting to attack.

"Swords out, shields up—we charge as soon as we can," Cortés commanded.

The rasp of steel grating on scabbards filled the air as seven men unsheathed swords in rough unison. A cold gust blasted through the valley, and the shrill whistle of the wind raised his hackles.

"Gentlemen, let us follow the sign of the Holy Cross and by this, we shall conquer," Cortés said. He bid his horse forward with a gentle spur, and the rest of the formation did likewise. Diego's every sense was focused—like a snake poised to strike, like a rabbit ready to flee—and when they rounded the corner, he spurred his horse into a gallop with a rough kick.

He covered almost one hundred paces before he reined his horse into a slow walk at the brow of a small hill. He looked for the enemies that should have been hiding behind the wall but did not see a single Indian anywhere. Yet there were so many obstructions in the landscape—rolling foothills, steep mountains, deep valleys, thick forests—it was hard to know if they truly were alone. The wind picked up with a newfound intensity, and he squinted to keep his eyes open.

"Where the Indians at?" Diego asked.

The only answer was the howl of the wind.

"Sheathe swords," Cortés said in a tight voice. He set off at a slow trot for the distant foothills. Despite his unease, Diego spurred his horse forward so he could ride abreast of the others. He shivered and his eyes cast about frantically for a sign of something living.

"Indians to our east," Cortés said.

Diego glanced to the side. The Indians were out of crossbow range and few in number; he counted only fifteen. He could tell they had weapons of some kind but could not recognize them from afar. He was not sure he would recognize them up close either.

The sharp blaring of a conch shell caught him unawares, and he turned to his countrymen in confusion. It took a moment to realize the Indians had blown the conch. He whipped his head in their direction, surprised to see the Indians were now sprinting for the horizon. Cortés kicked his horse into a faster trot, and the rest of the horsemen followed.

Cortés pointed at Diego and Felipe. "Capture them."

Felipe spurred his horse into a canter and Diego did the same, albeit a few moments later. The belated reaction gave Felipe the chance to gain ten paces, and the distance proved difficult to close. Determined to catch up, Diego raised himself to a half-seat. He gained a single pace for his efforts. Frustrated, he settled back in his saddle and looked ahead.

The Indians were within crossbow shot now, but they had done little to change their behavior. Rather than forming a defensive position, they continued to run straight. Diego almost pitied them. At least rabbits knew to run in zig zags when chased.

Felipe slowed his horse and shouted something about uneven ground as he unsheathed his sword. Before Felipe could finish his sentence, the Indian he had been chasing turned around and smashed a bladed weapon into the horse's muzzle. The animal whinnied in pain as the weapon dug deep into its flesh, and blood poured out of the wound like water from an open spigot.

The mare bucked so hard Felipe almost buried his blade in her flank, and the Indians quickly encircled the hapless pair. One warrior smashed a weapon against Felipe's calf, another slammed a club against his sword hand. Felipe screamed as the bone snapped, and the sword dropped from his useless hand.

The mob, voracious and galvanized by success, swallowed the horseman whole. Hungry hands sprung from everywhere to pull Felipe off his steed. He gave one last weak cry as he was torn from his saddle and thrown to the ground. His horse, now lame, did not fare much better and collapsing to the ground amidst a melee of clubbing and spearing.

Diego, desperate to avoid being consumed by that same mob, drew the reins so hard that his horse reared in protest. He shot his hand out to grab hold of the saddle horn as the horse tottered backward and caught a brief glimpse of the Indian charging toward him. His eyes went wide as the Indian jumped high in the air, swinging a strange club with sharp, glittering edges. The weapon sank into his horse's throat, slicing through flesh and skin like a knife through butter.

The horse's neighing gave way to a sickening gurgle, and the animal crashed onto its side. Diego screamed as something deep inside his leg snapped and fumbled for his sword in a haze of pain. He stopped. The sword was pinned beneath him.

A great numbness overcame him, and he rested his head on the grass. It would have been nice to see his parents one last time. How would they react when they learned their son had died alone and scared in some country they had never heard of?

The wind picked up again, carrying cheers and whoops to his ringing ears. He thought about all the times he had reveled in victory with his fellow countrymen and surprised himself by laughing. Such a strange thing, that a savage would share any customs with a Christian. His laughter caught in his throat when an Indian warrior stepped into sight and laid his sword on Diego's neck. The edge of his weapon was so sharp it stung, and Diego prayed for salvation.

A simple flick brought the weapon to life and opened the arteries in his neck. His life water rushed out, and there was nothing he could do to stop it. All he could do was gurgle weakly and cling to his memories of home and family as everything went dark.

~ ~ ~

Cortés studied the Indian sword by candlelight. Doña Marina said it was called a *macuahuitl*. Even with her help, he found the name difficult to pronounce. Smaller than his own sword by two hands and carved from wood, the weapon did not look lethal at first glance. However, owing to the glass shards embedded in the side of the weapon, the *macuahuitl* had a cutting edge that could put a sword to shame. He had never known any of the Indians to fight with such a weapon, and it was another reminder that he had been a fool to enter Tlaxcala with such a small force and such limited information.

He made a quick outward slash, admiring the way the *macuahuitl* sang as it sliced through emptiness. The simple weapon had helped kill two men-at-arms and two lightly-armored horses in a matter of seconds, an incident unimaginable a few days prior. Lord knew he had been fortunate not to lose more of the cavalry. The slaying of Diego and Felipe had enraged the scouting party beyond reason and they cut down every single Indian involved in the attack, only to discover they had attracted the attention of an Indian force numbering in the hundreds. With only four horsemen at his side, Cortés did not even need to give orders for a retreat.

Cortés laid the *macuahuitl* on the floor of the tent. He had hoped the Tlaxcalteca would be interested in forging a pact, and he was sorely disappointed by their intransigence. Following the skirmish, a small party attacked the company last evening and only fled when they were fired upon with the gunpowder weapons. The Tlaxcalteca had been humbled but not defeated, and he prayed his defenses would be strong enough to hold them off if they attacked again.

Unable to sit still any longer, Cortés stood and made for the tent exit. He peeled back the tent flap and was surprised by how much light flooded the interior. The sun must have risen at least half an hour prior. Soon, the morning fog would lift, and the day would warm. He prayed his men would be able to withstand the heat.

Cortés looked at the two guards stationed outside his tent. One asleep, the other so focused on rubbing his arms he did not know he was being stared at. Under different circumstances, Cortés would have reprimanded them, but yesterday's events had shaken faith in his command.

Many took issue with his decision to enter Tlaxcala. He trusted that most of his men would honor their vows, but he recognized that it would be wise to employ a gentle touch in the meantime.

He stepped out of his tent to tie back the tent flap. The guard who had managed to stay awake, Olea, jumped to his feet and offered a hasty apology.

"Tell the other officers to meet me here," Cortés said. Olea rushed off to do his bidding. Alone with the sleeping guard, Cortés decided some prodding was called for and woke the sleeping sentry with a gentle kick.

Cortés watched the bewildered guard come to and stepped back into his tent afterward. He took a swig of water to slake his thirst. He could not have slept more than an hour or two last night. Exhaustion clung to him like a wet cloak. His mind felt sluggish, his senses groggy, but he knew it would pass. Even if the water and the cold failed to rouse him, he was sure the Tlaxcalteca soon would.

He bent down to pick up the *macuahuitl*. The glass cutting edge made it light and easy to handle, but a hard parry would render the weapon almost useless. While a man in cotton armor had good reason to fear a *macuahuitl*, a man in full steel armor had little cause to do so. *A shame that most of my men make do with chain mail or quilted cotton.*

Pedro de Alvarado entered the tent, offered a terse greeting, and sat on a stool. Whereas officers like Puertocarrero would dress in full regalia simply to strut about camp, Pedro would rush into battle with nothing more than a hauberk, a helmet, and a light shield. Not that he lacked the money for better armor; he simply enjoyed the thrill of battle too much to protect himself from the danger of it.

31

A minute passed before Ávila, Olid, and León entered the tent. A few words were exchanged, but quiet pervaded the tent otherwise. Another minute passed, but no other officers arrived.

Cortés pushed down his anger and cleared his throat, "I believe we have waited long enough for the other officers, so they will have to forgive us for conferring without them. I am glad to see you are all dressed for battle." He meant it. Ávila, Olid, and León all looked as if they could take a lance to the chest without suffering anything besides a bruise. A small movement from any of them made their rerebraces, tassets, and vambraces clank together in beautiful unison. "Does anyone have news worth reporting?"

Silence.

"I must know how my officers feel about our current predicament," Cortés said in a clipped voice.

Olid picked at his sunburnt forehead and flicked a ball of dead skin at the tent wall. "The men believe you have led us into grave danger," Olid said. "They are calling you a—"

"A Carbonaro," Ávila finished. "The Tlaxcalteca were supposed to welcome us with open arms but have done everything they could to repel us since we entered their lands. If the Indians do not desire friendship with us, there is no reason to stay in Tlaxcala. The Indians here will give us grief long before they give us gold."

Cortés pursed his lips. "We did not come to Tlaxcala for gold. We came here to form a pact. We will get no more gold from the Mexica unless we can field a proper army so we must ally with the Tlaxcalteca."

León narrowed his eyes. "We would still have the g-gold the Mexica gave us had you not sent it all to Spain."

Cortés bristled. "Sending the gold to the crown will win us royal support. Nothing we do here matters if the crown does not recognize our winnings in these lands."

Ávila laughed. "What winnings?"

"Right now, our losses should be our greatest concern," Pedro cut in. "Cortés, how do we win the Tlaxcalteca to our side?"

"Slinking away to avoid confrontation will do us no good," Cortés said. He stared Ávila in the face. Ávila held his gaze, his eyes smoldering with indignation. "The Tlaxcalteca are a fierce, bellicose people; that is why they will make good allies. But they are not ready to ally with us yet—"

"What makes you think they ever will be?" Ávila asked, his color rising. "The Totonacs told us the Tlaxcalteca would welcome us with open arms, that the Tlaxcalteca would be eager to join a march on Tenochtitlan. Instead, they have harassed us ever since we entered Tlaxcala. Savages cannot be trusted to see reason. It is foolish to seek their friendship."

"The march will fail if we cannot win them to our cause!" Cortés pinched the bridge of his nose, took a deep breath, and laid a hand flat on his thigh. "The Potons were hostile to us when we first arrived in their lands, but we crushed them in battle and forced them to sue for peace. Now we must do so with the Tlaxcalteca. They may not want to ally with us now, but that will not matter if we are the ones who dictate the terms of surrender."

Pedro cocked his head toward him. "What is the strategy to force them to surrender?"

Cortés straightened. "We have an excellent defensive position with the river behind us and the clearing ahead of us; it would be folly to sacrifice that. Today, we hold our position, and wait for the Indians to attack."

Aghast, Ávila turned to the other officers. Seeing they did not share his disgust, he clamped his mouth shut and gritted his teeth. "Wait?"

"Yes, that would be the wise strategy."

"What will we do for supplies?" Saucedo asked. "There are not enough fish in the river to feed an entire army, and there is little foraging to be done nearby. Our food stores will not last long if we stay here."

"We will move when we exhaust our food stores," Cortés said. "Our situation is not ideal. But if we flee from Tlaxcala, we will gain little for it. Remember, there is a Mexica battalion waiting for us outside Tlaxcala. If we are so easily cowed, who is to say the battalion will not attack us after we depart Tlaxcalteca territory? Or that the Tlaxcalteca will allow us a safe retreat?"

"Well, if the choice is between running and fighting or standing and fighting, I vote for the latter," Pedro said. "My feet have more carbuncles than a ship has barnacles."

Based on the pained expressions of the other officers, Pedro was not alone in his suffering. Cortés bit back a laugh. It would be a blessing indeed if the company had such sore feet they could not soon be induced to march again. "We will prevail against Tlaxcala, but we must unite as one. We must strengthen our defenses—"

A horn blew in the distance, prompting the officers to freeze in place. A shrill screeching and a loud drumming followed. The other officers glanced at each other and then turned toward him.

"Form a pike phalanx around the perimeter with strong interior lines," Cortés said. "Make sure the tents cannot be lit aflame, and ready the gunpowder weapons. Go with God, all of you."

Cortés dashed out of his tent and rushed toward his horse, shouting orders all the while. He could not force the Tlaxcalteca to ally with him yet so he intended to do the next best thing: teach the Tlaxcalteca they did not want him for an enemy.

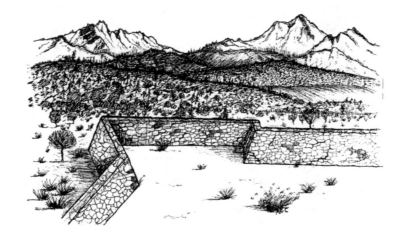

Tlaxcala Province

Chapter 4

Come evening, Xicotencatl the Younger usually made time to watch the sunset. He found no beauty in it today and focused on the carnage below.

His eyes drank in every detail of the battlefield, and he watched in frustration as a mixed assortment of projectiles rained down on his lightly armored troops. From his vantage point, he could view almost all the battlefield and what he saw broke his heart. Despite having the *teteo* completely surrounded, the Tlaxcalteca had been unable to break the *teteo* formation and had suffered severe casualties.

He sighed. Climbing up the cliff face had involved a great deal of risk, he slipped more than a few times on the rain-slicked handholds, and Xicotencatl did it solely to make sure he could see more than the other scouts. Now he wished he had stayed on level ground with his retinue, if only to spare himself a terrible sight.

At the onset of the battle, Xicotencatl had been convinced that dispatching the pale people would be a quick affair. Sure, the failure of yesterday's ambush gave him some cause for doubt, but victory seemed a certainty once he had the chance to assess their forces from up high. The pale people were so few in number that when they assembled in their wedge formation, Xicotencatl counted only four rows. The Totonac troops, assembled right behind the wedge, lent some much needed numerical heft, but the Tlaxcalteca army must have outnumbered them eight to one.

Within the first hour of battle, it became clear the *teteo* coalition was much stronger than it looked. The archers and spear throwers pelted the *teteo* front lines from the very outset of the battle, but few claimed any victims. He had been surprised to see the projectiles bounce harmlessly off heavy shields and thick armor, but the unexpected development did little to diminish his certainty that the Tlaxcalteca would prevail. He beamed with pride as the shock troops rushed toward the *teteo*... and gasped in horror as those troops fell before a volley unlike any he had ever seen.

Fire-sticks exploded in a rippling blast, arrows flew from behind shields, spears and slings rained down with startling precision, and the front lines of the Tlaxcalteca army disintegrated like dry leaves crushed underfoot. Carried forward by mass and momentum, the survivors charged over the bodies of their maimed and mutilated countrymen with little to no protection from the deadly onslaught. Volley after volley decimated their ranks, but still they charged forward.

They should have smashed through the *teteo* lines considering their speed. Instead, they were gored on the long spears of the front line or cut to shreds by the supporting ranks. Wave after wave assaulted the enemy line, but the *teteo* held firm as a stone wall.

The harsh wind tore at his sparse clothing and carried a distant clanking to his weary ears. Xicotencatl looked on in disgust as the pale people, covered in shiny armor and riding atop their gore-strewn beasts, swept through the main body of his army. The crazed beasts knocked aside grown men like they were stalks of corn.

Not a single beast had been slain during today's battle—the *teteo* had fitted all of them with heavy armor and rode in tight formations that did not slow until they were out of range of Tlaxcala weapons. Yesterday's feat, the slaying of two beasts, was not one that would soon be repeated. Xicotencatl clenched his fist. Too often the first battlefield triumph made the next one harder.

He studied his enemy's formation with a careful eye. The *teteo* line had proven surprisingly tenacious, and the dispersed Totonac troops had been most effective. As far as he could tell, the invaders had suffered few casualties, despite inflicting many on the Tlaxcalteca forces.

Down below, a Tlaxcalteca warrior shoved his way past the corpses gored on the long spears. The man charged at the *teteo* formation with a *macuahuitl* and was cut down in the flutter of an eyelid. He collapsed into the blood-soaked muck occupied by so many other dead men, still clutching his weapon. A few moments later, a servant crawled underneath the long spears to retrieve the *macuahuitl* and other discarded weapons. Once he filled the netbag, the servant would deliver the weapons to the Totonacs. Protected by heavy shields and thick armor, the Totonacs would lob the retrieved items into the Tlaxcalteca masses.

Xicotencatl winced and shook his head. The warriors brave enough to confront the long spears were dying just to deliver weapons to the enemy. He glanced at the gloaming horizon. The last rays of Tonatiuh would soon disappear from view and with it, all hope of victory. A deep sadness welled up in his chest. They had been fighting since sun up and had gained nothing for it.

Today was supposed to be a great victory. They were supposed to destroy the *teteo* coalition and dislodge the invaders by mid-morning. Instead, hundreds of Tlaxcalteca troops had perished in a vain attempt to regain territory still held by the *teteo* and many Tlaxcalteca were now retreating. Some warriors tried to retrieve weapons, only to be run down by the *teteo* beasts. Most were too battered to spare a thought for lost weapons and retreated with little grace or dignity. Watching them flee, he swore to lead the field troops during the next attack, come death or glory.

~ ~ ~

Pedro rubbed his temple and grumbled, "We were lucky to survive today's attack."

He stared at Cortés, tried to gage his reaction in the torchlight. Cortés looked neither angered nor saddened by his words. More than anything, he looked tired. His armor had too many dents to count, grime coated his hands, and the ugly brown bruise on his temple continued to ooze blood. The nearby officers looked no better. Lugo, Saucedo, León, Ordaz, Ávila, Olid... all had been asked to give too much today. It would not be long before they were asked to give more. Battle spared few considerations for the aches and pains of men. Cortés spared even less.

"We are running low on ammunition for the muskets and cannons," Cortés said. "We can only endure a few more battles before we run out completely."

"Maybe only a couple," Pedro replied. "Unless you know where we can find sulfur."

Cortés grunted and focused his attention instead on the small leg of dog meat in his hand. Food was even scarcer than gunpowder, and the men had to ransack the nearby settlements to supplement their meager stores. They found some food—a few lean dogs and some chewy figs—but it was not nearly enough.

"How are the horses?" Pedro asked.

"None dead, all injured in some way." Cortés took another bite of the dog leg, wincing as he swallowed. "Thank God none of them are seriously harmed. The Lord alone understands how grateful I am that we have armor for the horses."

Cortés handed Pedro the half-finished leg of dog. The dry meat glistened with his saliva, but Pedro cleaned the bone of all meat in seconds. His eyes darted about in search of more food. Seeing none, he gnawed on the bone's end. Winter in Badajoz could often be severe, but he could not ever remember being so hungry as he was now. Never had home felt so dear—or so far. "The armor must have taken a beating," Pedro said.

"From every manner of weapon. I have instructed the blacksmiths to repair the armor, but restoring it to a pristine state will be impossible."

Pedro's stomach growled. The meat had done more to whet his appetite than restore his energy. Every movement made his aching limbs cry out. Only a full-on feast could quell his hunger. He rubbed the nape of his neck and looked to Cortés. "When do we ride out?"

Cortés rolled his shoulder and massaged his legs. "Within half an hour."

The officers nearby groaned. Too tired to stand, most of them were sitting nearby, balming their injuries with salve and makeshift poultices. The physicians were so lacking in proper material they cut open the dead Indians to use their fat as balm. The battle had exacted a heavy toll; twelve Spaniards had died, along with thirty Totonacs and one hundred and twenty slaves. Hundreds had been injured in the fighting, and Pedro wanted nothing more than to rest his aching limbs. The slaves, the porters, the Totonacs, and the foot soldiers would do just that but the officers, some of the richest men in all the expedition, could not afford such a luxury. Instead, they would be riding out with Cortés to attack the nearby settlements. And if the officers proved stubborn, Pedro would be responsible for bringing them to heel.

Pedro studied the faces of the other officers. Lugo looked as if he were trying to sleep, Ávila looked as if he had aged a year, Saucedo looked... messy. No man looked their best after a battle, but his disheveled appearance surprised Pedro. Known more for vanity than fighting ability, Saucedo's self-grooming habits had earned him the title Saucedo the Neat, but the moniker seemed a cruel jape now. Hair once tidy and radiant, was now tangled and dirty, and a beard trimmed more carefully than a lateen sail had been fouled with gore and grit.

Pedro huffed and focused his gaze on others. Liberated from Pedro's arresting stare, Saucedo stood and made his way toward Cortés without even deigning a glance toward Pedro. "Captain-general, may we speak in private?" Saucedo asked.

Cortés picked at an inflamed pimple. "Camp is quite crowded, Saucedo. Privacy will be hard to find." He gestured to a nearby stool. "Sit. Tell me what is on your mind."

Saucedo smoothed his moustache and glanced at his shabby surroundings. After a moment, he took a seat on the proffered stool. "I do not see the sense in riding out to attack the Indians. We are all tired—"

"We need to force them to sue for peace," said Cortés. "When the Tlaxcalteca attacked our camp earlier today, did they seem ready to sue for peace?"

Saucedo pressed his mouth into a thin line. "No. But if we attack them tonight, will they not attack us tomorrow?"

"We want them to attack us tomorrow," Cortés said in a flat voice.

The officers shot each other confused glances. "We barely repulsed the attack today," Saucedo said. "Why would we want them to attack tomorrow?"

"Our food stores will not last forever. If the Indians are patient, they can starve us into submission. It would be the sensible strategy so we must give them a reason to reject patience. The Tlaxcalteca will not sue for peace unless we do great harm to them first."

"You only brave enough to fight savages when it's light out, Saucedo?" Pedro asked.

Saucedo flushed and turned to the other officers for support. None rose to his defense, and Pedro bit back a smirk.

Saucedo narrowed his eyes and shot Pedro a sour glare. "I am not scared to fight anyone. But riding out with mounted men, in the dead of night, to attack sleeping villagers should not be confused with some great undertaking." Saucedo turned back to Cortés. "The plan is to attack the poorly defended settlements, is it not?"

Cortés looked at him askance. "Only a dozen of us will ride out. Would you prefer to attack the well-defended villages?"

"Attacking villages in the dead of night to kill defenseless people is not honorable," Saucedo said.

Pedro scoffed. "Are you some errant knight? Honor is how you lose a war; killing the enemy is how you win."

Saucedo stiffened. "Captain, do you agree?"

Cortés offered a mirthless smile. "Saucedo, you worry so much. Did night raids never play a part in the Reconquista, the Crusades? These Indians have never learned the love of Jesus, and they will remain ignorant unless we take them as allies and educate them on the One True Faith. The Indians here are idolaters through and through; does not our Holy Book recommend that we smite false worshippers? You think Moses and Aaron blanched when they killed the idolaters? You think Joshua had tears in his eyes when he sacked Jericho? We are doing God's work here. There is nothing to feel guilty about."

Saucedo thumbed the pommel of his sword as he pondered an answer.

"Saucedo, you can stay behind if you are not stout of heart," Cortés said. "There is no shame in it. Not every man can fight for God."

Saucedo stilled. He dropped his shoulders and said in a low voice, "My commitment to God is absolute. I will join the night raid."

Pedro smiled, confident that he would not have to shame anyone into coming now that the most vocal

43

holdout had pledged his support. His intuition proved correct and when Cortés gathered men for the raid, not one man refused to participate. Pedro took a place near the head of the raid party, excitement coursing through his veins. It took almost twenty minutes to reach the pale, flickering lights on the horizon but that did little to dull his vim.

When they were fifty paces from the settlement, the first of the villagers emerged from their huts, most likely roused by the pounding of the horse hooves. Terrified screams rent the air, and an undeniable joy welled up within Pedro's breast. He loved carrying out God's work.

Tlaxcala Province

Chapter 5

Vitale wrapped his hand around the shaft of his weapon and watched as the Indian army charged toward the pike phalanx. Another minute and they would reach the front line. He tried to swallow. His mouth was dry as sandpaper, but his bladder was full to bursting.

He licked his lips. Complete madness, standing still as the Indians charged at them. If it weren't for the river behind camp, he might have already flung down his pike and fled for safety.

A unit leader shouted for everyone to hold steady as a group of falconets commenced firing. Cannonballs sailed overhead and plunged deep into the enemy lines. A pulpy mix of dirt and human was thrown into the air. Vitale gave thanks the Indians did not have any gunpowder weapons of their own.

His eyes watered as a thick plume of acrid smoke rolled over the front lines. For a few precious seconds, the enemy was shrouded from view. He prayed they would lose their nerve and retreat to the foothills. No such luck. When the smoke cleared, it revealed a horde of Indians charging across the clearing, fierce and angry as ever.

A volley of falconets, arquebuses, and muskets exploded to life. He grimaced as he saw chain shot tear a man's elbow off and tried not to think about what the Indians would do to him if they took him captive. A sharp whistling grabbed his attention, and he buried his chin in his chest.

Moments later, darts slammed into his thigh, his shoulder, and his stomach. Fortunately, none were strong enough to pierce his armor. He gave thanks once again that the Indian spears and darts were so ineffective against quilted cloth and chain mail. He risked a quick glance at the men standing beside him. As far as he could tell, none of them had been seriously injured by the volley.

The crossbowmen released a volley of their own, and the lightly armored Indians fell in droves. But still they charged, leaping and bounding past their maimed countrymen. Half a minute more and they would reach the pike phalanx.

Vitale dug his feet into the muddy ground. A terrible whirring filled the air as hundreds of throwing slings took to the heavens. A clay ball slammed into his ribs and he winced. The cracking and splintering of nearby pikes prevented him from dwelling on it, and he scanned the sky for incoming projectiles. A pikeman shouted that he needed a new weapon and men in the supporting rows hurried to comply.

The Indians were so close their charge was shaking the ground. Vitale stared into the faces of the men baying for his blood. Not a kind face among them.

"Lower pikes," shouted a unit leader.

Vitale lowered his pike to groin level. No Indian would be ducking under his pike today.

"Thrust!" shouted the unit leader.

Vitale's arms sprang forward. His target, a lithe Indian, swung his *macuahuitl* outward to bat the pike away, but the pike had too much mass and plunged into his abdomen. It passed clean through and impaled the Indian behind him. The pike shuddered as it punched through the man's rib cage, and the sheer force of the impact made Vitale stagger backward. His teeth clacked shut on his tongue, and he tasted blood.

The pike cracked as he tried to hoist it upward, and he yanked it backward to dislodge the spearhead. Vitale succeeded in removing the second victim, but the first one proved more stubborn.

Meanwhile, the mass of Indians stopped by the pikes grew to be as unruly and impenetrable as a wild thicket. Unsure what belonged to whom, the pikemen behind Vitale thrust their weapons into every part of the disorganized formation, and they were rewarded with howls so loud they blotted out the booming cannons and the rattling muskets.

A pikeman to the left of Vitale collapsed into the muck, grasping and clawing at his neck. A pair of Indian warriors rushed forward to finish the soldier off, but a new pikeman stepped forward and quickly dispatched both of them. The Indians yelled something, but it was lost in the din of a cavalry charge that tore through the Indian lines at half-speed.

"Front line, forward," shouted the unit leader. Vitale gritted his teeth, dug his feet into the mud, and managed to advance one full pace.

A spear drove into the ground between his feet, and he jumped in surprise. His footwear consisted of nothing besides boiled leather and soft padding—a spear could cut through that like a knife through Serena cheese. Vitale shook his head, yelled, and thrust his pike forward. He felt something catch on the other end, and it gave him a small thrill.

Is that normal? He had no idea, nor did he care. He had to stay focused. If the Indians broke through the line, the battle would be lost.

A rock smashed into Vitale's kneecap, and a sharp pain shot through his leg. He gasped, stumbled backward, and let go of the pike.

Indians tumbled into the new gap and a hand latched onto Vitale, pulling him down. He landed face-first in the mud and tried to push himself up. He lifted his head no more than a finger span before someone pushed him back down.

Mud filled his mouth and his nose, and a jolt of panic took him. He couldn't breathe! He turned his head to the side. No air, just more mud. Desperate, he flailed and kicked but gained nothing for his troubles.

Just when Vitale thought his lungs would burst, the person pushing him down stilled and fell to the side. Vitale rolled over and took a deep, shuddering breath. His throat burned, and his knee felt as if it were splitting open.

An Indian, bleeding out from a deep cut to the neck, twitched and convulsed half a pace away. Vitale grabbed a handful of mud and shoved it into the dying man's mouth. The sudden burst of energy quickly abandoned him, and he collapsed on his side moments later.

He rolled over to get a look at the man who had saved him from the Indian. Something about his countenance seemed familiar. Hard to be sure, though. Difficult, all of a sudden, keeping his thoughts straight. His eyelids were growing heavy, so heavy...

"Morla also had bad teeth," Vitale whispered right before he lost consciousness.

~ ~ ~

Solomon weaved through the mess of injured, dead, and dying soldiers strewn across the open field. The Christians had pushed the Tlaxcalteca back but suffered greatly for their efforts. Dozens of Spaniards were injured, some so badly they would die in a few days. He expected a great many to recover though. All of them had received visits from the physicians, and most of them were on the mend. Solomon wanted to believe his Christian captors would do the same for him, but he knew better. They cared about him to the extent it was convenient and not one iota more.

Solomon rubbed his cotton armor and made a du'a to Allah. The quilted cloth was surprisingly effective against darts and arrows, and he was most thankful for it.

Tonight, however, he was on the hunt for an item even more valuable than Indian armor: new footwear.

His rotted boots had been no match for the thick thorny vines they trudged through in the first pass and did not survive the desert crossing. For the past few days, he had made do with thin sandals he acquired in Xocotlan, and he had no intention of doing so any longer. Solomon could make do with the unorthodox Indian armor, but hurrying about the battlefield with nothing besides sandals would be no better than trying to cross the Mediterranean in a longboat.

He kneeled next to a supine soldier. Solomon gave him a small nudge and was pleased to see the Spaniard did not stir. He undid the laces on his right boot and waited. Not a peep. Solomon, almost giddy with joy, took the shoe in both his hands and pulled ever so gently. For his efforts, he was rewarded with a most terrible sound: a weak moaning.

Solomon sighed, stood up, and trudged off in search of his quarry. A dead man would not miss his boots one bit, but a wounded man would hanker after them like a lost pup in search of its mother. He passed half a dozen soldiers before he came across one that was suitably still.

He bent over and whispered, "Are you dead yet?"

Much to his dismay, the soldier responded by whispering the name of some woman. Solomon shook his head and made his way to a different row of wounded soldiers. Any man still cognizant enough to entertain thoughts of the other sex was cognizant enough to miss stolen boots.

A small *psst* sound made him freeze. Solomon turned in the direction of the sound and was surprised to see that one of the wounded men had propped himself up on one elbow. Even more surprising, the wounded man was staring right at him.

"That you, Solomon?" the wounded man asked.

51

It took Solomon a moment to realize the voice belonged to Vitale, a New Christian he had become acquainted with months prior. Relieved, he smiled and made his way over to the one soldier he could consider a friend.

He took a seat on a patch of cold damp grass next to Vitale. "May I offer you water? I am sure I can find a canteen somewhere."

Vitale smiled and slowly sat up. "If that was the case, you'd have pilfered it by now. I think I've drank enough, thank you much. Already passed water twice, and that's no easy feat when you're injured. Physician says I'll be healed in a few days." Vitale's grin faded. "Only reason I'm still alive is because of Morla, though."

Solomon searched his memory. The name did not ring a bell. "Morla is one of your countrymen?"

"He's the man who tried to steal my mother's necklace. Cortés tried to hang him back when we were still in Totonac lands, but Pedro stopped him. I can't tell you how much I wanted to kill Morla a few weeks ago. Now I owe him my life."

Solomon wondered if he could feel grateful to the Christians who forced him into slavery. Even if they freed him on the morrow and sent him back across the Atlantic on the first ship, he did not think he could find a place in his heart for gratitude. He had suffered too many years and lost too much to ever forgive.

"I was worried you wouldn't survive the march," Vitale added.

Solomon snorted. "I have seen more years than you, but I will see Mecca again, even if it is the last thing I do."

A brief silence settled over them. Chirping crickets and gurgling streams filled in the void, a primordial symphony that offered its bounty free to all.

After a minute, Vitale said, "At least you got something to go back to. I got nothing. I am nothing. All because of the Old Christians."

Solomon checked to see if any of the wounded men were listening. Most of them seemed to be asleep, and out of earshot for whispering, but it was reckless for the boy to speak so candidly.

"Vitale, you must—"

"Be careful?" Vitale asked. He laughed. "Been gettin' that advice all my life. My mother and father used to tell me that constantly, not that the advice helped them much. We used to stay together, back in Spain. We were the only New Christians in the entire town, but the neighbors never treated us bad. Probably helped that my father was the only doctor for leagues in any direction. He was a good doctor, too. Saved most of his patients. But there was one boy..."

Vitale cleared his throat and exhaled loudly. "He couldn't save. Nobody looked at us the same afterward. How could he save so many worthless patients but fail to save the son of the alcalde? Didn't make any sense—so they made it make sense. My father was a crypto Jew and killed the boy as part of some heretic ritual. Then the neighbor's cat died. No reason, as far as anyone could tell. After that, it wasn't just my father who was a wicked Jew—we all were. We should have moved. But we were too proud for that. And too poor."

Vitale rubbed his eyes and took a deep shuddering breath. "We were so poor my mother had to stay behind when my father went to help the patient in the next town over. I came with him, though. Had to, since I was supposed to follow in his footsteps and become a great physician, too. The patient we left town for died before we were even halfway there. And while we were away, another cat died. So the nice townsfolk got together and burned our house down. Maybe they knew my mother

53

was inside, maybe they didn't. Not sure how much it matters to her now that she's gone. The Old Christians left me with nothing to remember her by besides ashes and a measly necklace."

Solomon swallowed the lump in his throat. "They have not been so kind to me either. Perhaps the next world will be kinder to us."

"It's this world I'm most concerned with," Vitale replied. "And my place in it." Vitale went quiet. "I've always, always been poor. The Old Christians hold all the keys, but this campaign gives me the chance to make something of myself. I watched when Morla got strong up and didn't lift a finger to help him. If I'm bein' honest, I was disappointed when Pedro stopped the hanging. Morla coulda let me die today. Instead, he speared the Indian trying to kill me and saved my life, all because we're fighting under the same banner." Vitale sucked in his breath. "I have to put aside my hatred, my memories of life before. It won't help me here. I'm not sure it ever has."

Solomon's eyes widened. "Those memories should be more sacred to you than life. Our past is what gives us meaning and direction, what comforts us when we think about the travails of the future. Cast that aside, and you will truly have nothing."

Vitale rubbed a hand through his short hair. "So I'm supposed to live in the past? Pretend that nothing else matters and make it into some kind of escape?" He shook his head. "Day I look to my past for comfort, the day I forget how terrible it was. Cling to whatever make-believe you want. It won't help you here, won't change what is. You need gold if you want to change things."

Solomon narrowed his eyes. "Gold is all that matters, then? Chase after the world's riches all you want. Perhaps gold will buy you status and security. But with that comes envy and hatred, and one day the cutthroats will get together to decide how to take all you cherish."

"Then I'll live good until then." Vitale sniffled and cleared his throat. "Keep your great and glorious past—I need something real. I'm the seed of cowards who converted at the point of a sword, a Dutchman of low heritage, and I got no interest in dying poor."

Solomon shivered and blew out his breath. Earlier in the day, he had been ready to keel over because of the heat, but the scorching temperature seemed a distant memory now. It sometimes felt as if he spent all his time careening between extremes, and he often wondered if that would ever change. "Forgive me for being snide in the past," Solomon said. "I am not without faults."

Vitale grunted and leaned back on his elbows. "Leave me be, Solomon. We'll be marching again soon, so you best get some rest. There's talk we're running low on food and can't hold this position much longer."

Solomon nodded glumly. A cold wind swept through the field and cut through his cotton armor like a crossbow bolt through a Tlaxcalteca shield. The mere prospect of marching made his feet ache. He bid Vitale farewell and carried on his search as before, wondering all the while if he had lost something that could never be regained.

Tlaxcala Province

Chapter 6

Xicotencatl the Younger kneeled in the center of the room, painfully aware that he was the focus of attention. Even his own father sat in judgment. He kept his head down as he waited to be called upon and thought about what he should say to the distinguished lords. Three men too old to lead warriors would pass judgment on his campaign against the pale people. If he were found wanting, they could have him killed on the spot.

They would not kill me in front of my father. At least, he hoped that was true. The *teteo* invasion had upended everything. What he once considered impossible, now seemed ordinary.

"Xicotencatl the Younger, we have many questions for you," Temil said. Xicotencatl slowly stood and took in the sight of the lords in judgment. Father, a lord from before he could remember, sat on the far left, his rheumy eyes as watery and unrevealing as ever. The deep-set wrinkles on his face, however, seemed a touch more pronounced than usual. Was he worried for Tlaxcala or was he worried for him? Probably both.

The other lords, Temil and Catzin, sat in ornate chairs to the right of Father. And behind them, twelve guards stood at attention, ready to attack on a moment's notice.

"Many Tlaxcalteca are dead because of your conflict with the *teteo*," Catzin said, spitting out his words so fast that his chins shook.

Xicotencatl waited to see if Catzin would say more. After a lengthy pause, he replied, "It is not my conflict. It is our conflict."

Catzin scoffed. "You were the one who pushed for battle with the *teteo*. You insisted we take their envoys hostage, and you insisted we attack their camp."

Xicotencatl nodded. "That is true. And the War Council supported me because they knew the pale people share common cause with the wicked traitor Motecuhzoma."

The lords went silent, perhaps recalling that not so long ago, they cheered when Xicotencatl promised to bring the fight to the *teteo*. After an extended pause, Temil spoke. "The *teteo* claim they do not owe any allegiance to Motecuhzoma. They wish to see him cast down from his throne and mean to make war against the Mexica."

"And who will take his place on the throne?" Xicotencatl asked.

A small smile crossed Father's face but vanished so quickly that Xicotencatl wondered if he had imagined it.

"Surely those that ally with the *teteo*," Catzin replied.

Xicotencatl glared at the portly lord. Nowhere in Tlaxcala did the *teteo* have a more steadfast advocate. Catzin had protested loudly against the abducting of the Totonac envoys and insisted upon making peace with the *teteo* at every War Council.

"And how do we know that we can trust the pale people?" Xicotencatl asked.

"We can trust that the Mexica will exterminate us if we do not make common cause with powerful people," Temil countered. "The Mexica have punished our people with the cruelest of sanctions for years now. Our nation grows weaker with every new moon, and the Mexica nation goes stronger. How much longer can we resist their incursions?"

"I do not know," Xicotencatl said. "I do know the *teteo* are quite cruel. Think about what they have done to our warriors with their smoke and thunder weapons, what they have done to the villages with their night raids."

A number of the guards stiffened at the mention of the night raids, but Xicotencatl pressed on. "We cannot let our resolve weaken. We owe the dead vengeance. Every child killed by the *teteo*, every porter killed by the *teteo*, every warrior killed by the *teteo*—"

"Would any of them be dead if we were not at war with the *teteo*?" Catzin asked. "You have been the driving force behind battle strategy. Perhaps they would still be alive if you were a more able commander."

Xicotencatl's hand instinctively drifted to the place his war club should have been. He had been forced to relinquish it when he entered the room, and that was probably for the best. Braining Catzin would not win him allies amongst the Tlaxcalteca elite.

"Our campaign against the *teteo* has suffered many setbacks, and I do bear blame for that," Xicotencatl said. "Trying to ambush the *teteo* after they entered Tlaxcala was unwise; we should have attacked them before they ever set foot in our lands. I take full responsibility for that mistake."

The more he thought about the mistake, the more he wanted to smash his fist through something hard. Prior to the ambush, he worried the pale people would be so thoroughly routed that they would make for poor captives. Now he feared the *teteo* would rout his own forces if he did not find a better way to fight them.

Temil leaned back in his chair. "The *teteo* have been in Tlaxcala over half a month now and we have battled with them almost every day. Have you only made one mistake during that time? Do you have any regrets about letting the Otomi play such a large role in our fighting forces?"

Xicotencatl scratched his forehead. It would be easy to blame the Otomi. They were a marginal group in

Tlaxcala and few of the elites hailed from their ranks. Xicotencatl cleared his throat. "The Otomi are not Tlaxcalteca, but they have fought with valor and distinction. I am honored to fight alongside them and know they are as determined to eject the pale people from our lands as any of our warriors. Nonetheless, I must admit I fight alongside a Tlaxcalteca warrior who has been less than exemplary in carrying out his duties." Xicotencatl turned toward Catzin. "That man is Chichimecatecle."

Catzin's brow leapt upward. "You dare to insult my kin, your own deputy, in front of me, in front of this council?"

Xicotencatl started to answer but stopped himself. Father looked at him quizzically and Temil shook his head slowly, rapping his thin fingers on his jeweled armrest all the while.

"Honorable Catzin, I mean no disrespect," Xicotencatl said. "My deputy cannot be faulted for lack of bravery. However, his inability to follow commands is most troublesome. On our third day of battle, we managed to break the *teteo* formation. But when my men broke through the *teteo* lines, Chichimecatecle's forces did not follow us through the breach. Had he done so, victory would have gone to us that day."

Catzin snorted. "After the *teteo* ejected you from their camp, they carried out raids under cover of dark. How many villages did they attack that night?"

"Ten," Xicotencatl whispered.

Catzin leaned forward and jabbed a stubby finger at him. "Only five villages were attacked the first night. Breaking their formation led to more death and destruction, all so that you and your men could have the satisfaction of fighting the *teteo* with club and *macuahuitl*. What did we gain from it?"

Xicotencatl smarted as he remembered the indignation of having to call a retreat after breaking through the *teteo* formation. "I believe it is because we broke the *teteo* formation that they decided to relocate their battle camp. We inflicted great harm on their troops as they retreated from the river position and gained valuable information about their weaknesses. Most of the *teteo* we felled were brought down by our throwing slings, and we should make greater use of the weapon during the next attack."

Catzin rolled his eyes. "The *teteo* are now encamped on a hill and have a stronger position than ever. Why should we attack again? We can make peace with them, like we should have from the beginning."

"We would do a great dishonor to our dead by making peace with those who killed them," Xicotencatl said in a low voice.

"My subjects tell me they would rather be vassals than see their houses destroyed and their wives and children killed," Temil replied.

Xicotencatl blinked in amazement. "We are Tlaxcalteca. We grovel before no nation. We are an independent people—"

"We will not exist as a people if all our women and children are killed," Father said.

The air rushed out of Xicotencatl's lungs. Father had spoken out against him. His cause was lost. Xicotencatl knew with a sad certainty he would not be able to summon support for any more large-scale assaults on the *teteo* position. He ground his teeth and stared at the ground.

"We all know how bravely you have fought," Temil added. "But what do we gain by continuing to fight? Even if we prevail over the *teteo*, the Mexica would be sure to attack us before we could recover our strength. We must sue for peace and soon."

61

Xicotencatl took a deep breath and looked up. Every detail of the room came into sharp focus. The hard-set expressions of the guards, the resigned posture of the lords... and Xicotencatl knew he could not make peace yet. "I would like permission to make one last assault on the *teteo* position. We will attack at night with a small party so we can catch them unawares. Victory will gain us control of their weapons and give us the power to establish ourselves as the most dominant nation in all the One World. Should the night attack fail—" His voice cracked, and he took a moment to regain his composure. "I will lay down my arms and encourage others to do the same."

The lords conferred amongst one another. After what seemed an eternity, Father finally leaned forward to speak: "Permission granted."

~ ~ ~

Chicahua crept forward under cover of dark with the rest of the men. He had trained as a warrior since childhood and long considered himself immune to the terror that seized weaker men on the eve of battle. Nonetheless, fear had found a place in his heart, and the flutter in his stomach only grew worse as the march progressed.

The prospect of battle with the *teteo*, powerful as they were, had little to do with his unease. Their weapons—the thumping, the popping, the neighing, the ripping—were intimidating at first, but Chicahua no longer found their weapons frightening. He had not suffered a single injury on account of those weapons, and that could not be mere happenstance. The gods had special plans for him, and he had every confidence they would keep him safe in any and all battles.

Knowing the gods would look after him was not enough to calm the flutter in his stomach, however. Fighting battle at night was unnatural. None of the elders could remember the last time it had been done. As far as

Chicahua knew, it had never been done in their history. And with good reason.

Night shrouded everything in darkness and hid the enemy's face. Few things could be more terrible in battle. When the enemy was anonymous, it was easy to do ugly, terrible things. It was even possible to mistake a friend for the enemy.

All his life, Chicahua had been taught that battle had to be fought in a way the gods would approve. This need to fight honorably dictated not only when he fought, but how he fought. Archers and spear throwers aimed to kill, yet infantrymen were supposed to capture enemies so they could be given Flowery Deaths. Of course, there were always some who gave in to their bloodlust, but Chicahua prided himself on never killing an enemy on the battlefield.

Not so long ago, his countrymen had lauded his restraint, but there would be no such praise tonight. Everything had changed now that the *teteo* had come.

They fought without honor and killed wantonly on the field. The Tlaxcalteca had lost countless warriors to the *teteo* forces and could no longer fight the old way. Too many had died horrible, awful deaths, twitching and convulsing as they bled out from wounds that were burnt and ripped in impossible ways.

Most of the generals had lost their appetite for battle and Xicotencatl was one of the few lords still willing to fight. But he intended to do more than fight. He intended to win, even if it meant attacking at night and killing enemies on the battlefield.

Some of the nearby warriors slowed their pace as the incline of the hill became more challenging. Chicahua did the same, careful not to get too far ahead of his countrymen.

He studied the *teteo* camp formation for weaknesses, his heart pounding all the while. He could not see much in the darkness besides a few dim lights, but he did hear some scattered barking. Chicahua wondered if that meant the *teteo* were awake. He hoped not. The Tlaxcalteca needed every advantage they could get, and he hoped they would at least have surprise on their side.

But even if they did not, Chicahua was confident the battle would be a success. The Givers had assured all of them that the power of the *teteo* waxed and waned with the rise and fall of the sun. When the sun was gone, they could only make battle with their hornless stags and would be unprepared for a raid.

A blinding flash of light, followed by an eruption of horrendous noises, took him by surprise and Chicahua threw himself to the ground. Pops and thumps filled the air and countless Tlaxcalteca fell to the earth screaming.

He patted his chest and legs. Once again, the *teteo* weapons had left him unharmed. He looked to his side. A childhood friend lay by him, drooling like a senseless babe and pale as death. What was once a knee was now an ugly stub spurting bright blood.

New strength coursed through Chicahua's body, and his fear vanished. He would not let his friend die here. No, he would carry him to safety and get him treatment. Nobody deserved a death like that.

They were in the middle of the crossfire so it would be dangerous to carry him back to safety, but Chicahua was not afraid. The *teteo* weapons could not hurt him. They had tried to kill him many times before and failed every time. They would fail again.

He hoisted his friend onto his back and took a small step forward. His friend was heavy, but Chicahua was the strongest man in all his village. He knew with an unimpeachable certainty that he would carry his friend to safety. And afterward, he would return for vengeance.

The strain in his back eased, and his footsteps became more certain. He managed nine whole steps before a small piece of metal burst through his skull, killing him instantly.

Tlaxcala Province

Cholula Province

Chapter 7

Chimalli pushed aside a small branch and strained his eyes to make out the main entrance in the Tlaxcalteca defenses. Located almost half a long-run ahead, he could just barely identify the outline. If he moved forward a few hundred paces, he would not have to squint as much but that would place him at even greater risk of capture. Truth be told, he was already taking a significant risk by climbing in the tree to join the other scouts. It was in many respects an unnecessary risk as there were no shortage of Mexica warriors he could have delegated the task to. But if battle with the *teteo* was a certainty, Chimalli wanted to study their formation firsthand.

Tezoc would probably chide him for taking an unnecessary risk, but he was not here to reprimand him. *I wish he was here.* Chimalli pushed the idea from his head. His commander was needed in the Valley of Mexico, and there was no sense wishing for something that could not be.

He leaned against the tree trunk and kneaded the stiff muscles in his lower back with his free hand. The shift in weight elicited a groan from the pine branch under him, and he moved his right foot to a different branch. A nearby scout shot him a concerned look, but the others stayed focused on their duties.

Perhaps I should send another scout into Tlaxcala. Ten days had passed since he had received any intelligence from inside Tlaxcala, and the last report had been most interesting. The Tlaxcalteca had attempted to attack the *teteo* camp under cover of dark, but the audacious assault floundered under sustained fire from the *teteo*. Thereafter, there were no more Tlaxcalteca attacks, and the *teteo* burned the nearby villages with impunity. Then all fighting stopped completely. Chimalli had sent numerous scouts to investigate the matter, but the last five had not returned. If they had been captured by Tlaxcalteca forces, he doubted they had died well.

A scout, perched a few branches higher, whispered, "Movement near the wall's entrance."

Chimalli readied his knife. A row of five men emerged from the entrance, riding the giant hornless stags the *teteo* had used to such devastating effect against the Tlaxcalteca. His heart sank as he took in the sight of a monstrous animal with a body half the length of a canoe and legs as large as oars. He had prayed the Tlaxcalteca would kill the *teteo*, that the stories about their beasts would prove false, but it appeared he had asked for too much.

Three rows of mounted men emerged before he remembered he should mark the tree. He hurriedly added horizontal notches but kept his eyes focused on the *teteo* forces. Not until the sixth row became visible did he spot any men who walked on their own two feet. These unmounted men marched shoulder to shoulder in a row of eight, and he added a small diagonal slash to the new notch to indicate the change.

All the while, men continued to stream through the entrance of the wall, clad in armor that glittered like polished jade. Even more jarring than the armor's appearance, was the sound it made. Every foot step prompted a din of clinking and clanking that grated on his ears. Their spear-axes and long spears made little in the way of noise but they glittered brilliantly in the midday sun, and their long knives moved in a wavy line redolent of a meandering river.

Next came the Totonac warriors. The scouts hissed with disapproval, but Chimalli remained quiet as he took count. For the sake of space and efficiency, he now used one notch to represent twenty rows. He expected to stop after five notches or so but, much to his surprise, men continued to stream out of the Tlaxcala entrance.

Chimalli frowned. The Totonac section had grown while the *teteo* were in Tlaxcalteca territory, but that made no sense. If a large contingent of Totonac troops had entered Tlaxcala during the past few weeks, his scouts would have spotted them.

He squinted to see better. Many of the Totonacs were carrying light shields but did not wear any quilted cloth. That did not make any sense either. The Totonacs did not lack for cloth and knew it had great value as armor. He realized with a sickening certainty that the warriors lacking cloth, the ones he foolishly assumed were Totonac, could only hail from one nation: Tlaxcala.

Chimalli tried to swallow, but his mouth was dry as sand and his throat would not cooperate. An alliance between the Totonacs, the *teteo*, and the Tlaxcalteca could not bode well for Mexico. By the time the last row of Tlaxcalteca emerged, it was clear they constituted the bulk of the *teteo* coalition. If Chimalli had counted correctly, the Tlaxcalteca warriors were four thousand strong which meant the *teteo* were now marching on Tenochtitlan with an army of almost six thousand men.

Chimalli blinked. Maybe his eyes were playing tricks on him. The other scouts may have come to a different figure. "Itzli, how many did you count?"

"Six thousand. Seven thousand, if you include the porters and the servants."

Chimalli shook his head and suppressed a flare of anger. The *teteo* coalition outnumbered his own contingent by a factor of two to one. If his forces ever intimidated the *teteo*, they certainly would not do so now.

"They could reach Tenochtitlan in three days, if they hurry," Itzli said in an awed voice.

"They will not hurry to reach Tenochtitlan," Chimalli replied. "An army that large needs many supplies, and Cholula is only eight long-runs away so they will head there first. Pray for our allies in Cholula. They will be in no position to refuse the Tlaxcalteca and their *teteo* allies."

~ ~ ~

Pedro rolled his shoulder and gently prodded the muscle with his weary fingers. Apparently, a few hours of marching had undone the healing work brought about by twenty days of peace with the Tlaxcalteca Indians. While the pain in his arm was nowhere near as bad as the night he received the sling injury, it worried him that his shoulder had yet to make a full recovery. *I should take certain soldiers into the city and search for an apothecary.*

Considering the size of Cholula, scouts counted over five thousand houses, Pedro trusted he could find at least one apothecary. Moreover, the Choluteca Indians seemed friendly enough. The envoys that visited camp yesterday brought all manner of foodstuffs and the Choluteca had done nothing to harass their camp, which is more than could be said for some of the other Indians they had conferred with.

A sudden pain flared up in his shoulder again. He closed his eyes and clenched his fist. It would have been better if he had been injured by a spear or an arrow. There would have been more dignity in that. An edged weapon would have given him a scar at least, some kind of mark a woman could marvel over. But instead of a scar, he had a barely visible wound that hurt at random intervals and refused to heal in a timely manner.

Doña Luisa, his new wife since the peace agreement with Tlaxcala, coughed. Pedro sighed and turned toward her. She stood in the corner of the tent, wearing an airy skirt and a loose tunic. He massaged the nape of his neck, wondering if he would ever get used to the Indian style of dress. He wore neither shoes nor a shirt, but he still had on more articles of clothing than his wife. Doña Luisa's attire would have been outrageous in Spain but here in the New World, her style of dress was decidedly conservative.

Doña Luisa said something in Indian and Pedro rolled his eyes. "I don't understand savage."

She stepped forward, pointed at his shoulder, and then poked herself in the arm. Before he could respond, she kneeled next to his stool and blew on his shoulder. Her cool breath sent shivers down his arm. She gently prodded his forearm, slowly working her delicate fingers upward. A small groan escaped his lips.

He closed his eyes and took a deep breath, relishing the sweet relief her fingers brought. In a moment, all that changed and a searing pain shot through his body as three sharp fingers suddenly stabbed into his shoulder. His eyes flew open and he saw what almost looked like a smile on her face. He grabbed her by the arm and pulled her toward him.

Her grin quickly vanished but what replaced it, he could not recognize. He expected her to appear frightened or remorseful, but her steely expression reflected little in the way of emotion. He squeezed her arm harder and a twinge of pain flashed across her face. It occurred to him she might not have meant to hurt him, and he loosened his grip on her arm.

A noise outside the tent grabbed his attention. "Pedro, may I step inside?" Cortés asked.

Pedro unhanded Doña Luisa and rubbed his injured shoulder. "Come in."

Cortés brushed past the tent flap and stepped inside. "Doña Luisa, it is a pleasure to see you," Cortés said. "How fare you?"

Doña Luisa said something in Indian. Cortés cocked his head toward Pedro. "I see you have not been teaching her much Spanish. Doña Marina can teach her a few words, should it please you."

Pedro grunted. "You want all the Indians speaking our tongue?"

Cortés smiled. "We can discuss the matter later. Please dismiss Doña Luisa. We must speak privately."

Pedro nodded, gestured to Doña Luisa, and then pointed at the tent flap. She furrowed her brow, pointed at herself and then outside. He nodded again and snapped his fingers for emphasis. She scowled and stormed out of the tent. Pedro was not sorry to see her go, but he was a bit confounded that Cortés thought she might listen in on their conversation. Few could worry about the machinations of the Indians as much as Cortés.

Pedro stretched his good arm. "You know how to say sorry with a head nod?"

Cortés did not bother to answer. Instead, he seated himself on a stool across from Pedro and asked, "Do you remember the Xaragua massacre?"

Pedro arched his brow. He could not remember the last time someone asked him about Xaragua. The mere mention of it could quiet a tavern. "Of course I do. Amazing how up in arms everyone can get because some governor burns a few Indian chiefs."

"More than a few, Pedro. Governor Ovando bound and burned eighty chiefs that day, eighty chiefs who had already agreed to make peace." Cortés drummed his fingers against his thigh. After a trice, he added, "Do you think any of the settlers were upset that the Crown recalled Ovando?"

Pedro frowned. "Hard to say. Same settlers who grumble about the Crown being overly sentimental with the Indians were quick to piss on Ovando's grave. No easy task, being the scapegoat for an entire colony."

Cortés twirled his mustache between his thumb and his forefinger.

"Why is Xaragua on your mind?" Pedro asked.

Cortés clasped his hands together. "The Tlaxcalteca have a long-standing enmity with the Choluteca. They say the Choluteca are allies to Motecuhzoma and must be punished for depriving Tlaxcala of much needed trade goods."

Still seated on his sleeping mat, Pedro reached forward to grab his boot and flipped it upside down. A bug the size of his thumb tumbled out and scrambled off in search of safe haven. He crushed it with his shoe before it could get even halfway to the tent flap. "Punished how?"

"The Tlaxcalteca feel that every nobleman in Cholula should be put to the sword."

Pedro stiffened. "Have you tried convincing them to feel otherwise?"

"If the Tlaxcalteca were amenable to our blandishments, it would not have taken half a month and a dozen battles to make them bend the knee," Cortés replied.

Pedro laughed. "Good point. Skewered more Indians than I can count during those night raids." A sudden pain flared up again in his shoulder. He winced and said, "I swear if I find the Indian who hit me with the sling, I will cut his throwing hand off and stuff it down his throat."

Cortés looked at him askance and shook his head. In a low voice, he said, "The Tlaxcalteca are threatening to abrogate the agreement we made in Tlaxcala if we do not capitulate to their demands. They are threatening to march their entire army back to Tlaxcala should we refuse to kill the Choluteca."

"The Indians are making demands of us?" Pedro asked. "That's completely backward—they could not beat us in battle, so they get to decide which battles we wage?"

"They know we cannot march on Tenochtitlan without them," Cortés said. "And since we have already taken leave of their lands, reprisal worries them little."

Pedro curled his lip in disgust. First the Totonacs, and now the Tlaxcalteca. No matter where the Indians hailed from, they were incapable of putting aside their own interests when it came to alliances. "Cortés, we do not need them. You have convinced yourself the only way we can defeat the Indians is with other Indians, but you are forgetting our many triumphs. We beat the Potonchan Indians, we beat the Tlaxcalteca Indians—"

"The Mexica are more powerful than any of them," Cortés interrupted. "If the Tlaxcalteca abandon our cause, so will the other Indians. Our campaign would be mortally weakened, and we would be forced to make a retreat to the coast or push toward Tenochtitlan. Even if we were strong enough to take Tenochtitlan without the Tlaxcalteca, we could never keep it."

Pedro sucked in his breath. "Why would we want to keep Tenochtitlan? What happened to building new ships and returning home with the gold?"

"With the Tlaxcalteca as allies, we do not need to return home. We can make this place our home and establish a dynasty that will last for centuries. We could be the masters of this New World... but none of that will come to pass without allies. Our alliance with the Totonacs failed to give us the army we needed, and we cannot let our alliance with the Tlaxcalteca fail." Cortés picked at a scabbed over blackhead and said in a low voice, "We must do as the Tlaxcalteca insist. Otherwise, the march will fail and the Mexica will kill us."

Pedro narrowed his eyes. Cortés had failed to mention that retreat was not a viable option because he beached and scuttled the fleet. The omission did not surprise

Pedro; Cortés had an impressive ability to forget unpleasant details. Pedro puffed his chest out and leaned back. "If you already know what needs to be done, why did you come here?"

"The Crown punished Ovando for his part in the Xaragua massacre because he never provided an adequate justification for his actions," Cortés explained. "We must give the men a story that makes them feel we had no choice but to kill the Choluteca lords."

Pedro cracked his knuckles. "And you want my help, creating this story?"

Cortés shook his head. "Leave that to me. I will, however, need your help disseminating the story to others. And I must know if anyone questions it. Can you do this for me?"

Pedro stared into Cortés' earnest face. If he was the slightest bit ashamed at making Pedro party to his lie, he did not show it.

Pedro rubbed a hand through his hair. If Cortés was right, and the massacre was going to happen anyway, Pedro saw no reason to tell the others the full truth. It would only complicate things, and the company already had enough problems with mutiny. Pedro cleared his throat and said, "Of course, I will help you."

Cortés smiled and squeezed Pedro's hand. "I knew I could count on you."

Cortés stood, made a quick farewell, and then departed. Meanwhile, Pedro stared at the bug he crushed, wondering if he actually needed to kill it. The bug had done nothing to harm him, the bug probably would have left him alone... he shook his head. It could have been poisonous. Certainly strange-looking, judging by its crushed remains. Wings the size of his thumb and eyeballs as big as calluses. Something like that was not meant to live.

Cholula Province

Chapter 8

Malintze waded through the crowded streets of Cholula, taking careful note of every detail. Ever since she had been a child, she had heard stories about the city of wisdom. The traveling merchants loved to regale crowds with stories of the city, but she realized now that no secondhand account could capture the magnificence of the stone pyramids, the towering houses of adobe and clay, or the stunning statues carved in the likeness of the gods.

And while the merchants always raved about the bustling market, even the most flattering description could not communicate the sheer energy created by thousands gathering in one giant confluence to barter and banter. The promenade of feted customers had swallowed her much the same way a rushing river might, and she sometimes only caught glimpses of the goods being sold at the many stalls. A flash of obsidian jewelry here, a twinkle of polished jade there, but most startling of all, twenty bound women. The raw misery in their eyes reminded her of what she had escaped, and she gave thanks once again that she had been able to rise above her former station in life.

True freedom, however, was still not within reach, and she had no choice but to help Cortés destroy the city. It would only be a matter of time until the market was choked with smoke, and she wished she had something pretty to remember the city by. Perhaps the street artist could oblige her with a sketch or a painting. She sighed. There was no time for that now. She had important matters to attend to.

Cortés had sent her on a very specific, if simple, mission. He wanted her to talk with some of the local people in Cholula. It mattered little what she said or they said. It was all for theatre. The guards transporting her into the city were none too bright, and even less competent, but that was ideal because they had to believe she had uncovered a plot against the army by talking with some random local. Cortés honestly believed that was all it would take to convince his countrymen the Choluteca had sinister intentions, but she had some doubts. Sure, the simpletons transporting her through the market would believe her, but anyone who could believe such a simple story had to want a simple story.

Not that her input mattered. The men had already decided what was going to happen. Her job was to act out a fantasy for those who needed it. Malintze cast a darting glance toward her unwitting accomplices. If her "guards" noticed, they gave no indication of it. Instead, they gushed over the various beauties of the city—the clean, hard-packed walkways and the towering, stone structures—as they discussed the many reasons Cholula compared favorably to Valladolid. She wondered if their affection would prevent them from taking part in Cortés' massacre. She doubted it. Men rarely let love stand in the way of violence.

"Surely a fine woman deserves some fine items," a vendor called out in Nahuatl. Malintze turned in the direction of the voice. The vendor, a woman only a few years older than her, had a stall set up a mere ten paces away and stood in front of a plain green curtain. The vendor waved her over. Drawn forward by a sense of politeness and a budding curiosity, Malintze made her way toward the stall. By the time her moon-eyed guards realized she had left them behind, she was already five paces ahead, and they rushed to catch up with her.

Terror seized the vendor, and she froze like a startled deer. Malintze spoke to the guards in Spanish and let them know there was no reason to cause a scene.

The guards relaxed, and the vendor flashed Malintze a grateful smile before gesturing to the table with a grand wave. "Peruse the items laid out before you. I am sure you will find something to your liking."

Malintze nodded. The artisans of Cholula were famous throughout the One World. Rumor had it that Motecuhzoma used Choluteca plates, and Malintze had to concede the praise was well-deserved. Tiny figures adorned each pot's rim, and beautiful swirls of color pulled her gaze into the center of each plate.

"What do you like best?" the vendor asked.

"All of it," Malintze replied.

The vendor laughed. Malintze rubbed the bulge of a vase, impressed by the smooth finish and the creative blend of colors. The idea that rampaging soldiers might destroy the vase made her throat tighten, and she withdrew her hand.

She started to offer a farewell, but the woman stopped her and said, "I have something you will like."

The vendor picked up a small comb and placed it in Malintze's palm. Carved from mahogany, the comb's rich brown hue was finished with a reflective sheen that made every color pop and shine. The handle amazed her most of all. Carved in the shape of a butterfly, the wings radiated power and freedom. She reached out to stroke the splendid wings, and the smooth feel of the wood set her heart in a flutter.

"I have never seen such a nice comb," Malintze said in a choked voice. With reluctance, she handed it back. The woman nodded and urged Malintze to lean over the table. Despite being unsure what the woman intended, Malintze complied with the odd request.

The woman gathered up Malintze's hair in both hands, and the intimacy of it made Malintze stiffen. She could not remember the last time she let herself be so vulnerable with someone, and it took a moment to get her heart rate under control.

She focused on the beautiful pottery to calm herself. The vase nearest her was adorned with small animals, and she squinted to make out the coiled snake, the swooping eagle, the butterfly emerging from a damaged cocoon, the sad dog with the drooping head, and the sleeping deer cuddling with a newborn.

The vendor withdrew her hand. "Lift your head up."

Malintze did as instructed and found herself gazing into an obsidian mirror. Her dark reflection was startling, repulsive almost, but her heart softened when she saw what the vendor had done with her hair. Not only had she tied it in a bun, she had buried the comb in her hair so that the prongs were hidden from view, leaving only the butterfly handle visible.

Malintze tucked an errant strand of hair back and patted the bun with the palm of her hand. "You are a very talented artist," Malintze muttered and handed over a maravedí. The woman frowned and made no move to take it. Embarrassed, Malintze remembered that cocoa beans were the common currency in the One World. *Have I become Spanish?* She patted her dress and realized she had not thought to bring cocoa beans.

Malintze looked to the guards for assistance and noticed that one of them had taken off his plumed helmet. During the walk to market, he had complained bitterly about the helmet, claiming it was too small for use in battle or peace, and she realized it would be the perfect way to pay the woman.

Malintze explained to the soldier she would need his helmet. He stared at her like she had blasphemed, and she reminded him that she spoke for Cortés and that compensation would be provided. After hearing that, he needed no more convincing and relinquished the unwanted helmet without another word of protest.

Malintze offered the plumed helmet to the woman, and her eyes went wide as a Choluteca dinner plate. She tried to offer Malintze more items—the vase with the animals, the vase with the bulge—but Malintze refused to accept any of it. The vendor, however, was not to be dissuaded and encouraged Malintze to step behind the table.

As soon as Malintze did, the woman brushed back a curtain to reveal a small room. Malintze blinked in surprise. Her guards seemed equally surprised, and the one that had agreed to give up his helmet attempted to follow the vendor into the room.

Malintze held up her hand to stop him and let both her guards know they needed to stay outside. To preempt their objections, she quickly added that she needed to discuss female matters with the vendor. They flushed cherry red and agreed to stay outside.

The woman closed the curtain, and Malintze looked about the small room. The walls were made of clay, the floor of dirt, and there was nowhere to sit other than a small wooden stool.

A private space behind a stall was nothing unusual, but she had no idea that some vendors might use the space as a home. The entire room was probably no more than ten steps across. She glanced at the partition, certain that it was much too thin to shut out the sounds of the market. Despite the noise of the afternoon crowd, a small child lay curled up in the corner on a thin reed mat, snoring and occasionally fidgeting.

"What is your name?" asked the vendor.

In a small voice, she replied, "Malintze."

"Surely a high lady like you must go by Malintzin."

The woman's need to be respectful made her gut twist with pain. "You are a friend. You must call me Malintze," Malintze said. "And what should I call you?"

"Mazatl." She laid down the helmet on the one stool. Malintze's eyes drifted once again to the small, sleeping child. "My daughter," Mazatl explained. "Her name is Malinalli."

Malintze's heart skipped a beat. "So young," Malintze whispered. Her chest tightened and each breath became painful. Desperate, she turned to the woman. "Do you have any *octli*?"

Mazatl smiled slyly and grabbed a beaten, worn jug that had been hidden behind a much nicer jug. Malintze shook her head. The vendor spent all day working on fine crafts, and the nicest *octli* jug she could afford was a shoddy piece of misformed clay.

Mazatl sat on the ground and took a sip from the jug. She puckered her lips and closed her eyes. "It is still good," Mazatl said and passed the jug to Malintze.

Malintze took a on the ground and tipped the bottle back for a long drink. It had been months since she had drunk *octli* and the viscous elixir, a heady concoction derived from sap and fruit, was exactly what she needed.

After three large gulps, she handed the bottle back. "Have you lived here long?" Malintze asked.

"All my life."

Another sharp twinge. "Didn't you ever want to leave?"

Mazatl exhaled loudly. "I had an opportunity once. I could have lived in Tenochtitlan. But I did not want to raise a daughter there. Such terrible things happen in that city."

"Terrible things happen everywhere," Malintze said.

"Not in Cholula," the woman replied. "This city is very peaceful, very safe. I would not want to raise my daughter anywhere else."

Malintze's throat clenched as if a cord had been wrapped around it. Once the *teteo* and the Tlaxcalteca were finished with the city, Cholula would be inextricably linked to bloodshed.

Mazatl took another sip from the *octli* bottle before placing it in front of Malintze. "What brings you to Cholula?"

"I translate," Malintze said. "I was given to the *teteo* when they won an important battle, and I help them speak with us people here."

Mazatl gaped at her in shock. "You are a captive?"

"The *teteo* do not mean to give me a Flowery Death," Malintze said as she leaned forward to pick up the *octli* bottle. "They worship in a different way."

Mazatl nodded but did not seem fully convinced. "The *teteo* do not seem peaceful," Mazatl said. "It is wrong for them to bring an army here and take so much of our food. If a drought comes, we will all starve because the *teteo* will have left us with no food."

Malintze rubbed the worn *octli* bottle with a calloused thumb. "Motecuhzoma has invited the *teteo* to Tenochtitlan. We have only stopped here to rest and will soon leave Cholula."

The relief that flashed across Mazatl's face was unmistakable. She reached out for the *octli* bottle, and Malintze returned it with some reluctance.

"The *teteo* are so strange," Mazatl continued. "They smell awful and wear the oddest clothing. And their beasts are so messy."

Malintze laughed. She had become used to the *teteo* clothing, but their odor and their beasts still made her uneasy. "The *teteo* do not come from our world," Malintze said. "One day, I may see their world. The *teteo* have promised me freedom when they no longer need me."

Mazatl shook her head and wagged her finger. "You must come to Cholula when that happens and find me. There is no better city for a home. A nice woman like you could have anything she wants here."

"Could you ever leave here?" Malintze asked.

As soon as she asked the question, she knew she had erred. To let the woman know what the *teteo* planned for the city would be incredibly dangerous, not to mention foolish. Cortés would surely punish her, and Mazatl would very likely share the information with others.

Eventually, word would reach Choluteca forces and that would help no one. The *teteo* and the Tlaxcalteca had most of the city surrounded, and the Choluteca army would be no match for Cortés' army—Malintze was quite confident Cortés could sack the entire city if he wanted to. For now, the leadership had made plans to kill only the lords of Cholula, and she did not want to give them cause to kill even more people. But if she could convince the woman to leave on her own accord...

"Never," the woman answered.

Malintze winced like a knife had been stabbed into her back. "But if you had to?"

Mazatl shook her head and squeezed Malintze's hand. "You must leave the *teteo* when you are free—"

"I am not the one who needs to leave!" Malintze shouted as she flung aside Mazatl's hand. The bottle of *octli* tipped over, and the drink spilled onto the floor. The puddle blossomed into an ugly, distended stain and the woman who had been so friendly, the woman who could never leave her beloved home, looked at Malintze like she was a monster.

Malintze's resolve broke and she rushed out of the room, flinging the curtain back to make her escape. The guards were too busy playing dice to notice the commotion so she took a moment to close the curtain and compose herself. She tapped the nearest one on the shoulder, and they both turned toward her. Malintze opened her mouth to speak but found herself unable to form the words Cortés had given her earlier in the day. She swallowed the lump in her throat and tried again, but the results were the same.

The guards looked at each other in confusion, and one of them reached for his sword with his dirty hand. Her heartbeat slowed to a crawl as she studied the grime and the mud and the blood caked onto those fingers. All the terrible things the *teteo* could do with their hands came rushing back to her and words came pouring out of her in a wild torrent: Motecuhzoma had ordered the Choluteca lords to attack the *teteo*, and the kind noble woman had offered her a life in Cholula to entice her to defect.

The eyes of the *teteo* went wide as carriage wheels, and they insisted upon immediately returning to camp. She let them know she had to stay behind or the vendor would become suspicious but urged them to return and promised to find her own way back. They were surprisingly receptive to her instruction, perhaps they wanted to claim credit for discovering the plot, and hurried off without a backward glance.

Numb, Malintze staggered through the beautiful streets of Cholula, passing smiling families and massive stone edifices. She stared at her feet, ashamed to be healthy and alive, ashamed of everything that brought her to this point in life.

Biting back tears, she gathered her thoughts as she took stock of her new surroundings. Malintze had somehow wandered into a large garden filled with a beautiful assortment of flowers, shrubs, and trees. Not more than a few paces away stood an oak, young and strong and perfectly content to live at peace with the rest of the world. Something about that infuriated her, and she stormed toward it.

She unsheathed the comb from her hair and attacked the tree. The comb broke and so did she. She gave in to the tears and attacked the trunk with her hands and her feet. Spent, she leaned up against the tree in exhaustion, her fingers bloody and her feet throbbing.

Mazatl and her daughter had so little but because they had each other, they would always have more than her. Malintze had no family; no one who cared for her, no one who would console her when she cried. She slumped to the ground and tried not to think about the fate that would befall Cholula.

Cholula Province

Chapter 9

Vitale took a deep breath to calm his racing heart and scanned the crowded plaza. The prospect of battle always threw his body into disarray—his hands turned clammy, his mouth went dry—but fear had nothing to do with it this time. No, it was anger that made his heart pound against his ribs like a hammer against an anvil.

When Vitale first heard about the treachery of the Choluteca, he had been too shocked to feel angry. The army had been encamped next to Cholula for almost a week, and the Choluteca had been nothing but kind in all their interactions. During mornings and evenings, the Choluteca even brought the army food and water. Sadly, the kindness was a cruel ruse and Cortés informed the company last night that Doña Marina had uncovered a plot against the army.

Vitale squeezed the hilt of his sword and joined a group of soldiers making a circuit around the courtyard perimeter. Lords of Cholula milled in the shadow of Quetzalcoatl's temple, and moving amongst the enemy felt safer in a group. Most of them did not look all that dangerous. Their lack of weapons and their extravagant robes did little to inspire fear, but Vitale knew it would be folly to let his guard down.

He did not know, however, what the lords were discussing every time they pointed at him and his fellow soldiers. It unnerved him to be the subject of their attention, and he wished he could understand their whispering. For all he knew, they could be admiring his sword or discussing the best way to take it from him.

He ground his teeth. In a few minutes, it wouldn't matter. The Choluteca had been foolish enough to believe Cortés would not discover the plot, and they had been foolish enough to let Cortés enter the city with an armed guard. If the Choluteca weren't so treacherous, he might have pitied them for thinking that Cortés brought a hundred Spaniards and a hundred Indians into the city just to make a farewell speech.

They deserve what happens next. In many ways, they deserved worse. Plenty of the Indians had received him and his countrymen with violence, but at least they didn't rely on perfidy. What kind of people would offer succor and greetings before attacking?

The depravity of it made his blood boil. Nonetheless, he was glad Cortés would allow them a chance to repent. Not a single Choluteca would be harmed, so long as the traitors in the courtyard could admit to their treachery. However, if they refused to do so, orders would be given to kill all of them. Honor might stop good people from resorting to treason, but only violence could keep the wicked in check.

The wind carried a distant voice to his ears, and Vitale looked in the direction of the noise. Cortés had started speaking, but none of his words made any sense. Vitale reached for his helmet. He would hear better without it but could not bring himself to take it off. Much safer to keep it on.

He studied the crowd as they received the translation of Cortés' speech. He expected to see anger and righteous indignation but saw furrowed brows and quizzical expressions instead. That seemed wrong but he did not dwell on it, turning his attention toward the men blocking the exits. Most of them had already been blocked, and it would not be long until all of them were blocked. Even if the Choluteca tried to escape responsibility for the plot, they would not be able escape retribution.

The loud crack of a harquebus scattered his thoughts. The battle signal given, Vitale ripped his sword from its sheath. He lunged out at the nearest target: a Choluteca man who tried to stop the blade with his bare hands. The rapier minded little and buried itself deep in the man's rib cage, so deep it caught on bone. The Choluteca's eyes rolled backward and he fell backward, ripping the hilt from Vitale's grip. Vitale scrambled forward, dug his heel into the man's chest, and wrenched his sword out.

A loud wailing prompted him to turn around. Some fool of a child was screaming something nonsensical and shaking a bloody corpse. Vitale advanced toward the kneeling child but kept the sword down at his side. The boy was young, no more than eight, and offered no defense other than unchecked streams of tears and phlegm. Vitale raised his sword, surprised but relieved the boy had made no attempt to run or hide. To let him live out the rest of his life as an orphan would be cruel so there was only one thing to do.

He swung the sword down but something fast and sharp smashed into his face before it could connect. Vitale staggered to the side, dropped his sword, and collapsed to the ground. His shoulder went numb, and he rolled onto his side. Something had hit him in the eye, or near the eye, and he knew what an injury like that could mean. He squeezed his eyes shut and waited for the pain to pass. A minute passed, then another, before he finally summoned the courage to open his eyes again.

Up above, he saw only blue sky and white clouds. He pulled off his helmet to check his wound and a wave of horrible sounds assaulted his ears. All around him, screaming and crying. Vitale covered his ears to block out the sounds, but the feel of his wet sticky hands turned his stomach. He held up his hands, realized for the first time they were covered in grit and gore.

His gorge rose up and he leaned over to retch, bringing him face to face with a disfigured corpse. The bile caught in his throat as he took in the dead man's ugly grimace, and he turned away.

His thoughts flew to the orphan boy. Was he safe? He lifted his head and cast his gaze in every direction. The boy was gone. He had vanished, like ash scattered by the wind, and only the memory of him remained.

Vitale stood, his head throbbing like it had been split open. Nearby, Tlaxcalteca warriors chased down a group of Choluteca women while Spanish soldiers hacked their way through an unarmed crowd. The battle was, in truth, a massacre and the longer he watched, the more convinced he became that far more than a few Choluteca lords would be dead by day's end.

~ ~ ~

Cortés wrinkled his nose as the smell of ash and rotting bodies invaded his nostrils. The bloodbath had only lasted a few hours and most of it was a blur now. Apparently, he had given orders for the Temple of Quetzalcoatl to be burned, but he had no recollection of that now. He knew, however, he would never forget the sight of the Choluteca priests flinging themselves off the giant pyramids, or the noxious aromas released by thousands of corpses exposed to the sun for days on end.

Reports indicated that two thousand Choluteca had been killed. Most had been killed by the Tlaxcalteca, two days passed before they ran out of captives to sacrifice, but Cortés doubted such details would matter to Motecuhzoma or his subjects. No, they would concern themselves only with vengeance and would draw little distinction between his brave soldiers and the conniving Tlaxcalteca warriors.

Cortés stepped over a dead body crawling with flies. The flies did not take kindly to his presence and took to the air in an angry buzz, revealing a corpse robbed of eyes as well as lips. *This is the price of an alliance with the Tlaxcalteca; this is the price of my ambition.*

Cortés shaded his eyes to peer out into the distance. Up ahead, a group of soldiers had propped up a dead woman to throw knives at her bloated, distended body. Owing to the heat, many of the soldiers wore nothing besides light armor and some wore no armor whatsoever. He knew he should reprimand them for their lack of caution but could not summon the energy to do so. Whatever fighting spirit Cholula once possessed had been utterly destroyed by the massacre. The bulk of the killing had ended three days before, but most of the survivors had yet to emerge from their homes.

Cortés pursed his lips and turned to Pedro. If Pedro noticed the staring, he did not show it. Instead, he kept his attention on the dilapidated pyramid that dominated the courtyard. To reach the top of it would mean climbing over a hundred grass-choked steps, but more impressive than the pyramid's height was its sheer mass. From a distance, the Pyramid of Quetzalcoatl could be mistaken for a hill, and the fastest man in the army needed a whole minute to race along a single side of it. What with all the bodies and blood slicks, it would probably take much longer now.

Pedro pointed at the temple situated atop the Pyramid of Quetzalcoatl. "Think we'll find anything besides ash up there?"

Cortés tilted his head back to study the temple better. The stone walls were stained with soot but looked undamaged otherwise. A ravishing was not enough to topple something so mighty; it would have to be destroyed brick by brick. "Perhaps some charred bodies also," Cortés replied. "But one day, we will put something beautiful atop it."

Pedro laughed. "If the Indians don't kill us first."

Cortés frowned. How Pedro could be so blithe toward death and violence never ceased to surprise him. Nonetheless, he did have a point. The Mexica could not let the massacre at Cholula simply go unanswered, and Cortés gathered it would not be long until his scouts reported sightings of a massive Mexica army. If they were lucky, within the next day or two. The plains near Cholula would be an excellent place to fight, and the army could not tarry in Cholula overlong.

Sooner or later, the citizens would regain their fighting spirit, and he needed to make sure his army was far away from Cholula when that happened. Angry citizens did not make a professional army, but they could still throw rocks and swing clubs.

Cortés said farewell to Pedro, grabbed a nearby torch, and walked toward a deserted marketplace. Every item of value had been filched already, but that did not stop his eyes from roaming. One always had to be alert when away from camp.

A flock of crows took to the heavens as he entered the marketplace. The sheer number of bodies splayed out on the pavement stopped him cold. The killing was never supposed to reach this section of the city but once the bloodletting began, it had proven difficult to stop. His gaze drifted to the vacant stalls. A few days before, the place was more crowded than a church nave on Easter day. Would life ever return here?

A soft groaning reached his ears, and he glanced to the side. His eyes widened. A still-twitching foot was poking out from behind a curtained stall. Cortés unsheathed his sword and approached with his guttering torch held high. He edged around an overturned table and broken vases, then stopped in front of a crooked partition.

He could still go on his way, pretend nothing was amiss. He could keep being ignorant... but not if he looked inside. Cortés sighed. He had never been one to shy away from the ugliness of life, and he could not do so now. He flung the curtain back and peered inside the ransacked dwelling.

A dead woman lay in the middle of the floor, cradling a barely breathing girl. For some odd reason, she wore a plumed helmet. Cortés furrowed his brow. How would she have acquired something like that? His eyes drifted downward, but he wished he had kept them fixed on the helmet instead. The small child wore only half a dress, and everything below her waist was torn and ravaged. By Christian soldiers or Tlaxcalteca soldiers, he did not know.

Either way, he knew he was responsible. They all fought under his banner and one day, he would be called to account for the atrocities carried out in Cholula. If not by Motecuhzoma, then by Spanish authorities.

His lip trembled. Governor Velázquez would turn Cortés into an Ovando given half the chance. Could he count on well-heeled court officials to defend him from slander and hearsay? Of course not. Those grandstanding pampered lords would be more than willing to accept his gold and drag his name through the mud. He took a deep breath to calm himself. Under no circumstances, could he allow that to happen. Everyone had to understand that the Choluteca deserved their fate.

The girl moaned weakly. Cortés stepped back and took quick stock of his surroundings. Not a soul in sight, despite all the bodies.

He cocked his head toward the girl. She was small, and he could easily carry her to camp. Finding a physician would only take a few minutes, but a lifetime of recuperation could not restore what she had lost. More likely a physician would prolong her suffering. And even if a physician somehow pulled her back from the brink, Cortés knew she could never make a full recovery. She would always remember and never forgive. She would want justice, plain and simple.

He cursed under his breath and advanced toward the girl. He gritted his teeth and stabbed the sword into her barely moving chest. Her breath caught, and her sudden stillness sickened him. Cortés pulled the sword out and turned away. He did not need to see anymore; what he had already seen would haunt his sleep for many nights to come. He waited for his heart rate to slow and kneeled so he could find something to clean his sword.

Cortés tossed aside half broken pots, but the shattered remains of a painted vase gave him pause. He picked up some of the broken shards to study them better. On one shard he spotted a hissing serpent. On another, a screeching eagle. Pure chance positioned the snake—fangs bared, poised to strike—and the eagle—swooping down with talons extended—in adversarial poses. He carefully laid the pieces back down. Mighty predators so rarely crossed each other but when they did, the struggle had consequences for even the smallest of prey.

Tenochtitlan

Lake Chalco Area

Chapter 10

"Tahtli, what's wrong?" Cotton Flower asked.

Motecuhzoma angled his head toward his daughter. Her round face, normally bright and joyous, was marred by angst. It was possible she had heard about the *teteo*-Tlaxcalteca alliance or the massacre at Cholula, but he doubted that was the cause of her downcast expression.

She was far too young to understand the importance of either, but she was not so young that she failed to notice his distress. He had not broken fast for three days now, and his gaunt features must have caused some worry. Considering the demands that came with raising an army, weeks could pass before they saw each other again. He hoped she would not begrudge his absence.

He reached across the stone table and gave her hand a squeeze. "Forgive me, daughter. I have much on my mind."

Cotton Flower frowned. "Like what?"

How it is probably folly to march beyond the mountains, as everyone advises, to attack the teteo. He smiled and said, "Matters of state you need not fret about. Many more years will pass before you must concern yourself with such things."

Cotton Flower nodded, her gaze fixed on the table's playing board. "Will it take many years to learn how to *patolli*?"

Motecuhzoma laughed. "*Patolli* will bring you a lifetime of joy, but learning it will take considerably less time. How much do you know about the rules?"

Cotton Flower squeezed her lower lip between her thumb and her forefinger. "I know that I win if I get all the playing beads to the end!"

Motecuhzoma smiled. "That is one way to win. Whether you are playing *patolli* or pursuing your ambitions, having the proper pieces in play will help you achieve victory. But to win, it is also important you protect what you cherish." Motecuhzoma picked up a nearby bag and emptied it on to the table. Twelve turquoise beads spilled out, along with six pieces of green jade and six pieces of lavender jade. He grabbed a turquoise bead and held it up for his daughter to see. "Getting all of the pieces where you want may seem like a simple matter but it almost never is. Should I roll and land here—" he pointed to the eight white triangles on the *patolli* board—"then I lose a piece of jade."

Cotton Flower's eyes went wide. Motecuhzoma chuckled and said, "An appropriate response. After all, jade is very precious, and I have only six pieces in my treasury. If I lose all six pieces, I lose the game. After all, how can you persist after you have lost all that is precious?"

Cotton Flower nodded and Motecuhzoma continued, "As you can see, there are many triangles on the board. Moving my pieces around is quite dangerous. But there is also another danger."

Cotton Flower scratched her head. "What?"

"The opponent. In this case, you. It is important to note, however, that an opponent can only strike at certain times." Motecuhzoma pointed to the four squares in the middle of the board. "Should you ever place a piece here, I will be able to attack it."

Cotton Flower laughed. "I will never place a piece in the center then."

"Sometimes, you must. To win, you must be willing to expose yourself to risk." Motecuhzoma took a moment to place a playing bead next to a white triangle, thinking of the many risks he had exposed himself to as Great Speaker. "Let's pretend I rolled a one. What should I do?"

Cotton Flower furrowed her brow and studied the board. "You must move the bead onto the white triangle, and give up your jade."

"I could do that. But there is another option that lets me keep my jade. Any time I roll a one, I can move a new bead onto the board." To demonstrate, he moved one piece from the keep into the starting position. "Cotton Flower, sometimes it will seem like we have no choice but to charge into danger, but if we take time to evaluate every choice available..."

Motecuhzoma trailed off as he realized the import of his words. He beckoned to a nearby servant and instructed him to bring Tezoc to a quiet corner of Patolli Park. By the time Tezoc arrived, Motecuhzoma had already explained the rules twice over and instructed a trusted servant to play with Cotton Flower. He said farewell to his daughter, kissed her on the head, and made his way to Tezoc.

Tezoc bowed his head and offered a warm greeting that Motecuhzoma cut short. "Tell me, how much of the army do you think we will lose in a battle with the *teteo*?"

Tezoc straightened. "I cannot say with confidence. I can say, however, that the massacre in Cholula demands an answer and that our allies will abandon us if we do not punish the pale people for their actions—"

"Some advisors tell me we could lose half our forces," Motecuhzoma said.

Tezoc pressed his lips into a thin line and stared at the ground. "It is likely we would lose even more than that. We have never been able to beat Tlaxcala in open battle and now that they are allied with the *teteo*, it will be even more difficult to prevail over their forces."

"There may be a way to avenge Cholula without destroying our army," Motecuhzoma said. "But it would mean granting the *teteo* and the Tlaxcalteca entry to Tenochtitlan."

Tezoc stared at him askance. "I do not see how that will help us avenge Cholula."

"Because once they enter Tenochtitlan, it will be easier to kill them."

"It could also make it easier for them to kill us," Tezoc said, his voice low and his words clipped. "Consider what they did in Cholula after they entered the city."

"It is because of what happened in Cholula that we must grant them entry. The plan is not without risk. But once they enter Tenochtitlan, we can trap them inside the city."

Tezoc narrowed his eyes. "That would mean trapping armed warriors inside our city."

"Their best weapons will be useless," Motecuhzoma replied. Tezoc arched his brow and Motecuhzoma said, "Every report we have received from Cholula tells us that the *teteo* did not use their stags or their thumping weapons; perhaps they cannot use the weapons in close quarters. If we are to believe the survivors, it seems the Tlaxcalteca did most of the killing. The weapons they use are not so different from ours. If the Tlaxcalteca can slay countless people with *macuahuitl* and club, who is to say we cannot do the same?"

"Killing warriors is more difficult than killing defenseless merchants," Tezoc countered.

"Even warriors can be ambushed. It may take weeks, even months, before the opportune moment presents itself. But at some point, they will let their guard down, and that is when we will attack."

Motecuhzoma drove his fist into his palm for emphasis and waited for the Cutter of Men to respond.

After a brief pause, Tezoc said, "The plan does have some merits. So long as they are in Tenochtitlan, they cannot raise troops from our enemies or terrorize our allies. It may be the best option from a military standpoint. However, there are enormous political risks involved. If we attack the *teteo* when they are unsuspecting, a great victory is possible. But if the attack happens under different circumstances, many citizens could die. The warriors will never forgive you, even if we kill all the *teteo*. Our people will hate you for ages for letting them come into our city. Are you prepared to take that risk?"

Motecuhzoma glanced at his daughter. She wore a grin as wide as Lake Xochimilco as she counted out a roll, and her giddy enthusiasm made his heart turn white. He hoped she could always be happy and full of joy, but the *teteo* threatened every aspect of her future. Their power needed to be curbed. Otherwise, every daughter and every son of Tenochtitlan would be at risk. Motecuhzoma sighed and patted his advisor on the shoulder. "A Great Speaker who is not willing to jeopardize his throne for the sake of the nation does not deserve to sit on a throne."

~ ~ ~

Pedro rolled over on his thin sleeping mat. Damn dogs were making it impossible to sleep. Not long ago, he was most grateful the company had been blessed with such alert sentries. Everyone had been sure the Indians would counter-attack after Cholula, but weeks had passed and the Indians had yet to retaliate. Now that it was clear the Indians lacked the nerve to meet them on the battlefield, it was hard to muster the same goodwill toward the barking. He sat up and surveyed the inside of his tent. Still bright out so he must not have slept for long. Pedro sighed and stood up.

He stepped out of his tent, grateful to see scree and dirt. For the past week, he had seen nothing but snow and ice. If he could go the rest of his life without climbing through another mountain pass, he would die a happy man. Thankfully, the march to Tenochtitlan would soon be over, and the company could take some much needed rest in the Valley of Mexico. Already they were close enough to the Indian capital that if he squinted his eyes and ignored the harsh glare of the nearby lakes, he could make out some of the buildings of Tenochtitlan.

He sauntered through camp to let his eyes to adjust to the mid-day brightness. Some sort of procession was drawing near and the dogs were baying even louder now. A sudden anger seized him, and he grabbed a rock. He wheeled around to throw it at the nearest dog, but the sight of Ordaz, a fellow officer, gave him pause.

"Quiet those damn dogs, won't you?" Pedro asked.

Ordaz smiled and stuck two fingers in between his grubby lips. He made a shrill whistling sound, and dogs all throughout camp quieted.

Pedro tossed the rock aside and took a deep breath, reveling in the newfound silence. Long as he lived, he would never understand dogs. It did not seem right that an animal so vicious could be so tame, so eager to obey. "Thank you, Ordaz. Hard to think with all those dogs barking."

Ordaz laughed. "Did not know you did much thinking."

Pedro cocked his head toward Ordaz. "Climbing halfway up some mountain does not give you license to insult your betters."

Ordaz's face reddened. "I came within two lances of that summit—"

"I know, I know," Pedro said. "There were rivers of fire and flaming stones. Really, you must stick to more believable lies."

Before Ordaz could respond, a courier cut in to let Pedro know that he should report to Cortés. Pedro tipped his head toward the red-faced Ordaz and departed for Cortés' tent, studying the smoking mountain that Ordaz allegedly climbed. Capped with snow and referred to as Popo-something by the Indians, Pedro reckoned it would be impossible to get within twenty lances of the summit, let alone two. He blew out his breath and followed the courier into the tent.

A swarm of attendants were helping Cortés dress in his finest armor. Pedro stood in the corner as he waited for them to finish. Marina entered the tent a few moments later, and Pedro offered her an elegant bow. She scowled and stood on the opposite side of the room.

Pedro chuckled and walked toward her. "Good afternoon, my lady. How fare you?"

She sighed. "I am tired. I did not sleep good last night."

Pedro reached for her hand, but she snatched it away before he could grace it with a kiss. "I'm so sorry to hear that. The cold is preventing many of us from sleeping well. It does not help we must always be ready for an Indian attack." Pedro tutted and flicked out his tongue to lick his dry lips. "I think you could use a man to keep you warm and safe at night."

Marina's lip curled upward. "I did not sleep well because a man try to come into my tent last night." She stared at him and added, "He sound like you."

Pedro shot a quick glance at Cortés, deep in conversation with an attendant about some trivial matter. "Perhaps it was a dream. Do you often dream of me?"

Marina flared her nostrils, and her cheeks flushed with indignation. "I dream that something terrible will happen to man that try to enter my tent. I think Cortés would do many things to that man."

Pedro laughed. "I think not. Cortés is a good Christian and knows the value of forgiveness." He leaned forward and whispered, "He has forgiven me many sins, and I think he could find room in his heart to forgive me again."

Marina nodded. "Yes, Cortés is most forgiving. I sleep with a knife and if I had to use it on man that enter my tent, I think Cortés would forgive me. You think so, too?"

Pedro offered a thin smile, bowed once more, and stepped out of the tent. He shook his head and rubbed a blister on his hand. To be insulted by Ordaz and Marina in the same day was nothing short of scandalous. A duel could help right things, though. Violence had a unique ability to instill respect amongst the soft-hearted.

He was still mulling the thought over when Cortés burst out of the tent in full regalia and walked in the direction of the Indian procession. A large retinue, one that included Marina, trailed behind him, but he made no attempt to slow his pace. Pedro cursed under his breath and trudged after them. When they were in Totonac lands, Cortés always made sure to include him in his retinue. Now he surrounded himself with so many Indians that one could mistake him for a chief of some kind. It might be good, for his sake and for Cortés, if he killed a few of the Indian attendants.

Cortés and his retinue came to a stop a pike's length from the Indian procession. Pedro pushed his way to the front of the group so he could stand in the same row as his captain-general. If Cortés noticed the jostling, he did not give any indication of it and focused his attention on the Indian procession.

Pedro let his hand drop to his sword hilt. With most processions, the Indian chief would have stayed inside the litter, but this Indian found it important to stand for some reason. And unlike many of the other chiefs they had met, this one seemed fleet of foot. His massive headdress— bright as a tucan's beak and big as a half-sword—would probably slow his movement, but the same not could be said for his thin robe or his embroidered loincloth.

"Is this Motecuhzoma?" Cortés asked.

Pedro furrowed his brow. He had not even considered the possibility. If the Indian king was stupid enough to leave his capital city without a proper army, he deserved to be taken hostage.

"I do not know," Marina replied. "I will ask the Tlaxcalteca." A loud and lively discussion followed. After a trice, Marina said in Spanish, "They say it is not Motecuhzoma. Say he is too short and too thin."

Cortés scowled and stared at the standing Indian. "Are you Motecuhzoma?"

The imposter straightened and said something only the Indians could understand. "He claim to be Motecuhzoma," Marina explained.

Cortés cocked his head toward Marina. "It seemed as if he said quite a bit. I would like a verbatim translation."

Marina nodded and said, "He says, I am Motecuhzoma, I am your servant."

Cortés laughed. "My servant? That is most convenient. Don Carlos will be most eager to accept Motecuhzoma as a vassal."

"Cortés, it is a common phrase," Marina said. "It is like my house is your house. It is what people say to be polite—"

"Tell my servant to prove he is Motecuhzoma or leave my camp," Cortés said in a curt voice.

Marina pouted like a child denied sweets. Nonetheless, she passed on the statement. The imposter made no motion to retreat and did not even acknowledge her words.

Cortés narrowed his eyes and said, "We shall see Motecuhzoma. We shall not fail to look him in the face. We shall hear what he has to say, and we will not be deceived by some silly imposter."

107

Once he heard the translation, the imposter gave a small bow and retreated to his litter. The Indian servants lifted him up and carried him away without a word of farewell. Cortés stood statue-still as the procession disappeared from view, and his retinue gradually dispersed as the minutes dragged on. Pedro was about to excuse himself when Cortés gave a loud sigh and sat down on a nearby rock.

"I must say, I do not understand the Indian king at all," Cortés said.

Pedro glanced at the others to see if they might respond and started when he realized they had all left. He cleared his throat and gave his attention to Cortés once more. "What do you mean?"

"I thought he would attack us when we were still in Cholula. Instead, he sends a delegation to let us know we are still welcome guests in Tenochtitlan. He must wish very badly to make an alliance with us, so why bother with a silly imposter?"

Pedro shrugged. "Maybe the Indians wanted to know how we would react to meeting their king."

Cortés twiddled his mustache. "I suppose that would be important to know. God as my witness, I must admit I am surprised the Mexica have not tried to thwart our march."

"The battle at Cholula cowed the Indians," Pedro said, his voice brimming with confidence. "They know not to fight us, and they know we wish to confer with their king."

Cortés shrugged. "Or they mean to ambush us once we enter the city. We know they keep a great deal of gold in their capital, but I truly do not know why they have been so welcoming of us. How can we beat an enemy we do not understand?"

Pedro furrowed his brow. "Well, by killing them."

Cortés looked at him askance, but his serious expression soon gave way to a hearty chuckle. "Ah Pedro, I can always count on you for sharp insights." He laughed again and said, "You must know I am very grateful for your company. I would have been most sad had you stayed behind in Villa Rica or left for Spain with the gold. I shudder to think of what might have happened had you never joined the expedition."

Pedro grunted. "I shudder to think what happens if we give the Indians our trust. If you think they intend to ambush us, we should not enter their city."

Cortés scratched his chin. "We could encamp outside their city, but I suspect that many of our men tire of camp life. What with the rains and the heat, they do have cause for grievance. Considering how close we came to mutiny in San Juan de Ulúa and Villa de la Veracruz, we ought to be mindful of their wishes."

Pedro snorted. He assumed that scuttling the fleet would have allayed fears of mutiny, but he had misjudged Cortés' character. Much as an Inquisitor would always worry about false converts, so too would Cortés worry about dissension.

Cortés shot him a wayward glare. "Do you disagree?"

"Not at all," Pedro said. "Our experience in San Juan de Ulúa was trying for everyone."

"Indeed, and the march has not been much kinder. We could traipse through the countryside to find more allies, but we might lose the allies we already have."

Pedro nodded. A few days ago, the Totonac porters decided they needed to return to the coast. Some speculated they lacked the strength for another mountain crossing, but Pedro suspected they had more nefarious reasons.

"Do you think the Mexica could beat us, if they attacked us in Tenochtitlan?" Cortés asked.

"Of course not," Pedro replied. "But the Indians could be foolish enough to think they could prevail and that's dangerous. You put too much faith in their smarts."

Cortés covered his heart with both hands. "Pedro, you must not take such a dim view of all the Indians. Of course we can trust them to see reason. Have we not seen proof of their genius all throughout our march? A few weeks ago, we marched into territory divided by a wall as long as a Roman aqueduct. A few days ago, we stayed in a city with more pyramids than Seville has cathedrals. In a few days, we will enter a city built on water and meet with the leaders of the most powerful kingdom in all the New World."

Cortés stood up and wrapped an arm around Pedro. He beckoned to the glittering lake that dominated the horizon. "The city in the middle of that lake has enough gold to make us rich as a Roman emperor. If we can convince the Mexica to give us their riches, we stand to win a treasure the likes of which no Spaniard has ever gazed upon. Ballads will be sung about our great deeds for centuries to come, and countrymen of every persuasion will laud our heroics. Surely a prize that great is worth some risk."

Pedro gazed out at the lake. The sun's glare had not become any kinder, and he could hardly see Tenochtitlan. God's honest truth, he cared little about the appearance of the city. As far as he was concerned, the residents of Tenochtitlan could build all the ugly temples they wanted, so long as they were willing to share their gold. He chewed the inside of his lip. The Indians were a surly and untrustworthy lot, but Cortés had managed to bring them to heel in Tlaxcala, Cempoala, and Potonchan. Perhaps he could do the same again in Tenochtitlan. For his sake, and for the sake of his countrymen, Pedro hoped so.

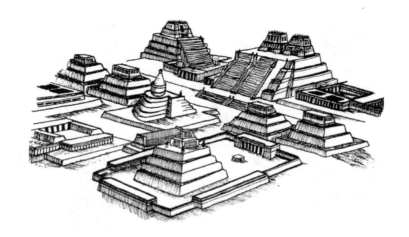

Tenochtitlan

Chapter 11

Cortés gazed over the edge of the stone causeway. It was built a lance above the water, and he reckoned a fall would not hurt overmuch. Nonetheless, he suspected a tumble would be fatal since his heavy armor would ensure he sank to the bottom of the murky lake. He shuddered. What kind of people would build a city in the middle of a lake?

Whatever their reason, the Mexica were obviously blessed with gifted architects. The stone causeway would put the Romans to shame, one section of it stretched for nearly two leagues, and not one corner of the city touched dry land. He took a deep breath. By mid-morning, he would be entering the floating city with his army.

And when we leave the city, we will possess an incredible fortune. He shaded his eyes to study the army's formation. Foot soldiers made up the bulk of his army, and the various contingents were separated by a single row of eight horsemen riding abreast. It had taken half an hour to assemble his men in the proper arrangement and, had it been necessary, he would have spent half the morning organizing them.

He wondered what Motecuhzoma, Great Speaker of the Mexica nation and undisputed leader of the Triple Alliance, felt when he looked upon Cortés' army. Hopefully fear. The Great Speaker also had an eye for pomp and flair, so the careful organization was probably not lost on him. Motecuhzoma perhaps had too much interest in such matters—Cortés and his men had been standing on the causeway for almost an hour because they were being treated to an extended dirt-kissing ceremony.

Cortés' mare, Arriero, pawed the ground, and he dismounted so he could rub her neck and whisper comforting words.

Whether it was the chilly lake breeze or the waiting that bothered Arriero, he did not know. Doña Marina did not seem bothered by either, and her remarkable composure was just another reminder of her impressive strength. He reached out to squeeze her hand, but a quick glance from her made him think better of it.

"Do you remember what I told you?" she asked. "About the way Motecuhzoma will speak?"

He nodded. "Yes, yes. In opposites, I remember."

"Not with everything but with much. If he says he has greatest respect for you, he has little respect for you. If he insults himself, it is to show you his greatness."

Cortés rubbed his beard. "Our nobles employ quite a bit of false flattery, too. Usually have to bring out some wine to get some honesty."

Doña Marina furrowed her brow and said, "He could use many honorific titles to address you, but he would do same with any visitor. The praise is hollow so do not think much of it."

Cortés nodded. "Thank you for the explanation. I am in your debt."

She looked at him askance. "Are you in Aguilar debt, too?"

Cortés turned away from her. He did not want to explain again that Aguilar had to be included even though she was a better translator. There were some aspects of Spanish culture she would never fathom.

Up ahead, a series of conch shells blared in unison. He clambered onto his mount for a better view and was delighted to see that the army was finally moving again. As the rearguard trudged forward, he realized the stone causeway often gave way to removable wooden sections.

If the Indians removed the wooden planks, his army would be unable to escape the city on foot.

A sudden gust made him shiver. He cast his gaze toward Tenochtitlan. Woe to the Indians if they sabotaged the causeways to trap his army. Much as he wished to preserve peaceable relations, he abhorred duplicity and would raze Tenochtitlan to rubble if he had to.

He glanced at the canoes floating nearby. Some were so large they could accommodate dozens, others were so small they could only carry one person, but all of them sat low in the water. The lake seemed shallow in most places and many of the boatmen plied the placid surface not with paddles but with long poles. Nonetheless, he doubted it would be possible to walk or even swim to shore from Tenochtitlan. *We should build some shallow-draft ships.*

Cortés pulled on his beard. Judging by the sheer size of the city, tens of thousands lived inside Tenochtitlan. A city that large had to have many items on hand, and he hoped he could find cordage and cloth in Tenochtitlan's Great Market. If not, it would have to be sent from Veracruz. It would take a few weeks to build the fleet, but that would be more than enough time to convince the Indians to accept him as their lord.

Cortés craned his head backward to make out the lazy spirals of smoke that wafted upward from the pyramids and the houses. He had never entered such a large city before and figured it had more people than Seville or Granada. He knew for a certainty, however, that even the highest battlements of his hometown could not match the height of the stucco-covered pyramids or the blocky palaces of Tenochtitlan. *How could a place this beautiful stay hidden for so long?*

The causeway soon gave way to a very wide and very beautiful avenue, and flat-roofed houses, crafted from pale adobe and dark stone, now flanked him on every side. Curious onlookers studied his army from behind ledges and half-open windows, but they offered no kind words of welcome. Instead, they muttered and whispered. If the Mexica intended to ambush his army, a signaler would be hidden amongst the onlookers. He peered into a sea of unfriendly, cold faces. Not a single person offered any type of greeting. *So why are they letting us enter their city and meet with their sovereign?*

The army ground to a halt, and the vanguard stopped in front of a large group of Indians. Cortés tensed and dropped his hand to his sword hilt. If the Mexica meant to ambush his army, the soldiers would make sure they paid dearly for the mistake. Not one crossbow needed to be loaded and not one gunpowder weapon needed priming; he hoped for peace, of course, but that was no excuse to shirk battle preparations.

The loud bang of a drum prompted him to glance backward. A litter-bearing delegation was approaching his army from the rear. He turned his horse around and ordered the rearguard to stand at attention. He kept a hand on the hilt of his sword and watched as a group of attendants, dressed in splendid cotton robes, swept the avenue with long bushy brooms.

Much as their colorful robes demanded attention, it was the jade-studded litter that captivated him. Coated in silver and gold, it was festooned with feathers as long as his forearm and wreaths woven entirely from flowers. The attendants stopped twenty paces away and lowered the litter to the ground with a practiced grace.

Cortés dismounted and gestured to his translators. Today, Doña Marina and Aguilar would be more valuable than his guards. He handed the reins of his horse to a nearby servant as a man stepped out of the litter.

Taller than him by half a hand, the man had a well-defined midsection and thighs the size of tree trunks. Besides the small wrinkles around his eyes, few of his features betrayed age. His thin beard, trimmed short, contained no gray hairs and if there were any on his scalp, they were completely hidden by his massive, green-feathered headdress.

As far as Cortés could tell, the man carried no weapon. His finely embroidered loincloth was much too skimpy to do so and he wore no other article of clothing, save a shoulder-draped robe and some thick sandals. What he lacked in clothing, however, he made up in piercings. Plugs the size of plum pits dangled from both his ear lobes, and a brilliant gold labret hung from his lower lip. The man strode toward him, utterly sure of his power and his wealth. Cortés' heart skipped a beat. The man in front of him could only be Motecuhzoma.

~ ~ ~

Malintze watched in horror as Cortés tried to embrace Motecuhzoma. Only close kin could touch the Great Speaker, and three Mexica guards stepped forward to stop him.

Cortés' guards grabbed their swords and shouted abuse at the Mexica guards. Her heart skipped a beat as a *teotl* pulled on his sword to unsheathe it, and Malintze shouted in Spanish, "Cortés, you cannot touch the Great Speaker. It violates all custom."

Chastened, Cortés took a step backward. He lowered his hands and his guards let go of their swords. He adjusted his cuirass and looked at Motecuhzoma. "Are you him?" he asked. "Are you Motecuhzoma?"

Malintze took a moment to let her heart rate slow, and translated the statement into Nahuatl. Malintze knew she should refer to him by his honorific title, but she could not bring herself to do so. She remembered all too well what her village had suffered on account of Motecuhzoma's demand for tribute.

Motecuhzoma frowned at her, and she dropped her gaze. Custom dictated that she stare at her feet while she was in the presence of the Great Speaker, but she could not bring herself to do that either. Instead, she stared at his sharp nails. Not so long ago, those talons had reached into her life and plucked her away from her home and her family.

"Yes, I am he," replied Motecuhzoma.

She passed on the words to Aguilar and studied Cortés' reaction. His eyes brightened as if he had been reunited with a distant relation, and he reached under his tunic to remove a pearl necklace that he then offered to Motecuhzoma. The Great Speaker eyed the necklace with some suspicion, but he eventually bid Cortés over.

Cortés approached Motecuhzoma with slow, measured steps, and the guards grudgingly allowed him to pass. A great many wrinkled their noses as he passed, but their reaction was tame compared to certain attendants. One remarked that the foul odor of the *teteo* had his nostrils burning, and she gave thanks that none of the Spaniards could understand Nahuatl. Through it all, Motecuhzoma stayed silent and let Cortés lower the necklace onto him.

Once Cortés retreated to a safe distance, Motecuhzoma took a small sniff of the necklace. If he found the odor offensive, he did not show it. He did, however, wave over an attendant who brought not one but two necklaces. Red snail shells adorned one necklace, and eight golden nuggets adorned the other one. Every nugget was carved in the shape of a shrimp, and she did not have to peer to make out the spindly legs or the antennaed head. She sighed. The artistry would be entirely lost on the *teteo*. She had lost count of all the times they had smelted priceless treasures to create their ugly ingots.

"To give away so much gold, you must be a truly powerful lord," Cortés said. "Let me take a moment to demonstrate my power for you."

Cortés gestured to his soldiers as she translated, but she was only halfway through when cannon fire split the air. Men and women screamed in terror, startled babes took to crying, and a white cloud of rank odor enveloped the crowd. The smell of rotting eggs flooded her nose, and she covered her coughs with her hand. Burnt wading landed on her arm, prompting her to gaze upward. All around her, tiny cinders were drifting to the ground in lazy spirals.

Judging by the faces of those nearest, the cannon volley had left many of the onlookers deeply unsettled. Motecuhzoma, however, seemed more irritated than frightened and whispered something that prompted a bout of laughter amongst his attendants.

Cortés turned to her for explanation. She flushed and said in Spanish, "I did not hear what said."

Before Cortés could respond, Motecuhzoma turned and set off at a leisurely pace. Cortés trailed behind him and ordered the rest of the army to follow. Doña Marina fell into step beside Cortés and let her eyes rove over the city landscape.

Much as she hated the Mexica, she had to admit they had built a beautiful city. The layout of the city was simple and intuitive, and a lovely smell of fresh-baked corn cakes and blooming flowers blanketed every neighborhood. Most impressive, though, were the canals. Oarsmen plied their placid waters with ease and, despite the abundance of vessels, traffic moved through the canals with remarkable speed.

After a few minutes, Motecuhzoma passed through a gap in a crenelated wall to step into a large courtyard completely devoid of canals. What it lacked in canals, it made up with massive structures. Looking around her, Malintze spied six pyramids and six temples, as well as a ball court and a towering skull rack. A great pyramid made of stucco and *tezontle*, taller than a full-grown cypress, caught her gaze. *This must be the Sacred Precinct.* She wondered how many tribute victims had

119

been put to death in this very same precinct, how many of her people had climbed the great stairs that led to the Sacrificial Block.

Motecuhzoma stopped in front of an ornate veranda and gestured to the entrance. "This is the palace of Axayacatl, a Great Speaker long before me. This will be your home while you are in Tenochtitlan. I know my enemies have told you that the walls of my house are made of gold, that the floor mats in my room are gold and that I claim to be a god. The houses, as you see, are made of stone and lime and clay."

Motecuhzoma lifted his arm and poked himself in the ribs. "See that I am flesh and blood, just like you and all other men. You must not give thought to these stories of divinity. You must take them as a joke, as I take the story of your thunder and your lightnings."

Cortés' eyes narrowed when he heard the translation. He replied, "We are most glad to meet with you. We come at the behest of a great monarch, Don Carlos of Spain, and we are honored to speak with you. Don Carlos has every wish to enter into friendship with you and the only stories of divinity we concern ourselves with involve our lord and savior, Jesus Christ."

Motecuhzoma smiled. "You have traveled very far to be in my company and must be very tired. I shall go now to the other palaces I possess, but you shall be provided with all that you and your people require. We will speak again later in the day. In the meantime, please enjoy the food my servants will soon bring to you. We know your people are used to finer fare, but we hope you will not be disappointed by the meal we have prepared for you."

Once she translated the statement, Cortés answered, "We appreciate your kindness and bid you a warm farewell. Please call on us soon."

As she passed the statement to Motecuhzoma, Cortés ordered some scouts to explore the palace interior, and they poured into the foyer like water into a breached hull. Confident the scouts would not soon return, she bided her time by studying the building exterior.

The palace reached a height of at least eighty hands and had a length that could rival four *carracks*. Despite the enormous dimensions of the building, she had serious doubt it could accommodate Cortés' army.

Nonetheless, his soldiers seemed quite taken by the luxurious palace. Men nearby were discussing how to pry the precious stones out of the hulking facade, but most were content to evaluate it in respectful silence. Malintze understood their admiration well. Never in all her life had she beheld such a magnificent building, let alone stepped inside one. But as beautiful as it was, she knew it could not stand before the *teteo* weapons. Their cannons would pulverize the stunning assortment of jasper and turquoise and marble to dust, and all the artistry would be for naught.

A few minutes later, the scouts returned to let them know that it was safe to enter the palace. Cortés ordered his men to find lodging inside, and then held out his arm for her. Malintze arched her brow in surprise but took his arm anyway. They entered together, and a brief sense of wonder washed over her as the sheer size of the foyer dawned on her.

She assumed the soldiers would give them time to explore on their own, but they rushed inside seconds afterward. The cavernous room was soon filled with the din of soldiers letting down their heavy loads and men rushing to find unoccupied sleeping places.

Cortés left to mediate some conflict. Malintze stood alone in the middle of a giant room packed with noisy soldiers. A sudden urge to explore the palace seized her, and she made her way to the nearest stairwell.

Once she stepped inside, the lavender and dun walls gave way to a beautiful mural that depicted the birth and death of the world. The *teteo* would probably find the image frightening, but it did not bother Malintze in the slightest. Creation and destruction often went hand in hand. All Nahua people understood that the world had already been destroyed four times before. Life often gave way to death, and vice versa. If she had learned anything from Cholula, it was that nothing good or bad could last forever.

Malintze traced her hand along the mural, awed by the sheer size of it and frightened by it also. She stopped in front of a painted figure wearing a diadem. A Speaker of some kind, if she had to guess. The Speaker clasped a bloody heart and struck a pose both triumphant and defiant. Moving on, she spotted the same figure in a much different pose. More chastened than exultant, the Speaker kneeled and pulled at tufts of hair. She furrowed her brow. The painted figure shared an undeniable likeness with the Axayacatl statue outside, and she wondered if the tapestry was intended as a historical collage.

Perhaps Motecuhzoma placed them in the Palace of Axayacatl because the long-ago Speaker had some special meaning to the people of Tenochtitlan. A Great Speaker had to take an interest in political symbolism, but she would not put a more sinister motive past him. Ever since the Totonacs had seized Motecuhzoma's tribute collectors, she knew it was inevitable that the Mexica would go to war with the *teteo*. The only question was how much they played at peace beforehand.

Malintze picked at her nails. She wanted so very much to climb the stairs and explore the rest of the palace. If she were a free woman, she might have. But she had yet to gain true liberty and still had an obligation to the *teteo*. They still needed her translating abilities and she had not forgotten that if their cause failed, so too would her bid for freedom.

She turned around and descended the stairs. Stepping into the foyer, she noticed that a delegation of Mexica servants had entered the palace to distribute food. Succulent dishes made from duck and fish and corn were laid out on dazzling floor mats for the *teteo* and Tlaxcalteca. Cortés' men tore into the food without second thought, attacking and grabbing like they were starved animals. They smacked and belched with abandon and the longer she watched them eat, the more convinced she became the *teteo* would be more at home in a wild garden then they could ever be in a civilized setting.

They were animals, plain and simple. But despite all her reasons not to, she felt safe around them. After all, animals could be quite useful on the battlefield.

Tenochtitlan

Motecuhzoma sat on a stone bench and peered out at the Palace of Axayacatl. Yopico's Temple offered an excellent vantage point and Motecuhzoma was glad that his brother, Cuitlahuac, had joined him. Nonetheless, his brother did not seem to enjoy the view much and paced back and forth like a captured ocelot.

"We should attack the *teteo* now," Cuitlahuac growled.

Motecuhzoma gestured to the Palace of Axayacatl with an open hand. "The *teteo* appear to be installing weapons in the window sills. Most of them have yet to take off their armor. Many of our warriors will die if we attack now."

Cuitlahuac flicked his gaze toward the palace, muttered under his breath, and then turned back to Motecuhzoma. "We never should have let them enter the city. We should have marched on them before they reached Tenochtitlan and fought them like men."

Motecuhzoma sighed. "The Potons and the Tlaxcalteca raised mighty armies to attack the *teteo* and fought gallantly. The Potons were crushed and the Tlaxcalteca now serve the *teteo*."

Cuitlahuac snorted and resumed his pacing. Some time later, he said, "We have the biggest army in the One World—"

"Having the biggest army did not help us defeat the Tlaxcalteca," replied Motecuhzoma. "We cannot simply charge into conflict with the *teteo*. Fighting the *teteo* the same way the Tlaxcalteca and the Potons did means suffering the same casualties. Sheer numbers might allow us to prevail but if we lost half our army to the *teteo*, do you truly think the Purepecha and the Huastecs would hesitate to attack Tenochtitlan?"

Cuitlahuac pursed his lips and sat next to Motecuhzoma. He squeezed the stone lip of the bench as if he were trying to throttle it, his muscles bulging and shifting as he applied more pressure. Cuitlahuac could heave and squeeze all day, but the stone bench would not give an inch. A copper axe would probably leave nothing more than a small gash in the stone, but some of the *teteo* weapons could obliterate the bench in the flutter of an eyelid.

Motecuhzoma shuddered and grabbed his brother's shoulder. "The *teteo* have made a grave mistake by entering our city. We can cut off their food and their escape at any time; that must mean something."

"Or maybe we made a mistake by allowing them into our city." Cuitlahuac blew out his breath and rubbed his palm. "Who is to say our guests will not launch a surprise attack?"

"The *teteo* are brutish, but they are not stupid. To attack us now that they are trapped inside our *altepetl* would be akin to kicking a hornet's nest. No, more foolish than that. It would be like kicking a hornet's nest after stepping on an arrowhead."

Cuitlahuac chuckled and let his shoulders drop. "I apologize for being so critical. I hate seeing the pale people here, in our Sacred Precinct. And the way you..."

"Charm and fete them?" Motecuhzoma finished. "Every kind word I say about them sticks in my throat. But my pride is a little thing compared to the well-being of our confederacy. Sooner or later, the *teteo* will let down their guard. When they do, we will fall on them without mercy."

Cuitlahuac nodded. "Let more of the *pilli* know what you intend. Otherwise, they will whisper in secret."

"The details of a plot are not meant to be well-known," Motecuhzoma replied.

He turned his head to take in his surroundings. No quadrant of the city could compare in beauty to the Sacred Precinct. The zoo and the library and the gardens were all beautiful in their own ways, but the Sacred Precinct exuded a martial glory that could not be matched. Did the *teteo* notice it also? No doubt the Tlaxcalteca had told them the Sacred Precinct was an evil place where Givers tore the hearts out of Tlaxcalteca warriors. In retrospect, Motecuhzoma had to wonder whether any of them were worthy sacrifices. Vermin did not deserve an honor as great as a Flowery Death.

"Cuitlahuac, do you know of a good poison master?" Motecuhzoma asked.

Cuitlahuac stiffened. "I may. Why?"

"The *teteo* and their allies will be utterly reliant on us for food. We ought to exploit that. How long do you think it would take to gather a quantity great enough to kill seven thousand men?"

"Months. And if they take meals at staggered intervals or employ poison testers, a large-scale poisoning might not be possible." Cuitlahuac tilted his chin upward and looked Motecuhzoma in the face. "Did you have a particular type of poison in mind?"

Motecuhzoma smiled. "Tree frogs excrete a most interesting substance, one that can incapacitate an able-bodied warrior without compromising his senses. A poison like that would give us ample opportunity to teach our guests about Mexica hospitality, would you not agree?"

~ ~ ~

Pedro stopped in front of the Great Pyramid and gazed upward. A hundred and fourteen steps to reach the summit. He shivered. The pyramid didn't sit right with him, and neither did the rest of the city.

The others did not seem to share his attitude. Four days they had been in the city and during that time, he heard nothing but rapturous praise of Tenochtitlan. He was tired of hearing about the Indian women who dyed their teeth red, the massive market where legged fish were sold a stone's throw from common fruits, the cisterns with running water, and he wished they would quit their nattering.

Pedro appreciated beauty as much as anyone and there were certain aspects of the city he liked. In Spain, most streets were choked by refuse and waste but here in Tenochtitlan, streets were swept daily. Better yet, most of the avenues were straight and parallel so navigating the city took little effort or thought. Nonetheless, he refused to swoon for the city as the others had. Someone had to stay vigilant.

Today especially, since Motecuhzoma had offered to take a party of twenty up to the top of the Great Pyramid. Pedro would not have volunteered himself but since Cortés had accepted the invitation, he didn't have a choice.

He licked his lips and put his foot on the first stair. Puny little thing could barely fit his foot. He sucked in his teeth and put his other foot on the stairwell. Only one hundred and thirteen more to go. Glancing to his left, he realized that his compatriots were making better progress than him. Cortés, León, and Saucedo were both far ahead of him, along with the fifteen guards who were also taking part in the excursion. Even Marina had climbed farther up the stairs than him.

Pedro gritted his teeth. He was not about to let an Indian woman show him up. He marched with newfound urgency. He made it halfway up the stairs before he tripped. He grabbed a nearby statue to steady himself and took in his surroundings. He instantly regretted it, and his stomach clenched tight as a maiden. A small gust reminded him how easy it would be to fall and his heart skipped a beat. At this height, a fall would either kill him or, worse, lame him.

He let his breathing slow down, released the statue, and looked to see if anyone had seen him trip. Motecuhzoma, Cortés, León, and Saucedo were too far ahead to notice, but Marina was only a few steps behind him.

He muttered obscenities and resumed his upward march, cursing the thin air all the while. He was a few steps short of the summit when a cloaked man came to the edge and shouted something in Indian. León, Cortés, and Saucedo were bent over from their labors, but they straightened after Motecuhzoma joined them on the ledge.

Pedro stiffened and turned to Marina for a translation. A sullen look crossed her face, and she stopped a few steps behind him.

"What did he say?" asked Cortés.

"He said temple on top of pyramid is sacred and I am not allowed in because I am woman," she said in Spanish.

Pedro chewed the inside of his cheek. Under different circumstances, he might have laughed at her misfortune but with Aguilar still in the palace, Marina was their only translator.

"Why did you wait to tell us this?" Cortés asked Motecuhzoma.

Motecuhzoma shrugged and said something to Marina. She translated, "He say he has much on his mind as Great Speaker and forgot to mention it."

Cortés huffed. "It would be most unjust to ask a lady to climb down these precarious steps by herself. Would you be so kind as to let her rest near the summit as you show us your beautiful temple? We know you to be very kind and hope you can grant us this small favor."

Motecuhzoma conferred with some of his guards. He nodded and retreated to some other section of the summit. Not much later, Cortés ordered some men to stand guard over Doña Marina and Pedro resumed his climb, one hand out for balance and the other wrapped around the hilt of his sword.

When he reached the ledge, he could see Motecuhzoma was still standing close by and had fixed his beady eyes on the out-of-breath Cortés. Motecuhzoma whispered something to the nearby guards that prompted a bout of enthusiastic nodding.

Cortés coughed and shouted, "Doña Marina, can you still hear us?"

A tense silence followed. Then a small voice answered: "Yes, Cortés."

Pedro let go of his sword hilt and glanced at Motecuhzoma. His idolaters were scowling and muttering amongst each other, but they quieted once they heard Motecuhzoma's stern voice.

"Motecuhzoma says you must be tired from the climb," Marina translated.

Cortés laughed and said between haggard breaths, "Tell him we Spaniards are immune to fatigue."

Motecuhzoma furrowed his brow as she translated, and his idolaters looked at Cortés as if he were a wingless animal that had attempted flight. After a trice, he stepped aside and bid Cortés forward.

Cortés coughed one last time and advanced toward the ledge on the opposite side of the pyramid. Pedro fell into step beside him, as did León and Saucedo. They stopped next to the ledge and took in the stunning view. Whereas the others were quick to remark on the beauty of the snow-capped mountains and the verdant valley, Pedro stayed silent and focused his attention on the lake. Evening was only half an hour away, but hundreds of boats were still loading and unloading at the dock; Indians loved commerce even more than gypsies loved mysticism.

Peering out into the distance, he spotted something that looked like a dike. He did not understand why the Indians would build one in the middle of a lake, but he recognized that it was an impressive feat of engineering. The dike was three leagues long, and he could not think of anything in Spain that could rival it. Certainly nothing in his hometown. Badajoz had some nice castles but neither the Alcazaba nor the cathedral could compare to the Great Pyramid.

Pedro made his way to the opposite ledge. Much more lake on the other side but more causeways on this side. He focused on the one closest to the palace of Axayacatl. Compared to the others, it was mostly straight and rather short. It had a few removable sections but if they had to escape the city in a hurry, they would be hard-pressed to find a better option. Cortés had plans to build a lake fleet but it could take weeks, if not months, before that was completed. In the meantime, the western causeway offered the best escape route.

Cortés cleared his throat and said in a slightly raised voice, "Doña Marina, please tell Motecuhzoma that we would like to know more about his beautiful shrines."

A smile crossed Motecuhzoma's face and he guided Cortés toward the two shrines located atop the Great Pyramid. Pedro, León, and Saucedo trailed behind them. They were ten paces from the temples when a strange smell washed over them.

Pedro took a deep sniff. The thick stench of iron filled his nose, but that didn't make any sense. He had yet to meet the Indian who knew anything about iron, and he doubted they would use their temple for smelting. Saucedo and León were both seized by violent coughing fits that slowed their pace. Pedro did not wait for them and followed Cortés and Motecuhzoma inside the red shrine.

The odor inside the temple was far stronger. He breathed in through his mouth to avoid gagging. Torchlights illuminated the temple's interior in vivid detail, and he beheld a floor so caked in blood it brought to mind Moses' first plague. Pedro kneeled to examine the gore better. Numerous cracks and fissures had been filled in with congealed blood, so much so that he struggled to pick out the floor patterning.

He shivered and looked up. An Indian was standing in the corner of the temple and stared at him with vacant eyes. Open sores covered both his arms and his long, uncombed hair extended past his shoulders. Disgusted, Pedro turned toward León and Saucedo. Their eyes went wide as they took in the pagan bloodletting, and Saucedo's coughing fit returned with a newfound fury. When he finally recovered, he crossed himself and whispered a prayer while León muttered something about an Inquisition chamber.

"Doña Marina," Cortés said, "please tell Motecuhzoma that I do not understand how a great and wise ruler can fail to recognize that he worships evil idols. Tell him that he must desist the foul practice of human sacrifice."

Marina shouted out her translation from the pyramid steps and the temple went quiet. Pedro reached inside his boot for the small knife tucked inside it. Made no sense for Cortés to insult the Indians here of all places, but he wanted to have the knife ready in case he needed to throw it.

He took a quick count of his countrymen. Fifteen were on the summit with him, and the three waiting on the stairs with Doña Marina were all within shouting range. The Indians were twenty in total and had little in the way of armor. Victory would go to whoever attacked first.

Motecuhzoma's guards reached for their clubs and whispered to one another, but Motecuhzoma stilled their tongues and their hands with a small gesture. With the Indians quiet once more, Cortés continued, "Do me the favor of allowing a cross to be placed on this pyramid and let us divide off a space where we can set up an image of Our Lady. You will see, by the fear that your idols have of her, how grievously they have deceived you."

Marina's soft voice carried Cortés' harsh words to Motecuhzoma, and the serene face of the Indian king gave way to a disgusted sneer. "If I had known that you were going to utter these insults, I would not have shown you my gods. We hold them to be very good for they give us health and fertility and all the victories we desire. We are bound to worship them and make sacrifices for them, so I pray you do not say another word to their dishonor. Leave this temple now as I must make penance."

Motecuhzoma gestured to the stairs and stared at Cortés.

Cortés nodded and broke eye contact to appraise the Indian guards. "I ask your pardon if it be so." He made his way toward the ledge, and Pedro hurried after him. In his haste, Pedro dropped his knife, and he stopped to pick it up. Much to his dismay, his countrymen did not bother to wait and made their way down the stairs without him. Pedro cursed and rushed toward the ledge. The long flight of stairs gave him pause, and he glanced back at the Indians.

Seeing none were close, Pedro put his knife away and slowly made his way down the stairs. His hesitant, faltering steps allowed the others to get even farther ahead. He wanted to call out for them to stop, but his pride would not let him. Why were they going down the stairs so fast? How could his own countrymen abandon him?

He pushed aside the dark thoughts, rubbed sweat from his brow, and picked up his pace. By the time he caught up with Cortés and the others, they were nearly at the bottom of the stairs, and Pedro's clothing was soaked with perspiration. Not one word was uttered, and the silence made it easy to brood on his growing indignation.

He heaved a sigh of relief when they finally made it to level ground, but the loud blaring of a conch made him freeze.

"What was that?" León asked.

"The signal for evening festivities," Marina explained. "Sacrifices will be carried out soon."

Pedro snorted. "Maybe we should send up a priest and give them another catechism."

Saucedo and León shared a brief look but said nothing. Cortés offered a weak smile and said, "Rome was not built in a day. Come, let's return to our quarters."

Cortés led the way and by the time they reached the palace, Pedro's anger toward León and Saucedo had all but vanished. His anger toward Cortés had only grown, though.

As they were about to step inside the entrance, Pedro said, "We should speak in private, captain-general."

León, Saucedo, and Marina stopped and looked to Cortés for guidance. He gave them permission to go ahead, dismissed the guards, and turned toward Pedro. "Yes?"

"You could have killed us all, insulting their idols like that," Pedro said. "We're damn lucky they didn't try to throw us off their heathen pyramid."

Cortés smiled. "Are you scared of the Indians now?"

Pedro clenched his teeth together to keep from answering. *I'm scared your reckless tactics will get us all killed.* He closed his eyes and took a deep breath. "Cortés, you cannot think of the Indians as friendly and gentle. They would kill us all, if they had the chance."

134

Cortés narrowed his eyes. "Pedro, I can assure you that I understand that many of the Indians harbor ill-feelings toward us."

Pedro threw his hand up in the air. "Then why did you insult their idols?"

"I needed to see how they would react. Tell me, what did the guards do when they heard the translation?"

"They reached for their weapons—"

"But they stopped at Motecuhzoma's urging," Cortés finished. "It is likely there are many in Tenochtitlan who wish us harm. We need to know how well Motecuhzoma can control his people."

Pedro pinched the bridge of his nose. Cortés' willingness to gamble his own life, and the lives of others, never ceased to surprise. "When will we take leave of Tenochtitlan?"

Cortés looked at him askance. "When we have more gold."

Pedro scoffed and fought the urge to roll his eyes. "And when will that be?"

"In a few weeks' time, tribute collectors will return to Tenochtitlan with gifts of gold," Cortés replied. "Motecuhzoma has agreed to share it with us so long as we promise to leave his subjects in peace and depart Mexico when sailing winds are fair."

Pedro frowned. The massacre at Cholula must have terrified the Indians for Motecuhzoma to agree to such a terrible deal. Then again, the Indians had been free with their gold even before the massacre, so it did make some sense the massacre would make them more generous. It wasn't like the Indians had the power to stand up to them anyway.

"When do you think Montejo and Puertocarrero will reach Spain?" Pedro asked.

"My hope is they have already arrived. The pilot gave me his word he would get the ship to Spain no later than October."

Pedro rubbed his chin. Once the gold reached Don Carlos, Christians would flock to Mexico from every corner of the kingdom, eager to lend their talents and weapons to Cortés' cause. Waiting for them to arrive would be a trial of its own, but the army would not lack for water or shelter in the city. All things considered, it did seem preferable to setting up camp in some random locale.

Pedro stared at the Great Pyramid. He wondered what it would feel like to be hauled up those stairs and have his heart cut out for some chanting audience. Couldn't be much worse than being offered as an *auto-da-fe*. He ran his tongue along his teeth. The Indians had probably never heard the term, but he knew that many of his countrymen would be eager to educate them. Sooner or later, all of Mexico would belong to Spain.

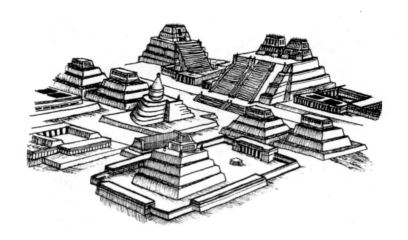

Tenochtitlan

Cortés rubbed his cold hands together. The sun would soon set, and the chill pervading the small room would only worsen once it turned dark. He glanced at his officers, studying their features for weakness. About five minutes before, a messenger informed Cortés that Mexica tribute collectors had killed six soldiers and a Spanish officer, not to mention some Indian allies, in a skirmish near Fort Veracruz.

When Pedro heard the news, he responded by smashing a chair against the ground. Having taken some time to pace, he seemed calmer now. Saucedo, ever softhearted, had resorted to tears and sniffling, mumbling something inaudible every now and then. Olid and León, on the other hand, had gone quiet as church mice and stared at the floor as if it were a scrying glass.

"Is Escalante really dead?" Saucedo asked in a ghost of a whisper.

Cortés nodded. "His wounds were mortal. We lost seven of our countrymen to the Mexica, along with some Totonac allies." He doubted his officers cared much about the Totonacs, or the dead foot soldiers. Escalante was not all that popular—he came from a town almost nobody knew and did not call Extremadura home—but his rank and his wealth had accorded him a level of respect amongst Cortés' inner circle. To lose him to the Indians, in a skirmish of all things, was unconscionable; infantry and slaves were supposed to die in minor battles, not important officers.

Olid shook his head and looked up. "They were in a fortress. How did the Indians scale the wall? How did they get through the gate?"

Cortés blew out his breath. "Escalante left Fort Veracruz with a small party so he could confront a group of Mexica tribute collectors. No one who stayed inside came to harm."

"What kind of Christian gets himself killed trying to prevent savages from killing each other?" Pedro muttered. "Damn idiot deserves his fate."

Saucedo jumped to his feet and glared at Pedro. He reached for his sword, but León pulled Saucedo back into his seat before he could even touch the hilt. Pedro grunted and went back to pacing.

Olid pushed his hair back. "How can we be certain the news is true?"

Cortés glanced at the runner who had brought them the terrible news. He had marten-dark skin and probably knew nothing about the Lord. "We have no reason to distrust him," Cortés said. "He would gain little by deceiving us, and his report is much too detailed to dismiss it out of hand. Escalante is dead, and the Indians now think they can kill our kind with impunity. We must disabuse them of this notion and fast."

The room went quiet. Saucedo stopped crying, Pedro stopped pacing, León stopped whispering, and Olid stopped fussing with his hair.

"Hear, hear," Pedro said, his eyes glittering with mirth. "We should gather all the leaders of Tenochtitlan in some central plaza and cut them all down, like we did at Cholula. The Indians will never cross us again."

Cortés glanced at the other officers. Much as he was relieved that none of them rushed to offer their support, he was disappointed none of them had the temerity to denounce Pedro's proposal.

Cortés cleared his throat. "We sacked Cholula because Doña Marina discovered a plot. Our cruelty helped restore order but if we try to do the same here, we will inflame violent passions in every corner of the city. And since we have not finished building the lake fleet, that would be most unwise."

"We have to do something," Pedro replied. "It's not right, letting savages get away with murder. Let's send Doña Marina to the market, see if she can discover a plot—"

"Enough of that!" Cortés thinned his lips, amazed at Pedro's lack of tact. "It will be many weeks before we leave Tenochtitlan, and we must preserve good relations with the Indians. Those responsible must be punished, but a massacre will not serve our interests and would only incite rebellion."

Cortés glared at his officers, daring them to disagree. León and Saucedo could not match his stare and turned away. Pedro did not even acknowledge his glare and resumed his pacing, muttering all the while. Much to his surprise, Olid held his gaze and said, "Perhaps we should take Motecuhzoma hostage."

Cortés' eyes went wide. *Have all my officers gone mad?* He puffed out his chest and straightened. "Trying to take Motecuhzoma hostage right now would be the height of folly. He always travels with a large guard, and any attempt on his person would be met with fierce resistance. But even if we managed to take him hostage, we gain little from it. He's our golden goose—take him hostage, and we forgo untold sums of gold."

León furrowed his brow. "If we take him hostage, his subjects will g-give us more g-gold."

Cortés cocked his head toward León. "We do not know that for certain. We do know, however, that Motecuhzoma can check the worst impulses of his

141

countrymen, and that he has already given us a great amount of gold."

Pedro sneered. "So what do you propose we do, Cortés?"

Cortés scratched his chest. If emotions weren't so raw, he would have reprimanded Pedro for being snide. "Some of the Mexica who were involved in the attack are traveling to Tenochtitlan right now. Once they have arrived in the city, I will ask Motecuhzoma for a personal audience and inform him that he must hand over the guilty party to keep peace with us."

Saucedo scratched his head. "But you said we need to preserve relations with the Indians. You would be making an empty threat—"

"Motecuhzoma does not know that," Cortés cut in. "Do any of you plan to tell him?"

Silence. Despite heated arguments of past, Cortés trusted the men to keep faith with him. Not because he put great stock in their honor. More because he knew they would gain nothing by betraying him.

"So, we are gambling justice on a bluff?" Pedro asked.

Cortés smiled. "I do not intend to settle for justice. We will have vengeance, and payment will be in the coin of our choosing. But no matter what recourse we pursue, it is essential that the guilty party be punished in a manner both severe and public. Otherwise, the Indians will never respect our authority."

Saucedo nodded. "A hanging then?"

Cortés shook his head. "No. A hanging would be far too lenient. We need to strike terror into the heart of any Indian who has ever contemplated violence against our kind."

Olid rubbed his chin. "What did you have in mind?"

His officers exchanged long glances but, one by one, they all turned toward Cortés. A warm sensation spread through his breast. They were deferring to him, just as they were supposed to.

"Are any of you familiar with Joan of Arc?"

~ ~ ~

Motecuhzoma watched as the Spaniards erected a small wooden structure on the roof of the Palace of Axayacatl. The *teteo* had lived inside Tenochtitlan for almost a month, and their stay had passed without event. A few trying incidents, but nothing that would blacken his memory forever. Now, for the first time, Motecuhzoma wondered if he had made a terrible mistake by allowing the *teteo* into Tenochtitlan.

Qualpopoca, leader of the attack that killed the Spanish lord, must have felt that he had made a terrible mistake by entering the city. Qualpopoca had been in the city less than an hour before Cortés approached Motecuhzoma to let him know that he needed to take Qualpopoca's retinue into custody. Motecuhzoma had objected, but Cortés was immovable: he knew that Qualpopoca had been involved in the attack and, worse yet, his men knew.

Cortés had refrained from making an outright demand, but his implicit threats made it clear that violence could only be avoided if Qualpopoca was handed over. Motecuhzoma wanted so very badly to refuse Cortés' request, but he could not endanger the city's citizenry just to protect some provincial lord.

Much better to hand over Qualpopoca and continue amassing poison to kill the *teteo* and their allies. Many in his inner circle disagreed, but Motecuhzoma trusted them to not do anything rash. He would not blame them for being tempted, however. Qualpopoca was a hero and deserved better than the *teteo* would give him. Judging by the screaming last night, Qualpopoca had received little from the *teteo* besides pain and suffering.

143

Teteo stepped onto the roof of Axayacatl's Palace carrying bundles of kindling. Motecuhzoma squared his shoulders and glanced at the others who had joined him on the palace balcony. Cuitlahuac was seething, but Tezoc and Cuauhtemoc watched it all with a stony face. Motecuhzoma studied Cuauhtemoc's features closely.

His kin by blood, Cuauhtemoc's soft features belied a steely mettle and implacable ambition. Motecuhzoma had every confidence the nation would one day benefit from his talents; he had less confidence, however, that the nation would benefit from today's events.

"The *teteo* are bringing Qualpopoca onto the roof," Tezoc said.

Motecuhzoma turned toward the window. Blood streamed down Qualpopoca's face, and his feet dragged along the ground as the *teteo* carried him out. Motecuhzoma sucked in his breath as the rest of Qualpopoca's retinue were hauled outside. Shreds of skin and flesh dangled from useless limbs, and he doubted any of them could walk unassisted.

"They used their dogs on the prisoners," Cuauhtemoc said in an even voice.

Motecuhzoma shook his head. He hoped they had not shown weakness. No matter how terrible the torture, a Mexica man could not give in to whimpering and pleading. To do so would bring dishonor upon the nation as well as themselves, and the last thing his subjects needed was more cause for shame.

Motecuhzoma tightened his grip on the balcony railing as the *teteo* wrapped a chain around Qualpopoca and secured him to a wooden post. A few moments later, his son and his attendants were led to other posts.

"Let it be fast," Motecuhzoma whispered, over and over again.

A group of *teteo* bearing torches stepped onto the roof, and his stomach tightened. Motecuhzoma ordered a

144

servant to hide his daughter lest she see or hear what happened next.

Heart pounding, he watched the *teteo* set the kindling alight. He prayed the fire would quickly grow into an inferno, prayed that the suffering Qualpopoca and his retinue would soon end.

The fire did not heed his wishes. Not even a Great Speaker could change the malevolent nature of a fire, and he could do nothing besides watch as the tiny flames crawled toward the hapless victims.

A small crowd of subjects had gathered in the plaza, and they gasped when the first wisps of smoke became visible. He counted only forty people in the courtyard but suspected the crowd would soon grow. The *teteo* must have agreed because they had barricaded every window and entrance to the Palace of Axayacatl. Motecuhzoma wished he could barricade them in there forever, but he knew enough of the *teteo* weapons to understand that would not be possible. And while a mass poisoning was possible, it could take months to stockpile an adequate amount. In the meantime, he would have to pray the gods would forgive him for letting the *teteo* have their way with Qualpopoca.

Metal links tied Qualpopoca and the others in place, and the shiny material sparkled whenever it caught the light. The men shifted and squirmed to escape the budding blaze, setting off clinks and clanks that echoed in his ears. Small flames licked at cracked feet, prompting shrill screams that made his hackles stand on end. He closed his eyes and prayed for mercy. When he opened them again, a plume of white smoke had engulfed Qualpopoca and the others, sparing all onlookers the horrid sight of their anguished expressions. It did not, however, herald an end to the suffering of Qualpopoca and his countrymen. The ear-splitting screams gave way to gut-wrenching coughs so loud they blocked out the crackle and pop of the burning branches.

Perhaps angered by their impudence, the flames leapt upward and the bewildered *teteo* staggered backward. *Teteo* armed with buckets of water rushed toward the fire, desperate to assert their dominance over it, but the conflagration had grown beyond control. Nourished by blood and suffering, the fire proved impossible to tame and swallowed up Qualpopoca's retinue with startling speed.

Twenty buckets of water later, the sated fire succumbed to fatigue. With the curtain of orange and red finally vanquished, onlookers everywhere could behold the charred corpses of seventeen brave men.

"They were heroes," Cuauhtemoc said. "They reminded all of us the *teteo* can and must be killed. Let us pray the gods honor them in the afterlife."

Motecuhzoma nodded. He could not think of anything else to say and neither could anyone else so they departed, leaving him alone on the balcony, staring out on seventeen charred bodies, wondering if he had made a terrible mistake. His countrymen might never forgive him, his city might never forgive him, his own family might never forgive him for handing over Qualpopoca. No matter. So long as the *teteo* were not allowed to escape the city, none of it would matter.

He took a deep, bracing breath. Whether it took months or years, Motecuhzoma would make sure the *teteo* paid for what they did today.

Part Two
The Stay
May-July, 1520.

Lake Brigantine

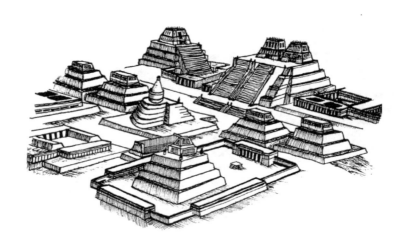

Tenochtitlan

Chapter 14

Tezoc sat cross-legged on the deck of the moored ship and ran his hand along the tar-coated planks. The pale people called the water-house a brigantine and had already built four to explore Tenochtitlan's lake system. Months had passed since the *teteo* finished the first one, but that had done little to make them any less mystifying.

Nonetheless, he could recognize the brigantines were superior to Mexica boats. Whereas a large canoe could usually hold no more than fifty people and never had more than one level, the brigantines could accommodate up to seventy-five people and had multiple levels. Perhaps most disconcerting were the "sails." They appeared to be giant sheets of cloth but expanded to gigantic proportions in the wind and allowed the ship to scud across the lake like a water beetle.

He did not understand it much himself, but he had not dedicated himself to the task either. There wasn't much point. In a few weeks, the poison would be delivered to the *teteo* and their allies.

It had not been easy, gathering up enough poison to incapacitate seven thousand men, but the Mexica were nothing if not resourceful. For far too long, the *teteo* and the Tlaxcalteca had exploited Motecuhzoma's goodwill, and the people of Tenochtitlan had grown weary of the unpleasant guests.

Tezoc tried to part the deck planks with his finger and let out a loud sigh when he realized he could not. So much seemed to be out of his control. He wished there was time to create a slower-acting poison, anything which caused immediate symptoms was functionally useless, but there was no more time for experimentation. The Flayed Festival would soon happen, and the religious authorities insisted that the *teteo* be put to death during the celebration.

Besides, they could not keep plying the pale people with gifts of gold, nor could they keep convincing the *pilli* to tolerate their impudent demands. And even if they could, the arrival of nineteen *teteo* ships on the eastern coast made it urgent they act soon. Letting them unite with their countrymen in Tenochtitlan would be folly in the extreme.

The sharp caw of an eagle overhead made Tezoc start, and he shaded his eyes to study the thirteen skies. Too bright to see anything. He turned to see if anyone else had noticed the sound. He frowned. None of the men or women on deck gave any indication they heard anything amiss.

Nonetheless, he did notice that the *teotl* on the opposite side of the deck, the one called Aguilar, was pointing at him. Tezoc scratched his head. *Probably interested in my piercings.* Whatever it was, he insisted upon talking about the matter with the translator woman. She did not seem to share his interest and when he grabbed Malintze's arm to get her attention, she slapped his hand away.

Tezoc chuckled and walked in their direction. The *teotl's* face lit up, and he puffed out his chest as Tezoc approached.

Tezoc stopped in front of Malintze and gestured to Aguilar. "Your *teotl* friend seems most interested in me."

Malintze scowled and said, "He wants me to give you a sermon."

Tezoc grinned. Their speeches about Jesus and eternal punishment would ring in his head long after the last *teotl* had his heart torn out. "Your accent is quite interesting, Malintze. You come from the south, correct?"

Malintze stiffened. "I did not know you had an ear for accents. Did you gain this knowledge in your travels as a peaceful merchant?"

Tezoc laughed. "Since when do merchants herald peace? First comes the trader, then comes the warrior."

Malintze pursed her lips and stared at his braid. She had to know it meant he belonged to an elite military order, but she gave no indication of fright or angst. Were he a younger man, he might have taken offense. Not now, though. These days, there was nothing he appreciated more than an enemy who lacked good sense.

"Why did you stay behind on the ship?" Tezoc asked. "Doesn't your master need help with translating?"

Malintze crossed her arms. "There is no need for a translator on a hunt."

Tezoc nodded. He could not fault her logic. Violence rarely needed translation.

Malintze tilted her chin upward. "Why did you stay behind? Doesn't your master need guarding? Hunts can be dangerous. What if he comes across a snake?"

Tezoc peered out at the small island where Motecuhzoma and the *teteo* were hunting. Motecuhzoma had hunted there numerous times, with the pale people and without, and had always returned unharmed. All the same, it did feel wrong to stay on the ship while Motecuhzoma traipsed around the island with the pale people.

Tezoc shrugged and turned back to Malintze. "Motecuhzoma has eyes sharp as an eagle and knows how to handle a weapon. Remember, he has won many victories for Tenochtitlan and has done a great deal to expand our confederacy."

A grave look passed over her face. "I know."

Tezoc furrowed his brow. He had not expected such a serious reaction.

"The *teteo* can protect Motecuhzoma if need be," Malintze added. "Look, they are returning with him now."

Tezoc turned toward the dock. True to her word, Motecuhzoma and Cortés were both walking back to the ship. Their guards followed behind them, but they appeared surprisingly comfortable with one another. Not only did they walk side by side, they matched each other in terms of stride. To the casual observer, they may have looked like friends and perhaps, under different circumstances, a mutual respect might have formed.

Had the *teteo* not formed a pact with the Tlaxcalteca and the Totonacs, the Mexica might have been able to reach some sort of agreement with Cortés and his soldiers. Motecuhzoma could have been convinced to provide gold for military service and the pale people could have lived like royalty... Of course, none of that would come to pass now, and it would only be a few short weeks until all the *teteo* who defiled Tenochtitlan were slaughtered.

Those on the coast would be more difficult to kill, but Tezoc trusted that his countrymen could raise an army equal to the task. If the gods were kind, they would allow him to lead that army. The pale people had been coddled much too long.

A few moments later, Cortés and Motecuhzoma were back on the brigantine and the ship departed for Tenochtitlan. Rowers pulled the ship forward with great heaves, and the unfurled sails quickly caught the wind. He studied the strange fabric closely. One day, the Mexica would have to learn how to use sails in their own fleet. When they did, there would not be an *altepetl* in all the One World that could resist them.

Tonatiuh was still high in the sky when they reached Tenochtitlan, but Tezoc wanted nothing more than to return to his home and take rest. Nevertheless, he could not shirk his duty and fell into step beside Motecuhzoma as they disembarked at the Tetamazolco dock.

They walked down the hard-packed dirt avenue together. When they were a safe distance from the brigantine, Tezoc asked Motecuhzoma, "How was your island excursion?"

"Most informative. The bolts they fire with their snapping bows fly straight and fast, but they are cumbersome in the extreme. In the time that a child could nock and shoot three arrows, a snapping bow can fire only two."

Tezoc licked his lips. *My troops will find that information very useful.* Tezoc understood why the *pilli* were aggrieved by Motecuhzoma's decision to host the *teteo* for so many months, but he wished they would at least admit that Motecuhzoma had gained valuable information in that time.

He doubted they would, though. Too many *pilli* cared only about green jade and social status. Tezoc sometimes wondered if Motecuhzoma's somber demeanor was caused not by the outrages of the pale people, but the incessant nagging of the *pilli*. They concurred, of course, that the invaders should be killed but objected most strongly to any method that involved deception or subterfuge. Much better to send the *teteo* the shield and the arrow, and then make war on them. Tezoc understood the value of pomp and ceremony as well as any Mexica warrior but he saw no sense in broadcasting their intentions beforehand, not when they were dealing with such a dishonest and immoral enemy.

"If the poison fails, we will have to eject the *teteo* by force," Tezoc said. "Can padded cotton keep our warriors safe from their snapping bows?"

Motecuhzoma shook his head. "Only a wooden shield will do. What did you learn about their ship?"

153

Tezoc recalled the feel of the smooth planks and the mottled pine resin coating. "It will not burn easily. But it can burn. We will need oil though, lots of oil."

~ ~ ~

Cortés took a sip of his wine and set his goblet on the table. The wine, and his three lunch guests, had been sent all the way from Villa Rica, but his guests had traveled in chains. The journey from Villa Rica to Tenochtitlan was not a short one, but Cortés insisted on the chains. Men pledged to Narváez could only be trusted to a certain extent.

Guevara's flesh still bore evidence of his mistreatment and despite being freed from his manacles hours prior, he was still rubbing his chafed wrists. Vergara and Amaya, on the other hand, seemed to forget all their earthly troubles once they clapped eyes on Tenochtitlan. They walked through the avenues in a daze and when they were brought inside the Palace of Axayacatl for a banquet, Cortés made sure they were all treated to a rich spread of turkey, pheasant, and partridge. Their eyes went so wide that Cortés half-expected them to pledge fealty on the spot.

"I hope the meal and the drink were to your satisfaction," Cortés said. He dipped a corn cake in a petite bowl filled with green and red sauce. "The lake scum has a taste reminiscent of Manchego cheese, no?"

Vergara and Amaya nodded enthusiastically, but a sharp glare from Guevara made both of them stiffen.

"Pray tell," Cortés said, "has Narváez ever provided you anything of the sort?"

Amaya scoffed. "The stingy bastard could put a Jew to shame."

Cortés put a hand over his heart and feigned dismay. "I fear his master, Governor Velázquez, is cut from the same cloth. Such a shame when Christians cannot extend their own kin love."

"Almost as shameful as being stuffed in a cage and carried for countless leagues," Guevara muttered.

"Yes, I must beg pardon for the actions of my subordinate," Cortés said. "Sandoval can be a bit overzealous in his duties." Cortés took another sip of the spiced wine. God, how he had missed the taste. It had been months since he had a proper drink. "Sandoval is, however, an honest man. He tells me Narváez has been sent by Governor Velázquez to arrest me. Is this true?"

Vergara and Amaya looked at one another but stayed silent. Guevara issued a loud burp and leaned back in his wooden chair.

"It is most certainly true," Guevara said. "Narváez has anchored at San Juan de Ulúa with a fleet of nineteen ships. Over eight hundred Spaniards fight for him. You would be wise to release us, and submit yourself to his mercy. Governor Velázquez has many questions for you, chief among them why you have not shared any of your winnings, and why you founded a colony when you expressly forbidden from doing so."

Cortés buried his dirty fingers deep in the folds of a napkin to hide the tremor in his hand. Two hundred and fifty Spaniards had followed Cortés into Tenochtitlan while one hundred and fifty had stayed behind in Veracruz. Even if he consolidated all his forces, he would still be outnumbered almost two to one by Narváez's forces.

"Narváez could bring to bear eight thousand men, and I would not fear him," Cortés said. "What does a righteous man have to fear from an unlettered ladrone? I have God and justice on my side."

"And the Indians," Vergara said, prompting laughter from Amaya.

Cortés smiled. "Yes, one must not forget about the Indians. Tens of thousands have already pledged their loyalty to me. Narváez would be most unwise to cross me."

Guevara's lip curled upward. "You've allied with savages?"

"I am a stranger in a strange land; surely you do not seek to fault me for making allies amongst the locals. Look around you some." Cortés gestured to the grand interior of the Palace of Axayacatl with a sweep of his arm. "The natives of these parts are of much greater intelligence than those of the islands. Tell me, have you ever seen a city more beautiful than Tenochtitlan?"

Silence fell over the table. "It is like something from a Tale of Amadis," Vergara said in a quiet voice.

Except Amadis never had to contend with enemies half as vicious. Cortés had lost count of all the sacrificial ceremonies he had seen. "I could not agree more," Cortés replied. "The city has no equal in all of Europe. But the Indians here are not just clever. They are incredibly generous, also. In these past few months, this company has gained more gold than any company in all the New World or the West Indies."

Guevara snorted. "Amazing how blessed the condemned can be. Seems every man set to hang has some fortune hidden away, some fortune they are eager to share if they can be granted clemency."

Cortés smiled mirthlessly. Guevara knew nothing about desperation. He had no idea what it was like to wake up in the dead of night in a cold sweat, to spend hours tossing and turning because sleep offered no respite. To spend entire days fretting about the machinations of the Indians, Governor Velázquez, his own officers...

Cortés snapped twice and waved the servants over. Three covered plates were laid down in front of Amaya, Guevara, and Vergara. Cortés nodded and the makeshift lids were removed, revealing glimmering ingots of gold stacked a hand high.

"Yes, Guevara, we truly are blessed. God smiles upon this expedition..." Cortés raised his hand high in the air and slammed it down on the table. Vergara jumped and Cortés had to hide a smile as he pulled his hand back. "And He would strike down those who would seek to sabotage it. I am but an instrument of God, but I do not lack for great wealth. I can be a most generous patron, ask any of my men."

Just do not ask the men I have had to punish for insubordination, or the common soldiers who gripe of poor compensation. Cortés flattened his trembling hand and stared into Guevara's rutted face. Red from sun exposure and dotted with ingrown hairs, Guevara was about as pleasing to gaze upon as a horse's maw, but Cortés refused to break eye contact. Almost a minute passed before Guevara finally blinked and turned toward his fellow companions.

"What would entering your service entail?" Amaya asked.

Cortés grinned. "That you accept the gold I am about to give you."

Guevara grunted. "Presents do make nonsense of troubles. What else would you ask of us?"

"That you travel back to the coast with the gold and let others know of my generosity," Cortés added. "You have spent many weeks in Narváez's company now. Surely you must know which officers can be persuaded to defect. Speak to them for me, let them know I am curious about Narváez's plans. Do this small favor for me, and I will give you a king's ransom."

Guevara, Amaya, and Vergara exchanged long glances. After a lengthy silence, Guevara leaned forward and said, "We would be happy to assist, captain-general."

Tenochtitlan

Chapter 15

Xicotencatl waited outside Cortés' room. Located on the highest floor of the Palace of Axayacatl, the room offered a sweeping view of the Sacred Precinct and Xicotencatl suspected that Cortés spent a great deal of time taking in the sight.

How the *teteo* were still enamored of the city was beyond him. He could concede that Tenochtitlan had some charming qualities—the market brought together people from all over the One World, and the zoo contained every manner of animal—but that did not stop him from missing Tlaxcala. Tenochtitlan was too crowded and bustling, the people too duplicitous and conniving. He longed to return to Tlaxcala, to feel the cut of the wind as it sliced through craggy foothills, to hear the trill of merry birds in an open field.

He looked at Chichi and wondered if he also missed Tlaxcala. Once known as Chichimecatecle, his former deputy now insisted everyone call him Chichi since the *teteo* seldom used his full name. If their refusal to address him by his proper title bothered him, he did not show it.

A guard stepped out of Cortés' room and escorted Chichi and Xicotencatl to Cortés. He sat behind a high table, hands folded and shoulders squared. He offered a small smile as they approached but his translator, Malintze, could not be bothered to do so. Instead, she sniffled and wiped at her puffy, red eyes.

Cortés said something in his strange tongue and Malintze translated, "Cortés hopes you are both well."

Xicotencatl forced a smile. Not so long ago, Cortés and Xicotencatl had been mortal enemies. For the good of both their people, they had been able to set aside animosity, but their alliance would always be one of necessity, never love. "Tell him we are flattered by his concern," Xicotencatl replied. "We wish him good health also."

Cortés nodded when he heard the translation. "How do your warriors fare?"

Xicotencatl pursed his lips. Tlaxcala had lent four thousand warriors to Cortés' cause and, despite promises made months ago, not one of them had been given a chance to strike down a Mexica warrior. Nonetheless, they had all been given the pleasure of quartering together in a palace much too small to accommodate multiple armies. So inadequate was the palace for their massive numbers that his warriors had to build barracks on the roof, as well as the inner courtyard, for the sake of accommodation. Unfortunately, the wooden barracks provided little protection from the rain. Inclement weather often forced his men to take shelter inside the building, much to everyone's discomfort.

"My warriors are eager to make battle against the Mexica," Xicotencatl said. "We have been away from Tlaxcala a long time, and many wish to see their families again."

Cortés nodded. "It is high time we make a move against Motecuhzoma then."

Xicotencatl straightened. Were the *teteo* no longer blinded by gold? Had they finally discovered some courage?

"What did you have in mind?" Chichi asked.

Cortés' voice betrayed no emotion, but Malintze's composure cracked under the weight of his words. She paused to dab at her eyes and said, "Cortés would like to know if the brave men of Tlaxcala would be willing to take part in a raid to steal Motecuhzoma's children."

Xicotencatl stiffened and looked at Chichi. Judging by Chichi's gaping mouth, he was also surprised by the turn in conversation.

"To what end?" Xicotencatl asked.

"Cortés must leave the city soon, but he cannot leave unless he knows that Motecuhzoma has been accounted for," Malintze replied. "Cortés cannot have him stirring up trouble while he is away."

Xicotencatl narrowed his eyes. "Why not take Motecuhzoma hostage instead?"

Malintze turned to Cortés. He said something in his strange tongue, but Malintze did not pass along his words. Instead, she responded to Cortés in Spanish. He did not honor her with an answer and stared at her until she had to turn away. Head down, she said, "Motecuhzoma has too many guards and has a very unpredictable routine. We must take his children hostage so he will surrender himself to us."

"Motecuhzoma lays his head down in many different places," Chichi said. "How do we know the same is not true for his children?"

"The *teteo* have been watching them for many days and believe the younger ones keep a more fixed routine," Malintze said. "Most of them sleep in the Palace of Motecuhzoma the Younger. That palace is well guarded and hard to sneak into. However, some of his children sleep in the Palace of Motecuhzoma the Elder. Those children will be easier to take."

Xicotencatl cracked his shoulder joints. For months, the *teteo* had occupied themselves by playing cards and smelting gold. Some never ventured outside the Palace of Axayacatl and those that did always travelled in groups of ten or more. Now they suddenly wanted to risk all their gold, their own lives even, on an audacious bid to seize Motecuhzoma's children.

"What is happening on the coast?" Xicotencatl asked.

161

Much to his surprise, Malintze did not turn to Cortés to translate his question. Instead, she answered herself and said, "New *teteo* have arrived in Mexico. They are many in number and mean to disrupt the campaign against the Mexica."

Xicotencatl furrowed his brow. Why would the new *teteo* wish to sabotage Cortés? Perhaps Xicotencatl's countrymen were not the only ones with divided loyalties.

"The *teteo* are led by a *teotl* named Narváez," Malintze continued. "Narváez is unpopular with many of his deputies, and Cortés believes they can be persuaded to fight for him. If they join his cause, he can bring more men to Tenochtitlan, and we will all be safer."

Xicotencatl nodded. He did not relish the prospect of having to interact with more of their kind, but he understood the value of winning more soldiers to the cause. He glanced at Cortés. Dark bags had formed under his eyes, and his wan pallor reminded him of rancid tallow. His angst was clear as day. Whether it was born from fear the raid might fail or fear that Narváez would sabotage his plans, Xicotencatl did not know.

"When does Cortés hope to seize the children?" Xicotencatl asked.

Malintze turned to Cortés. They exchanged some words, and she said in Nahuatl, "When the moon goes dark."

Xicotencatl blinked. The dark moon was only a few days away. He glanced at Chichi who seemed positively giddy about the turn of events. Did the man really relish the prospect of danger that much? Had the battles with the *teteo* taught him nothing about the folly of charging into conflict?

"How many men will be needed?" Xicotencatl asked.

"Fifteen Tlaxcalteca men will be needed. Five *teteo* have already volunteered, and Cortés trusts that you know

162

which warriors would be most suited for this… task." Malintze stopped to clear her throat and dab her nose. "Cortés would be honored if you took part in the raid."

Xicotencatl sucked in his teeth. Of course the *teteo* would want him to take part. It would be extremely dangerous, and he trusted they would be none too sad if he were killed during the raid. He had never been able to feign much love for their kind and wished every day his people had refused to make common cause with the *teteo*.

He wondered if he should refuse to join the raid. It would be a mark against his courage, but the *teteo* could not be allowed to think he would do whatever they asked. But if he refused to take part, he could not, in good conscience, ask any Tlaxcalteca warriors to join the raid. And Tlaxcala had to take part.

Tlaxcala had been at war with the Mexica for generations. For decades, they had suffered at the hands of the Mexica with no hope of reprieve. With the princes and princesses of Tenochtitlan in Tlaxcala custody, Xicotencatl's people would finally be able to negotiate from a position of strength. No longer would they simply have to suffer the sanctions that led to so much death and illness, and no longer would they have to accept being cut off from their old allies.

He let out his breath and looked at Malintze. "Tell Cortés my men will be ready by the new moon. I am honored to help."

~ ~ ~

Cortés shivered and clenched his teeth to stop them from chattering. The room was cold as a Medellín winter. He would be warmer without the heavy mail, but he could not bring himself to take it off. If the raid failed, the Mexica would probably try to force their way into the Palace of Axayacatl, and a *macuahuitl* could easily cut through unprotected flesh.

He took a deep breath. He still had time to call off the raid. Leaving Tenochtitlan and surrendering himself to Narváez would be the safest thing to do. But if Cortés let Motecuhzoma and his family be, could he trust the Mexica not to attack his forces as he traveled to the coast? Could he trust Narváez to take mercy on him if he surrendered? Probably not. And that's why the raid had to succeed, why it would be folly to call it off.

For days now, the Tlaxcalteca and the Spanish had trained tirelessly just for this mission and the constant drilling had to count for something. God would not let them fail, he was sure of it.

Cortés tore his gaze away from the Palace of Motecuhzoma the Elder and glanced at Pedro. Bastard gave no indication of being cold or anxious. Life would be easier if he were Pedro; life would be easier even if he were some lowly foot soldier. At least then he would not have to worry about Narváez. If that low-born degenerate figured out how to hold an army together, Cortés stood to lose everything.

He clenched his fist. Once he had Motecuhzoma under lock and key, he would make his move against Narváez. Damned fool had to be mad. Why else would he insist that Cortés surrender to his authority? He would die before he gave any of his riches to Narváez, but first he would kill. No man—not Narváez, not Governor Velázquez, not Motecuhzoma—would thwart his great cause.

"Why are there so few sentries outside?" Pedro asked. "Madness to put only four sentries near an entrance."

"Most of the sentries stay inside so they can patrol the halls," Cortés replied.

Pedro snorted and kept his gaze fixed on the Palace of Motecuhzoma the Elder. Had Pedro better knowledge of Nahuatl, Cortés might have included him in the raid. But Pedro could not participate in the raid any more than he

164

could; only Spaniards who could understand Nahuatl would take part in tonight's battle.

Cortés rubbed his eyes and studied the stronghold where so many of Motecuhzoma's children slept. It was roughly similar in size to the Palace of Axayacatl, and he prayed that it had a similar layout. Besides the essential information—the prince slept on the third floor on the west side of the building, the youngest princess slept on the third floor on the east side, and the older princess slept on the second floor on the north side—the Tlaxcalteca knew little about the building they would soon enter. Scouts could only glean so much from a distance.

It was apparent to all, however, that the sentries had to be killed for the plan to succeed. He glanced at the nearby hourglass. Not much sand left.

Cortés cleared his throat. "Doña Marina, tell the archers to fire once they are ready."

Ever dutiful, she passed along his words. She had many misgivings about his plan, but he knew she would never plot against him. He wished the same was true for all his subordinates.

The Tlaxcalteca nodded and nocked their bows. In terms of vantage point, the archers could not ask for a clearer line of sight. Not only would they be firing from a darkened room at the highest level of Axayacatl's Palace, they would be firing upon targets who moved in predictable circuits. Better yet, some of those targets would be stationary.

The twang of eight arrows releasing all at once made him start. He whipped his head toward the sentries. Not a single one still standing. He squinted and shaded his eyes. One was still moving, he could raise the alarm—a single arrow shot out of the dark and punched through the man's chest with a satisfying thump.

Three pintail honks were made in quick succession, and the next step of the plan went into effect. Five

Tlaxcalteca, shorn of all clothing, emerged from the Palace of Axayacatl and raced toward the dead sentries. Meanwhile, men on the roof lowered reinforced planks into position. Cortés smiled as he watched the Tlaxcalteca warriors cross the makeshift bridge that now connected the Palace of Motecuhzoma and the Palace of Axayacatl. Nobody could accuse the Indians of cowardice.

His heart racing, he looked back to the Tlaxcalteca who were busy stripping the dead sentries and changing into their attire. They could be spotted at any moment— if they had not already been spotted. Perhaps they were walking into a trap. He pushed the thought from his mind. It would do no good to think on such dark matters.

Once the Tlaxcalteca changed into the proper outfits, a new group of men rushed out of the Palace of Axayacatl and carried the bodies out of sight. Meanwhile, two Tlaxcalteca warriors took up post near the entrance of Motecuhzoma's palace while the others patrolled the nearby grounds. By the time they finished getting into position, the last of the Tlaxcalteca warriors had traversed the makeshift bridge and it was being drawn up again.

The men who had crossed over unfurled long ropes and hurriedly tied them around the roof scuppers. Once they finished, the others slipped the braided loops around their waists and tested the knots with prying fingers. If the ropes failed, many brave men would plunge to their deaths.

"God protect them," Cortés muttered.

The warriors checked each other's knots and advanced toward the ledge. Their countrymen lowered them into position, and the climbers surrendered themselves to gravity. Not a single knot slipped, and Cortés watched, amazed, as a handful of men silently scaled the palace wall. He let out his breath. He should have had more faith. God kept Daniel safe when he ventured into the lion's den, and He would do the same for the Tlaxcalteca.

Cortés crossed himself and turned to Pedro. "I, for one, am proud to call the Indians our allies today."

Pedro furrowed his brow. "They're not our allies. They're our servants."

"Call them what you will. They are undeniably brave."

Pedro scoffed and opened his mouth to respond, but a strange sound made him stop. Both of them turned in the direction of it. The Tlaxcalteca archers were pulling at their hair and gesticulating wildly in the direction of the Palace of Motecuhzoma. One of them was already deep in conversation with Doña Marina, and Cortés gritted his teeth as he waited for a translation. His index finger started twitching uncontrollably, and he bunched his hand into a fist.

A few moments later, Doña Marina turned toward him. Ashen-faced, she said, "Xicotencatl and Chichi have gone to the wrong room. They are on the balcony of the servant quarters, and we have no way to signal them. Unless they realize their mistake soon, we cannot help them."

Tenochtitlan

Chapter 16

Xicotencatl untied his rope and shook out his hands. Finally on the palace balcony, but his palms burned as if they had been doused in flame. He prayed to the gods for strength and pushed thoughts of weakness from his head. The raid would not fail. His forebears had carried out countless raids, though none half as daring, and they would grant him strength.

He readied his *macuahuitl* and looked to Chichi. Armed with a two-handed club, his former subordinate and long-time rival stared fixedly at him. Xicotencatl straightened and gestured to the heavy curtain partition. Chichi nodded and made his way toward it. Xicotencatl followed close behind.

The curtain grated against the rod as Chichi brushed it aside, and the sound made his hair stand on end. Xicotencatl held his breath as he stepped inside and quietly surveyed the dim room. Was the darkness playing tricks on his eyes? He had been told there would be an ornate bed in the center of the room and that the princess slept alone. No matter where he looked, he did not see a bed, but he did count eight sleeping forms. Some rested on reed mats while others lay on the floor, and he doubted they would stay asleep much longer.

Eyes wide, Xicotencatl turned to Chichi. They were in the wrong room. He looked at the balcony, his heart pounding. Perhaps they should climb back up. He took a step in the direction of the curtain partition, then stopped.

Scaling the wall would take time and energy, and those resources were too valuable to waste. If anyone would know where to find the princess, it would be the people in this room.

Xicotencatl touched Chichi on the shoulder and gestured to a nearby figure. Moving on the balls of their feet, they made their way toward the supine figure. When they were a few paces away, Xicotencatl held up a hand to stop Chichi.

Chichi furrowed his brow and looked to him for explanation. Xicotencatl held up three fingers and put one down after counting to twenty. Chichi tried to move forward, and Xicotencatl grabbed him by the shoulder. He counted to twenty and put another finger down. Assuming the other warriors had made it to the right rooms, they were probably binding and gagging their captives by now. He wished them luck and put down his last finger.

Knowing no reason to delay further, Xicotencatl advanced upon the sleeping figure. He kneeled next to the man and raised his *macuahuitl*. The man stirred as the shadow of it passed over his face, and Xicotencatl clamped his hand over the man's mouth. His eyes flew open, and he tried to yell. Xicotencatl smothered the noise with his palm and raised the *macuahuitl*. The man went still, and Xicotencatl slowly pulled his hand back.

"Where is the princess?" Xicotencatl whispered.

The man stared at him blankly.

Xicotencatl lowered the *macuahuitl* so that the sharp edge rested against the man's neck.

"Where is she?"

"The room to our right," the servant whispered. "The next one over."

Xicotencatl nodded. "Who are you?"

"Nobody. A palace servant."

Xicotencatl pursed his lips. The others had to be servants also, and Motecuhzoma would not care overmuch for their lives. The servant trembled, and the *macuahuitl* opened a small cut on his neck.

Should I open his throat? As long as the servant drew breath, he could raise an alarm. Then again, he could prove useful alive.

Xicotencatl pulled the man close. "Wake the others, quickly and quietly. You are no longer a servant; today, you go free."

The man blinked and hurried off to do his bidding. Chichi leaned close and whispered, "I hope you know what you are doing."

I hope so, too. One by one, the servants came awake and fixed their attention on him.

"Brothers and sisters, I am Xicotencatl the Younger, and I hail from the nation of Tlaxcala." Xicotencatl waited for the enormity of his words to register with the group. He bit back a smile as their mouths dropped open. "The evil tyrant Motecuhzoma Xocoyotzin has probably told you many terrible things about me, that I have nothing but hate and violence for the *pilli* of Tenochtitlan... and it's true." Chichi gaped at him in shock, and Xicotencatl raised his voice just a little higher.

"How can I not?" Xicotencatl asked. "The wealth of the Great Speaker is known all throughout the One World, but who benefits from that wealth? The Tlaxcalteca do not—Motecuhzoma means to make beggars and slaves of us all. Do you benefit from his great wealth? Motecuhzoma and his kin rest their heads on leather pillows and stay warm with fur blankets stuffed with eiderdown and cotton. You sleep on the cold hard ground and have nothing to rest your head on besides a thin reed mat. It is unjust and it ends tonight. Is there anyone here who does not wish to be free?"

Xicotencatl swept his gaze across the room. Not one servant offered an objection.

"Good. Tonight, we take back our freedom. Does this room open into a hallway?"

Silence. The servants shifted and fidgeted, but not one offered advice. After a long pause, one finally spoke up and said, "There's no way to open the door from the inside. There are two guards posted near the door, and they will not let down the barricades before morning."

"Then we will break down the door!" Eyes glittering, Xicotencatl held up his *macuahuitl* and grinned. "Chichi and I will deal with the guards."

~ ~ ~

A loud bang roused Cotton Flower from her sleep. She sat upright, her heart racing.

"What was—"

An even louder bang interrupted her, followed by a splintering of wood that gave way to panicked shouting and running.

Cotton Flower grabbed the guttering torch and hurried toward the hallway to investigate, but a bloodcurdling scream stopped her cold. She looked around her room, desperate to find some place to hide. Her eyes jumped to the bed. She could hide underneath, but what would she do with the torch?

No, she had to keep the torch in hand. She might need it as a weapon. Cotton Flower hurried toward the dressing screen. Halfway there, something grabbed her from behind and tossed her backward.

The torch clattered to the floor, and she landed beside it with a hard thud. She screamed but a hand flew to her mouth and trapped the noise inside. Desperate, Cotton Flower sank her teeth into the dirty, meaty fingers. The man howled and slammed his fist into her stomach. Dazed and short of breath, Cotton Flower rolled over and crawled toward the torch.

Her attacker grabbed her ankle and pulled her backward. He turned Cotton Flower over and slapped her. Blood filled her mouth, and her cheek burned like fire.

He flicked blood off his hand and raised his club. "Bite me again, little princess, and I will bash your head in. Do you understand?"

She nodded and slashed out her arm to rake him across the face. He caught her wrist, pinned it under his knee, and then slapped her again. Tears flooded her eyes.

"Stop, Chichi," yelled a deep-voiced man. "We need her alive. "Bind her limbs—the servants will not distract the guards for long."

The deep-voiced man, a tall warrior with a thick Tlaxcalteca accent and a glittering *macuahuitl*, tossed rope toward Chichi who set his club down to tie her wrists together. She cried out as the rope dug into her skin, and Chichi shot her a menacing glare.

He reached for her face and she cringed, thinking he was going to slap her again, but he surprised her by stuffing a dirty rag into her mouth. Tears streamed down her face. This had to be a dream. She was a princess, she was descended from royalty; warriors stood guard outside her room just to keep her safe.

Cotton Flower yelled at him to stop, begged for mercy, but all that came out was a garbled muffling. The tall one came over and tied her ankles. Together, the two of them lifted her up and carried her toward the balcony.

They flung aside the curtain partition, and the cool night air instantly enveloped her. For a moment, she felt calm. That sense of tranquility did not last long, though. Without warning, they hoisted her upward and tossed her over the balcony railing.

She tried to scream, but everything happened too fast. She landed in the middle of a giant net, unhurt but very confused. The men holding the net stretched it taut and a *teotl* clad in shiny armor grabbed her arms, slung her over his shoulder, and ran toward some place she could not see.

Cotton Flower fixed her gaze on the Palace of Motecuhzoma. The men who had barged into her room were clambering over the edge of her balcony, but Chichi slipped and fell to the ground. The other man, the tall Tlaxcalteca warrior, dropped to the flagstone pavement and helped Chichi to his feet. A terrible anger seized her, and she prayed the gods would strike them both down.

Cotton Flower repeated this one simple wish, over and over. Out of the dark, a sling came whirring. Her heart leapt. The sling sailed over Xicotencatl and Chichi and she realized, with a start, that it was heading for her.

She squeezed her eyes shut and tensed her body. Cotton Flower heard something snap as the throwing sling wrapped itself around flesh and bone, and the *teotl* screamed so loud it made her ears ring. He fell to the ground and dumped her on the flagstone tiles. The teotl yelled curses in his strange language and tugged at the sling wrapped around his knee.

This is my chance to escape. She rolled onto her side. The canal was not that far away. She had no idea how she was going to swim with bound hands, but anything seemed better than letting the *teteo* take her. Cotton Flower rolled over again. She could smell the canal now, and the pungent aroma of algae and lake scum made her heart turn white.

Just when she was sure nothing could stop her from reaching the canal, a new *teotl* picked her up and hoisted her into his arms. She kicked and wriggled and fought, but none of it mattered.

The *teotl* sprinted for the Palace of Axayacatl, and she prayed he would be felled with a sling. The gods, however, did not answer her prayer, and the *teotl* passed through the entrance unharmed. Cotton Flower stilled as she realized a terrible truth: her father's men had failed to protect her. Unless she could find some way to escape, she had no choice but to reconcile herself to life as a hostage.

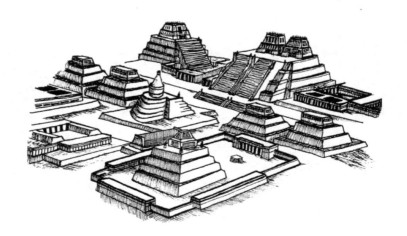

Tenochtitlan

Chapter 17

Motecuhzoma stared at the deep gash in his palm. No longer oozing blood, the initial pain had abated, and he felt only a small sting when he closed his hand. It would probably hurt more in the days to come, and he would curse himself for knocking aside the drinking glass with his bare hand. But right now, he could do nothing besides curse himself for letting the *teteo* steal his children.

Three of them seized—all within the course of one night. It beggared belief. He could not think of any event more shameful in all his reign. In his own life. Tears filled his eyes, and a lump formed in his throat. He had taught Cotton Flower how to *patolli* months ago. He was supposed to play with her regularly, but the duties of the throne beckoned so he put off lessons. The memory of her smile chilled him. She might never look at him that same way again.

"Brother, how do you fare?" Cuitlahuac asked.

Terribly. His emotions alternated between violent rage and despondent grief with such volatility that he could not predict which would get the better of him. Motecuhzoma blinked away the tears and gazed at his brother, gazed at all the advisors who had gathered for tonight's discussion. Tezoc, Cuauhtemoc, Cuitlahuac, Milintica.... this could be the last occasion where they were all gathered in the same room.

"What did the captured warrior say?" Motecuhzoma asked.

Cuitlahuac looked down. A heavy silence filled the air. Eventually, Tezoc cleared his throat and said, "He demands you surrender yourself to the *teteo* and the

Tlaxcalteca. He says if you refuse to do so, a captive will be killed each night until you change your mind or until…"

"They have no captives left," finished Milintica.

Motecuhzoma winced. He had always known the *teteo* cared little for proper custom, but he had never suspected they, or the Tlaxcalteca, would sink to such barbarity.

"Are the rest of my children safe?" Motecuhzoma asked.

Cuauhtemoc nodded. "They will be guarded by Eagle Warriors tonight and depart for Tetzcoco at dawn."

Motecuhzoma let out his breath. The relief that flooded through him was so overpowering that his composure cracked for a moment. He closed his eyes and did his utmost to project the stoic strength that once came naturally.

"Good," Motecuhzoma replied. "I am entrusting the care of my children to you, Cuitlahuac. I am in no position to carry out my duties and must resign as Great Speaker."

The room went quiet. Dumbfounded, Cuitlahuac and Cuauhtemoc stared at each other while Tezoc slowly shook his head.

Milintica stared at Motecuhzoma as if he had committed sacrilege and sputtered, "You cannot resign. It is unprecedented. No Great Speaker has ever resigned—"

"No Great Speaker has ever had his children abducted by his own guests," Motecuhzoma said.

During the past few months, Motecuhzoma had tricked himself into thinking that he had lulled the *teteo* into a false sense of security. News of the abduction had turned that certainty on its head, and he castigated himself for being so foolish. He sucked in his breath and looked at Cuitlahuac. "You were right. We never should have let the *teteo* into our city."

Cuitlahuac's eyes went wide. His surprise soon gave way to dismay, and anger distorted his features.

"We still have the poison," Tezoc said. "We can make sure they do not march out of the city. Give us another week, and we will have enough to kill all of them."

Earlier in the day, the same news would have made Motecuhzoma's spirits soar. Now he just felt tired. He recalled the agonized screams of the captured warrior, the way he screamed and begged once they started using the knife on him. Motecuhzoma did not want to imagine how his children might react if the *teteo* did the same to them. "Do what you must," he said. "I will surrender myself to the *teteo* before sun up and make sure my children are safe."

Cuitlahuac threw his arms in the air. "Surrendering yourself to the *teteo* will avail your children little. Do not give yourself to such evil people. It will only cause suffering."

Motecuhzoma rubbed the cut in his hand. The shape of it reminded him of a snake's fang. He had let the *teteo* put their poison in him, but he was not going to let the same happen to his children. "The *teteo* may not free them but we know what will happen if I do not give myself to the *teteo*," Motecuhzoma said. "I cannot leave them at the mercy of the *teteo* when I know I can help them. They are the future of this city, and their safety means more than my freedom."

"How will we carry out the poisoning if you give yourself to them?" Tezoc asked. "They are utterly reliant on us for food, and you will depend on them in turn. If we give them poisoned food, they will very likely pass it along to you."

"That is another reason I must give myself to the *teteo*," Motecuhzoma replied. "If I do not surrender to them, who will make sure my children do not eat the poisoned food? I can only protect them if I surrender myself."

Cuitlahuac slammed his hand down on a table. "You cannot—"

"He must," Cuauhtemoc said. "If the children consume the tainted food, they will show symptoms long before any adult. A mass poisoning will not be possible if the invaders learn too early of our intentions."

Cuitlahuac reddened and stormed toward the exit. He paused before Cuauhtemoc and said something indiscernible. Before anyone could even ask him to speak up, he exited the room.

Cuitlahuac would not be the only one sickened by his choice. Motecuhzoma knew and accepted that many would lambast his decision. None of it mattered. He cared only for the well-being of his children. Nothing mattered more than their safety.

Milintica's face brightened. "The poison could be key to saving you and your children from *teteo* captivity."

Tezoc scoffed. "We do not even know what day the poison will be ready."

Milintica shot him a caustic glare. "We do not need to know the exact day. We just need to find a way to let Motecuhzoma know which dish is poisoned. Surely I do not need to explain how to carry out a poisoning to you."

Tezoc looked down, shamefaced. He was about to respond when Motecuhzoma cut in and said, "Include double-flowered marigolds with the poisoned dishes." He stopped and took a moment to let his heart calm. "It has been my greatest honor to serve our nation, and I relinquish my position with a heavy heart. But before I do so, you must all promise me one thing."

Confused, his advisors glanced at one another and then looked to him.

"What do you need from us?" Tezoc asked.

"If the poisoning fails, you must not let the *teteo* leave the city alive," Motecuhzoma commanded. "Even if it means my death, you must kill them all. They have plagued our people for long enough."

Another painful silence followed his proclamation. He clenched his fist, and the gash in his palm stung with a newfound intensity. The pain made him gasp, but he did not open his fist. They needed to see his anguish, they needed to understand the seriousness of his purpose. They needed to—

"We will make the *teteo* rue the day they ever stepped into Tenochtitlan," Cuauhtemoc said. "Whether it takes a week or a year, we will slay Cortés and his countrymen."

Motecuhzoma closed his eyes and released his fist. Dispatching the *teteo* was no longer his task. The burden that had weighed so heavily on him these past few months had finally been lifted, but the relief that washed over him felt hollow and incomplete. Perhaps that was the only way a father could feel after losing his children.

He studied the expressions of his advisors. Indignant and heartbroken, all of them. Hopefully the mix of emotions would not sap their fighting strength. They needed to be strong to carry on the fight that he no longer could. He bid his honored advisors farewell and prepared to surrender himself to the *teteo*.

~ ~ ~

Solomon rubbed a sheet of sandpaper along a rough cut of wood. At his current rate, it would take hours to finish. Once he finished, he would be rewarded with an even rougher cut of wood. He massaged his back. The feel of his lacerated flesh sent shivers of revulsion through him, and he wished sometimes his wounds had never healed.

Bondage had not been kind to his body, and he looked forward to the day when he could take rest under the shade of high trees and bask in Allah's presence. Nonetheless, that day was not yet here so he blew out his

181

breath and resumed his duties. He would attract unwanted attention if he spent overlong catching his breath. Perhaps if he were inside he could rest as needed but in the courtyard of Axayacatl's palace, he was much too exposed.

He put down the cut of wood and blew on the sandpaper to dislodge errant wood filings, careful to keep the nearby soldiers in his line of sight. Why they wanted him to sand the cut of wood, he did not know, but he did not concern himself with the matter overmuch.

Ever since Motecuhzoma surrendered himself to captivity, the Christians had grown increasingly erratic in their behavior and their demands. To be fair, they did have good cause for angst. The Mexica had made no attempt to recapture Motecuhzoma by force, but they were not known for their docile nature.

If the Christians had any sense, they would have quit the city by now. They were determined, however, to extort more gold from their hosts and had convinced themselves that the Mexica would not attempt an attack so long as they held Motecuhzoma hostage. Why they had such confidence, Solomon did not know. They would learn their folly soon enough. Whether or not his Christian captors would admit it, a great reckoning was brewing.

Perhaps Cortés sensed as much because he was already making plans to leave the city with a portion of his army. However, the bulk of his forces, the Tlaxcalteca warriors, would stay in Tenochtitlan as he journeyed over the mountains. Apparently, there was some trouble on the coast, and Cortés needed to make battle against the Christians who had arrived in the New World a few weeks earlier. Solomon had serious doubts Cortés would prevail against his foes, but Solomon was not personally invested either way. The day he rooted for one group of

Christians over another would be the day he became a slave in spirit as well as body.

Solomon shuddered and glanced again at the soldiers. To his surprise, Vitale was standing among them and pointing at him. Weeks had passed since they had a real conversation, and he had no idea why Vitale would seek him out now. Nonetheless, he offered no objection when the soldier ordered him to follow him into the Palace of Axayacatl.

Cool air enveloped him as he stepped inside, and he muttered thanks under his breath. If Vitale heard him, he gave no sign of it as he made his way toward the stairs. Solomon followed behind but he could not match Vitale's brisk pace and quickly fell behind. He might have lost sight of him altogether but Vitale brought the trek to an abrupt halt by stopping in front of an open window. By the time Solomon caught up with him, his breath was short and his legs were aching. He sat down on a nearby crate.

"Need water?" Vitale asked.

Solomon chuckled drily and waved away his question. A sudden fit of coughing seized him, and he doubled over.

"Don't cough too loudly," Vitale said. "There'll be trouble for both of us if anyone sees us talking."

"How did you convince the soldiers to grant me leave?" Solomon asked between coughs.

"Told them I needed somebody who can speak Nahuatl," Vitale said simply.

Solomon nodded. He was by no means fluent, but he could hold a simple conversation in Nahuatl. He wiped sweat from his brow and let his breathing calm.

"Feeling improved?" Vitale asked.

Solomon grunted. "I fear my body is not what it used to be."

A pensive look came over Vitale's face, and he turned his gaze toward the horizon. "Wonder if it's possible to stay the same as we once was."

Solomon let out a quiet sigh. "I would give anything for things to be as they once were."

Vitale said nothing and stared out at the majestic mountain chain that cleaved the Valley of Mexico from the rest of the One World.

"Will you be staying in Tenochtitlan with Pedro or traveling to the coast with Cortés?" Solomon asked.

Vitale stiffened. In a hushed voice, he said, "Traveling to the coast. How 'bout you?"

"Staying here. I'm not sure my body has recovered from the last march anyway." Solomon forced a smile. "I probably would not survive the first mountain crossing."

"It's them soldiers on the other side of them mountains we ought to worry about, not ice and rock." Vitale thumbed the pommel of his sword. "Narváez brought eight hundred fighting men with him. Veterans, all of them."

"Is that so? I hear chaff often gets mixed in with the wheat."

Vitale pushed the skin back on his fingernails and stared at his dirty palms. "Rumor has it that Narváez is a zealous man. Some men in the company served him in the West Indies. When the islanders were slow to convert, Narváez raised an army and laid waste to their villages."

Solomon rubbed the nape of his neck. He had heard nothing of the sort, but the Christians committed too many outrages in the West Indies to keep track of them all. A part of him wondered if things had been the same when his people invaded Iberia. "Cortés is no stranger to cruelty," Solomon said. "Did you forget what he did in Cempoala? Tlaxcala? Cholula?"

Vitale narrowed his eyes. "Course not. But I know where I stand with Cortés. I tried to desert, and he granted

184

me clemency. Maybe Narváez would have done the same for me, but I got no way of knowing that."

Solomon could not fault his logic. As a free man, albeit a very poor one, Vitale did have cause to be concerned with his social standing. Solomon, however, would stay a slave whether Cortés or Narváez was in power.

Vitale turned toward him. "I need you to take something for me." Solomon arched his brow and waited for an explanation. Instead of answering him, Vitale dug inside his knapsack and pulled out the necklace he used to wear around his neck. He held out his arm and said, "It's my mother's necklace—"

"It belongs to you," Solomon cut in. "Do not burden me with it."

Vitale's face hardened. "I've burdened myself plenty on your behalf." He held out the necklace once more. "Please take it. I don't know if I'll…"

Solomon's gut twisted. "It will be safer in your keeping."

"Narváez commands more men. The necklace will be safer with you."

The necklace glimmered in the afternoon light. Solomon fingered the hem of his shirt. Maybe it wouldn't be wrong to take the necklace. Maybe he could fix it for him. No—that wasn't his duty. "Won't the Indians be marching with you? Cortés has had months to make alliances with the Indians. He should have a bigger army than Narváez."

Vitale shook his head. "The Tlaxcalteca have no interest in marching to the coast to battle with some upstart *teteo*."

"And the Totonacs?" Solomon asked in a weak voice.

"Fat Chief is aggrieved that Narváez has seized the town center of Cempoala for himself, but he probably hasn't forgiven Cortés for destroying his temples. Cortés thinks he can rally support from the village folk, but it may not be enough."

Solomon scoffed. "It would seem Cortés' genius strategy of humiliating his own allies has backfired, would you not agree?"

Vitale shrugged. "Cortés has won over some of Narváez's officers. More might defect, maybe enough to even the odds. Besides, he's gotten us this far, right?"

"Cortés is going to get you and all your countrymen killed. Allah as my witness, he is a degenerate. Every gamble that pays off just encourages him to bet more, and soon he is going to chance it all—"

"I know. That's why I need you to take the necklace."

Solomon went quiet. After a half-minute passed, he reached for the necklace. He brought it up to his good eye for a closer inspection. A woman's face had been carved into the pendant's center, but he doubted it could do justice by Vitale's mother. He could make out nothing of her features, nothing about her heritage or her nature, yet the boy treasured it all these years because it was all he had. His lip quivered.

"When we were in Tlaxcala, you told me it's important to hold on to the past. I didn't want to believe you, but then Cholula happened..." Vitale cleared his throat and said, "Well, I get what you mean that the past don't stay past. Long as that's the case, we oughta hold on to the good parts, too. My mother didn't come from no great family, never led no great movement, but she was a good person. I wanna know she'll be remembered." Vitale wiped his eyes and blew out his breath. "I'm counting on you to keep the necklace safe."

Solomon swallowed the lump in his throat. "I used to trade in slaves." Vitale paled and stared at Solomon as if he were some type of rabid mastiff. "I traded in everything, when I was a merchant," Solomon explained. "Started off with crystals and carpets. But the market changes so much from port to port. Sometimes, an item that would sell for a fortune in Algiers would not sell for half a *maravedi* in Barcelona. It is so very important to have something everyone wants, and there is always a market for slaves."

Vitale's face darkened. "Why are you telling me this?"

"You have always wanted to know about my past, and I think I should give you a full accounting since..." Solomon trailed off.

Vitale blinked and exhaled through his nose. "Keep good health, Solomon. Who knows, maybe you will see Mecca one last time."

Solomon smiled weakly, and Vitale bade him farewell before disappearing down the stairs. Solomon stared at the necklace he had been gifted. The clasp was broken and the chain was rusting, but nothing else appeared damaged. He resolved to fix the necklace, to give it a new clasp and hide away all the blemishes, regardless of how much time or energy it would take. Solomon knew others might regard it as a worthless keepsake, but he knew better. He would fix it, and everything would be right again.

Totonac Province

Tenochtitlan

Chapter 18

Malintze tucked a strand of hair behind her ear and studied the Totonac kneeling in front of Cortés' high-backed chair. His left hand was misformed, two fingers were smushed together like lumps of unformed clay, and pimples dotted both his cheeks. Was he shivering on account of the cold?

What with the intense heat of the day, the still night air could have a queer effect on the body. *Maybe he's scared.* He did not lack for cause. Cortés' reputation for violence must have preceded him, and she would be none surprised if the boy feared for his well-being. The hurried march from Tenochtitlan to Totonac lands had left all of the *teteo* exhausted and tired, but that just meant they were less inclined toward patience and more toward violence.

"Doña Marina, tell the boy to stand," Cortés commanded.

"Our Speaker asks that you please stand," Doña Marina told the boy in Nahuatl. The boy winced and muttered something unintelligible as he stood up. She wished she could understand his tongue, but Nahuatl was the only language they had in common. Fortunately for them, few of the Spaniards could understand Nahuatl.

Cortés rapped his fingers on the chair's armrest and made a quick appraisal of the trembling boy. "What do you know about Narváez's forces?"

Malintze almost rolled her eyes at the question. The *teteo* had the strangest habit of assuming everyone thought and acted like them and seldom bothered to adjust their speech or actions for others. She contemplated the best translation and then said in Nahuatl, "Our Speaker is honored that you have come to our camp to tell us about the *teteo* on the coast. You must be tired from your exertions so please accept some food and water. Can you please tell us more about the *teteo* that arrived in the water-houses a few weeks ago?"

The boy's face brightened at the mention of refreshments and he straightened. "Food and water would do a great deal to revive me, and I am most grateful for the offer." He paused and wiped sweat from his brow. "The Speaker of Cempoala was at first inclined to be friendly to the *teteo* that arrived a few weeks ago. The *teteo* Speaker said they wanted to ally, but they have been most disrespectful in their conduct. They have no respect for Cempoalteca holy places, and they have used many of the women roughly. Many of the village folk have little love for Cempoala, but they worry the *teteo* who follow the Narváez man might do the same to their people."

Cortés had also been very contemptuous of the Cempoalteca holy places but so far as she knew, Cortés' men had behaved themselves with the Cempoalteca women. Narváez's inability to do the same suggested he had less concern for diplomacy or less ability to control his men. Either way, it was good for Cortés. She glanced at the Totonac boy. It would be prudent to make sure he received his proper due before she translated anymore.

"He can tell you about Narváez's forces, but he will need food and water first," Malintze said in Spanish.

Cortés huffed but gave orders for turkey, corn cakes, and water to be brought forward. She asked the boy if he was pleased with the offerings and pretended to listen as he offered thanks. As soon as he finished speaking, she turned to Cortés and told him of the situation in Cempoala.

Cortés' eyes brightened at the mention of the rift between Fat Chief and Narváez. He learned forward and scratched his chin. "Where does Narváez place his falconets and lombards?"

Malintze translated the question as the boy took a swig of water and looked at her strange when she said falconets and lombards. She explained to him that she was referring to the thunder and lightning weapons, but that meant nothing to him either.

Malintze tucked her tongue in her cheek. Cortés would not be pleased by the boy's ignorance. "He regrets to inform you that he does not know where those weapons are," she said in Spanish.

Cortés narrowed his eyes and asked if the boy knew of the whereabouts of Narváez's cavalry.

"Do you know where we can find the giant hornless stags?" Malintze asked.

Seeing the boy's confusion, she explained that she was asking about the *teteo* on the coast. He shook his head no.

Cortés' face darkened. "Does this boy have any useful information to offer?"

"Our Speaker is sad you cannot tell us much about the *teteo* on the coast," Malintze translated. "Where can we find most of them? Are any of them sick? Have they allied with the local people?"

The boy tore his eyes away from the food-bearing servants and let her know that none of the *teteo* looked sick, but they did smell as if they were wasting away from some terrible disease. He also let her know that the bulk of Narváez's forces could be found in the town center of Cempoala and that Narváez had been unsuccessful in making alliances.

She passed on his words to Cortés and waited as Cortés discussed the news with his officers. Not much later, Cortés leaned forward and asked, "Where does Narváez sleep?"

Malintze passed on the question and received an answer almost immediately: "Narváez has taken the main pyramid in Cempoala for himself and sleeps on top of it. Men with snapping bows and long knives sleep nearby. He thinks a total of thirty men guard the pyramid."

Cortés thinned his lips at the mention of the main pyramid. Almost a year ago, he had ordered his men to march up the pyramid and desecrate the religious temples in order to punish the Cempoalteca for their duplicity.

Had Narváez any tact, he could have capitalized on the lingering resentment to cultivate a mutually beneficial relationship. Instead, he had abused the goodwill of his hosts and could no longer count on Fat Chief's support.

Whether that meant Cortés was lucky or that most of his countrymen were brutes with little talent for diplomacy, she did not know. Either way, she hoped Cortés would be more circumspect in the future.

"Doña Marina, please let the Totonac villager know we are most grateful for his help," Cortés said. "Please tell him to take as much food and water as he wishes. Let him know that any Totonacs who join us in the fight against Narváez will also benefit from our munificence."

The boy cautiously made his way toward the servants holding the food. He reached out for a parcel of corn cakes but declined to take possession of the bag just yet. Instead, he puffed out his chest and turned back to Cortés. "Cortés has done many favors for the village folk, and we are glad to offer him our aid. If we could offer more warriors to his cause, we would. But we have no more fighting men to spare, for they all marched with Cortés when he first left for Tenochtitlan."

Cortés' face curdled when he heard the translation. He squeezed the arm of his chair so hard his knuckles went white as maguey buds, and he stiffened as if his honor had been insulted. "Tell the ingrate we appreciate his honesty, and let him know we are heartbroken the village folk will not be honoring their promise to help us in times of need. Tell him to make himself scarce and that he should pray we do not decide to raze any Totonac villages after we have dealt with Narváez."

Malintze's stomach dropped. Surely Cortés could not mean any of that; surely he could not be so petty or foolish. But the more she studied his hard-set expression, the more she realized she had only the faintest grasp of his thinking. Not long ago, she had considered him staunch in his beliefs and fearless in the face of danger. Now she knew she had just never seen him truly tested, and she had to wonder why she ever bought into his facade.

I wanted it to be true. For better or worse, she finally recognized him as a conniving opportunist. But what did that make her?

She turned toward the Totonac boy. She would not foul his ears with the nonsensical threats of a desperate man. "Cortés is most grateful for your help and insists you take as much food and water as you'd like," she said in Nahuatl. "Cortés will confront the *teteo* in Cempoala and put an end to their outrages."

The Totonac boy offered his heartfelt thanks and scurried off with the food. She looked back to Cortés. He was lucky to have enemies like Narváez and Motecuhzoma. Otherwise, his cause would have failed long ago.

~ ~ ~

The chained captive groaned and muttered something Indian. Pedro furrowed his brow and wondered if he should call in a translator. Probably not worth it. The Indian could not raise his voice above a whisper and had stopped speaking sensibly half an hour prior.

Never in all his life had Pedro seen a man react to torture worse. The man started screaming as soon as he saw the burning evergreen logs and only screamed louder once they were pressed against his stomach. He raised such a racket that Pedro had been tempted to gag him; the only thing that stopped him was his interest in the man's confession.

Pedro cracked his knuckles and kneeled in front of the Indian. Tenochtitlan was filled with thousands of Indians just like the one in front of him, and Pedro was somehow supposed to hold the Palace of Axayacatl with a force of one hundred and twenty Spaniards. Yes, he had the Tlaxcalteca Indians to help him, thousands upon thousands of them, but he knew better than to trust them. All the same, he did find it interesting the Tlaxcalteca were so convinced the Mexica would soon attack.

"You know, I think you owe me an apology," Pedro said. "My ears are still ringing from all your screaming."

The Indian mouthed something inaudible, gawping like a beached fish. Pedro studied the burns on the man's stomach. His marred and mottled skin reminded him of a burnt orange peel, save the fresh scabs and bloody lesions. All things considered, his wounds did not look that bad. He would probably struggle to stand upright, but the Inquisition would have done far worse to him.

"The other Indian didn't say a word, and we tortured him for hours," Pedro said. "How come you started talking so fast?"

The Indian stared into the distance with glassy eyes. Pedro frowned and pressed his finger against an open wound. Besides some writhing and inaudible mumbling, the poke did nothing to make the Indian more lively.

Pedro shook his head. He withdrew his finger and wiped the blood off on his boots. "Thought all you Indians were supposed to be strong. You sure you're an Indian?"

The captive, still lying on his side, tried to curl into a ball. Pedro tutted and reached for the small gold labret that hung from the captive's ear. He stroked it tenderly, like a mother might a sleeping babe. "Will never cease to amaze me, how much gold you Indians have. Not fair really. What did your people do to deserve so much gold?" Pedro withdrew his hand and scratched his cheek. "God willing, it'll be ours soon enough."

The Indian sputtered something nonsensical and Pedro laughed. "You're not one for conversation, I'll say." Pedro took a swig of his water and patted the chained Indian. "I appreciate that you were quick to confess, though. You did us a great favor by letting us know the intentions of your wicked countrymen."

The Indian stilled. Did the savage understand Spanish? Pedro smoothed his mustache and leaned toward the Indian. "We will act on the information you gave us very soon. When all your countrymen gather in the plaza for your wretched festival, we will cut them down like stalks of wheat. All because you let us know they're planning to kill us."

The Indian whimpered. Pedro smiled. The savage understood him! "Without your help, we would have never discovered the plot. None of the other captives said a word about the Indians making plans to burn us out of the palace. At least, not until you started blathering about it."

The man winced. In hindsight, it had been a bad idea to interrogate the Indians in the same room, but what could be done about that now? Once Pedro realized his mistake, he moved the captives into separate holding areas, but he could not put smoke back in a chimney. Besides, everyone knew the Indians were plotting some kind of perfidy. The interrogations were a formality more than anything else.

The Indian closed his eyes. Pedro licked his lips and said, "You seem smarter than most your lot. Tell you what, I will set you free if you say a few words in our language."

The Indian made no attempt to speak. Pedro narrowed his eyes. "Just a single word."

Not a peep from the Indian. Pedro sighed and crept closer to the chained man. "If the Indians plan to smoke us out of the palace, don't say a word."

Silence.

"If the Indians intend to drill their way into the palace, don't say a word."

Silence.

"If the Indians have no plans to kill us whatsoever and simply wish to carry out their festival, don't say a word."

Silence. Pedro sucked in his teeth. The Indian had confessed to everything less than an hour ago. Why was he being so quiet now? Pedro gazed at the man's wounds. Ugly and fresh, but nothing deadly. Pedro glanced at a smoldering brazier. It still had some live coals. Reheating the log would not take overlong.

Pedro licked his lips and wiped his nose. "Say a single word in any language, and I will set you free. Stay silent, and I will use the log again."

The Indian sighed but made no sound otherwise. Pedro shrugged and made his way toward the log. The Indian had only himself to blame for his current predicament. Pedro had no idea if his confession meant anything, but he knew what it meant to be ignored. Crossing the Atlantic had been one of the greatest trials of his life, and he did not risk his life just to be disrespected by savages.

Cortés had left him in charge of Tenochtitlan and Pedro intended to do right by his command. The quiet Indian, Motecuhzoma, the people of Tenochtitlan—they all needed to be put in their place. It was not his fault the Indians could not understand anything besides violence.

A warm feeling spread through his chest. The Flaying Festival would be the perfect time to strike; the Indians would be unarmed and too consumed with their savage rites to take any mind of his men. It would be Cholula all over again, except better. He lifted the log out of the brazier and tapped the end to make sure it was safe to hold. A little warm but nothing excruciating.

As for the other end... well, the Indian would find out soon enough. It would only be a few more days until the Flaying Festival, but that would be plenty enough time to refine his interrogation skills.

Cempoala

Juan pricked his ears. He could make out little noise other than Narváez's snoring and the drum of the rain—not since childhood had he experienced such a torrential downpour—but he had to stay vigilant. Cortés' army could attack at any moment, and it seemed wrong to try to sleep. More than wrong. Impossible really.

The other men did not seem to share his fear, confident that common sense would deter Cortés from attacking. After all, Narváez had twice as many Christians fighting for him, plus the support of Governor Velázquez. Some of the officers were so confident that Cortés would not attack that they abandoned their watch posts to retire to their sleeping quarters. The dereliction of duty shocked Juan, and he was sure Narváez would mete out punishments once he heard the news. Instead, Narváez snapped at his servant for waking him up and reminded him that only a halfwit would try to make battle in a downpour so he cared not one whit if his officers decided to seek out dry shelter.

Despite all his grumbling that he would never sleep a wink if others kept disturbing him, Narváez resumed his snoring within minutes. In different circumstances, Juan might have laughed. But much as he wanted to make light of the situation, his angst denied him that reprieve.

Juan was no stranger to battle. His first introduction happened early in life, when he still lived in Kongo. His uncle had tried to seize Father's throne by means of force, his surprise attack had nearly succeeded, but Father prevailed. Not that he was ever the same afterward. Consumed by paranoia and suspicion, Father saw enemies everywhere and friends nowhere. So, when word reached him that Juan had accidentally discharged the Portuguese musket right at his brother's chest, there wasn't anything to explain.

After all, Father already knew the truth: Juan had tried to kill Henrique because he wanted to inherit the throne. It did not matter that Juan was just a boy and that the throne was little more than a fancy seat to him. It did not even matter that the musket failed to discharge; Father knew. And because Father could never be dissuaded from anything, it was decreed that Juan should join the missionaries on their journey to the mysterious place called Europe.

Juan sighed. Twenty long years had passed since that dark day and home was a distant place on the other side of the world. He had dedicated his life to washing away the sin of Cain, forged himself into a weapon for Christendom, but the New World had awakened long-buried memories. The fireflies, the rain, the heat—all of it reminded him of what used to be.

He sat up and stared into the distance. The darkness made it difficult to see more than a stone's throw out, but he could sense the trees and took comfort in their presence. He had lived with the Old Christians for so long he had forgotten there were still places in the world where the trees reached higher than the spires, and beasts still prowled at night. Tonight, however, he suspected the prowling would be done by two-legged beasts.

Juan pulled at a loose curl of hair. Why was Narváez so sure that Cortés would not attack? For the life of him, he could not understand it. Joshua had to march seven days through the desert before he reached Jericho, but that did not stop him from putting the city to the sword. God tested men with adversity and rewarded them for rising to the occasion. Narváez, however, must have disagreed because he insisted Cortés would surrender himself to justice instead of attacking.

Juan shook his head. Narváez made a show of praying daily but somehow failed to understand that God did not suffer fools lightly. Juan glanced at the men sleeping beside him. Ten men were sleeping on the summit, twenty men near the base, but only two stood guard. The rest of the army was scattered throughout Cempoala, and Juan doubted they could quickly rally to the pyramid if Cortés attacked. Hopefully it would not come to that. A terrible sin for Christians to fight each other.

He grabbed his boots and fastened the laces. The rain was beginning to lighten and now was as good a time as any to relieve himself. He reached for his drawstring, but a distant shouting gave him pause. He peered into the distance. Had he imagined it?

The sound came again, closer this time. He rushed toward the sentries. "Did you hear that?"

The sentries looked at him askance. "Hear what?" the shorter one asked.

Before Juan could answer, a man shouted that something was coming their way. Juan cursed and raced to the pillar where he had stashed his armor and his sword. He had just finished slipping on his brigandine when a bedraggled figure stumbled into the torchlight at the base of the stairs.

"What's the matter, Hurtado?" asked a drowsy soldier.

Hurtado raced up the steps instead of answering, ran straight for Narváez's sleeping quarters, and then shouted at the top of his voice, "Cortés is coming!"

Men who had been dozing on the pyramid's summit instantly came awake, and a call to arms was made. A careless kick sent Juan's helmet flying off the edge of the flat-topped pyramid into the dark. He snatched up his sword as an unfamiliar voice cried out, "Long live the King!"

Juan crossed himself and unsheathed his sword. A soft rumble of hurried footfalls reached his ears, but he could not guess by sound alone how many men were tromping through the dark. He could tell, however, that the noise was growing louder. He glanced at a nearby torch. It gave off little smoke as it burned, but it did not give off much light either. A bevy of flaming torches kept the summit well-lit, but darkness hid everything more than a stone's throw out.

Juan sucked in a deep breath through clenched teeth. Was there any worse place to be than the pyramid ledge?

Somebody gave orders to douse the lights, a command quickly forgotten once the first of Cortés' men came into view. Their beards were wild and unkempt, their armor tarnished and dirty, and they ran as if they had the Devil at their backs. They swept past the disorganized guards at the base of the pyramid without even pausing to break their stride, and the few men who tried to fight were quickly dispatched. In a matter of seconds, Cortés' men sped up the wide flight of rain-slickened stairs and crashed through the mess of soldiers who tried in vain to stop their advance.

Juan yelled and ran toward the melee. He stabbed his sword into an exposed forearm and his victim jerked in surprise. Juan pulled the sword out with a vicious tug and leapt backward to avoid a copper-tipped spear. He stumbled and fell to the ground. A man Juan had practiced drills with landed beside him, clutching his innards and screaming like a man possessed.

Juan jumped to his feet and parried a sword blow that missed his knee by a finger's breadth. He slashed his sword upward and caught the tip of the man's chin with the edge of his rapier. The man howled and dropped his sword to the ground.

Much to Juan's surprise, the man then rushed toward him and slammed him against the temple wall. Pain arced through his back, and he thrust his sword forward. The blind jab only enraged his assailant more, and the man responded by grabbing Juan by the throat and pinning his sword arm against his body.

Juan drove his knee upward into the man's groin. The grip around his neck loosened, and Juan pushed himself off the wall with a kick that sent him barreling into the man's midsection. His opponent stumbled backward, tripped over a soldier splayed out on the ground, and went tumbling over the edge of the pyramid. Juan whispered a silent prayer of thanks and ran for the pyramid steps.

The pyramid would soon be overrun but if Juan could reach the main body, he could rally men for a counter-attack. He stopped when he saw the short-haired man climbing up the stairs, rapier in one hand and shield in the other.

The soldier beckoned to Juan with his sword. "Drop your weapon, Moor."

Juan tightened his grip on his sword hilt and retreated a few steps. The soldier had an Andalusian accent, but he lacked a coat of arms and proper-fitting armor.

"I am no Moor," Juan said. "I am a Christian from Kongo."

The soldier furrowed his brow and dropped his sword a fraction. Sensing an opportunity, Juan rushed forward to attack. The soldier parried the first blow, and Juan buried his fist in the man's stomach. While he was still dazed, Juan bludgeoned him over the head and rushed past him.

When he reached the bottom of the stairs, something hard and heavy smashed into Juan's foot. He fell to the ground and dropped his sword to keep from landing on it. He looked backward to see what had hit him. The short-haired soldier had slid his shield down the stairs to trip him. Juan cursed himself for rushing past the soldier so fast but gave thanks the soldier was too dazed to make his way down the stairs.

A sudden blaze caught his eye. The stone temple had a thatch covering, and Cortés' men had lit some of it aflame with their torches. Not content to let the fire spread on its own, they encouraged it with greased-soaked rags and careful prodding. None of Narváez's men tried to stop them. Most had already surrendered. Those that had not done so were hiding inside the burning temple. Cortés' men blocked the one entrance but made no attempt to enter. There was no need. If the heat did not kill the men hiding in the temple, the smoke would.

Juan held his breath as the voracious flames enveloped more thatch. Narváez and his personal guard had been sleeping inside the temple. He knew none of them well, but he prayed he would have the good sense to yield. God clearly favored Cortés' cause, and it would be folly for Narváez to deny the inevitable. Not a single person moved and the men, whether they owed allegiance to Narváez or Cortés, stood rapt as the fire grew and the smoke thickened.

Almost half a minute passed before a handful of ragged figures emerged from the burning temple. Narváez—recognizable only because of his fiery red beard and his two-handed broadsword—collapsed to his knees and let his weapon clatter to the ground. He held a hand over his right eye and shouted something at his tormentors. They responded by cuffing him across the face and hauled him down the pyramid steps.

Juan tensed as Cortés' men came closer but did not try to hide. Narváez had been captured and the pyramid had been taken; now was the time to yield, not crawl away to some dark corner. Once they reached the base of the pyramid, Cortés' men propped up Narváez and searched his person. They wrenched out the papers Narváez had hidden under his shirt and examined them closely.

Narváez muttered that he needed a surgeon for his ruined eye, prompting laughter amongst Cortés' men. Juan had not expected that reaction and furrowed his brow. How could men favored by God be so callous? He did not dwell on the matter long. God worked in mysterious ways.

One of Cortés' men made his way over to Juan. He pointed his spear at Juan's chest and said, "My name is Gonzalo de Sandoval, and I am the chief constable of Villa Rica de la Veracruz. Will you yield to me?"

Juan stared at the man's gold-rimmed cuirass. He had not seen gold that rich for many years. Not since he last gazed upon Father's person... Juan cleared his throat. "Yes, I yield."

"Good. If Narváez had done the same when we first put the question to him, he'd still have his eye." Sandoval spat and shook his head. "Narváez is your commander no more; you fight for us now. Refuse and we will put you in chains. Agree and we will reward you with immense riches. What will your choice be?"

Juan coughed and wiped his brow. He thought of his brother Henrique, so determined to be a bishop of Kongo. For as long as Juan could remember, his brother wanted to take the cloth. Juan loved God just as much as him, but he never felt that same calling. He was a soldier for God and had a duty to expand Christendom, even if it meant forsaking the vow he had made to Narváez. He stared at the man pointing a spear at him and said, "My name is Juan Garrido, and I would be honored to fight for Hernando Cortés."

Tenochtitlan

Chapter 20

Tezoc had never been a great dancer or singer. All the same, he appreciated both art forms and knew he was being treated to the best of both with the Flaying Festival. Over four hundred dancers had assembled in the main plaza of the Sacred Precinct and thousands had gathered to watch the rotating procession. Onlookers would be expected to clap and encourage the dancers but the musicians—using drums, flutes, bone fifes, and conches—were responsible for setting the tempo.

Much as he enjoyed the performances, Tezoc was glad he was not one of the performers. Being the Cutter of Men came with enough responsibility, and he did not need any more. He had quite enough to worry about with the *teteo* and Motecuhzoma and Tlaxcala.

Thankfully, he would not have to worry about the *teteo* or the Tlaxcalteca much longer. The poison masters had finally amassed a quantity large enough to dispatch all the *teteo*, as well as the Tlaxcalteca, and the poisoned food would be delivered to them within the day.

The plan was fraught with risk, Cortés was still away from the city and the Tlaxcalteca employed many precautions when it came to their meals, but Tezoc knew of no better option. Perhaps Motecuhzoma could have helped them devise a better plan, but his counsel was no longer available to them. Soon though, very soon, Motecuhzoma would be restored to his former position, his children would be returned to safety, and Tenochtitlan's unwanted guests would be sacrificed to the gods.

Tezoc bit his lip and rubbed the nape of his sweat-dampened neck, wondering if the tension in his shoulders would ever go away.

Chimalli, standing to his right, leaned toward him and shouted, "Tezoc, I think you could use a good massage."

At least that's what he thought he said. Hard to be sure since the drums and conches were so loud.

"The best massages take place in private settings," Tezoc shouted back.

Chimalli said nothing but gave his hand a discrete squeeze. A warm sensation spread through Tezoc's stomach, yet it soon gave way to dismay and discontent. Life would surely improve once the guests were killed, but Tezoc and Chimalli would still have to hide the truth about their relationship. Tezoc sighed. He wondered sometimes if he could enjoy a better life elsewhere, but he could disavow his nation no more than he could do without water.

Frustrating as the norms of his people could be, his heart would always be Mexica. Moreover, he had a duty as the Cutter of Men to always fight for his nation, and service came before all else. Tezoc flexed his hand. How long would it take to master a *teotl* weapon?

A lifetime, for all he knew. He wanted so very much to test his skills with a *macuahuitl* against an armed *teotl*, but he doubted he would soon get the chance. Nonetheless, he was grateful the poison masters had given his people a way to incapacitate the *teteo* still in Tenochtitlan. Once they and all their allies had been killed, plans could be made to attack the *teteo* encamping near Cempoala.

Tezoc glanced at the Palace of Axayacatl and prayed the poison masters would do right by their trade. Taking the building by force would take weeks and would cost many warriors their lives.

Something moved in front of the palace windows, and he shaded his eyes to see better. Boards were being fixed to the window frames. He turned his gaze elsewhere. Some windows were completely boarded over. A chill passed through him. Only an enemy that expected to be attacked improved their defenses.

Tezoc turned his gaze toward his countrymen to see if anyone else had noticed. None of them were even looking in the direction of the Palace of Axayacatl. A distant clanking reached his ears, but the music was so loud he could not be certain what he heard. Moreover, the Sacred Plaza was filled with so many onlookers that his field of vision had been compromised. He tilted his chin upward to see more, but it did little to improve his line of sight.

He grabbed Chimalli by the shoulder and yelled, "Lift me up so I can see over the crowd."

Chimalli shouted something back, but he could not hear a word of his response. Frustration mounting, Tezoc pointed upward until Chimalli understood. Chimalli recruited a random bystander, and the two of them lifted Tezoc so that he could see over the crowd.

Nothing obstructed his view now, but what he saw was so shocking he struggled to believe his own eyes. Not only were the *teteo* and the Tlaxcalteca forcing their way through the crowd, they were blocking every exit in the Sacred Precinct. Tezoc shouted and pointed, desperate to draw the crowd's attention. A few nearby noticed his frantic motions and scooted away. The rest ignored him and shaded their eyes to see the dancers better, bobbing back and forth to see past the many obstructions.

Tezoc's mouth went dry as he watched a *teotl* unsheathe a large, glittering sword. Frantic, Tezoc looked for something he could use to silence the drummers. The crowd needed to know what was going on, they needed to know the exits were being blocked. A spear, a sling, a rock—he would have thrown his own sandal if it would have made a difference. But no matter where he looked, he saw not a single weapon that he could use. The only weapons were in the hands of the enemy, and Tezoc knew better than to expect mercy from them.

A *teotl* shoved and shouldered his way to the center of the dancing procession and raised his sword high. Before others had the chance to even realize what was happening, he swung the sword down and lopped a man's head off. Screams rent the air, and the crowd scattered like kernels of corn thrown into the wind. The man who had been helping Chimalli hold Tezoc fled, and Tezoc fell to the ground. His shoulder exploded with pain, but his cry was lost amidst the din.

Chimalli hauled him to his feet, and they dashed toward the nearest exit. As they rounded the side of a pyramid, the exit came into view. A group of *teteo*, clad in metal armor, stood between them and safety. Tezoc skidded to a halt and grabbed Chimalli's arm. A man far ahead of them tried to charge past the *teteo*, and they gored him on a long spear with contemptuous ease.

Tezoc's stomach dropped. He tried to think of a place they could hide. By this point, all the exits had to be blocked. His eyes darted to the wall that surrounded the Sacred Precinct. Twenty hands high, it would be difficult, but not impossible, to scale. The Tlaxcalteca, however, had realized the same and were shooting arrows and throwing spears at anyone who came within a few paces of the wall.

A sharp crack split the air, and Chimalli screamed in pain. Tezoc turned toward his second in command, confused and terrified by the sudden turn of events. Chimalli was doubled over and a light sheen of sweat covered his face... and he was bleeding!

Tezoc rushed forward to help. He draped Chimalli's arm over his good shoulder, and they hobbled toward the nearest pyramid. Tezoc paused at the first step. Anyone could follow them up the stairs, and there would be no place to hide on the summit other than the temple.

He cast his eyes to the wall once more. A mother threw her child over the wall and tried to scramble up herself, only to be pulled down by her hair and bludgeoned to death by Tlaxcalteca clubs. Tezoc swallowed. Better to take a chance on the pyramid than the wall.

He helped Chimalli up the stairs and by the time they reached the summit, his heart was racing and his breath came in short gasps. Chimalli was in an even worse state, clutching his stomach and groaning weakly. Tezoc blinked the sweat from his eyes and kneeled so he could examine Chimalli's wound. Flecks of black powder dotted the wound—a small, round hole in his midsection—but the black powder was conspicuously absent from the wound in his back. He wiped from his forehead. Chimalli had been hit with some kind of projectile, but it passed through his body so easily it left no trace besides black powder. Tezoc's fingers hovered over the wound. If ever there was a time he wished he were a healer, it was now.

A loud scream reached his ears. He staggered toward the edge of the pyramid and beheld the carnage. A Mexica noble lay motionless as the *teteo* ripped all the gold off his person and ravished a woman in plain view. Itzli, second in command to Motecuhzoma's own brother, tried to run toward the wall. A wicked sword slash opened his stomach, and he tripped on his own entrails. A Jaguar warrior, one of the bravest men Tezoc had ever met, begged for his mother as the Tlaxcalteca pinned him down and hacked at his calf with a *macuahuitl.*

The taste of bile flooded Tezoc's mouth, but he could not look away. All his life, he had been told there was nothing higher than martial glory. Battle was a rarefied

211

art, a way to honor the gods and do right by kin, and possessed a beauty only civilized people could understand. But the scene in front of him was downright horrifying, ugly and barbaric in a way that made him ashamed he had ever taken pride in his title as Cutter of Men. Perhaps most horrifying was how much he recognized himself not in the victims but the attackers. He had lost count of all the raids he had taken part in, all the battles against recalcitrant nations, all the times he had spilled life water to sate his ambitions.

He wiped his cheeks and turned back to Chimalli. He had to get him somewhere safe. Bloodlust didn't just bring out the worst impulses in a warrior—it also sharpened the senses. Sooner or later, someone would check the pyramids for survivors. Tezoc had failed in his duty as the Cutter of Men but at least he could do right by Chimalli, his brother-in-arms and his partner in life.

He took a deep breath and pulled Chimalli to his feet. Chimalli grimaced but made no objection otherwise. They quit the temple's dark interior and hobbled onto the well-lit summit. The warm sun, usually a tonic for Tezoc's weary body, felt odd against his cool skin. Perhaps it would be better to hide inside the temple. He dismissed the thought. If they hid there, it would only be a matter of time before the enemy found them. Once that happened, the best they could hope for would be a quick death.

Tezoc turned away from the mayhem and cupped both his hands together. Chimalli looked at him in confusion.

"Put your foot in my hand," Tezoc said. "I am going to push you up so that you can climb onto the temple roof."

Chimalli looked at him skeptically. "I am heavier and taller than you. I should be the one to push you up."

Tezoc smiled and shook his head. "It is the heart that makes one strong, not the bulge in one's arm." Tezoc stroked Chimalli's cheek and swallowed the lump in his throat. "Put your foot in my hand, and climb onto the roof. That's a command, and you will obey it."

Chimalli nodded. For a brief moment, his lip quivered. Before today, Tezoc could never have imagined Chimalli doing such a thing, but nothing about today was right or normal.

Ever dutiful, Chimalli put his foot in Tezoc's hand, and Tezoc hefted him upward so that Chimalli could grab the ledge.

Tezoc's injured shoulder burned with an intensity that brought tears to his eyes, and his back felt as if it would buckle at any moment. Nonetheless, he continued to push Chimalli upward and kept his arms rigid as stone. Keeping his arms steady required enormous effort, but he did not dare let them shake. To let Chimalli fall onto the stairs, or off the pyramid's ledge, would be as bad as killing him.

The strain in Tezoc's back increased, like heat trapped inside a simmering pot, and just when he thought he would collapse, Chimalli found a handhold and pulled himself onto the roof. A strange desire to laugh overtook Tezoc, and he rubbed his sore muscles with an aching hand.

"Jump so I can grab your hand," Chimalli said. "I am going to pull you up here."

Tezoc sobered and dropped his shoulders. It was time to tell Chimalli the truth.

"Do not waste your strength trying to pull me up," Tezoc said. "You are wounded, and you will only hurt yourself if you try to help me."

Chimalli shook his head. "Stop talking nonsense. It is not safe down there."

"I will be fine," Tezoc said. "Find somewhere to hide and stay safe; that is my final command to you. Live, so you can fight another day. Take care of my son and know that my love for you—"

Tezoc staggered forward as something slammed into his shoulder. His vision swam and he collapsed against a stone pillar, clutching his wounded arm.

An arrow the length of his shin jutted out of his shoulder. A quick glance let him know it was a Tlaxcalteca arrow. He gritted his teeth. His people had never taken to the bow with the same enthusiasm as the Tlaxcalteca. Perhaps that was why his people had never been able to overcome Tlaxcala. He moved his shoulder a fraction, and a bolt of pain shot through his arm.

A loud shuffling reached his ears. Tezoc unclenched his teeth and shouted, "Stay on the roof, Chimalli! I am still your commanding general, and I am telling you to stay there!"

The shuffling stopped, and Tezoc breathed a sigh of thanks. He stood and scanned the plaza for his assailant. Another arrow could hit him at any moment, but he did not care anymore. His life was already forfeit. Much to his surprise, no archer took aim at him. Confused, he scanned the courtyard for his assailant and spotted a Tlaxcalteca warrior at the base of the pyramid.

Tezoc puffed out his chest. If the warrior had seen Chimalli climb into his hiding spot, his second in command would not be safe for long. Tezoc had to keep him safe, but he was in no condition to make his way down the stairs for a fight with a much younger man. But if he had learned anything from his time training warriors, it was how to goad men into violence. Tezoc cleared his throat and shouted, "Come and fight me you whoreson! Learn how a real warrior fights."

The warrior stiffened.

"What's the matter—does having a mother of easy virtue make you hard of hearing?"

The warrior raised his club high, screamed, and sprinted up the stairs. Tezoc allowed himself a small smile. His hand drifted to the arrow in his arm.

Touching it made him light-headed, but he was the Cutter of Men and would not go to his death defenseless. The Tlaxcalteca had done a great wrong to his people—he would kill at least one before he died.

He clenched his teeth and felt along the shaft for a crack or a defect. Near the arrowhead, he found the defect. Whatever archer shot him had not taken proper care of his arrows. Tezoc sucked in his breath, pressed his thumb against the small crack, and snapped the arrow shaft in two.

The pain made him go weak in the knees, and he closed his eyes to keep the tears from spilling out. By the time he could open them again, the irate warrior was halfway up the stairs.

Tezoc held the jagged arrow shaft down by his side. It would not be much of a weapon, but it would have to do. The man yelled something unintelligible, and Tezoc squared himself for impact. The warrior was fast, and Tezoc had no idea how he was going to get past his club. He would have to duck under it. Or at least try to.

He squatted down and readied himself for a quick drop. A flash of color caught Tezoc's eye. Moments later, a sandal smacked into his enemy's face. Chimalli's sandal had too little mass to inflict serious injury, but it surprised the Tlaxcalteca warrior and that was enough.

Tezoc lunged forward with the broken arrow shaft and plunged it deep into the man's innards. Momentum carried Tezoc forward, and he latched onto the Tlaxcalteca warrior as he fell.

They tumbled down the stairs in a messy embrace, and the fall pushed the arrowhead deeper into Tezoc's arm. A fiery pain erupted in his shoulder and, for a moment, it was all he could think about. Then he cracked his head against a stone stair and there was no pain at all, only numbness.

He reached the bottom of the stairs battered, broken, and bloody. Footsteps came toward him, some part of him knew that meant danger, but he was powerless to move. He gazed up at the thirteen skies, reveling in the serenity and tranquility that had stolen over him.

A shadow passed over Tezoc, and an indistinct figure stared down at him. Tezoc made no attempt to crawl or beg or bargain. He just waited. Soon enough, the figure obliged and raised an arm to deliver the killing blow. A few moments later, everything went dark.

Tlaxcala Province

Tenochtitlan

Cortés dug his foot into a soft patch of dirt and let his gaze rove over the rolling foothills that dominated the Tlaxcalteca landscape. It had rained a few hours prior so the ground was still damp and mud clung to his boots like a woman to her lover. Only thing worse than waiting was waiting in poor weather. And the only thing worse than waiting in poor weather was waiting in poor weather while Tenochtitlan tore itself asunder.

Cortés chewed the inside of his lip and cursed himself for leaving Pedro in charge of Tenochtitlan. Attacking the Mexica unprovoked was bad enough, but attacking while forces were divided was downright idiotic. Half of Tenochtitlan was now laying siege to the Palace of Axayacatl, and Cortés could do nothing to help.

Returning with a fraction of his force would be a fool's errand, and he had no choice but to stay in Tlaxcala as he waited for the scattered scouting parties to rally to his banner. Thankfully, the Tlaxcala would be lending more soldiers, a thousand more, but he had no idea when the rest of the Spanish troops would arrive. Rangel and his men should have returned yesterday, and Cortés prayed they had not come to harm. He also prayed the army would soon be united, that Pedro and his forces could hold the palace for a few days more, but most of all he prayed for God's favor.

Cortés exhaled and focused his attention on the fencing match between León, Saucedo, and Escobar. León had many faults—he had once been disloyal to Cortés, he had a slight stutter, he counted Governor Velázquez amongst his relations—but his fencing skills were above reproach. For near on a minute, León had managed to hold off Saucedo and Escobar with a combination of parries and thrusts that inspired envy as much as awe.

"I think León will get the better of his opponents," Cortés said to Sandoval, forcing some lightness into his voice. "Care to wager on the outcome?"

Sandoval ran a hand through his hair. "I predict that Saucedo and Escobar will prevail. But let's not quibble over a sum. Gold has no place in a friendly contest."

Cortés laughed. "I must protest. Gold occupies a place of importance in any contest of consequence. But if you lack for confidence, we need not put down coin."

Sandoval extended his arm. "Let's shake on the matter then. I wager that León will lose."

Cortés grudgingly took his hand. What was the point of gambling if there was nothing to be gained? While he pondered the question, Saucedo landed a lucky strike against León, bringing the match to an end.

Cortés narrowed his eyes and turned to Sandoval. Much to his surprise, Sandoval did not gloat or boast about Saucedo's victory. Instead, he offered perfunctory praise to Saucedo, but praised all of them for bringing glory to Spain with their swordplay. Only after he finished lauding their abilities did he finally deign a glance at Cortés.

"The risky gambit seldom succeeds," Sandoval said, his voice as dry as cassava bread.

Cortés rubbed his shoulders. Sandoval had said as much yesterday, when he advised Cortés against returning to Tenochtitlan. Cortés heard him out, but he had no intention of following such foolish advice. To not return would be tantamount to abandoning the gold, not to mention his pledged allies. No, that he could not do.

"León, do you have the energy for another bout?" Cortés shouted.

León stiffened and looked to Escobar and Saucedo. When neither of them said anything, he stared down at his sweat-stained tunic and wiped his forehead with the back of his elbow. After a long pause, he looked up and said, "Of c-course, captain-general."

Not so long ago, León had been loath to refer to him as such. But that was many months ago, back when León was still loyal to his accursed uncle, Governor Velázquez. Thankfully, time in the brig had made him realize the error of his ways.

Cortés clapped and motioned to Saucedo and Escobar to put their helmets back on. "You will see, Sandoval. Fortune favors the bold."

Saucedo, Escobar, and León put down their visors and the fencing match recommenced. León took the offense early on and quickly dispatched Escobar with a slash down the front of his mail. Ever a fair sport, Escobar yielded and León focused his attention on Saucedo. The two circled round one another, eying each other like hungry scavengers.

"Have you thought about what I said?" Sandoval asked. "In regard to returning."

Cortés squared his shoulders. "Yes, Sandoval. My answer is the same: we will not forsake our allies or the gold. Once the rest of our countrymen join us, we will return to Tenochtitlan as swiftly as possible."

"If the Mexica wished to have our kind in Tenochtitlan, they would not be attacking Pedro and his men."

Cortés pulled at a loose thread on his tunic. "Once we return to Tenochtitlan, we can sort out the situation. Thanks to Narváez, we now have a hundred horses and hundreds of fresh troops. The Mexica will have to negotiate, whether or not they want to. And we still have their king."

"Pedro has their king," Sandoval corrected. "Has it done him much good?"

Cortés opened his mouth to respond, but a loud shout cut him off. He grabbed his sword hilt, yet soon realized there was no cause for alarm: Saucedo's shout was one of pain, not fear. A smug grin split Cortés' face once he realized León had prevailed, just as he predicted.

Cortés offered hearty congratulations to León and then said to Sandoval, "Pedro does not have Doña Marina. She will speak to the Mexica for us, and we will negotiate a peaceable settlement."

A dark look passed over Sandoval's face. "The Mexica do not want peace anymore, and no amount of honeyed words can bring their loved ones back."

Cortés crossed his arms. Why was Sandoval being so obstinate? Did he doubt Doña Marina's skill? *Perhaps he doubts me.* Cortés studied Sandoval's features. Still soft but that made sense considering his age. Younger than most of his officers by almost a decade, Sandoval had earned a place in his inner circle by dint of loyalty. Some of the officers with deeper pockets and familial connections resented Sandoval for his humble background, but Cortés never paid much mind to such matters. Medellín men had to stick together.

"What would you propose we do?" Cortés asked.

"I propose we lay siege to Tenochtitlan. We can sabotage the dikes to cut off their supply of fresh water, and we can encircle the lake to cut them off from trade. Grief and anguish can cloud the mind, but hunger and thirst will remind the Indians what's important. Sooner or later, they will have to sue for peace."

Cortés nodded. Tenochtitlan grew some of its own food but the vast majority did come from outside the city. Sabotaging the dikes would be difficult, but the cannons would help. Deprived of food and freshwater,

Tenochtitlan would surely fall… but it would take weeks, if not months.

"We have thousands of allies in Tenochtitlan," Cortés said. "Most of them are Tlaxcalteca but many hail from home. Do you think we can rescue them without sending in a relief party?"

Sandoval's features hardened into granite. "They created a mess for themselves, and they must extricate themselves from it. God helps those who help themselves."

Cortés blinked. He had always known Sandoval to be colorless, but he had never known him to be so cold-hearted. "The Tlaxcalteca will abandon our cause if we let thousands of their warriors die."

"The Tlaxcalteca have far too much interest in our success to abandon our cause. But even if they did, we could find new allies. Tetzcoco has long taken a back seat to Tenochtitlan, and there are many Tetzcocans who wish to see Tenochtitlan brought low."

Cortés tutted and wagged his finger. "Sandoval, you have much to learn about Indian affairs here. The leadership of Tetzcoco could not be allied more closely with Tenochtitlan. Cacama was put in power by Motecuhzoma, and I doubt any in his inner circle wish to betray their benefactor."

"Cacama had good reason to be loyal to Motecuhzoma, but Cacama's brother has never had cause to be loyal," Sandoval replied. "Ixtli could have been the ruler of Tetzcoco, had it not been for Motecuhzoma's politicking. As it stands, Ixtli controls Tetzcoco's northern domain and must wish to control more. He would make a good ally and could lend thousands of warriors to our cause."

Cortés ran his fingers through his beard. Most of the officers had no interest whatsoever in Indian matters, and he had not expected such a cogent response. Had he more officers interested in regional affairs, the campaign could have avoided some costly setbacks. How many hours had he spent winning the loyalty of fickle men like León, mollifying bleeding hearts like Saucedo? What if he had been able to spend that time discussing strategy and politics with the likes of Sandoval? Cortés sighed. It did no good to think about what could have been.

He had to play the hand he had been dealt. Pedro was brash and violent, but he was loyal and Cortés owed him a great deal. To abandon him and his men to the Mexica would be cruel, not to mention unpopular. And much as Cortés wished the Tlaxcalteca were more servile, he had no wish to abrogate the alliance.

Nonetheless, he did respect Sandoval's ability to put aside sentiments and focus only on the practical. Perhaps that would be the best way to win the gold.

Cortés frowned. Sandoval had not mentioned the gold once. Cortés cocked his head toward his fellow Extremeño. His tunic was faded and stained, his doublet torn and tattered, and his boots were scuffed and dirty. He wore no insignia on his person, and his rapier bore no special markings or engravings. His manner of dress was as plain as his speech, and his thick country accent rendered him *persona non grata* in many social circles. How a man like Sandoval could neglect to mention the very thing every Medellín family dreamt of was beyond his comprehension.

"What do you think will happen to the gold we left behind in Tenochtitlan?" Cortés asked. "If we lay siege to the city, instead of entering it."

"The gold cannot be recovered and we must focus on winning other riches—"

"Enough, Sandoval!" Cortés said, his voice louder than intended. León and Saucedo turned his way, and Cortés offered them a thin smile. Once they broke eye contact, Cortés added in a low voice, "Do not ask me to forsake my gold and my men. We have an obligation to our fellow Christians and our Indian allies. Come what may, we will return to Tenochtitlan to save our men and our winnings."

Sandoval opened his mouth to respond, but Cortés silenced him with a wave of his hand. He had no more patience for ridiculous suggestions. Men like Sandoval never took risks and always contented themselves with the low-hanging fruits; it would be foolish to put a great deal of stock in his counsel. Pedro was not without faults, but at least he would never suggest anything as ridiculous as forsaking the gold. Cortés shook his head. Perhaps it was a good thing he did not have more officers like Sandoval.

~ ~ ~

Pain. That was the first thing Chimalli felt when he woke up. Then, once the physical pain relented, anguish. Even now, he could hardly believe the turn of events. During the course of one day, Tenochtitlan had lost some of its most distinguished citizens.

But it was Tezoc's death that hurt most. Worse yet, that was the one he could have prevented. If Chimalli had known that Tezoc would refuse to follow him up, he would have never climbed onto the temple. His heart pounded against his chest as he remembered the sight of Tezoc tumbling down the pyramid stairs.

He had lost consciousness before Tezoc reached the bottom, but Chimalli knew Tezoc could not have survived. Chimalli's hand drifted to the small hole in his side. It burned as if chilli had been stuffed inside, and he wished he were unconscious again. To sleep and never wake again would be a great blessing.

"You should not touch the wound," someone said. The voice sounded distant and muffled, like it came from far away and had passed through many layers of cloth.

Chimalli turned toward the voice. He could see the blurry outline of someone, but he could make out no distinct features. He spread his hand flat and pressed his palm down on the sleeping mat. Soft, very soft. And smooth. Fur of some kind, from a rabbit most likely. He strained his ears for noises. Besides the breathing of his anonymous companion, he heard little. He sniffed the air cautiously, filling his nostrils with the smell of stale sweat. He coughed and sniffed again. A faint aroma of flowers and incense lingered in the air, but it faded with every breath he took.

Slowly, his vision came into focus, and Chimalli realized he had been sequestered to some sort of private room. He vaguely remembered being dragged off the pyramid temple, being tended to by concerned shadows, but it was all a blur, indistinct as smoke on a foggy day. He blinked and focused on the dark figure sitting cross-legged next to him. It was Cuauhtemoc, the proud warrior-general who had promised so long ago to kill Cortés.

"Where is the healer?" Chimalli asked, his voice raspy and weak.

"There are many to attend to these days," Cuauhtemoc said. He sighed and rubbed his kneecap. "Do you need anything?"

I need Tezoc back. Chimalli's eyes watered, and he closed his eyes to block the tears. Cuauhtemoc took hold of his hand and squeezed. "I will leave, if you need to rest."

Chimalli shook his head and swallowed the lump in his throat. "How many days has it been since…"

"Two days."

Two days and his side still burned. He prayed he would soon recover. He needed to be able to fight again. "Have we taken the palace?"

"Not yet," Cuauhtemoc said. "The Tlaxcalteca and the *teteo* are most determined to keep it."

Chimalli sucked in his breath. "I should be out there, helping the warriors storm the palace, not lying here like some invalid."

Cuauhtemoc scratched his forehead. His voice hushed, he said, "The attack has been halted."

Chimalli's blinked and tried to sit up. He grimaced with pain, and Cuauhtemoc gently pushed him back down. "Why has the attack been halted?" Chimalli asked between ragged breaths.

"Because we have lost many warriors trying to take the palace. Fortunately, we have hunger and thirst for allies. Once they have had more time to take their toll, we will attack."

Chimalli suppressed a flare of anger. Everyone was always waiting to attack the *teteo* but never actually attacking. And when they did, they lacked proper resolve. Was he the only one who had lost someone during the attack? He prayed his countrymen would find their strength again and finally put an end to the *teteo* threat. "What has happened with the *teteo* that left for the coast?"

Cuauhtemoc's face darkened. "They are heading back here, and they are bringing Tlaxcalteca reinforcements. In a few days' time, they will be back in Tenochtitlan."

Chimalli's blood ran cold. He could think of nothing worse than more *teteo* and Tlaxcalteca entering the city. "We need to stop them."

"They are many and they are strong. The *teteo* are twelve hundred in number, and they are marching with at least a thousand Tlaxcalteca warriors. Even if our sovereign was not captive and our people were not beset with grief, it would be difficult to raise an army quickly enough to stop them."

A tear leaked out of Chimalli's eye. "So, we are going to let the *teteo* and Tlaxcalteca back into our city? Will we charm them with more gold?"

Cuauhtemoc thinned his lips. "A few days ago, a group of *teteo* tried to cross the mountains to reach Tenochtitlan. They were only forty in number, and we fell on them with half a thousand. We captured all of them..." Cuauhtemoc trailed off, his voice heavy and pregnant with angst. "But we lost many. Four for every *teotl*. This will not be an easy fight, you must know that."

Chimalli winced. If his people could not find a way to even the odds, thousands upon thousands of his countrymen would have to die to kill all the *teteo*. "Is it agreed the fight will continue?"

Cuauhtemoc nodded. "We have no choice but to allow the *teteo* and Tlaxcalteca back into Tenochtitlan. However, they will be honored guests no more. They are barbarians and will be treated as criminals."

Chimalli mulled his words over. Criminals were punished in a variety of ways and the most serious transgressions were resolved with a heavy rock to the back of the head. Nothing would bring him more pleasure than carrying out such punishment himself, but he could hardly ball his fist, let alone pick up a stone. He hoped the others who were wounded were making better recoveries than him. Otherwise, Tenochtitlan would be in no position to give battle to the barbarians.

"The barbarians won't have much interest in standing for judgment," Chimalli said. "Once they secure the gold, they will flee the city."

Cuauhtemoc smiled mirthlessly. "The worst criminals never wish to face judgment. But they are mistaken if they think escaping Tenochtitlan will be a simple matter."

Chimalli ground his head into the fur matting. "They will escape in their water-houses—"

"Their water-houses are no more," Cuauhtemoc said. "We burnt them to a crisp."

Chimalli stilled. It would have been nice to see the water-houses burn. Tezoc had spent so much time studying their weaknesses and strengths; he deserved to see them burn more than anyone else. Grief seized him again, squeezing his heart so hard he was sure it would burst. But it didn't and his breathing eventually subsided. After a moment, he asked, "Do we know if Motecuhzoma is still alive?"

Cuauhtemoc stared out the window slit, shame and anger scrawled across his face in equal measures. "We can only hope. Some believe the *teteo* can be convinced to return Motecuhzoma, but they have not offered to do so thus far. But even if the *teteo* give us back all the hostages and return all the fine gifts, we cannot grant them clemency. Blood must be paid in kind."

Chimalli took a deep breath. He had dedicated his life to service and authority, but all that mattered now was vengeance. "Has Tezoc been sent off yet?"

Cuauhtemoc let out his breath after a long pause. "He was cremated yesterday. He is survived by his son, Tlalli. And you." Cuauhtemoc patted his arm. "Take rest and recover your strength, Chimalli. I know you were… close with Tezoc, but you must not let grief cloud your thoughts."

Chimalli's breath caught. What would happen to him and Tezoc if he told others… he did not finish the thought. Tezoc was dead and no longer had to worry about the judgment of his countrymen. "How long have you known?"

"Many years," Cuauhtemoc answered.

Silence filled the small room.

"How come you never reported us?" Chimalli asked.

Cuauhtemoc shrugged. "I did not think it important. Tezoc was a good man. He taught me, when I was still a student in the House of Lineage. I learned a great deal from him about leadership and responsibility. I will miss him, as will many others." A wistful look passed over Cuauhtemoc's face, and he reached for the braid tucked behind his left ear. Tezoc had the same braid—it was an honorific granted only to warriors who distinguished themselves in combat. Cuauhtemoc lowered his hand and said in a quiet voice, "I owe him a great debt, and I intend to slay the men who cut him down. Will you make good on your debt to Tezoc also?"

Chimalli thought on Tezoc's final words. He told him to take care of Tlalli. The boy had lost his mother years before and with Tezoc now gone from his life, Tlalli had no one who would look after him. He needed a father, not a warrior. But Chimalli could not be a father to him. He did not know how to be caring or loving anymore. There was too much anger in his heart now. Chimalli cleared his throat and said, "I will give up my own life if that is what it takes to kill the *teteo* and their allies."

Cuauhtemoc patted his chest and stood up. "I will find a healer to change your poultice. We need you strong again soon. The barbarians cannot be allowed to escape."

Cuauhtemoc said farewell and left the room, leaving Chimalli alone with his grief and his hatred.

Tenochtitlan

Chapter 22

Cotton Flower jumped as the sound of distant explosions reached her ears. The popping and thumping of the *teteo* weapons had become frighteningly familiar—those terrible weapons roared to life during every major attack on the palace—but the sounds were usually much closer. She whimpered and bit her lip. She hated that sound. It was the reason why the warriors had been unable to rescue her, the reason why so many wailed and screamed during the quiet hours.

"Hush, my child," Tahtli said and pulled her closer. "I am here, I will protect you."

She nodded and curled up closer to him, causing her chains to chafe against her raw skin. A few weeks ago, she would not have thought to question such a simple statement. To do so would have been outrageous. Tahtli wasn't just her father; he was Motecuhzoma Xocoyotzin, the venerable Great Speaker of the most powerful nation in all the One World. To doubt Motecuhzoma was an insult to everything proper. At least, it used to be. She had only seen ten summers, but she now knew there were things even the Great Speaker could not control.

Tahtli rubbed her back and whispered comforting words. He used to do the same, whenever she had a nightmare. Sometimes he sang lullabies, sometimes he related the creation legends. Whatever he said, it was always new, always different. But that was when she was still a princess, back when she did not need constant comforting. Now he just muttered over and over that he would protect her. Cotton Flower wished he would go back to saying histories and fables, if only to know that nothing had changed, but could not bring herself to say the words. She needed to hear that someone would protect her, that someone still cared about her well-being.

Cotton Flower sighed and closed her eyes. Exhaustion suffused her every muscle, but she refused to give in to drowsiness. The reprieve offered by sleep was just as false as it was dangerous. Had she simply been paying attention when the warriors first snuck into the palace, they would have never taken her captive.

Her heart pounded as she remembered the way Chichi had grabbed her, how smug he looked when he slapped her. He would pay for that one day. "Tahtli, what do the explosions mean? Is the palace being attacked?"

Tahtli shook his head. "The explosions would be louder and more numerous if there was a battle outside." Tahtli's voice, once majestic and proud, was now colored by grief and defeat, so much so that it seemed painful for him to speak. "The explosions are a signal of some kind," Tahtli explained. "It could mean *teteo* are getting ready to enter our city, or it could mean *teteo* are getting ready to leave the city."

"Will we be rescued soon, if the *teteo* leave the city?" Cotton Flower asked in a breath of a whisper.

Tahtli stiffened. After a long pause, he squeezed her shoulder and muttered, "Of course."

Cotton Flower nodded. She wondered how her siblings were faring. When they were first taken hostage, they were all placed in the same room. Devoid of all natural light, the cramped space offered little in the way of comfort or privacy, and they had been forced to huddle together for warmth. Much as it pained her to know that her siblings had also been taken hostage, seeing their faces and sleeping next to them had provided a strange comfort.

The comfort proved false. When the men came to take her to a separate room, her siblings were powerless to stop them. The men did things that left her torn and bloody, the *teteo* and the Tlaxcalteca both, and no amount of pleading made them stop. Then a soldier named Juan Caño intervened and placed her in a room with Tahtli. The visits stopped after that. Cotton Flower sniffled. She hoped her siblings had been spared some of her suffering.

A din of distant clattering and shouting reached her ears. "Tahtli, what is that sound?"

"*Teteo* are marching into the city," Tahtli said in a flat voice. "Let us pray it is only a few and that they did not bring any Tlaxcalteca with them."

Cotton Flower did not pray for that, but she did pray the gods would strike down the men who had violated her—that they would all suffer terrible, horrible deaths—and that everything would go back to the way it used to be.

The din outside grew louder. She frowned. She did not hear anything that sounded like battle. "Tahtli, why is nobody attacking them?"

"They are waiting for the right time to strike," Tahtli said.

Cotton Flower shivered. She was tired of spending all her time in a dank dark room, straining her ears for every tiny sound and studying every corner of the torch-lit room. She missed the feel of the sun on her back, the laughter of her siblings, the certainty that all would be well. "When will that be?"

Tahtli sighed. "I do not know."

Cotton Flower's breath caught. Never in all her life had she ever heard her father utter such terrible words. She snuggled closer to him. "Why are they here?"

"The *teteo* want our gold, and the Tlaxcalteca want ven..." Tahtli trailed off. After a moment, he cleared his throat and said, "The Tlaxcalteca want our mantle. They wish to see the Triple Alliance cast down and hope to see the Tlaxcala nation rise up. They wish to control the One World and would make us their slaves."

Cotton Flower blinked. The Mexica had ruled the One World for generations and received tribute from every nation of note. The Tlaxcalteca had to be soft in the head to think they could ever eclipse the might of the Triple Alliance. She could trace her lineage back to the founding of the Republic. Could any Tlaxcalteca princess say the same?

She opened her mouth to say as much, but the words did not come. The blood in her veins had done nothing to protect her from the lecherous brutes that had taken her captive, but it had everything to do with her captivity.

Cotton Flower sat up so she could look Tahtli in the eye. His face was lined with wrinkles and covered in grit. The imperial air he once projected had all but vanished, replaced with weariness and dejection. "Will they get what they want?" Cotton Flower asked.

A hard look passed over his face. "No," he said, his voice full of strength and certainty.

Warmth welled in Cotton Flower's stomach and, for a few precious moments, she forgot all the terrible outrages she had suffered. She leaned toward Tahtli and whispered, "Let's escape when the invaders are sick."

Motecuhzoma tensed. His eyes darted to every corner of the room, searching either for eavesdroppers or some way to escape, and drank in every detail of their cramped surroundings. After some time, he relaxed once more. "There will be no poisoning," he said, his voice flat and uninspiring again. "The *teteo* and the Tlaxcalteca committed a most terrible sacrilege, and our people will never treat them as honored guests again. The invaders know they cannot count on us for food anymore and will treat anything we give them with suspicion."

Tears formed in Cotton Flower's eyes. How were they going to escape if poisoning was no longer feasible?

236

Every attempt to take the palace by force had been repulsed. Her stomach growled, and she licked her chapped lips. She could not even remember the last time any of the guards had brought food or water. "Tahtli, what will we do?"

"We will stay alert," Tahtli said. "Eventually, an opportunity to escape will present itself. When it does, we must not hesitate. To spend the rest of our lives in captivity would be a fate worse than death."

Cotton Flower nodded. She did not want to think about pain and honor and death anymore. She rested her head on Tahtli's chest and closed her eyes. She could not take pride in her title as a princess anymore, but she was still proud to call Motecuhzoma her father.

~ ~ ~

Pedro sat across from Cortés in a room with boarded-over windows and thick curtains strewn about the floor. The space reeked of smoke and sweat and Pedro wanted nothing more than to leave. Nonetheless, he stayed seated and waited for Cortés to speak.

When the others heard that Cortés had returned, a chorus of cheers had broken out inside the Palace of Axayacatl. Some of the men had broken down in tears when Cortés entered the building and lauded him as if he were Jesus returned. Pedro had been a bit more demure in his welcome. Glad as he was to have Cortés back, he knew the captain-general might hold him responsible for the Indian uprising.

Cortés sighed loudly and took a sip from his canteen. Pedro's throat tightened as he watched Cortés down the water. Nonetheless, he knew better than to ask for a swig. Better to wait for Cortés to speak first and see where he stood with the captain-general.

"Would you care for something to drink?" Cortés asked in a level voice.

Pedro nodded and cleared his parched throat. "Of course, captain-general. Fresh water has been right scarce since the Indians turned on us."

Cortés stood up and crossed the short distance that separated them. He held out the canteen, and Pedro reached for it with a shaking hand. Pedro could not remember the last time he drank something that wasn't tainted with salt or dirt. On the nights where he actually managed to sleep, he dreamed not of women, not of gold, but of water. Fresh, gleaming, glittering, clean water.

His throat quivered a little as he accepted the canteen, and he unscrewed it with trembling fingers. Pedro took a deep breath to calm his nerves. He had lost count of all the hours he had spent fantasizing about this moment, all the hours spent dreaming about this sweet ambrosia, and thanked Cortés again. His hands shook as he brought the canteen to his lips, and he tipped it backward for a drink. A flash of movement alerted him to danger, but he barely had time to widen his eyes before Cortés smacked the canteen to the ground. The small metal container clattered loudly on the alabaster foundation, spilling its sweet contents on the grime-streaked floor.

Pedro—for one brief shameful moment—thought about throwing himself to the floor and lapping up the small puddle. Sheer force of will kept him in place, but he could not stop himself from bunching his hands into fists.

Cortés grabbed his sword hilt. "Give me a reason," Cortés hissed through gritted teeth. Pedro dropped his shoulders and unclenched his hands. His throat was dry as sandpaper and his stomach as empty as Cortés' canteen—it made no sense to fight Cortés. Right now, at least.

Pedro turned toward his captain-general. Surely there was no sin as terrible as wasting water. Even if it took years, he swore to get revenge against Cortés one day.

238

"Why did you offer me your canteen if you did not intend to let me drink from it?" Pedro asked in a low voice.

"Why, Pedro, did you let the Indians gather in the courtyard for the festival if you did not intend to let them celebrate it?"

Pedro suppressed a flare of anger. Had Cortés really wasted water just to make some roundabout point?

"Cortés, they were planning to attack—"

"How do you know that, Pedro?" Cortés shouted. "You cannot speak Nahuatl, and Doña Marina was not here to help you translate. How am I supposed to trust that you uncovered a secret plot?"

Pedro shifted in his seat. "Doña Marina is not the only one who understands Nahuatl. Many of our countrymen are familiar with the language now and know how to speak with the Indians here."

Cortés narrowed his eyes. "Strange the Indians would confess their intentions to you so freely. How did you get them to render such a true account?"

Pedro rubbed his ear, remembering how the Indian screamed when the burning evergreen log was pressed against his stomach. Never ceased to amaze him how much men could sound like women when begging for reprieve. "Cortés, what does that matter? The Indians confessed—they would not have done so if there was no plot."

Cortés narrowed his eyes. "It does matter, Pedro. Pretend otherwise, and I will coax agreement from you the same way you coaxed confessions from the Indians."

Pedro swallowed. He wanted to believe that Cortés would not torture a fellow Christian, a fellow Extremeño, but he knew better. Cortés did not care for a man's religion or his heritage; he would ally with the leaders of a thousand different Indian nations and reject all his Christian countrymen if that's what it took to win the gold. He could tolerate any number of sins amongst allies

239

or officers, any sin except disloyalty. That one could never be tolerated.

Pedro rubbed his palm. "I failed you, Cortés. I ruined your plan to win Tenochtitlan without bloodshed and beg your forgiveness. God as my witness, I swear to cut down your enemies and offer my unswerving fealty." Cortés stared at him skeptically. "I owe you my life Cortés, as does everyone here," Pedro continued. "Had you delayed in returning, the Indians would have killed all of us."

Cortés dropped his shoulders a fraction and leaned back. "Where is the gold?"

"I moved all of the gold to the highest floor," Pedro replied. "It's safe."

Cortés nodded. "That was smart. I will have a count done soon. How many ingots should I expect to find?"

Pedro scratched his head. "I do not know." Cortés' face darkened and Pedro added, "We have had other... concerns of late. The Indians tried to storm the palace many times over, and it was only through the grace of God we were able to repulse them. We cannot go to the Indians for food anymore, and they fall upon us like animals when we try to retrieve fresh water. God sustains us, but we have gone without food and water a very long time." Pedro's stomach grumbled and his eyes drifted back to the puddle. "Thirst and hunger, they do strange things to the mind. My memory fails me often, even in simple matters."

Cortés grunted and waved his hand dismissively. "No matter. I will have a count done soon." He rubbed his chin and exhaled loudly. "I am glad you kept the gold safe, and I will have Doña Marina speak with the Mexica soon. I do not think they will gift us gold anymore so we will have to trade for it. Motecuhzoma and his family are still with us, yes?"

Pedro nodded and rested his finger on his lips. *Should I tell him about the row with Motecuhzoma's daughter?*

Juan Caño had proven most determined to defend her honor and had even recruited some of the soft-hearted priests to his cause. Probably better to not tell Cortés. He would ask too many questions, and Pedro did not have the patience for another interrogation.

"Do you have something you wish to tell me?" Cortés asked.

Pedro sighed. "I do not think the Indians have any wish to trade with us. We have already won a great deal of gold. We ought to leave the city right away—"

"You are in no position to be making suggestions," Cortés interjected. Pedro went quiet and ground his heel into the floor. After a trice, Cortés added, "The horses and the men need time to rest. Besides, Narváez's men are most keen to explore the city and see the market. We will leave Tenochtitlan soon, but not until we have gained more gold."

Pedro furrowed his brow. Cortés had a habit of charging into danger but never blithely. Something had changed, and Pedro wanted to know what.

He studied Cortés' carefully. Splotches of mud covered his clothing, and his mouth was pinched tight with worry. He had bags under his eyelids, and the whites of his eyes were shot through with angry red veins.

"Why do we need more gold?" Pedro asked.

Cortés shot him a withering glare. The facade cracked after a few moments, and his face softened once more. He sighed and said, "Narváez' men make up the bulk of the army, not counting our Indian allies. They will make good soldiers, but their loyalty did not come cheap."

Pedro's empty stomach tightened. "How much did you promise them?"

Cortés twirled his mustache and sat down again. "Narváez offered sixteen thousand reals to any man who killed me, and I promised the same to every man who pledged loyalty to me."

241

Pedro's eyes widened. Cortés must have been mad to offer that much. Even if he forced every foot soldier and officer to forego their winnings, there would still not be enough to pay all of Narváez's men such a massive sum. "Cortés, where do you expect to find this king's ransom? We have no idea if the Mexica have that much gold." *And even if they did have that much, they would not give it to us.*

"What was I supposed to do?" Cortés asked, punctuating his "I" with an angry finger jab. "Narváez's men numbered almost a thousand! I made a sally against him with only three hundred of our countrymen. We succeeded because we captured Narváez early on, and because I was willing to be generous with defectors. My actions saved us and the expedition. This entire march would fail if Narváez had arrested me, and everything we have won would be for naught." Cortés stopped and took a deep breath. "Do not think I was looking out only for my own interests, either. You are a signatory to the charter of Veracruz also, as is every other officer. Given the chance, Narváez would have arrested all of us for treason."

Cortés stared at the ground, perhaps contemplating what might have happened if Narváez had prevailed. Pedro did not think it worthy of much thought. He knew exactly what would have happened had such an outcome come to pass: Pedro, like every other officer, would have sworn his loyalty to Narváez and forsaken every vow he made to Cortés.

Pedro rubbed his temple and licked his cracked lips. Despite Cortés' antics with the canteen, Pedro was glad the captain-general had returned. Granted, he stank of desperation and arrogance, but he had brought food and water with him, both of which were in short supply.

Most important of all, he brought reinforcements, so many that Cortés had to appropriate another palace to lodge everyone. Perhaps it would be enough to pacify the Indians. Cortés did have a strange knack for being able to bend the savages to his will.

A scout burst into the room, drawing Cortés and Pedro to their feet. The scout made a quick salute and then said, "The Indians have sabotaged the causeways, captain-general. We can no longer leave the city on foot."

Cortés stared at the scout in shock. The scout shifted uncomfortably and waited to be excused. Pedro cleared his throat, and Cortés shook his head as if he were in a daze. He dismissed the soldier and turned to Pedro. He flashed him a pained smile and said, "It seems the Mexica agree we ought to stay a little while."

Pedro grunted. Peace interested savages no more than celibacy interested whores. The sooner Cortés realized that, the better. "How much food and water did you bring with you?" Pedro asked.

Cortés did not answer, staring at the barricaded window instead. Shafts of sunlight stabbed through the cracked and splintered boards, and Pedro doubted the latticework would hold much longer. He had lost count of all the barricades that had been destroyed during the Indian attacks.

They had surprised him with their tenacity. When the massed charges did not work, they lobbed flaming projectiles into the building and when that did not work, they resorted to doing both. Had it not been for the Tlaxcalteca, Pedro would have lost control of the palace long ago.

"Captain-general?" Pedro asked.

Cortés rubbed his forehead. "We have enough food and water to last a few weeks, if we ration carefully. Do not fret over much. We will make peace with the Indians soon enough. War can still be avoided."

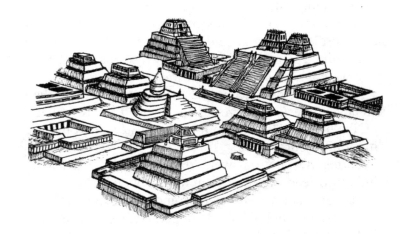

Tenochtitlan

Chapter 23

Chimalli pressed himself against the wall as the call of an eagle cut through the air. That was the signal—the barbarians were finally emerging from the palace. Chimalli's heart quickened, and he checked his *atlatl* to calm himself.

The *atlatl* was one of his favorite weapons. Light but deadly, the simple weapon could throw a spear thrice as far as any man. Many years had passed since he had been able to use an *atlatl* against an enemy, and he hoped the gods would guide his aim. He took a deep breath. Of course they would. The gods were just as outraged by the sacrilege of the barbarians, if not more so. Moreover, they had guided his arm true when he practiced with the *atlatl* earlier in the day and the day before that.

For the past week, he had done almost nothing besides practice since the *teteo* and the Tlaxcalteca refused to take part in a pitched battle. Instead, they made quick sallies in search of food or water but retreated as soon as they met organized resistance. Chimalli did not doubt he and his countrymen would force the barbarians to retreat back to the palace before day's end, but he hoped they would do more than that today. The barbarians had been allowed to draw breath for too long and if they tried to retreat, Chimalli and his countrymen would give chase. If necessary, they would raze their stronghold to the ground.

A distant tromping of feet reached his ears. He frowned. Whenever they made their sallies in the past, they usually left with eighty or so. What he heard sounded more like hundreds. No matter either way. The barbarians were not going to be allowed to escape any more than they would be allowed to sue for peace.

They were much closer now, and he could hear the clank of metal and the creaking of stretched bows. The clank had to be the *teteo*, the creaking had to be the Tlaxcalteca. Straining his ears, he also heard loud snorting. The hornless stags, if he had to guess. He wanted to peek his head around the corner to check, but he resisted the impulse. The risk of being seen was too great; they had to catch the barbarians unawares for the attack to succeed. No, he would stay hidden and follow orders, just as Tezoc had trained him to do.

Another eagle caw. Chimalli raised his weapon. When the next call came, it would be time to attack. He prayed to the gods for strength and tried to calm his twitching fingers. He would avenge Tezoc, and the nation, today.

The final signal was issued and all at once, sounds of battle—the howls of wounded men, the lusty screams of warriors, and the clash of stone against steel—filled the air. Chimalli leaped from behind cover and studied the pandemonium with a trained eye. The *teteo* and the Tlaxcalteca were bunched together in a tight mass with hornless stags at the front, *teteo* in the middle, and Tlaxcalteca in back. He aimed for the center of the mass and let his spear fly. Before it could land, he dove behind cover and grabbed another spear.

He peeked his head around the corner. The barbarians were being pelted by stones, arrows, and spears from every which angle, and the barrage was growing thicker with rapid speed. The *teteo* and the Tlaxcalteca tried to retaliate but as soon as they found a target, it disappeared or their aim was knocked askew by a well-placed projectile. He counted five dead Tlaxcalteca but spied only one *teotl* body on the ground. Anger flared inside him. To kill only the Tlaxcalteca would be unjust; the *teteo* had to suffer also.

He studied the crowd to find his target. A *teotl* with a snapping bow took aim at a boy taunting him from atop a roof. With a pull of his finger, the *teotl* released an arrow that punched through the boy's thigh like a needle through cloth. Chimalli growled under his breath; he had found his target.

He stepped out of cover, raised his weapon, and snapped his arm forward. The spear went flying out of the atlatl so fast he had to squint to see it. To his dismay, the spear embedded itself not in a teotl, but in some Tlaxcalteca warrior. Chimalli cursed and ran back for another spear.

The *teteo* and the Tlaxcalteca were closing ranks, and he could not find his target anywhere. He balanced himself on the balls of his feet to see better.

Something small whizzed past his ear, scattering all his thoughts. He scurried for cover and cursed himself for being so absent-minded.

Chimalli took a moment to catch his breath before he stepped out into the open. A smile cracked his face; the barbarians were in full-fledged retreat. One of the giant hornless stags had become separated from the column, and the rider tried, in vain, to calm the beast. Chimalli raised his arm to take aim. He whispered a quick prayer and let the spear fly. It sailed through the air effortlessly and buried itself deep in the animal's flank, just as he intended.

The beast screamed and reared violently. The rider—covered in shiny metal from head to toe—lost his balance and fell to the ground in a messy heap. Crazed with pain, the hornless stag barreled through the ranks of the barbarians and disappeared into an alley. Chimalli ran back for another spear but stopped before he picked it up. The barbarians were in retreat, their column in disarray, and he intended to give chase. An *atlatl* would not do for close-quarter fighting. Chimalli grabbed his club. Inlaid with obsidian glass and thick as three corn stalks, the club had served him well in numerous battles, and he prayed it would not fail him today.

He darted out from behind cover. Half the column had turned the corner, and it would only be a matter of time before all of the barbarians disappeared from view. They were in full-fledged retreat, harassed the entire time by the ambushers, and warriors everywhere were abandoning cover to chase after the enemy. Chimalli would have done the same but saw something he could not ignore: the *teotl* who had been thrown by the hornless stag was still moving.

Chimalli sprinted toward the dazed *teotl* and let loose a feral war cry. The *teotl* forced himself upright and fumbled for his long knife. Before he could pull it even halfway out, Chimalli smashed his club into the *teotl's* elbow.

The man screamed and staggered backward. Chimalli hit him again, this time in the temple, and the man's metal head covering crashed to the ground with a resounding clank. Somehow, the *teotl* stayed on his feet. Chimalli furrowed his brow and examined his club. Every shard of obsidian had shattered, and a large crack had formed near the haft of the weapon.

The *teotl* grunted and made a half-hearted charge. Chimalli jumped back and readied his club for a strike. Much to his surprise, the *teotl* did not try to press the advantage. Instead, he let his long knife hang down by his side and panted like a dog. He swayed on his feet but made no movement otherwise. Chimalli grinned and lowered himself into a fighting crouch. The *teotl* tried to do the same, but his legs refused to cooperate and he gave up. He took a few tentative steps backward and collided with the wall of a barricaded building.

Chimalli made a feint toward the man. The *teotl* pressed himself against the wall and swung his long knife wildly. It went wide of Chimalli by half an arm's length but cut through the air with a savage swish that made the hairs on his arm stand up. Such a weapon was not to be trifled with.

Chimalli took quick stock of his surroundings. The *teotl* could not count on any of his countrymen to help him any more than Chimalli could; everyone was much too busy rushing back to Axayacatl's palace. Chimalli made another feint toward the man. Again, the man swung his weapon out, but the sheer force of his swing left him panting and gasping.

The *teotl* slumped against the wall and muttered something incoherent. He tossed his weapon to the ground and said something about ransoming. Chimalli furrowed his brow. He understood few *teteo* words, but that one had been seared into his memory by the seizure of Motecuhzoma's children.

He stared at the *teotl*. Flushed red with exertion and shiny with sweat, blood dripped down his face and mixed with the thick, yellow hairs that hid his jawline from view. His cheeks were covered with minute holes and tiny spots. Could something like that happen naturally? Perhaps but it seemed more likely the man had done it to himself as some kind of bleeding rite.

Chimalli puffed out his chest. He did not care how the man gained the disfiguration. He did not want to learn his tongue or his custom and had no interest in taking him captive or selling him for a ransom. He placed his foot on the flat edge of the long knife. The *teotl* stiffened and gawked at Chimalli like he had suddenly grown wings.

"Blood debts can only be settled one way," Chimalli said in an even voice.

The *teotl* arched his brow and stole a glance at the sword. He dove for the weapon and Chimalli swung his club upward, catching the man in the nose. The blow sent him reeling backward, and Chimalli clobbered him with his club over and over until a sudden snap made him stop.

He stepped back and examined his work. The *teotl's* face reminded him of a crushed melon and the sight of the soft, mushy mess made his stomach roil. He checked his club. The crack near the haft had widened and long strands of blood dangled from it. He tossed the weapon aside and picked up the long knife.

Near as long as his leg but thin as his thumb nail, the weapon was surprisingly light. It was shiny also and caught the sun's glare whenever he tilted it. He ran his thumb over the material coating the hilt. Some kind of leather, if he had to guess.

A loud popping grabbed his attention. His countrymen needed him, and he could tarry no longer. Today, they would finally take back the Axayacatl's Palace. He ran along a lake canal and crossed the waterway bridge without even pausing to catch his breath.

Thirty more paces and he would reach Axayacatl's Palace, but he could not see the *teteo* or the Tlaxcalteca anywhere. Anger focused his senses. They had retreated to the safety of the palace and his countrymen were trying and failing, yet again, to storm their stronghold. He screamed in frustration and threw himself into the crowd of warriors jostling to get inside.

Something splashed onto his face, and he glanced to the side. The warrior next to him had collapsed, his neck split like a burst tomato. Chimalli grabbed the man's club and threw it at a barricaded window. It bounced off the wooden slats and tumbled to the ground. A few moments later, a *teotl* came to the window, wedged his thunder stick between two slats of wood, and pulled the trigger, toppling another Mexica warrior.

His countrymen threw every item imaginable— burning chunks of wood, heavy stones, and light spears—

at the boarded-over windows but their efforts availed them little. As soon as they broke a window plank, a group of *teteo* stepped forward, fired thunder sticks, and then retreated so that others could repair the breach.

Pelting the building with rocks and shouts would be pointless; better to force his way in. If any man—Mexica, Tlaxcalteca, or *teotl*—tried to stop him, he would cut them down with his long knife. He bellowed a warning to his countrymen and then pushed and shoved his way to the front of the crowd. He was barely halfway through when a great cheer went up—his countrymen had brought down a portion of the palace wall!

The crowd surged through the breach and cries of victory filled the air. Those cries were cut short as one, then two, then three, then four booms went off in quick succession. Chimalli dove to the ground as an unseen force tore through the crowd and smashed into an adjacent building with a crashing so loud it made his ears ring.

The ringing faded, replaced by anguished howls. He put a hand on his pounding head and sat up. The breach was ten paces away and beckoned like a light in the dark. Some warriors nearby proved unable to resist the urge and made a mad dash for it. Eight charged through the breach, full of confidence and bravery, only to be bowled aside like stalks of corn as some monstrous chain tore through flesh and bone.

His head lolled backward, and the palace's full profile came into view. Flashes of light were coming to life in nearly every window now, and the screams grew louder. An arrow buried itself half a pace from his thumb, and he drew his hand back. How had the arrow gotten so close? Just moments ago, he had been standing in the middle of an excited throng of warriors. He swiveled his head to the right and the left. He could see none of those warriors now. In their place, he saw only ugly corpses and dark puddles. A man with half a jaw stared at him with glassy accusing eyes, and he dared not hold his stare.

Looking behind him, he found the throng of excited warriors. Except they were no longer excited; now they were scared and confused and retreating. A deep sadness overcame him. Once again, the *teteo* and the Tlaxcalteca had proven too mighty to defeat. Perhaps it was hopeless to fight them. A stranger pulled him to his feet. He should have pushed him away. Instead, he fell into step beside him as they both ran for safety.

His bloodlust and confidence forsaken, he ran as if he were being pursued by mounted *teteo*. The afternoon high—striking the hornless stag and killing the *teotl*—felt hollow and meaningless now. He rounded a corner and caught a glimpse of the palace as he turned.

The building had suffered no end of abuse during the past few weeks; the deep gashes in the stone facade and the black scorch marks all bore testimony to that. Nonetheless, he spotted only one breach in the wall. He had every confidence the *teteo* and the Tlaxcalteca would spend all night repairing it, and he had no idea if his countrymen would be able to force their way through again. Even if they did, what would it matter? The popping, thumping weapons would cut down every warrior who made it through.

His gorge rose up unbidden. The barbarians could hold the palace for months if they had enough food and water. He cursed the Mexica architects who conceived the near impregnable building and cursed the *teteo* for defending it so well.

Chimalli gritted his teeth. So long as the barbarians stayed in the palace, they could not massacre his countrymen the way they did during the Flaying Festival. He knew it would only be a matter of time before they attempted another sally and prayed the next one would also fail.

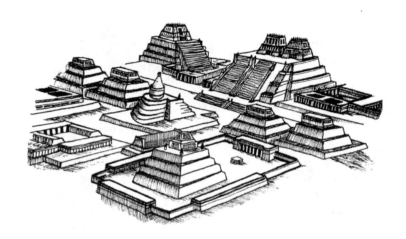

Tenochtitlan

Cortés ran his tongue along his teeth. His mouth was dry as wool and his teeth were coarser than sand. He could hear water lapping at the edges of a nearby canal when he strained his ears. At least, it seemed so. He did not know how much he could trust his senses these days. Just last night, Cortés had been certain he saw Leonor, the mistress he left behind in Cuba, striding through the palace halls.

He glanced at the men standing behind the cannon. Judging by their drawn faces and chapped lips, the lack of food and water had taken a toll on them also. Or perhaps it was anger that had transformed their features. The seething, baleful glares wounded him just as much as they confused him. Was it his fault the Indians attacked? He had not forced Pedro to massacre the festival attendees any more than he forced Narváez's men to join his cause. Nobody wanted peace more than him. The transfer of power in Tenochtitlan was always supposed to be bloodless, but now they were trapped inside a Godforsaken palace because Pedro had been unable to control his violent urges.

Cortés clenched his fist, snapping the fish bone he had been rubbing for God knows how long. He stared at the broken thing, surprised by the destruction he had wrought. Cortés let out his breath and opened his hand. He crossed himself and lifted a wooden plank, only a finger span, so he could look upon the Sacred Plaza. Littered with debris and corpses, the grim sight chilled him like a gust of winter air.

If the twelve warriors milling about Yopico's Temple were disturbed by their surroundings, they did not show it. All of them were armed—some with bows, others with spears, most with slings—and he worried they might be planning some kind of attack. Yopico's Temple offered an excellent vantage point for an attack on the Palace of Axayacatl but, it was just as possible they wanted to parley. Cortés had no idea either way.

He studied the outline of the twelve figures in the fading light. One wore a giant headdress, similar to the one that Motecuhzoma wore when Cortés first met him, but he could make out none of their features in the gloam. He rubbed his dry eyes and blinked, half-expecting them to disappear while his eyes were closed. Much to his disappointment, all twelve of them were still there when he opened his eyes again.

"What would you have us do?" Sandoval asked.

Cortés bristled at the sound of his voice. Sandoval had warned him not to re-enter Tenochtitlan and probably blamed him for the current mess. Not that he would ever say such a thing aloud.

In some ways, it did not matter. Cortés sensed the reprimand lurking beneath his placid mien, like a snake hiding under a rock.

"Is the cannon primed?" Cortés asked.

"Yes," Sandoval replied. "But we are low on black powder."

Cortés stiffened. He knew they lacked for provisions and did not need to be reminded. He glanced at the cannon. The cold piece of metal had done more to help him than any of his officers. It did not plot against him, did not make foolish suggestions, did not cast judgement; it laid waste to his enemies and did as he bid. But cannons needed powder and shot, and both were running dangerously low.

"How many crossbow bolts do we have?" Cortés asked.

"Enough to fend off four or five more attacks."

Cortés nodded. The Mexica attacked them every time they stepped outside the palace and if he could not rally support for another sally, the bolts would be near impossible to retrieve. In times past, he would have ordered a random group of soldiers to retrieve the bolts. Now he had to explain that he was not favoring one faction over another and had to promise the malcontents even more gold to buy their obedience.

He rubbed his throat. By denying Cortés victory, the Mexica warriors were undermining his leadership more than Governor Velázquez ever could. Perhaps it would be good to strike a few of them down, if only to remind them of his power. He let down the plank and turned toward Sandoval. "What do you think they want?"

"I don't know," Sandoval said, his voice flat and lifeless.

Cortés grunted. Of course he did not know. None of his officers had any useful input to offer. They never failed to let him know that supplies were running low but seldom came to him with any solutions. Instead, they stared at him expectantly, as if he could snap his fingers to make powder and food and water reappear. He took a deep breath to calm himself. Soon, God willing, they would take leave of the palace. The portable bridge would be finished in a few days' time; his men lacked for necessities like food and water but not for carpentry tools.

He brought the fishbone up to his mouth and picked at the grime that coated his teeth. His hand trembled a bit, and the point stabbed into tender flesh. He winced and cast the bone aside. *Shouldn't have done that.* He stared at the discarded toothpick. The pale sliver of bone was not difficult to spot. The floor, once white as ermine, was now coated in brown filth and gray ash.

"Perhaps they wish to make peace," Cortés said.

Sandoval arched his brow. "Do they come bearing white flags?"

Cortés laughed bitterly. "Have you ever known Indians to use white flags?"

Sandoval shook his head. "Never. But I do not claim to know all their ways. I do not see why the Mexica would surrender when they are on the cusp of victory, though."

Cortés ran his thumb along his lip. The dead skin and thin scabs made for a rough texture, one reminiscent of frayed rope and crinkled leather. He gave thanks a mirror was not handy and ran his teeth along the detritus, rupturing a scab. He prodded and twisted but it clung so he pinched his fingers together to better impose his will. After what seemed an enormous effort, the scab finally relented, and he pulled it loose with a small tug. Blood rushed to fill the small cavity, and he assayed the carnage with a tentative tongue. It would heal, in time.

"Do you think we should fire on them?" Cortés asked.

"What would we gain?"

Cortés suppressed a flare of anger. Did Sandoval think himself some kind of jester? His penchant for answering questions with questions had become tiresome.

Cortés stared at the other men who had gathered around the cannon, waiting for one of them to speak. Not one obliged. God alone knew if they had been following the conversation. Many of the artillerists had gone hard of hearing—a few claimed they had lost all sense of hearing. Cortés did not know if he believed them. Surely God would not be so cruel as to take away that which He had given, not from those who had already sacrificed so much on His behalf.

"One of them put on a headdress," Cortés said. "He's important. It could be Cuitlahuac or Cuauhtemoc."

Those two warriors had caused him no end of heartache, and he prayed every day he would be able to repay them in kind. A part of him did wonder, however, if that day would ever come. Every attempt at dialogue had been rebuffed and every attempt at escape had been foiled.

The Mexica had drawn quite the noose around his neck. If he could not find a way to slip it, the entire campaign would fail. All the gold they had won, all the charters they had drawn up, all for naught. He could not let that happen. He would be cursed for eternity if he permitted such a terrible injustice.

"Or it could be an imposter," Sandoval said. Cortés looked at him in confusion. It took a few seconds for him to remember that Sandoval was talking about the Indian with the headdress. Oblivious to his confusion, Sandoval added, "Either way, we gain little by firing on them. If we waste our powder firing on small groups of Indians, we won't have any powder to fend off a massed attack."

Cortés shuddered as memories of the last attack came rushing back. The Mexica had come on thick as a plague of locusts and turning them back had exhausted precious powder. It would be an absolute disaster if they launched more attacks like that; the men were too weary and too rattled to keep fighting off such massive hordes. He cleared his throat and said, "Cut off the head of a snake…"

Sandoval stared at him askance. "We are not making battle against reptiles or slithering beasts; we are defending a crumbling building against irate warriors. We are greatly outnumbered and very short on supplies—I do not think we are in a position to waste shot."

"The Indians revere their leaders," Cortés demurred. While he would never admit as much out loud, he envied Cuitlahuac and Cuauhtemoc for being able to inspire such loyalty. They had legions of men willing to fight, kill, and die for them, all because of their noble lineage. Cortés could never inspire that type of devotion. His soldiers loved him so long as gold was plentiful and battles were few but as soon as the Indians turned surly, his countrymen forgot all their oaths and admiration. "We would be decapitating their leadership and crippling their ability to make war."

Sandoval squared his shoulders. "They do not need to be well-led to defeat us. They just need to make a few more massed attacks. Besides, we decapitated their leadership when we took Motecuhzoma hostage, did we not?"

Cortés grunted. Sandoval did have a point there. Taking Motecuhzoma hostage had done little to improve the behavior of his subjects. If anything, they had become more duplicitous and conniving.

"You say the Indians revere their leaders," Sandoval added. "We still have Motecuhzoma hostage. Let's use that to our advantage. Make the god your puppet and tell them to disperse."

Cortés turned toward the barricaded window. "Pedro did the same, when we were gone," Cortés said. "He had to threaten Motecuhzoma with a blade to make him cooperate."

Sandoval shrugged. "If he will no longer heed threats, we will have to use the blade on him. He has no value to us if he cannot bring his subjects to heel."

Cortés rubbed his scraggly cheek hairs. Sandoval's reasoning made sense. Perhaps he had one good officer after all.

~ ~ ~

Cuauhtemoc studied the outline of Axayacatl's Palace from the summit of Yopico's Temple. His countrymen had inflicted great damage on the building, and there were multiple breaches in the wall. Nevertheless, every attempt to seize it by force had failed.

For the life of him, he could not understand it. The more the palace weakened, the more determined the barbarians were to hold it. Cuauhtemoc wanted to believe that one more massed attack would be enough to finally overpower the barbarians, but he understood why the others were more skeptical. He had lost count of all the times overconfident warriors bragged that victory was close at hand, only for the barbarians to unleash some terrible volley that utterly devastated Mexica forces.

Cuauhtemoc was surprised the barbarians had not already fired their popping and thumping weapons. They seemed to have an endless supply of shot and never had any reservations about firing upon Mexica warriors in the past.

"Should we send an envoy their way?" Cuauhtemoc asked.

Cuitlahuac's face darkened. "And give the *teteo* another hostage? No, we will let them come to us."

Cuauhtemoc seriously doubted the barbarians would come out of hiding but kept silent. Cuitlahuac was Great Speaker now, and Cuauhtemoc knew better than to contradict him. Moreover, he could understand why Great Speaker felt it useful to attempt dialogue before launching another massed attack. Hundreds had already died trying to seize the palace—warriors they had grown up alongside, warriors who hailed from the most distinguished family lines—and the Mexica had little to show for it. Not a single captive had been freed and many feared the worst.

Cuauhtemoc brought his shield closer and thumbed his throwing sling. The night the barbarians kidnapped the children, he had brought down a *teotl* with his sling. The way the man screamed when it wrapped around his leg still brought a smile to his lips. His only regret was that he had not been able to bring down more of the *teteo*. Perhaps if he had, the children would still be safe and Motecuhzoma would have never surrendered himself. He sighed. He had more regrets than smiles these days.

"Something is moving on the palace rooftop," Cuitlahuac said.

Cuauhtemoc tightened his grip on the sling. He fixed his gaze on the distant ledge and was surprised to see Motecuhzoma come into view. His mouth dropped open. It had been weeks since he had last seen the former Speaker, but he looked as if he had aged a lifetime. Flanked on both sides by armored *teteo*, he carried himself like a careworn beggar.

"Let the Mexica hear," shouted Motecuhzoma. His voice echoed out across the courtyard, brittle but strong. Cuauhtemoc glanced at Cuitlahuac. His face was set in a hard grimace, and he shook with confined rage.

"The *teteo* believe we are not their match and that we should cease fighting. They believe we ought to spurn the arrow and the shield so that we can take heed of our people's suffering. They urge us to think of the poor old men and the women, the infants who toddle and crawl, who lie in the cradle and know nothing yet. It cannot be denied they will suffer if fighting continues, but great victories often require great sacrifices."

Motecuhzoma drew in a labored breath and added, "The *teteo* would have you believe they cannot be defeated, that they are immune to the pangs of hunger and the ravishes of thirst, but it is a lie. Their fighting spirit weakens with every hour. They are losing heart and cannot summon the energy to go on much longer. Just as my own strength is flagging, so is theirs."

Cuauhtemoc blinked in surprise and turned to Cuitlahuac. "Why are the *teteo* letting him speak this way?"

Cuitlahuac removed a hand from his bow and shaded his eyes. "I see only two *teteo* with him. They may not know our tongue."

Or your brother is doing as commanded. "You do not see the translator woman anywhere?" Cuauhtemoc asked, his voice colored by disbelief and confusion.

262

Cuitlahuac shook his head. "She may be hiding inside."

"If she is, can she even hear him?"

Cuitlahuac furrowed his brow and gave orders to a nearby warrior to climb onto the temple roof and look for anything amiss. Cuauhtemoc raised his shield and stared fixedly at Motecuhzoma. Standing upright seemed to require an inordinate amount of energy, and Motecuhzoma swayed on his feet any time a breeze picked up. Cuauhtemoc narrowed his eyes. Were the barbarians so depraved as to torture a Great Speaker?

"Terrible outrages have been committed against me, against my children, against our nation and the offenders must be punished," Motecuhzoma shouted. "Beside me stand two *teteo*. Like the rest of their countrymen, they are guilty of great crimes. They assume their armor protects them from justice and so long as they draw breath, they will continue to carry out terrible outrages— unless there are Mexica warriors brave enough to stand up to them. Let all those who can hear me take my words to heart: the *teteo* and the Tlaxcalteca must be killed. Do not let them charm you with promises of peace, and do not let concern for me stay your weapons. My life is already forfeit, but my passing will be easier if I know at least two *teteo* will join me in leaving this world."

Cuauhtemoc stiffened. Never in all his life had he been asked to do something so sacrilegious. How had things come to such a terrible pass? Dazed, Cuauhtemoc looked to Cuitlahuac for guidance. Tears brimmed in Cuitlahuac's eyes, and his brow quivered like a sapling in a storm. His voice, however, did not quaver as he issued his command: "We will honor my brother's last wish."

Cuauhtemoc nodded and moved his shield in front of him. Confident the *teteo* could not see his sling, he slowly swiveled his forearm to get the weapon spinning. Sweat beaded on his forehead. Motecuhzoma and the *teteo* were located almost fifty paces away, and he did not know if he could trust his aim at such a distance. If his aim were off by a few paces, he would hit Motecuhzoma instead of the *teteo*. He prayed his arm would not betray him and cursed the barbarians for bringing him and his countrymen to such a strange pass.

"On my signal," Cuitlahuac whispered. The line moved forward a pace, and the *teteo* called out something in their strange tongue. It wasn't important, whatever it was. Cuauhtemoc tightened his grip on the shield and advanced another pace.

"Now!" Cuitlahuac shouted.

Cuauhtemoc let down his shield and waved his arm above his head like he was trying to beat the air. He released the throwing sling and watched it sail toward the *teotl* standing to Motecuhzoma's right. It flew true as any he had ever thrown, but the *teteo* raised his shield long before it reached him, and the clay balls shattered against the shiny shield. Moments later, a spear crashed into that same shield, followed by an arrow that bounced off its rim.

The *teotl* stumbled backward but kept his shield high. The other *teotl* did likewise with his shield but instead of retreating backward, he rushed forward to grab Motecuhzoma and pulled him out of the path of an arrow. He failed, however, to remove him from the path of harm, and a rock that should have gone wide of Motecuhzoma smashed into his head. Motecuhzoma went limp, but he uttered no cry of pain as he fell toward the ground. The *teotl* ducked to avoid a sling and stole toward Motecuhzoma. A light spear went wide of his shoulder by a finger span, but the *teotl* paid it no mind. Undeterred and unharmed, he grabbed Motecuhzoma's wrist and pulled him toward safety.

Seeing the *teotl* drag Motecuhzoma filled Cuauhtemoc with a murderous rage, and he scanned his surroundings to find another weapon. He spotted a chunk of rubble nearby, crouched to pick it up, and lobbed the rock with all his might. He picked up another stone and was about to throw it when Cuitlahuac shouted for him to stop.

He turned toward his cousin, his breath short and his forearm burning. "We have done our duty," Cuitlahuac said. "They are gone from view and we can do no more."

Cuauhtemoc nodded and dropped the lumpy rock. A few moments later, the scout clambered down from the temple roof and dropped to a knee in front of Cuitlahuac. He hung his head and waited for permission to speak.

Cuitlahuac squared his shoulders and brought himself up to full height. "Did we…."

The scout shook his head. "The *teteo* draw breath still, as does Motecuhzoma. But—" The scout flushed and said no more.

"Tell me," Cuitlahuac demanded.

"Motecuhzoma has suffered a terrible injury," the scout said. "One we did not inflict."

Cuitlahuac narrowed his eyes. "What do you mean?"

The scout flushed, then glanced toward the warriors and attendants who had gathered beside Cuitlahuac. After a long pause, he whispered, "When they dragged him away, I saw the back of his loincloth. It was red. It looked like—"

Cuitlahuac silenced him with a wave of his hand. His face went hard as granite, and he squeezed his bow as if he were trying to throttle it. "The *teteo* have been given but a small taste of our fury today. If they, or their allies, try to escape we must fall upon them without mercy. They can keep the Palace of Axayacatl—they will die in there also."

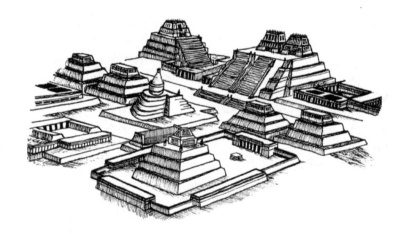

Tenochtitlan

Malintze rubbed the dirty cloth with her thumb and stared at Motecuhzoma's bedraggled figure. He did not cut an impressive appearance lying on his shoulder amidst waste and filth. Ugly patches of bruised flesh and festering sores had cropped up all along his body, like mushrooms on a rotting log, and she doubted he would live much longer. Despite his infirmity, the *teteo* had not seen fit to release him from his irons, and they clanked together whenever he made the smallest motion.

His cracked lips and his unkempt hair did little to improve his appearance. Try as she might, she could not remember what he looked like when he was still Great Speaker. Half a year had passed since he first greeted them in Tenochtitlan, but that memory belonged to a different time, a different life. So much had happened since then. When she first entered the city, she did so as an honored guest. Now she could not step foot outside the palace without an armed guard. As much as things had changed for her, they had changed even more for Motecuhzoma. When they first met, he had been the most powerful person in all the nation. Now he was a prisoner on the verge of death and would draw his final breaths in a room that stank of corruption and rot.

A small whimpering reached Malintze's ears. With some trepidation, she turned toward Cotton Flower.

The princess who once slept on luxurious cushions now slouched against the coarse stone wall as if it were a soft down pillow. She had somehow managed to fall asleep and fidgeted every now and then. Malintze's stomach churned. The princess had suffered a stunning fall from grace, one Malintze would not have wished on anyone, but one she had helped engineer. Perhaps it was inevitable that the rise of a village brat would mean the decline of a pampered princess, or perhaps little girls were never really safe from men accustomed to taking. Either way, Malintze could not help but feel a small twinge of shame whenever she looked at the girl.

She shifted in her seat and turned back to Motecuhzoma. The stool elevated her above the worst filth, but it did nothing to make the smell of the room any more pleasing. A chamber pot lurked in the corner of the room, full to the brim, and she wondered when it was last emptied. Weeks, for all she knew. Emptying chamber pots, retrieving food and water—all of it had become dangerous now that the Mexica attacked them every time they stepped outside the palace.

Malintze leaned forward to tend the bruise on Motecuhzoma's chest. She knew the warriors would suffer no peace entreaties but never imagined they would attack their own Great Speaker. Her hand shook a little, and she remembered why she came. She reached toward Motecuhzoma, armed with nothing other than a hand towel, but he raised an arm to stop her.

She pulled her hand back and tucked the cloth away. "Cortés has asked me to attend to you. Why are you refusing care?"

Motecuhzoma blew out a shallow breath. "Fate has brought me to a terrible pass… and I no longer wish to live," he said in a weak voice. "I regret that I ever put stock in the words of the *teteo*. You will, too."

Malintze narrowed her eyes. "Do not presume to know my future. It does not belong to you, nor will it be decided by you."

Motecuhzoma chuckled weakly. "What makes you so sure you will have a future? You are trapped in this palace the same as I am. The warriors would sooner die than let you escape."

Malintze brushed her hair back and glanced in Cotton Flower's direction. Still asleep but squirming like she was in the midst of a nightmare. Whatever she was dreaming about, it could not be much worse than her waking world. "What did you say to the warriors when you were on the roof?" Malintze asked.

A small smile crossed Motecuhzoma's face. "I let them know they have a duty to kill all the *teteo*, as well as the people who ally with them."

Malintze nodded. She feared he might do something like that. She had warned Cortés against letting Motecuhzoma speak to the warriors, just as she had warned him that she would not be able to hear Motecuhzoma unless she went outside with him. He had ignored her on both counts, insisting that she listen from a barricaded room where no harm could come to her, but he had yet to admit to any error. If he ever did, it would be a minor miracle.

"Mexica warriors are nothing if not dutiful," Malintze said. "I am sure they will do their utmost to follow your orders."

She clamped her jaws shut to keep from saying more. Much as she wanted to tell him about the portable bridge—to let him know that she and all the occupants of Axayacatl's palace would soon take leave of Tenochtitlan—she could not bring herself to do so. It would be cruel, like ripping the wings off a butterfly to watch it kick and squirm.

"Why do you make common cause with the *teteo*?" Motecuhzoma asked.

Malintze furrowed her brow. A Great Speaker was not supposed to take an interest in the inner thoughts of a lowly slave girl. But the arrival of the *teteo* changed that, just as it had changed so much. "I grew up in a small

269

village called Painalla. My Tahtli was an important man, but he died when I was young. Some time later, my mother found another husband… but he never cared for me the way Tahtli did." Malintze paused to steady her voice. "It would not have mattered, even if he did. I had a brother, and boys always matter more than girls."

Malintze ran a hand through her long dark hair. She wondered if her brother had hair as dark as her own. If she saw him again, she would be hard-pressed to recognize him. "My village never had much to offer your tribute collectors, and we had even less after the drought. The elders assumed your tribute collectors would ask less of us once they learned what happened to our harvest, but they were wrong. To deny the Great Speaker his deserved tribute would be a great injustice, so we had to find a way to make up for the shortfall. I do not think it took my step-father long to decide that I would be sold and my brother would not." Malintze sighed and shook her head. "No, I do not think it took my step-father long at all to reach that decision."

Motecuhzoma put a hand over his stomach. A new bout of pain seized him, and he grimaced. After a moment, he whispered, "As Great Speaker, many decisions fell to me. Which *altepetl* would be attacked and which would be spared; which village would be exempted from tribute payments and which would be punished. I know now many of those decisions were wrong, but none seemed so at the time." Motecuhzoma closed his eyes and took a deep breath. When he opened them again, his eyes had lost some of their luster. "Every decision felt justified, all because I thought I knew what the future held. I truly thought I could see beyond the bend of the river."

His face softened and he shook his head. "I know now we have little power to chart our own destiny. We can ply the waters of fate to hurry our progress or change our direction, but the boatman cannot go against the current any more than he can change the course of a river. Had I recognized as much when I was still Great Speaker, I would have made very different decisions."

Malintze mulled his words over. She had agreed to serve as translator almost a year before, and her life had changed drastically since then. She had gained many privileges on account of Cortés, but she was by no means a free woman. Cholula had not been her choice any more than the sacking of Cempoala, but she had been forced to partake in both. And if she survived the flight from Tenochtitlan, she would have to assist with even more destruction. Cortés would always ask her for more, and she would always say yes; to go back to life before would be a fate worse than death.

"I am not long for this world," Motecuhzoma said. Malintze started. She agreed, she suspected he would expire on the morrow or the day after, but had not expected him to recognize as much. "The journey to the next world will be easier if I know my children will be looked after."

Malintze froze. Perhaps it would be good to let Motecuhzoma know that she counseled Cortés against the raid, that she sought out Caño's aid solely to help Cotton Flower. She opened her mouth to say as much, but the words did not come. She stared at her cracked fingernails. Reminding Motecuhzoma what had happened to his daughter, reminding him how little power she had to curb the violent impulses of Cortés and his countrymen, would do him no good in his current state.

She wiped her cheek, confused by her mix of emotions. As Great Speaker, Motecuhzoma had levied tribute payments and war upon the most helpless of people, robbing Malintze, and countless others, of her family, her innocence, her home. She hated him and all his ilk and had spent countless nights fantasizing about

271

his downfall. Nonetheless, the rage that once consumed her had faded, tempered by grief and guilt. Motecuhzoma had done terrible things as Great Speaker—she could live a hundred years and never cause half as much havoc— but she knew she also had blood on her hands.

She cleared her throat and said, "I cannot promise anything... but I will try."

Motecuhzoma nodded. "What will happen to me, after I pass?"

Malintze pulled at a frayed cotton thread on her tunic. She had never worn anything half as fine in Painalla or Potonchan. The loose tunic covered her stomach, her breast, even her shoulders, and marked her as an important woman in any crowd. Vendors clamored for her attention when she strode through a market and would-be suitors shot her longing glances, all because she wore clothing that kept most of her body hidden. It scared her sometimes, how much interest she now inspired. But just as Motecuhzoma was powerful only if he had his rich cloak and his ostentatious diadem, she was powerful only if she wore long skirts and loose tunics. "I do not know what will happen to you," she whispered.

Motecuhzoma sighed. "The death of a Great Speaker is always a solemn occasion. Tradition holds that a Great Speaker must be laid out on the divine hearth and then cremated. I hope I will also be given this honor."

Malintze swallowed the lump in her throat. What would happen to her own body when she died? She doubted the Mexica would give her any special honors. More likely they would desecrate her body and her memory. And if they took her alive... She shuddered. It did no good to think about it.

"When I was still Great Speaker, I took part in many sacrificial rites," Motecuhzoma said, his voice weak and his face wan. "Only the gods know how many deaths I have presided over, for I could never tally them all. They blur together, like trees on a distant shoreline. My city has seen so much death these past few weeks, so much that I wonder: will anyone remember my passing?"

Malintze smoothed her dress. "We cannot control how others will remember us," she said, surprised by the confidence in her voice. "As you tell it, we have little control over the events in our own lives. I think we can control how we confront death, though. For your own sake, for your daughter's sake, confront it with dignity and grace. You may not have the power you once had... but you still have that power at least."

Malintze stood up. Clad only in his bloody loin cloth and bound like some common thief, Motecuhzoma looked small. Weak even. She hoped she would not suffer as much in her final hours and gave thanks that fate had not brought her to the terrible pass it had brought Motecuhzoma.

~ ~ ~

Juan Garrido crossed himself and adjusted his breastplate. He had tucked three gold bars under his cotton armor, and they weighed heavy on his chest. He was tempted to take them out, if only to make breathing easier, but that would be folly in the extreme. The gold was safe so long as it was on his person—moving it to a knapsack created needless risk and leaving the gold behind would be an affront to everything Holy. God had not guided him to Tenochtitlan so he could refuse His munificence.

Many of the men claimed God had abandoned them, some even had the temerity to suggest God was punishing them, but Garrido knew better. God had tested them with confinement in Axayacatl's palace, and he would reward His faithful flock by guiding them out of the city under cover of dark. Who else had sent tonight's fog, if not God?

Garrido glanced at the Christians standing beside him. Not all of them were pure of heart, and he prayed those of little faith would realize the error of their ways. God would not save those who ignored his teachings and such men would have little protection against the heathen Indians. Garrido shuddered. He did not want to imagine the horror of being hauled up the steps of a pyramid, only to have his heart torn out for some cheering audience. At least an *auto de fe* victim would strengthen the One True Faith with his death; a sacrifice victim had no such assurance. Garrido squeezed the hilt of his sword and kissed the blade. He would be counting on its sharp edge to keep him safe tonight.

An officer whispered something to some of the men standing in the vanguard. Hushed muttering ensued and Garrido straightened. A few moments later, the mounted men urged their horses forward and departed the palace's safety for the outside world. Garrido sucked in his breath and prayed the Indians would not notice the muffled clop of cloth-wrapped horseshoes. Even if they didn't, could thousands of warriors, soldiers, and slaves really make a stealthy escape?

He crossed himself again and focused on the line of soldiers standing in front of him. It would not be long before they also had to step outside. Everything was still quiet outside, and he prayed the Indians were still ignorant of their movements. The line in front of him shifted forward, and he fell into step behind them.

His heart pounding like a *ngoma* during a funeral ceremony, he marched out of the Palace of Axayacatl with the rest of his Christian brethren. The chill of the still night air took him by surprise, and he clamped his teeth to keep them from chattering. He gazed up at the night sky and tried to guess how many more hours of dark God would afford them. Impossible to know, what with the fog. The stars were just dim lights, and the moon was completely hidden from view. He gave thanks again for the fog. It would do as much to facilitate their escape as the dark, if not more.

Ahead, a horse nickered and was quickly shushed. If he squinted, Garrido could make out certain riders but nothing besides that. They were only forty paces ahead, but that might as well have been half a league. The column made a sharp turn, and he caught a fleeting glimpse of the other column. Not a single man carried a torch, and he hoped the person who was guiding the column had good eyesight. Departing the palace in multiple columns—some through the foyer entrance, others through the wall breaches—made for some complicated logistics, but he understood the logic of it. Time was their enemy tonight. The sooner they departed Tenochtitlan, the safer they would all be.

Off in the distance, a duck honked loudly. Garrido's heart skipped a beat. Was the honk a signal? He stared ahead. The structures nearest Axayacatl's palace had been leveled earlier in the month, but the flat-roofed buildings near the water's edge were still intact. If the Indians meant to ambush them, they would probably hide there. He kept his eyes fixed on the nearest ledges and suppressed a shiver.

He hugged his shield tighter, wishing it were made of steel instead of wood and boiled leather. If the Indians attacked, would it really be enough to keep him safe? Garrido doubted it. The Indians had launched so many attacks against his Christian brethren that many who once had full-body shields now had to make do with scraps of wood half an arm long.

He stepped onto the canal bridge, surprised the Indians had left it intact. Were the Indians trying to lure them out of the palace for an ambush? He would not put such cleverness past them, but he prayed that was not the case.

He glanced down at the still lake water as he passed over the canal. The lake was not especially deep, but the creatures inside it made it more frightening than a rushing river. What kind of fish had legs? It was an affront to everything Holy, and Garrido had not been surprised to learn that the legged fish quickened many stomachs.

He stepped off the bridge onto hard-packed dirt. The leveled buildings were so close he could reach out and touch the razed remains. Many Christians had given their lives to bring those buildings down. Had it not been for their sacrifice, he doubted the column could have made it to the first canal safely. He knew better than to relax his guard, however. The column still had four more canals to cross over before they reached the causeway. And the closer they got to the causeway, the more exposed they would be.

Garrido stepped onto the next canal bridge. The wood groaned, and he prayed God would lend his strength to the bridge. The pack horses, loaded with ingots worth thousands of reals, and the cannons, so heavy they could be used as ballast, still needed to cross. Somewhere behind him, a man coughed into his arm. Garrido glanced at a nearby building. Two stories high and crafted from clay, the building appeared to be a house of some kind. Had the Indians inside heard the cough?

He ran his thumb along the sword guard and stepped onto the next bridge. Often times, the Indians hid on the flat-topped roofs and dropped rocks so heavy they could crush a man's head like a kola nut. What if one of those rocks landed on the canal bridge? He shuddered and kept an eye out for movement. He spotted nothing amiss, but that meant little. Heathens were nothing if not sneaky.

The vanguard ground to a halt at the head of the causeway as the portable bridge was lowered into place. It was an impressive feat of engineering, crafted almost entirely from the ceiling beams of Axayacatl's palace, but it was an unwieldy one also. Transporting the bridge required the labor of more than a hundred and fifty porters, and Garrido had no idea how those men were supposed to move such an ungainly device while being fired upon. If they were fortunate, none of them would have to discover the answer to that question.

Buildings flanked Garrido on every side now. None of the sallies had levelled the structures this far out, and he braced himself for attack. God alone knew how many times the Indians warriors had used the flat-topped roofs to ambush soldiers who had gone out in search of food and water. Even children took part in the attacks, lobbing stones and darts from any rooftop they could climb onto.

Garrido balanced himself on the balls of his feet to try to see over the ledges. No luck. He looked over his shoulder to check the progress of the column. The middle guard had stopped but the bulk of the rearguard had yet to cross the third canal bridge. Garrido furrowed his brow, surprised at how far he could see. If he strained his eyes, he could even make out the outline of Axayacatl's palace.

His mouth went dry. The fog was thinning. He gazed up at the stars. The once dim lights were now shining like polished ingots. Garrido looked back at the portable bridge. It still hadn't been lowered into place. He closed his eyes and prayed.

Now, more than ever, they would need God's protection. Thousands of men could not make an orderly retreat in a dark and unfamiliar city, nor could they protect themselves from warriors who hid on flat-topped roofs and rained down deadly projectiles. If the Indians attacked, the vanguard would have to make a mad dash along the causeway, and he did not even want to imagine the chaos that would entail.

He opened his eyes and took a deep breath, pushing his chest out so much the bars of gold pressed against his breastplate. God would protect him. He had ushered them safely out of the palace—why would He abandon them now?

A mounted man held up his hand to let the vanguard know the portable bridge had been lowered into place, and the marching resumed. Garrido let out a quiet sigh. Not a moment later, a shrill voice cut through the night's silence, and the ambush began.

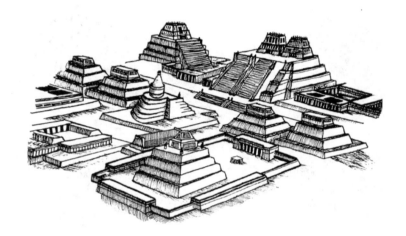

Tenochtitlan

Chapter 26

Cuauhtemoc closed his eyes just before the splatter of
blood hit his face. Disoriented, he shuffled backward and
raised his shield. Something smacked against it, and his
arm went numb. He roared with indignation and lunged
forward with the shield, propelled by his own warriors as
much as his rage. Cuauhtemoc could not see the man he
crashed into but felt him drop to the ground and knew
what he needed to do next.

Turning his *macuahuitl* lengthwise, he raised it high
above his head and brought it down with all the force he
could muster. The man, a dark-skinned porter, threw up
his forearms to protect his face, and Cuauhtemoc's
macuahuitl sank deep into unprotected flesh. Gaping slits
appeared in both his forearms as Cuauhtemoc wrenched
the weapon out.

The porter's howl rent the air and Cuauhtemoc kicked
him in the groin, kicking and kicking until the man finally
rolled out of his way. A moment later, a Tlaxcalteca
warrior came rushing at him with murder in his eyes.

Cuauhtemoc slashed his *macuahuitl* outward, and the
man bent backward to dodge the blow. He moved too
slowly, and the *macuahuitl* tore through his exposed
throat with brutal ease. The warrior collapsed onto the
hard-packed walkway, writhing like a burning snake.

Cuauhtemoc sank into a crouch, ready for the next
warrior to attack. Much to his surprise, none obliged and
his would-be attackers made a disorganized retreat to the
Palace of Axayacatl. In the past, the sight would have
filled him with impotent rage. Now it brought a ragged
smile to his face, and he raised his *macuahuitl*

triumphantly. A loud cheer went up from his men, and a warrior rushed forward to give chase. Cuauhtemoc held up his arm to stop him.

"Later," Cuauhtemoc said. "First, we must see to the others."

The warrior, a thick-set man with biceps as big as melons, nodded and resumed his place in formation. Cuauhtemoc turned around and strode to the back of his squadron. His personal bodyguards followed in his wake but the rest of the warriors stayed put, weary from the battle's exertions.

He had two hundred men when he fell on the rearguard and had expected to lose at least a third of his men in the attack. A quick headcount let Cuauhtemoc know the vast majority of his men were still standing, and he estimated that he had lost no more than a fifth of his force. Nevertheless, they had cut off half the rearguard from the rest of the army. Preventing the other barbarians from escaping would be more of a challenge, but he knew his countrymen would not shirk from the challenge.

He stared at the army's backline, only forty paces ahead. Many of the barbarians were crowding at the city's lakefront as they tried to gain a foothold on the causeway. Cuauhtemoc smiled. The barbarians were no safer on the causeway than they were inside the city. In some ways, they were less safe. Boatmen could attack the barbarians on both sides once they reached the causeway, but neither the Tlaxcalteca nor the teteo could turn back so they threw themselves deeper into the morass. Their fighting formation had lost all coherency. They fought not as a determined group but as desperate individuals, shoving and elbowing their own countrymen aside to chase a mirage of safety.

"Mexica brethren, catch your breath," Cuauhtemoc said. "We will make another attack soon."

The warriors cheered, and Cuauhtemoc ordered some nearby men to rip out the plankings for the first canal bridge. The men did so with glee, whooping and cheering every time a heavy beam sank beneath the murky waters.

Cuauhtemoc wiped sweat from his brow. Motecuhzoma's plan was succeeding beyond anyone's wildest expectations. The hornless stags were useless in the narrow streets, and the thumping weapons had not gone off once the entire night. Weak from hunger and thirst, the barbarians had no interest in fighting defensively and scurried through the streets like frightened mice. The battle had become a rout and might become a massacre yet, if his countrymen pressed the offensive.

Cuauhtemoc glanced at his warriors. Glistening with sweat and covered in life water, some were so exhausted by their exertions they were bent over. Much as he wanted to give them more time to catch their breath, he knew he could not. They could not give the barbarians a chance to reorganize and had to attack the rear line while it was still in disarray. He raised his *macuahuitl* and watched his men lower themselves into a sprinting position. He slashed his arm down, and his warriors flew forward like bolts fired by snapping bows.

He sprinted as fast as he could but could not keep up with some of the younger men and fell to the middle of the pack. None of his warriors said a word, and they rushed along the canal bridge like a strong gust through an open field. Only one more canal to cross before they reached the army's rear.

Cuauhtemoc pushed himself to run faster, sure that his men would slow now that the enemy was closer. Much to his surprise, the squadron leaders picked up their pace. Cuitlahuac smiled and squeezed the hilt of his *macuahuitl*. Bloodlust inspired courage just as much as it inspired depravity.

283

A handful of *teteo* and Tlaxcalteca warriors turned around as the squadron neared, but most were so focused on the causeway melee they did not hear the danger until it was too late. His warriors smashed into the rear like an axe head against a tree trunk, prompting howls and curses that made his heart turn white.

A few paces ahead, a boy dressed in nothing but a loin cloth threw himself at a fully armored *teotl* with such force he carried the man off his feet while a warrior with arms as thin as corn stalks dislodged teeth with a bloody club. Cuauhtemoc roared with delight and threw himself into the fray by leaping over a corpse and smashing his *macuahuitl* into an upraised blade.

The thin steel blade wedged itself firmly into the *macuahuitl's* thick wooden plank and, confident the blade would not be able to slice all the way through, Cuauhtemoc pushed downward with the *macuahuitl*. The *teotl* dropped to a knee and pulled desperately on the hilt of his weapon to dislodge it. Cuauhtemoc kicked the *teotl* in the chest, and he fell backward with a cry.

Falling helped dislodge his blade, but it did the soldier little good: a nearby warrior jammed a spearhead so deep into his chin it disappeared completely. Cuauhtemoc kicked him one more time for good measure and searched for his next foe. A shout alerted him to danger, and he leaped sideways to doge the axe-spear of an angry *teotl*.

Cuauhtemoc's guard rushed forward to defend him, and the *teotl* stabbed him in the sternum. Enraged, Cuauhtemoc smashed his *macuahuitl* down on the *teotl's* exposed wrist, prompting an agonized scream that was cut short by a melee of club blows.

A flash of long dark hair near the water's edge caught his eye. No warrior would have hair that long. He pushed deeper into the enemy's formation in pursuit. He shoved a *teotl* warrior aside with his shield and cut down a

Tlaxcalteca with a slash of his *macuahuitl*. He caught another glimpse of hair and his heart skipped a beat.

Cotton Flower always kept her hair long. If she was still alive, she would be in the column, not Axayacatl's palace. Cuauhtemoc roared out her name, and a startled girl with long dark hair turned his way. His breath caught as he took in her appearance. Just a few rows ahead, he had no trouble making out his niece's swollen nose, her split lip, or her bruised cheek. A dangerous rage took hold of him.

Cotton Flower was daughter to Motecuhzoma, and the heir to an ancient lineage. Only through marriage to her would the next Great Speaker gain legitimacy and rescuing her took priority over any other task.

Without thinking, Cuauhtemoc threw himself into the thick of the crowd. A Tlaxcalteca lunged toward him, and the tip of his spear missed Cuauhtemoc's hip by a finger span. Without thinking, Cuauhtemoc smashed his *macuahuitl* into the man's neck. His victim went limp and collapsed to the ground.

A moment later, a *teotl* slashed out at him with a heavy, two-handed blade. Cuauhtemoc ducked but did not drop his shield fast enough to spare it damage. The shimmering blade sliced through his wooden shield like a dagger through vellum and cleaved the rim clean off.

Motivated by desperation as much as anything, Cuauhtemoc vaulted forward with his shield and slammed into the *teotl*. The *teotl* grunted and staggered backward. A surprised shout, followed by a great splash, let him know the *teotl* had fallen into the nearby canal.

A guard helped Cuauhtemoc to his feet, and Mexica warriors surged forward to surround him. He muttered thanks to his guard and took quick stock of his surroundings.

Most of the barbarians were stretched out along the length of the causeway, harassed on all sides by warriors

285

who fired upon them from their canoes, but small pockets could still be found within Tenochtitlan proper. Some of the barbarians retreated into residential neighborhoods, only to be set upon by outraged citizens. Others tried to yield, only to be cut down by irate warriors.

The *teteo* and Tlaxcalteca still held Tepantzinco, the headway that controlled access to the causeway, but Cuauhtemoc doubted they could keep it much longer. Their defensive formation grew weaker by the moment, and his countrymen were quick to exploit every new gap.

He caught another glimpse of his niece. Three rows ahead, but her captors were pulling her deeper into the column. If they managed to get her to the causeway, there would be no saving her. Cuauhtemoc glanced at the men nearest him. Three of his guards had been slain, and two had been wounded, so he had only five men to protect him now.

He raised his weapon for all to see and forced his way through his own men to reach the enemy's backline. A line of angry spears greeted him, and he bent backward to dodge the spearhead that almost took him in the chest. He shuffled backward and urged one of his guards to hand him a signal conch.

All too eager to comply, a guard shoved a pearly pink conch into his breast. Cuauhtemoc grabbed the precious shell and jammed it against his lips so hard he tasted blood. He made four short blasts in quick succession, blowing with all his diaphragm, and the harsh blare blotted out the piercing screams and the loud clangs.

The spearmen exchanged worried glances and huddled closer together. Cuauhtemoc grinned. They could not have made a worse move.

A loud hissing filled the air, and a thick storm of arrows, slings, and darts rained down on the enemy's backline. *Teteo* dropped to the ground like felled saplings as warriors fired upon them from the safety of their canoes, and the spearmen were forced to take cover under their shields. The move brought them little reprieve as Mexica warriors then lunged forward with heavy spears to gore the vulnerable *teteo*.

In some cases, spearheads broke against hard metal armor, but most of his warriors knew better than to aim for the *cuirasses*, training their lances on throats, eyes, and arm pits instead. In a matter of moments, the two rows of *teteo* spearmen were wiped out, a victory that seemed impossible the week before.

Cuauhtemoc blew the conch twice to signal a halt to the fusillade and ran forward with his warriors to attack the column's backline. A Tlaxcalteca warrior slashed at him with a *macuahuitl*, but Cuauhtemoc ducked under it and buried his *macuahuitl* in the man's belly. The man collapsed to the side, wrenching the *macuahuitl* from Cuauhtemoc's weary hands, but he did not bother trying to retrieve the weapon. Instead, he pulled out his stone dagger and shoved his way through the column, stabbing and jabbing anything vulnerable but pushing aside anything heavy with his shield.

He heard Cotton Flower call out for him and the sound of her voice, the sheer proximity of it, made his heart leap. Cuauhtemoc tossed aside a man who sought to slow his progress and studied the mess of men to find his niece. Only one row of soldiers separated them now. A *teotl* slashed at him with a long knife, and he twisted to the side to avoid the wicked blade. Cuauhtemoc's foot caught on something, and he fell before he could catch himself. He landed on a wounded man and rolled over to cover himself with his shield.

The *teotl* raised his long knife to make the killing blow, but one of Cuauhtemoc's guards stabbed him in the armpit before he could bring his weapon down. The *teotl* screamed and retreated into the thick of the disorganized column. Cuauhtemoc grabbed a long knife and slashed at everything in front of him. His strokes were inartful, sloppy even, but deadly all the same. His guards rushed forward to support him, and a spray of blood filled the air as his countrymen cut through the backline of the enemy.

Perhaps recognizing that it would be futile to try to make their way across the crowded and sabotaged causeway, the men who were supposed to hold Tepantzinco threw themselves into the lake to swim for a distant shore. Some sank like rocks, but those strong enough to keep their heads above water were quickly discovered by the boatmen. Cuauhtemoc was tempted to throw himself into the water to give chase to the cowards, but he had to save his niece first. He slashed at a teotl only half an arm's length away, missed, and was about to draw back his arm to make another slash when someone hit him in the abdomen.

He stumbled backward and raised the long knife to bludgeon the person wrapped around his waist. Not a moment too soon, he realized the person was Cotton Flower.

He cast the long knife aside and picked her up in his sweat-lathered arms. All thoughts of violence abandoned him, and he rushed away from the causeway to find somewhere safe. He crossed over two canal bridges, and would have run over twenty more if necessary, but a small whimper made him halt.

He lowered Cotton Flower onto her feet and dropped to a knee in front of her.

"How fare you, princess?" Cuauhtemoc asked.

She flinched at the mention of her title, and his pulse quickened. He brushed aside her dirty hair and looked into her sad eyes. Phlegm dribbled out of her bruised nose, and he wiped her face with a trembling hand. He noticed the scabbed blood on her thighs, and his stomach tightened.

288

The rapid pounding of footsteps let him know his harried and out-of-breath guards had finally found him, and he stood up to greet them. "Escort the princess to a healer," he said, motioning to the two nearest ones. They nodded and hurried Cotton Flower away before she could make a sound.

Cuauhtemoc swallowed the lump in his throat and turned toward his other guards. "Find new weapons. The fight is not yet over."

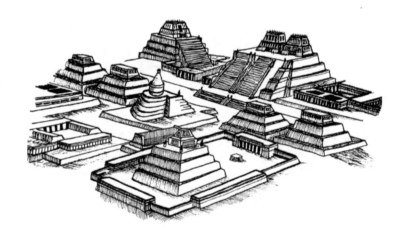

Tenochtitlan

Xicotencatl yelped as something sharp drove into his shoulder blade. His armor absorbed the brunt of the impact, but a painful scratching let him know the projectile had pierced the thick cotton stitching. He readjusted his shield and muttered a prayer.

Not that it would help much. The gods clearly did not favor their cause in this battle. The retreat was nothing short of a disaster. He had expected the fighting to be fierce, but he assumed the worst of it would take place in the city. Terrible as it had been, the causeway was a killing ground, and there was no place in the column more dangerous than the rearguard. Flanked on both sides by angry boat men, the men in the rearguard could do little besides cower under their shields as Mexica warriors savaged their backline.

Owing to the mess of dead bodies and the missing sections in the causeway, the column shuffled forward at a slow crawl, and Xicotencatl had no expectations of meaningful reprieve. What was he supposed to do once he reached the next gap in the causeway? He had only been able to cross the first one because of the portable bridge, but it had proven decidedly less portable than expected and would avail him none now that he already crossed over it. Countless Tlaxcalteca warriors had died trying to dislodge the bridge from the first gap, and he wanted to throttle the *teteo* who had told him they would be able to use it to cross all the gaps on the causeway.

A sling wrapped itself around the head of a nearby man, crushing the bridge of his nose like a ripe tomato. Xicotencatl grimaced and moved forward a pace. When he reached the next gap, he would need to jump it or take his chances in the water.

He studied the surface of the lake. Thousands of boatmen were churning it into a froth in their rush to paddle toward the causeway, but the smarter ones stayed back so they could fire on the column with their long-range weapons.

A wave of screaming distracted him, and he looked backward. His breath caught—a crazed horse was charging toward him! He threw himself to the pavement and curled himself into a ball. The horse's hoof smashed into the ground a hair's breadth from his head, and he squeezed his eyes shut. When he opened them again, the gold-laden horse had passed over him, and he caught a flash of its tail as the giant beast tumbled off the causeway.

He tried to stand up, but the stampede of men who followed in the wake of the horse proved equally crazed. A foot came down on his ankle and Xicotencatl screamed. He slashed out with his *macuahuitl* to punish the careless *teotl*. His swing went wide, and the soldier disappeared into the crush of men fleeing along the causeway.

The stampede ended as quickly as it began and Xicotencatl was suddenly alone, abandoned by the *teteo* and his own men. He cursed and tore his gaze away from the disorganized column to behold the horde of enraged Mexica warriors slashing and clawing their way through the *teteo* backline. It would not hold much longer. Too many of the supporting ranks had given in to the false safety of flight, and the handful of armored spearmen who had chosen to stand against the Mexica would soon be dead.

Xicotencatl reached for his injured ankle and winced as a bolt of pain shot through his leg. He grimaced, waited for the pain to abate, and reached for a discarded shield. The horse had punched a hole through the center of it, but the arched shield looked undamaged otherwise. He dragged it over his person and scooted toward the edge of the causeway. He could not jump a gap with his injured ankle, so he'd have to take his chances in the water. He glanced one last time at the backline and wondered if he should join the men who had chosen to stand their ground.

He exhaled and tossed aside his *macuahuitl*. He had no interest in dying for gold or Tenochtitlan. He wished only to return to Tlaxcala and surround himself with loved ones. He curled into a ball and rolled off the causeway with shield in hand.

The fall was not long, just a heartbeat or two, but the sudden collision with the cold wall of water robbed him of his breath and ripped the shield from his hand. Gasping and disoriented, he broke the surface of the water and took in his surroundings. The nearest boatman was nearly thirty paces away and much too focused on launching spears to take any notice of him.

Xicotencatl swam toward the shield and draped it over his head. He took a deep shuddering breath and expelled water from his nose. Rain had been scarce the past few weeks, and he could keep most of his head above water if he stood on the tips of his toes.

A small wave hit him in the face, making him choke and sputter. He spat algae-laden water from his mouth and jumped to avoid the next wave. His teeth chattered, and he thought of home to keep himself warm. He needed to make it back, and he needed to help his men get back there also. He prayed to the gods for strength and set off in the direction of the shore.

~ ~ ~

Cortés broke the surface of the water and wiped the muck from his eye visor. He had fallen off the causeway trying to grab a teetering Christian, an Extremeño from Narváez's expedition, but he did not see the man anywhere. Probably sank to the bottom of the lake, considering his heavy plate armor.

A high-pitched scream, followed by a loud splashing, prompted Cortés to turn around. A large wave enveloped him, and he spat out lake scum once it passed. Someone shouted his name, and he glanced in that direction.

A canoe filled with angry warriors was heading his way.

Cortés dove underneath the water and tore his way through the muck-filled darkness. His hand struck something solid and unrelenting, and he broke the surface of the water again. The causeway loomed before him; he had swum the wrong way! Cortés clenched his fist in frustration and went dizzy with pain. He had bent a nail backward when he raked his hand across the unforgiving stone.

Mexica warriors yelled out his name again, closer this time, and Cortés whipped his head toward the shore. It was at least forty paces away and the closer he got, the more obstacles he would encounter. He took a deep breath and plunged into the water, attacking the scummy surface with choppy strokes and angry kicks.

Muck clung to his eyelashes and his ingots pressed uncomfortably against his cotton armor, restricting his movement and his breathing. The shouts were getting closer. He begged his arms to move faster but it was no use. His hand was throbbing, his lungs were burning, and his legs were heavy.

A light spear sailed past his head, and he dove underneath the water again. He stayed under for half a minute and broke the surface with a great gasping. Something hit his shoulder, and he submerged himself once more.

Cortés could see nothing in the inky darkness, but he could hear angry shouting directly above him. Cortés groped for his rapier and tugged it from the sheath. He gently patted the boat's keel, probing for weak patching or rot.

A muffled shout reached his water-logged ears, and he abandoned the search. He prayed to the Lord for strength, grabbed the hilt with two hands, and pushed up with all his might. The Toledo blade punched through the boat's thin underside like a fist through parchment and caught on something that jerked and spasmed violently.

Sudden splashes broke out all around him. He wrenched the blade loose and swam away from the loud noises. When he finally broke the surface again, his lungs were screaming but his feet had finally found purchase.

He trudged toward the shore, a stone's throw away. A handful of Christians were wading through the water just ahead of him, not even a pike's length away, and he shouted at them to stop. Not one did.

Can they hear me? Impossible to know. The din of battle was so loud he could hardly hear himself. He waved his sword above his head and smacked the water in frustration.

The man nearest him turned and pointed behind Cortés. He turned around just as a club smashed into his helmet. Cortés went limp and did not offer any resistance as strong arms wrapped themselves around him and dragged him away.

He mumbled weakly as he was pulled into a canoe and tried to sit up, only to be pushed down by irate Mexica warriors. Someone wrenched the sword from his hand and tossed it overboard.

Shocked into action, he kicked the man nearest him and punched another man square in the nose. A painted warrior raised his club, and Cortés covered his face. He braced himself for a punishing hit, but the blow never came. Instead, the warrior shouted something, stiffened, and then fell to the side. Confused, Cortés opened his eyes just as an armored soldier dragged him from the canoe.

Mexica warriors surged forward to grab him but another Spaniard came forward, swinging a great two-handed sword that severed heads and opened stomachs, and forced the Mexica warriors to dive for safety.

The armored soldier, a Christian he hardly knew, pulled him toward the shore and shouted for others to help. Men rushed forward and dragged him through the water like a limp marionette. Once they neared the shore, he shouted for them to stop and pushed them away so he could stand on his own. He ordered some man he did not recognize to fetch him a horse and trudged forward on unsteady feet. Although the water only came up to his knees, each step required enormous effort. Thankfully, the pounding in his head was subsiding.

By the time he reached dry land, his knees were shaking, and he was grateful to have the reins of a horse shoved into his hands. He let some of the nearby men help him into the saddle and leaned forward to keep his balance. His head swimming, he muttered thanks and bid the horse toward the causeway. A disorganized crowd of men blocked his passage, and he did not trust the horse enough to force a way through. And even if he did, he did not trust the men to allow him through.

The neat procession that had departed Axayacatl's palace had vanished, replaced by a shameful mess of men who stumbled and ran along the causeway. Some were so desperate to reach the shore they jumped into the water and waded through the shallows to reach dry land. More than a few men who jumped off the causeway did not surface again, weighed down by heavy bars of gold or simple exhaustion.

Tears filled his eyes as he watched men and women plunge to their death, but he refused to look away. He watched as lombards and falconets tumbled off the causeway, crushing canoes as well as Christians, watched as horses and packs of gold sank to the bottom of the lake.

There had to be something he could do to save the battle! God had not given him a magnificent army just to let the Mexica destroy it. God would intervene, he was sure of it. He would send a wave that would scatter the canoes; He would send cavalry to clear the causeway of Mexica warriors.

Cortés waited but the Lord did not bless him with a miracle. The God that gave him the wit and the tact to turn Narváez's men to his own cause, to forge an alliance with the Tlaxcalteca, had abandoned him.

His stomach tightened, and he studied the faces of his men for strength. Streaked with blood, grime, and sweat, they were a sorry sight that gave him little cause for inspiration or pride. Unnerved by the unending, miserable stream of humanity that continued to pour off the causeway, the horse retreated backward. Cortés made no attempt to halt it.

His horse neighed, and he realized another mare was near. He glanced to his right, surprised but pleased to see Pedro sitting atop a borrowed mount. Cortés shouted Pedro's name, but his hoarse voice did not carry, and Pedro did not turn. Cortés spurred his horse into a trot, and stopped in front of Pedro.

"Where is the rest of the rearguard?" Cortés asked.

Pedro stared at the ground, his teeth chattering and his clothes torn.

Cortés leaned forward and lowered his voice. "Where are the people I entrusted to your charge?"

Pedro stiffened but kept his gaze fixed on the ground. "All of them are here," he said in a choked voice. "If some are not, forget them."

Cortés' eyes widened. Forget them? Surely Pedro did not believe it proper to abandon Christians in need of aid. Cortés straightened, anger building in his breast. His hands tightened around the reins, and he thought of all the terrible things he should say to Pedro. He sucked in his breath, determined to put the reprimand into words, but the harsh invective caught in his gullet like a jagged bone.

Pedro's hands were shaking. The brave Extremeño who prided himself on charging into battle had wet himself.

Cortés tore his eyes away from Pedro's scared figure and glanced at the cluttered causeway. There had to be hundreds strewn along it, and he did not want to speculate how many men had been claimed by the lake. Had he not told the men it would be dangerous to carry too much gold?

He swallowed the lump in his throat and thought of all the men he would never see again. Would he never see León again, the wayward officer who betrayed his own uncle to support Cortés' captaincy? Would he never see Saucedo again, the soft-hearted officer who spent weeks exploring an unfamiliar shoreline just to find the fleet? And what of the gold? Where was the pack horse Cortés had loaded a dozen boxes of gold onto?

"Gone," he whispered. Buried at the bottom of the lake, no good to man or fish. Was God so cruel as to smite the bulk of his army and his fortune, all in the same night?

Cortés mumbled a half-hearted farewell to Pedro as he brushed past him. He fixed his gaze on the dim lights of Tenochtitlan. He had spent eight long months there and knew the profile of the city so well that he could identify every pyramid and every palace by the shape of its dark outline. He knew the layout of the city better than he knew his encomienda, but it mattered not one whit. He never knew the hearts of the people who lived there, and he realized now that entering the city was a terrible mistake. The residents never had any love for him or his countrymen, and Cortés would never again be welcomed into the beautiful floating city where he had won and lost a fortune.

A volley of slings, spears, and darts arced through the air and a sharp-eyed soldier yelled a warning to the rest of the army. Without thinking, Cortés kicked the horse into a canter and made for a nearby tree.

He dismounted under its voluminous canopy, confident the thick network of branches and leaves would protect him from any more volleys fired by the angry boatmen. Some of his countrymen tried to return fire, but the water-logged muskets and crossbows were useless. Only the Tlaxcalteca succeeded in returning fire, letting loose a volley of arrows, spears, and slings that caught the boatmen by surprise.

The Mexica warriors who had been so eager to reach the shore slowed their pace. Some turned around altogether. Canoes crashed into one another, and the warriors who lacked shields jumped into the water. He gave thanks the boatmen were not better organized, but he doubted the Tlaxcalteca could hold them back much longer. He had marched five thousand Tlaxcalteca warriors into Tenochtitlan, but he would be surprised if a quarter of them survived the retreat.

Most of those warriors were strangers to him. He knew not their names, their ages, or their families and now the information was forever lost to him. He could not even say with confidence why they marched into Tenochtitlan with him. Perhaps they had been motivated by simple avarice, perhaps they hankered for glory, or perhaps it was something else entirely. It did not matter now. They were dead, and his great army was no more. His fortune was forfeit, and his standing with the men.... Cortés could not bear to think about it anymore. He had a retreat to organize.

The tears came sudden and unbidden as he realized the full scale of his defeat, and shame brought him to a knee. He leaned against the tree, hoping his men would not think less of him for giving in to weakness and cursing himself for ever stepping foot in Tenochtitlan. Cortés knew he would always be haunted by the tragic events of this sad night and prayed God would lend him the strength for vengeance.

Part Three
The Retreat
July 1520

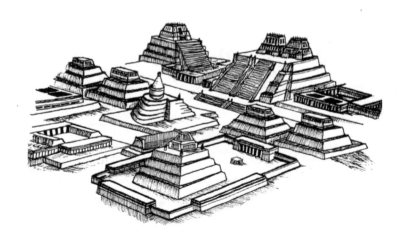

Tenochtitlan

Cacamulco Area

Tlalli adjusted the cloth wrapped around the lower half of his face and stepped over a dead Tlaxcalteca warrior. The corpse would not begin to decompose for another day or so, but a dizzying miasma already hung over it.

A light spear jutted out of the warrior's belly, and Tlalli assumed that had something to do with the foul smell. He doubted the man had died on account of the spear, though. More likely it was the dagger sticking out of his eye. A girl trailing behind Tlalli stopped in front of the corpse. Tlalli did not wait for her.

He had only fourteen years to his name, but he was on very intimate terms with death. Mother died bringing him into the world, and Father died in battle. Both deaths were glorious in their own right, and Chimalli was most insistent that Father had died well and honorably. Tlalli did not know if he could put stock by his word, however. Just saying Tezoc made Chimalli's face contort with pain and he apologized so profusely, so loudly that Tlalli knew something was amiss.

What it was, he did not know, nor did he expect to soon find out. Chimalli could keep his secrets; Tlalli intended to keep his distance. Chimalli had offered him a place in his household, and Tlalli rejected it out of hand. Better to not have anyone look after him than stay with the man who may have played a part in Father's death.

Tlalli dropped to a knee to better inspect a scraggly-bearded corpse. Most of the *teteo* dressed in light metal armor, steel as they called it, but the bearded teotl wore only cotton armor.

He shaded his eyes and looked up. Tonatiuh was still low in the sky, but scavenging would be much more difficult once the adults came out. Had it not been for the loud noises last night, Tlalli would have come out earlier. He wished that he had. The best items were probably gone by now, taken by braver and more desperate orphans.

The stinky corpse made a strange noise, and he stared down. The *teotl* was lying face down, but his collar bone was not touching ground. Tlalli craned his head. There was a small bulge under the man's cotton armor. Tlalli gritted his teeth and rolled the man over, setting off a small clanking. Tlalli frowned. He saw no metal on the *teotl's* person so why was he clanking? He patted the bulge on the *teotl's* chest, pleased to feel something solid and substantial.

He grabbed his knife, an obsidian dagger that once belonged to Father, and slashed at the cotton armor. The knife did not lack for a sharp edge, but the crisscross stitching proved difficult to saw through. He set the knife down and scooted forward, careful not to take his gaze off the dead man's glassy eyes. He half-expected the man to blink or grab his arm, but he remained still as a log as Tlalli reached under his armor. His fingers brushed against something cold and smooth, and he reoriented himself to get a better position. A chill passed through him as his elbow brushed against the *teotl's* cheek, but he pushed his hand in deeper so he could tug the mysterious item loose.

Much to his surprise, he found himself holding a bar of gold. He turned it over in his hands, confused by the crude shape. It must have been molded by human hand, but there was no artistry to it whatsoever. What was the point of melting a golden sculpture just to craft it into some simple, unassuming block?

Tlalli shrugged and dropped the slim bar into his netbag. He then reached under the man's armor to grab more. By the time he was done, he had pulled out five bars, each one heavy as a full-grown melon. He stared at the *teotl*. Had the man really thought he could make a quick get-away with five bars of gold tucked under his armor? If so, he had been a fool of the worst sort.

Tlalli picked up the netbag and lifted it to test the strength of the rush fibers. Carrying more than three bars would be difficult, but he did not need many anyway. When it came to buying food at the market, green jade and Quetzal feathers would be more helpful than gold. He stuffed two of the gold bars back into the man's armor and turned him over so that he was lying on his stomach once more.

He secured the netbag to his back, stood up, and made his way toward the causeway. A thick tangle of bodies blocked the entrance, and he stopped to take in the sight. Most were Tlaxcalteca, but he spotted *teteo* corpses amongst the pile also. Word had it that thousands of Tlaxcalteca had been killed during last night's battle, along with hundreds of *teteo*. Tenochtitlan had won a great victory, but barbarians like Cortés had been allowed to escape, along with Xicotencatl and Malintze. Worst of all, the fire-haired *teotl* who led the Flaying Festival massacre still drew breath. Tlalli hoped the warriors would give chase to the survivors, but he doubted any such chase would soon happen. Wounded warriors had to be attended to, and captives needed to be sacrificed.

Tlalli took a deep breath and placed his foot on the back of a dead porter. The stiff corpse proved a good foothold, and he picked his way through the pile of corpses without putting his foot down on solid ground once. He stopped in front of the portable bridge, still wedged in the first gap of the causeway.

He lowered a single foot onto the blocky, wooden planks. The boards creaked, but the bridge did not give in the slightest. He set his other foot down and took a small step forward, ready to jump if any of the boards gave way. Thankfully, the bridge held and made only a few creaks and groans as he walked across it. He took a deep breath once he had both feet on solid stone again. He looked over the edge of the causeway. A multitude of corpses stared back at him, bobbing on the water's surface like water lilies.

Many of the women wore extravagant dresses spun from fine cloth, and he figured they were wives of some kind. Many looked as if they came from the coastal lands or Tlaxcala, but some had skin as pale as *octli*. No matter where they hailed from, Tlalli knew that few of the scavengers would take an interest in them. Only poor corpses floated—corpses heavy with valuables rested amidst the muck.

A small groan made him start. He whipped his head to the side and spotted a *teotl*, only six paces away, who was still drawing breath. He made his way over slowly, his heart pounding like a festival drum.

He came to a standstill half an arm's length away from the *teotl* and studied him with a careful eye. Most of the *teteo* had skin white as maguey buds, but this one had skin darker than his own. His dark skin was just one quality that set him apart, though. He also wore a silver necklace, and his left eye was coated in a pale gloss.

Tlalli kneeled next to the *teotl* and held his knife at the ready. Careful not to take his gaze off the *teotl*, he reached for the necklace.

"Don't," muttered the *teotl* in Nahuatl. Tlalli jumped to his feet, dropping the knife. How did the *teotl* know Nahuatl? He narrowed his eyes and clenched his teeth. Nothing about the *teotl* made sense. He possessed no sword, he had skin dark as mahogany, and his hair grew in tight, dark curls.

His arm trembled a bit. He squeezed the hilt of his knife. The *teotl* only had a few hours left, that much was obvious. He had a *macuahuitl* buried in his stomach and could not move without assistance. To kill him would be an act of mercy as much as it would be an act of justice.

"Water... please," whispered the *teotl*.

Tlalli stiffened, shocked by the *teotl's* impudence. The teteo had taken his father, his childhood, his status, and now this *teotl* had the temerity to beg him for help? Tlalli slipped off the netbag and wrapped his hands around the bag's neck. He hoisted the bag up, his arm shaking from the effort of holding the three gold bars above his head.

"This is for my father," Tlalli said. He took a deep breath and slammed the netbag down with all his might. Not satisfied he had killed the *teotl*, he raised it and smashed it down on his face again. By the time he was sure the dark-skinned *teotl* was dead, his shoulder was burning, and the net was dripping with life water.

He gazed down at his feet, staring at the pool of red gathering around his toes, and the flecks of gore that dotted his bare shins. He stepped backward. The puddle was growing rapidly. Unless he could find a way to stanch the blood flow, it would surround him completely and make him dirty and smelly.

Tlalli put the bag down, careful to place it on dry stone, and bent over to grab the teotl by his cotton armor. He pulled up, rolled the corpse onto its side, and pushed it over. He did it over and over again until he finally maneuvered the corpse from the middle of the causeway to the edge.

He wiped the sweat from his eyes. The necklace dangled over the edge of the causeway, and Tlalli slipped it off the corpse with a gentle pull.

He held it up to better examine the craftsmanship. The silver chain was stained with blood and tarnished from exposure but, peering closely, he spotted what looked like a woman's face in the pendant of the necklace. She bore no likeness to any woman he had ever seen—she had a large nose and curly hair—and he wondered who she was. Perhaps the *teotl's* mother? He looked down at the man he had killed. He did not see much resemblance between his victim and the woman. Perhaps the carving was not supposed to represent the woman in her likeness.

Tlalli closed his hand around the pendant and hurled the necklace into the lake. It landed in the water with a gentle plop and made only a small ripple as it sank beneath the surface. Satisfied the *teteo* would never recover the item, he kicked the corpse into the fetid lake water.

The dark-skinned *teotl* hit the water with a great splash, but he did not sink to the bottom as Tlalli expected. No matter. The *teotl* would never again bother him or his people. He prayed the same would hold true for the rest of the *teteo* and their allies.

~ ~ ~

Xicotencatl gritted his teeth and trudged forward with the rest of the column. Two hundred times twenty of his men were dead. Men with families, men who had trusted him, all for naught. What would he say to the widows, when they asked him what happened to their husbands?

He did not know if he could admit that most of them died trying to flee a city they never should have entered. Such a death was neither just nor glorious. He sighed and wiped sweat away from his eyes. So many of the prominent men and women of Tlaxcala had high hopes for the alliance with the *teteo*. A crowd had gathered to watch them leave Tlaxcala, full of smiling children and proud wives. He doubted any such crowd would greet them on their return to Tlaxcala. If they made it back at all.

Xicotencatl and the rest of the survivors had left Tenochtitlan three days prior, and they had been harried by Mexica warriors almost the entire time. In total, the column numbered no more than eighty times twenty and while his forces outnumbered the *teteo*, he did not know if that would remain the case for long. Injured men dropped by the wayside with alarming regularity, and many of his warriors had come down with terrible fevers.

Every now and then, they came across an *altepetl* with food and water, but the locals were loath to share and quick to attack. Desperation had driven some of the men to eat grass, but even that was in short supply now. He shook his head and prayed the march would soon be over. They would be safe once they reached Tlaxcalteca territory, but the army was still many days out.

A sudden cramp seized his calf, and he limped out of formation to seat himself on a large rock. He took a moment to catch his breath and rubbed his aching muscles. He cursed the sun for bearing down on him with such unrelenting might and took in his surroundings as he waited for the pain to subside. Small shrubs and bushes dominated the barren landscape, but he spied little in the way of edible food. What it lacked in sustenance, it made up for in gravelly slopes and blocky boulders. The austere bleakness had a grim beauty that reminded him of home, but the narrow ridges and loose deposit did not make for easy marching. Fortunately, recent rains had swelled the nearby ponds so water was plentiful, but that did little to ease the sharp hunger pangs.

Xicotencatl rested a hand on his empty stomach, fantasizing about all the food he would eat once they were back in Tlaxcala. He would gorge himself on corn cakes and fowl and anything else he could get his hands on.

The cramp eased as he thought about all the pleasures that would soon be his, and he sucked in a deep breath. Only a few more days until they reached home. What he was going through now was no more than a fast, and he would be stronger for it. He allowed himself to become soft when he was in Tenochtitlan, and he needed to purge himself of weakness for the battles to come. Otherwise, the Mexica would surely prevail over Tlaxcala.

The faint aroma of corn cakes wafted toward Xicotencatl. He furrowed his brow. Was he imagining the smell? He took a deep sniff, but the smell was no more. He grunted and cast his gaze toward the *altepetl* in the distance. It was called Cacamulco, if he remembered correctly. The *altepetl* did not seem especially large, he estimated that no more than one hundred times twenty people lived there, and he suspected the townsfolk knew little of hunger. They probably ate corn cakes every day. For all he knew, they were gorging themselves this very moment.

Anger welled in his empty stomach. A few months ago, he commanded so many men he could have encircled the entire *altepetl* multiple times over to demand food and lodging. His once great army was just a shadow of itself, and he gained nothing from his time in Tenochtitlan save some new wounds. Every hostage of note had been recaptured by the Mexica or killed during the escape, and the great hurt his warriors had inflicted on Tenochtitlan during the Flayed Festival had been repaid many times in kind.

Xicotencatl massaged his temple. The march had been hard on everyone, himself included. His ragged armor was held together by threadbare stitching, and it would avail him little in a serious battle. The shield that helped him escape during the Sad Night had proven too heavy to carry for days on end, and he abandoned it in favor of a round shield five hands across. Even that had proven too burdensome to carry, and he traded it for a handful of food the day before. He had no shield whatsoever and had little to defend himself besides his *macuahuitl*. He did not want to think about what would happen when he was too tired to carry that.

An injured mastiff limped past him. He always thought of dogs as friendly animals, but the dogs he had grown up with could fit in the palm of his hand. The *teteo* dogs were six hands tall in most cases and had teeth as sharp as obsidian. They were vicious on the battlefield, and most of his countrymen gave the *teteo* dogs a wide berth. Xicotencatl had little love for the snarling beasts, but they had proven most useful in the battles against the Mexica. He suspected many of his countrymen owed them their lives.

He whistled and bid the striped mastiff over. The dog turned toward him, its eyes glistening with pain. He whistled again and patted his thigh. He knew not a word of Spanish, but he trusted the dog to recognize him as a friend. With some trepidation, the dog limped toward him, careful to keep its front paw elevated. The dog stopped in front of him and Xicotencatl slowly reached for the dog's wounded paw. It whimpered a little as he examined its paw but did not growl or bark.

Xicotencatl flipped the dog's paw over. A shard of obsidian was embedded in the dog's pad. Xicotencatl squared his shoulders and pinched the glass shard between his fingers. The beast stiffened and Xicotencatl froze. He stared at the dog's fat lips, waiting to see if the dog would bare its teeth. Confident the dog trusted him, he released his breath and pulled the shard out. The dog pulled its paw back and licked the bleeding wound. The dog wagged its tail, licked his hand, and trotted off to join the rest of the column.

He smiled and stood. His calf felt much better. He tested his leg to see if it could take his weight and, satisfied that it would not betray him again, he made his way back to the column's left flank. He had to be strong, and not just for his own sake. The others were looking to him for strength. It was his responsibility to guide them home. Moreover, he still had loved ones that needed him.

Gods be praised, his daughter had survived the flight from Tenochtitlan; unfortunately, her accursed husband had also survived. Xicotencatl did not doubt that the fire-haired brute would try to father children on her at some point, but he hoped he did not live to see that day.

A pained scream split the air. He cocked his head toward the sound, and his eyes went wide as he took in the sight of the volley raining down on the left flank of the column. The Mexica were attacking again!

More screams broke out, and the column bulged outward to escape the onslaught of darts, slings, and spears. The column swallowed Xicotencatl whole, and he was surrounded by panicked men on every side. The screams were louder now, and he had to push and shove to keep from being bowled over.

The *teteo* yelled something indecipherable, and the sharp crack of muskets broke out. New screams filled the air, but they were farther away and less panic-inducing. Nonetheless, the column had yet to slow its hurried pace and frightened men were peeling off to hurry down the gravelly slopes.

Teteo and Tlaxcalteca shouted at each other and the enemy, but not a single word escaped Xicotencatl's clenched jaws. Once again, he was fleeing for his life and more of his men were dying, all because the statesmen of Tlaxcala decreed it wise to ally with the impertinent *teteo*.

A mounted *teotl* rushed alongside the column's left flank. Xicotencatl could not understand any of his orders, but he knew the voice belonged to Cortés. The taste of bile filled his mouth. Too long had he been forced to listen to his unctuous pleas and his deranged fantasies. No *teotl*, save Pedro, deserved to suffer more than that one.

The gods must have agreed because it was right at that moment a rock smashed into Cortés' helmet. He reeled to the side but stayed upright in his saddle. Xicotencatl cursed under his breath. Once again, Cortés had been saved by his armor. Perhaps one day it would fail him. Tlaxcala had suffered greatly on account of Cortés' terrible ambitions, and Xicotencatl prayed every day he would be able to repay the *teteo* in kind.

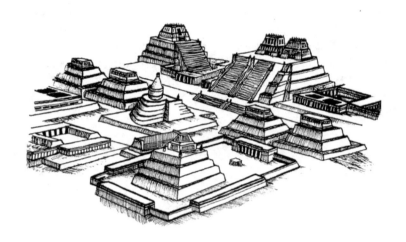

Tenochtitlan

Otampan Valley

Cuauhtemoc curled his nose as the smell of *teteo* came wafting toward him. How the *teteo* failed to notice their own stench never ceased to amaze him. When they first entered Tenochtitlan, their odor made almost as great an impression on him as their weapons. Having spent many weeks confined to Axayacatl's Palace, their stench had worsened and curdled into something sour. He was glad, of course, that so many *teteo* were finally being put to death, but he could do without the miasma and the screaming. He would have been gladder still if he could take leave of the city to pursue the fleeing barbarians, but he first had to confer with Great Speaker Cuitlahuac.

He shot a quick glance at Chimalli, pleased to see that the new Cutter of Men was also discomfited by the interminable waiting. The relish Chimalli took in the bloodletting was not lost on him, however. The loss of Tezoc had awakened a bloodlust in Chimalli that perturbed Cuauhtemoc as much as it saddened him. A grudge that consuming could never be satisfied.

Cuauhtemoc rolled his wrist and studied the procession of captives who had been gathered at the base of the Great Pyramid. As far as he could tell, the vast majority hailed from Tlaxcala. Most went to their deaths with a dignity and grace that inspired grudging respect. However, the *teteo* soldiers failed to summon the same courage and most of them had to be hauled up the stairs by means of rope and brawn.

Why did the *teteo* not understand the honor they were being given with a Flowery Death? What with all their nattering about the glories of heaven and the love of

Jesus, it seemed they had little reason to fear death. Nonetheless, not one teotl seemed eager to leave the present world and some fought against their captors so viciously they had to be clubbed into submission.

Cuauhtemoc picked at a scab on his chest and tried not to breathe in too deeply. What with the heady tang of freshly spilled life water and the rancid stench of *teteo*, keeping his latest meal down had proven challenging. It did not help that many of the captives soiled themselves once they clapped eyes on the sacred block.

A part of him was disgusted they would be so shameless in their final moments. Nonetheless, Cuauhtemoc had led enough men into battle and presided over enough sacrificial rites to know that men met death in a variety of ways. Cuauhtemoc could recognize a scream born from agony better than one born from pleasure, and he knew the same held true for his most trusted warriors. They had to realize, therefore, that most of the *teteo* screams had little to do with pain or surprise. No, they had a much more insidious cause: fear.

The *teteo* viewed death the same way Mexica royalty viewed ignominy, and the revelation unnerved him. The *teteo* would fight even when the odds were hopeless, simply because they feared death too much not to. What would it take to defeat an enemy like that?

"Is something on your mind?" Chimalli asked.

Cuauhtemoc blinked, surprised Chimalli had been able to read him so well. "Nothing," he muttered.

Chimalli grunted but did not press the matter. "Do you think Great Speaker Cuitlahuac will give us leave to pursue the barbarians?"

"I hope so," Chimalli said. "But he may want to keep one of us close. He has much to attend to in Tenochtitlan."

Just thinking about the challenges facing Great Speaker was enough to give Cuauhtemoc a headache. Great Speaker had to make sure the orphans and widows were provided for, that the wounded and infirm were attended to, and that neighboring peoples did not try to take advantage of Tenochtitlan's weakened state. Cuauhtemoc did not envy him in the slightest, but he did worry that Great Speaker Cuitlahuac might not rise to the occasion. He had never been known for a calm, deliberative nature, and Cuauhtemoc prayed that the diadem would temper his worst impulses.

Thus far, it had done little to make him less rash, and Cuitlahuac insisted upon celebrating his new title with a massive sacrifice of captured enemies. In ordinary times, the confirmation ceremony would be the time for a mass sacrifice, but nothing about the past few weeks had been ordinary. While Cuauhtemoc understood Cuitlahuac's desire to celebrate, he wished Great Speaker would dedicate more of his efforts to seeing victory through and less of his efforts to revelry.

"Are you willing to stay behind if Great Speaker does not grant both of us permission?" Chimalli asked.

Cuauhtemoc stiffened. "If I am ordered to stay, I will stay," he said in a level voice.

He prayed to the gods the Great Speaker would not be so cruel. The *teteo* would reach Otampan in a matter of days and when they did, they would be set upon by a massive force of sixteen thousand Mexica warriors. It promised to be a battle remembered by anyone of note, and he would never forgive himself if he did not take part.

A young boy came rushing down the steps of Yopico's Temple and stopped in front of Cuauhtemoc and Chimalli.

"Great Speaker Cuitlahuac requests your presence," the attendant said, his voice cracking as he said the last word.

Cuauhtemoc nodded and followed the boy up the stairs. Attendants who served a Great Speaker were rarely so young, and Cuauhtemoc had never come across one so youthful. Perhaps he was very talented, but it was more likely that he had been inducted into Great Speaker's service on account of expediency. Cuauhtemoc sighed. So many had died during the Flaying Festival and even more had died trying to storm the Palace of Axayacatl— would Tenochtitlan ever truly recover? The recent victory had provided a much-needed salve, but he suspected the trauma inflicted by the *teteo* and the Tlaxcalteca would echo for generations.

Cuauhtemoc crested the last few steps and Cuitlahuac's full profile came into view. He was seated on a magnificent, high-backed chair, but it was his diadem that commanded attention. The Quetzal feathers had come all the way from the Far South, and the green jade sparkled and shimmered like the nighttime sky. A long slash ran down the length of Cuitlahuac's torso, and his calf was wrapped in bandages, but his stoic expression reflected little in the way of pain.

That was to be expected, though. A Great Speaker could not afford to show weakness in front of his guards or attendants, and Cuitlahuac did not lack for either. Two guards stood in front of his throne while three stood behind him. All five of them had donned red face paint and striped orange cloaks, an honor granted only to men who captured a prisoner in single combat. Great Speaker would sooner die than show weakness in front of these men.

Cuauhtemoc and Chimalli stopped an arm's length from the nearest guards and dropped their heads out of reverence for Great Speaker.

"It pleases me that both of you are in good health," Great Speaker said, his voice dry and emotionless.

Cuauhtemoc lifted his head and offered a polite smile. "And it pleases us to see the diadem upon your head. We have every confidence you will do right by the nation."

318

The corner of Great Speaker's lip slanted upward. "I think Huitzilopochtli will be very pleased with the amount of tributes we offer him today," Cuitlahuac said, his eyes bright and his face warm.

"I think it would please him further if we captured the barbarians who escaped Tenochtitlan," replied Cuauhtemoc.

Great Speaker laughed. "Indeed it would. I would not be sending out so many emissaries to our allies if I disagreed. Word of our recent victory has spread to every corner of the One World, and none dare to ignore our summons now. Thousands of warriors are gathering at Otampan, and they will soon take the battle to the *teteo*. As we should have done so long ago."

Cuauhtemoc frowned. He had been skeptical of Motecuhzoma's conciliatory policy toward the *teteo*, but it had proven useful in luring them and their Tlaxcalteca allies into Tenochtitlan. Motecuhzoma erred when he assumed they would reform their ways once he had the chance to charm them, but he had been most wise to recognize they would struggle mightily to escape the city.

Chimalli cleared his throat, and Cuauhtemoc remembered himself. "Yes, it promises to be a most glorious battle, and we would be honored to lend our efforts to the victory," Cuauhtemoc said. He motioned to Chimalli and added, "Both of us would be greatly honored if you would allow us to partake in the battle."

Great Speaker narrowed his eyes. "Is there not honor to be found staying in Tenochtitlan and assisting with reconstruction?"

Cuauhtemoc shifted uneasily. "Of course there is—"

"Our city has suffered grievously on account of the barbarians. In some quarters of the city, *pilli* cannot go out for fear of attack. Some of our most holy sites have been violated. Restoring order will be more difficult if I let men of rank leave the city."

Cuauhtemoc went quiet. To his surprise, Chimalli spoke up. "Order will not take if we cannot give our *altepetl* security. To keep Tenochtitlan safe, we must take all *teteo* and the Tlaxcalteca captive."

Great Speaker turned toward Chimalli. "Do you doubt my ability to keep Tenochtitlan safe?"

A guard standing behind Great Speaker dropped his hand to his *macuahuitl.*

"Only a fool would do so," Cuauhtemoc cut in. "But many will sleep easier once they know all the barbarians have been captured. Let us take a few hundred men to Otampan so that we can help secure victory."

"We have near sixteen thousand warriors at Otampan, and a few hundred more will not make much difference," Great Speaker said. "Put aside your vanity, cousin. I have already sent many men to Otampan, and I cannot spare men who I need in Tenochtitlan. Are your ears closed to the poor old men and the women, to the infants who toddle and crawl? Do not doubt they will suffer if order is not soon restored."

"We do not need a large escort," Chimalli said. "We could both travel with no more than twenty guards each."

Great Speaker rapped his fingers on his thigh. "To travel with so few invites risk."

"A necessary risk," Cuauhtemoc said, surprising himself with the urgency of his voice.

"Necessary?"

"Many of the warriors at Otampan do not hail from Tenochtitlan. They have heard stories of how the *teteo* make battle but have not experienced it themselves. They could benefit from our counsel."

Great Speaker leaned back in his chair and blew out his breath. Were it not for his wounds, Cuauhtemoc suspected that Great Speaker would be leading troops into battle. He always had more appetite for issuing commands than building consensus. "You will have to travel light, if you are to make it to Otampan before battle breaks out," Great Speaker said.

"We need travel with no weapons other than our daggers," Chimalli said. "We can send heavy gear ahead with relay runners."

Great Speaker nodded and turned to Cuauhtemoc. "Are you of the same mind?"

Cuauhtemoc bunched his lips together. To travel without bow or spear meant they could do no hunting on their run, and they would be completely dependent on friendly locals for food. Water would be less of an issue now that the rains had returned, but the roads would be difficult to travel. And if they came across any brigands, they would have little defense against them. "I am," Cuauhtemoc said.

Great Speaker sighed. "You have my permission. Your absence will not be without consequence, though. See to it that the battle at Otampan is a success and return to Tenochtitlan without delay. Our great city has already lost too many warriors to Xicotencatl and Cortés."

~ ~ ~

Garrido shaded his eyes and drew a line in the damp dirt. He always had a good head for figures—Mother told him he knew how to count before he could run—but the sight in front of him beggared belief. Thousands upon thousands of Mexica warriors had gathered in the valley below, the first reports had come in yesterday evening, and the sight chilled him to his core. For days, the column had been hounded by small groups of Mexica warriors, and he had hoped they might find some respite once they took leave of the craggy foothills. It seemed, however, they had run out of the smoke and into the fire.

Try as he might, he could not count the assembled warriors in his head and had to draw lines in the dirt to keep track of all the multitudes. He counted fifteen thousand the first time, but that figure seemed impossibly large so he decided to do a recount. He had not yet finished, but he had already tallied twelve thousand men. He sighed. Even if only half of those men were warriors, they outnumbered the column by a significant margin.

He knew he could count on his Christian brethren to fight until their dying breaths, but he did not know if that would be enough. The Mexica had already wiped out more than half the army and those who had survived the Sad Night still needed time to recover. Less than a week had passed since they had left Tenochtitlan and food had proven scarce. A small helping of horse meat the day before had lifted his spirits some, but he longed for a proper meal of fish and bread.

Did Father suffer the same as him when he went on campaign? He must have. Father had enemies all throughout Kongo. He hoped his brother Henrique had followed his dream and taken the cloth. At least then he would be spared some of the same suffering so common to war. Garrido would never see either of them again in this life, but he trusted that he would see them in the next world.

A twig snapped nearby. Garrido pushed himself off the ground and balanced on one knee. He dropped his hand to his sword hilt and checked his periphery. The bulk of the Mexica army was two leagues away, but he needed to stay alert. For all he knew, the brush-covered foothills could be crawling with Mexica scouts eager to capture Christians fool enough to leave the main company. He backed away from the ledge and scanned the tangled bushes for life.

Behind him, a voice called out, "You got a reason to be out here?"

Garrido let go of his sword hilt and turned toward the soldier approaching from his rear. He furrowed his brow.

Something about the soldier's short hair and lilting accent seemed familiar. The soldier stopped an arm's length from him.

"I know you," the soldier said. "You're a Narváez man, aren't you?"

Garrido nodded, careful not to take his eyes off the crossbow the soldier balanced on his shoulder or the sheathed sword that hung from his hip.

"You clout me over the head the night we took Narváez hostage," the soldier said, his face darkening.

Garrido searched his memory and dug his foot into a soft patch of dirt. If the soldier tried to rush toward him, he would give him a face full of dirt for his efforts. "As I recall it," Garrido said, "you tripped me with your shield. I limped for half a week because of you."

The soldier grunted and extended his arm. "I go by Vitale. How 'bout you?"

Garrido shook Vitale's hand, surprised by the rough feel of his calloused skin. "Call me Juan Garrido."

Vitale looked at him askance. "You some kind of jester?"

Garrido shrugged. Garrido had been his moniker for as long as he could remember, and he no longer found it strange or flattering. "You'll never meet a Christian more serious than I."

Vitale muttered something under his breath and readjusted the crossbow on his shoulder. "How many warriors down there?"

"I counted fifteen thousand," Garrido said.

Vitale cursed and scratched at a scab under his eye. "Madness to attack a force that large."

"Better to fight in the open field than some mountain pass. They are doing us a great favor by letting us come to them."

Vitale furrowed his brow. "Why you think they doin' that?"

"Probably waiting for more supplies and men."

Vitale nodded.

"Fortunate for us the Mexica know nothing of cavalry," Garrido added. "Otherwise, they would never let us make battle on terrain so favorable to horses."

"Unfortunate for us that we needa' fight again." Vitale spat and shook his head. "Barely survived the last battle, and God knows we can't recover what we've lost. The gold is forfeit, our friends are dead..." Vitale trailed off.

He turned away from Garrido and stared at the ground, grinding his teeth and sucking in deep breaths through his nose. Garrido blinked, surprised by his sudden turn of emotion.

Vitale cleared his throat. "That night we first met, you said something about being Kengay, right?"

"I hail from Kongo," Garrido corrected.

Vitale wiped his nose. "Many Moors serve in this expedition. You on friendly terms with any of 'em?"

Garrido laughed. "I am a Christian. Why would I be on friendly terms with Moors? Unless they have accepted the One True Faith, I have no relations with them."

"Most of the Moors who set out with us from Cuba are dead," Vitale said in a flat voice. He fixed his bloodshot eyes on Garrido. "There's a Moor I owe a lot to, but I can't find him nowhere. He's blind in one eye and got a trinket which mean a lot to me."

Garrido arched his brow. He did not know how to make it any clearer to the soldier that he did not keep a close relationship with any of the Moors in the crew. Moreover, it was a mite disturbing to hear a Christian admit to fraternizing with heathens. "I have seen no such man."

Vitale sighed. "What do you think would happen to somebody, if they got left behind?"

They will have their heart torn out, and they will be feasted upon by heathen Indians. Garrido patted his crucifix. "Only God can know."

A look of disgust flashed across Vitale's face, but it was so brief Garrido wondered if he imagined it.

"Found any game?" Garrido asked.

Vitale shook his head. "Saw one rabbit, but my arrow went wide of it. I got much to learn about using a crossbow."

Garrido studied the weapon with a critical eye. Muskets were far more popular in Kongo than crossbows, and he had never understood the appeal of the cumbersome thing. "Is it not your weapon?"

"Some Genoan with a busted wrist lent it to me." Vitale licked his chapped lips. "What you learned with your scouting?"

"We're outnumbered," Garrido said simply. "But as Cortés always says: the more the Moors, the greater the spoils."

Vitale snorted. "Let's get back to the column. Easy to get ambushed out here."

Garrido nodded. The attacks had become more frequent as of late, and he suspected the Mexica warriors were herding the column toward the main army.

Vitale gave him his back and set off for safety. With some trepidation, Garrido fell into step behind the short-haired soldier. He hoped the other men had stouter hearts. Otherwise, cavalry and faith in God would not be enough to win the coming battle.

Otampan Valley

Cortés slowed his bloodied horse to a trot once he reached the thin copse of trees. The other riders did the same. They were nearly a hundred paces away from the fighting, and he trusted that the range, as well as the foliage, would protect them from archers.

His head throbbed so much he could hardly sit up straight, and he was grateful to have a mount under him. He scanned the fallow field for Mexica warriors, watched as the occasional gust of wind flattened the wild grasses. The desiccated trees could not hide a large contingent of men, and the flat landscape afforded few places to hide. Confident there were no enemies nearby, he let the horse catch its breath.

He adjusted his saddle position and studied the battle from afar. The rectangle formation of his men had proven resilient, and the sturdy pikes held the enemy in check. Nonetheless, both the right flank and the backline were losing strength. Porters, servants, and wounded men provided shield cover to the foot soldiers, but Mexica weaponry and simple fatigue had opened up gaping holes in the shield canopy. Worse yet, the Mexica had completely surrounded his army, and the sheer crush of men would soon overwhelm the pike formation. Cortés had minutes to turn the battle, if that.

A quick snap of his wrist flicked the blood off his borrowed sword. He checked his steed for wounds. The scrawny packhorse, requisitioned for lack of better options, was lathered with sweat, yet he espied no serious injuries. He trusted it to make another charge. But then what? The cavalry had ripped gaping swathes in the enemy's formation, but the Mexica had yet to quit the field.

Cortés' cavalry consisted of only two dozen horses, and smashing through the enemy line repeatedly had taken a toll on the horses as well as the riders. His elbow was numb from a hit he had taken on his shield, and his lance had broken hours earlier. They had been battling since early morning, and he was not sure how much more he could ask of his men.

A glittering on a small mound caught his gaze, and he shaded his eyes to peer into the distance. A small group of men, located in the enemy's rear, were waving a feathered standard back and forth. Nothing on the battlefield could match it in size or prominence.

He turned towards his officers. Only five had joined his sally, and he considered Salamanca to be the squadron's best horsemen. Nonetheless, he also put great stock by the abilities of Sandoval, Ávila, Pedro, and Olid. Would they join him for a charge against the standard-bearer, though? The standard-bearer would be well-defended and charging deep into the enemy's rear did involve considerable risk.

Cortés straightened in his saddle. El Cid would not hesitate in the face of danger, and neither could he. If his officers did not join him, he would make the charge alone. He pointed at the enemy's rear and said to his officers, "The battle standard is our target."

He spurred his horse into a canter and set off for the battle standard. A loud rumbling of hooves let him know the others had fallen in behind him, and the knots in his stomach slowly came undone as they charged across the empty field. His men had heaped bitter recriminations on him for the debacle that was the causeway retreat, but he would secure victory for them once more, and they would forgive him his mistakes.

They were thirty paces away by the time the battle chieftains realized they were being charged. Panicked men fled for safety, but the standard bearer stood his ground and turned to face them. His guards huddled closer to him, readying their clubs and their shields.

Cortés allowed himself a small smile. If the Mexica had pikes and gunpowder weapons, huddling might have made sense, but it made little sense for men armed with light weapons. He kicked his horse into a gallop and felt the rush of wind known only to riders. He raised his sword and shouted out a battle cry. They were ten paces away now, and he half-expected the Mexica guards to scatter. Instead, they rushed forward en masse.

The surprise charge did them little good. Cortés and his fellow riders burst through their line like water through a ruptured dam—not one warrior managed to stand against them. In less time than it took to call out the blessed name of Saint James, he split open a man's head with a slash of his sword, parried a blow from a light club, and bowled over a burly man with the flank of his horse.

Foreign cries filled the air. The sudden eruption of unintelligible voices distracted him none, and Cortés kept all his attention focused on the standard bearer. Anything that obstructed his path was cut down or knocked aside.

The standard bearer leapt to the side, but he did not move with nearly enough speed. He took the mare's shoulder right in the chest, and the violent collision snapped the battle standard's wooden handle.

Salamanca, following closely in Cortés' wake, leaned over to retrieve the standard and raised it to his chest. A magnificent bliss enveloped Cortés, but it was short-lived; a club smashed into his hand and bent two fingers so far back they almost touched his forearm.

Fiery tendrils of pain shot up his arm, and his breath came in short gasps. He turned the horse with his knee, aware now that he had charged too deep into the enemy's line. He slashed at everything around him with his one good hand and urged the mare forward with vicious kicks. She bolted forward like iron shot from a cannon, brutally shoving aside anything and everything in her path.

The horse emerged from the unruly crowd with a light spear sticking out of her armored flank, but she did not slow to a trot until they were almost fifty paces out. He glanced behind him.

None of the men in his squadron had sustained serious injury, but they trailed far behind him. Salamanca was nearest and carried the colorful battle standard under his arm. Cortés grinned, the pain in his hand forgotten, and slowed his horse so that Salamanca could catch up with him. He half-wished that some of the Mexica warriors would break rank to chase after the battle standard, but none dared to do so.

Instead, they screamed and shouted at one another. He understood little of their tongue, but he could recognize the confusion that was sweeping through the ranks. The onslaught of arrows, darts, slings, and spears that had been raining down on his troops for hours on end finally began to lighten. His heart swelled.

The warriors did not know where to aim without the battle standard!

Better still, they had no idea where to apply pressure. Reinforcements had lent some much needed heft to his army's right flank and the backline, but the left flank had weakened considerably. If the Mexica rushed forward with enough men, they could break through the pike formation and engage his men in hand-to-hand combat. But instead of rushing forward en masse, the Mexica warriors were peeling away to attack the reinforced backline.

A group of warriors ventured too far from the main body, and they were attacked by a pack of war dogs.

Cortés crossed himself. If God was kind, most of the mastiffs would survive the battle.

Salamanca pulled up beside Cortés and offered the battle standard. He reached for it with reverential awe. When he was younger, Father had regaled him with stories of the Legionnaires, and the lengths the Romans would go to in order to recover a battle standard. They would burn villages to the ground and they would charge into hostile territory, all to recover their sacred eagles. An *aquila* was the pride and joy of every legion, but the battle standard Salamanca had seized was so much more than that. It was the lifeblood of the Mexica army, and they could not coordinate movements without it.

Cortés pulled his hand back. "You keep it, Salamanca. You earned it."

Salamanca beamed like a boy invited to his first hunt. The rest of the riders joined them a few moments later, and the once mighty Mexica army descended into chaos.

Cortés glanced at his fellow officers. Strewn with blood and gore, their armor was dented in more places than he could count, but none had sustained serious injury as far as he could tell. "Ready your weapons," he said. "We must relieve pressure on the left flank before it fails."

The officers assented with small nods and weary mutters. Cortés took a deep breath and kicked the packhorse into a canter. He doubted the horse would survive the battle, but it did not matter. His army would survive and so long as he had an army, the campaign could carry on.

~ ~ ~

Cuauhtemoc could not believe his luck. He, with the help of Chimalli and others, had taken Xicotencatl captive! As a prize, the Tlaxcalteca warrior was more valuable than Cortés or Malintze, and Cuauhtemoc thanked the gods he had been deemed worthy of the great honor.

He tightened his grip on Xicotencatl's wrist and trudged forward with Xicotencatl's arm draped across his shoulders. Nearby warriors recognized Xicotencatl's limp figure and let up a great cheer as Cuauhtemoc and his guards forced their way through the maze of Mexica warriors. He did not join in the revelry, focusing instead on carrying Xicotencatl to the outskirts of formation, but every yip and holler made his heart leap with joy.

Xicotencatl groaned something inaudible, and Cuauhtemoc allowed himself a small smile. Xicotencatl had taken a club to the stomach and a hard kick to the head, but Cuauhtemoc hoped he still had the presence of mind to understand the cheering.

Over the next few days, Xicotencatl would be subjected to many gruesome rites and Cuauhtemoc wanted him to be conscious for all of it. Tlaxcala needed to suffer for allying with the teteo, and Cuauhtemoc could think of no better person to punish than Xicotencatl. He would be given a Flower Death, of course, but he would not be honored with drink beforehand. No, he would tortured in the most horrific ways possible and then have his heart torn out for a cheering audience. Never again would men of Tlaxcala contemplate violence against Tenochtitlan, not when they learned the fate of Xicotencatl.

Loud screams rent the air, and Cuauhtemoc snapped his head to the side as the hornless stags barreled through the Mexica army. Men were thrown aside like tufts of cotton, and panic swept through formation. A hard push unbalanced Cuauhtemoc. He fell to the ground, dragging Xicotencatl down with him.

Cuauhtemoc's head collided with a shield and stars filled his vision. Mere moments after he crashed to the ground, a wounded man collapsed on top of him. Cuauhtemoc tried to push himself up, but a foot caught his elbow, and he lost his balance. Another man landed on top of him, driving the air from his lungs. Thankfully, guards soon came to his rescue and hurled aside the wounded men to pull Cuauhtemoc to his feet.

Cuauhtemoc leaned on a nearby man for support while Chimalli shouted something at him. Still dazed, Cuauhtemoc could not make any sense of his words. He furrowed his brow and strained his ears. It sounded as if Chimalli had said the battle standard had fallen, but that could not be right. He glanced at the horizon.

A chill passed through him. He could not see the battle standard anywhere. He blinked and rubbed his eyes, confused. Never in all of living memory had a standard fallen during battle.

He sobered like a man doused with cold water. He searched the nearby faces for Xicotencatl, sure that he would find him among his guard or splayed out on the ground. But like the battle standard, Xicotencatl had disappeared. Panic seized Cuauhtemoc. How had everything gone so wrong?

Frantic, Cuauhtemoc swiveled around. Off in the distance, he spotted a limping figure. When the stags came stampeding through moments before, they had ripped a bloody hole through Mexica formation. Xicotencatl must have taken advantage of the disarray to run for safety.

The sight of his fleeing captive quickened his pulse, but he did not allow himself to give chase just yet. He needed to think. If he took a large contingent of men to chase after Xicotencatl, the mounted riders would be sure to notice them. No matter how many men he took with him, leaving formation would be dangerous. Letting him escape might be the best course of action. His stomach tightened. No, they had to recapture Xicotencatl, and they had to raise the standard again.

"Send some men to raise up the battle standard again," Cuauhtemoc said to Chimalli. "You and I will recapture Xicotencatl."

Cuauhtemoc sprinted after Xicotencatl. Chimalli fell in behind him, along with two guards. Cuauhtemoc was tempted to dismiss the guards, but he did not waste his breath. His energy was flagging, and he did not mind sharing the glory with either of them.

A stitch forced Cuauhtemoc to slow, and the two guards pulled ahead. They were twins, if he remembered correctly. One had just started a family; one had lost all his family in the Flaying Festival massacre. If such men could not be counted upon to fight bravely, none could.

Cuauhtemoc focused his attention on Xicotencatl. He was eighty paces ahead, but they were gaining on him with every footstep. Xicotencatl shot a quick glance backward and their eyes connected. For some strange reason, Xicotencatl smiled at him and started clapping his hands together frantically. Cuauhtemoc clenched his teeth together and forced himself to run faster.

Xicotencatl had nowhere to hide. Wild grass had taken root in the fallow field, but it reached no higher than Cuauhtemoc's thigh and would provide little in the way of cover. Xicotencatl could try to swim for safety if he made it to the river, but that was more than half a long-run away. He tripped on something and fell to the ground.

Xicotencatl stood and tried to whistle. Cuauhtemoc furrowed his brow. Who was he trying to signal? The Tlaxcalteca and the *teteo* were much too far away to come to his rescue, and the mounted riders were far more concerned with the battle than him.

Xicotencatl clapped his hands together repeatedly, wiped his lips on his shoulder, and stuck two fingers in his mouth. The piercing whistle made Cuauhtemoc start, and he tightened his grip on his *macuahuitl*.

It did not matter who Xicotencatl was trying to signal. They could not help him now. Cuauhtemoc was only fifteen paces away, and Xicotencatl had no weapon to defend himself. Even an Eagle warrior could not triumph against those odds, and Xicotencatl had to be delusional if he thought he could fight them off.

A dark blur of movement in the grass caught Cuauhtemoc's eye. He opened his mouth to shout a warning, but it was too late. A striped dog, big as a fawn but vicious as a jaguar, leapt into the air and bowled over a guard in the flutter of an eyelid. He screamed as the dog tore his flesh to shreds, but his loud protests soon gave way to a heart-rending gurgle.

The other guard rushed to his brother's aid and shouted a vile curse. Once again, the dog launched itself into the air and pulled the man to the ground by sinking its teeth deep into his unprotected shoulder.

Cuauhtemoc drew his shield close and grabbed Chimalli to hold him back. "He cannot be saved," Cuauhtemoc shouted. "Raise your shield—we must protect each other now."

Anger flashed across Chimalli's face, but he did as commanded. Cuauhtemoc sank into a crouch, and Chimalli did the same. He shot a quick glance at the Mexica formation. His countrymen were much too far away to help him now; signaling would be pointless.

The guard's agonized screaming stopped, and Cuauhtemoc tightened his grip on the shield. The beast would come for them now. He blinked to clear sweat from his eyes. The wind picked up, and he wrinkled his nose as the smell of offal and fresh-spilled life water overwhelmed his senses. He breathed through his mouth and scanned the wild grass for the dog.

"Is that you, Cuauhtemoc?" Xicotencatl asked.

Cuauhtemoc shot Xicotencatl a quick glance. Xicotencatl had armed himself with a *macuahuitl* and stood a mere ten paces away. Cuauhtemoc wanted nothing more than to rush toward him, but the dog kept him in check.

Xicotencatl adjusted his loin cloth and made his way toward a dead guard. "Tell me, how many Tlaxcalteca did you kill when your people invaded my country?"

"That was many years ago," Cuauhtemoc said.

Xicotencatl laughed and bent down to pick up something. "That makes little difference to me."

Xicotencatl raised himself to full height again. Cuauhtemoc figured he would pick up a shield, but Xicotencatl did something far worse: he picked up a knife. Cuauhtemoc cursed. A weapon like that would be easy to throw. Cuauhtemoc turned to face Xicotencatl.

He checked his periphery. He did not see the dog, but the grass was so high it could be hiding anywhere.

"Chimalli," Cuauhtemoc whispered, "we must—"

The dog burst out of the wild grass and leaped at Cuauhtemoc's unprotected flank. He moved the shield in front of him moments before the beast smacked into him, but the sheer weight of the animal knocked him backward.

A flint knife collided with his shoulder blade, and Cuauhtemoc fell to a knee a few paces from the slavering beast. It bounded toward him and lunged for his neck.

Chimalli swung his club toward the dog and gave it a glancing blow to the head. The dog snarled and clamped its jaws around Chimalli's shin. He screamed and hit the dog again. It yelped but did not relent. Cuauhtemoc smashed his *macuahuitl* down on the dog's back, drawing another sharp cry. Chimalli hit the dog in the head, and the beast finally went still.

A sudden rushing alerted Cuauhtemoc to danger, and he pulled his shield close. A wet smack made his breath catch. He glanced at Chimalli, and his eyes went wide. Xicotencatl was standing right behind him, and his

336

macuahuitl was buried deep inside Chimalli's neck. He gurgled something and swayed on his feet.

Cuauhtemoc's heart stopped and time slowed to a crawl as he watched Chimalli buckle and fall. Before he even knew what he was doing, Cuauhtemoc lunged toward Xicotencatl. The Tlaxcalteca warrior easily jumped out of the way and ripped out the *macuahuitl* that had been holding in Chimalli's life water. Cuauhtemoc slashed again, but Xicotencatl ducked underneath his swing and hit Cuauhtemoc with the flat of his *macuahuitl*. Cuauhtemoc staggered to the side and took a moment to catch his breath.

Xicotencatl bent over double to suck air down. His face was lathered with sweat, and his breath came in ragged gasps. Cuauhtemoc retreated a step and shifted his shield. Quick as a flash, Xicotencatl lunged toward him and swung the *macuahuitl* toward Cuauhtemoc's exposed ribcage. Not a moment too soon, Cuauhtemoc raised his shield. The *macuahuitl* smashed into it with so much force both wood and glass splintered.

Xicotencatl tugged on the hilt of the weapon to dislodge it from the shield, and Cuauhtemoc swung his *macuahuitl* upward. A sudden bolt of pain seized his arm, slowing his swing and making him cry out. Xicotencatl jumped backward and escaped with nothing more than a small slash on his stomach.

Cuauhtemoc gritted his teeth and waited for the pain in his shoulder to die down. Instead, it grew worse, like a blaze in the midst of dry season. He could not beat Xicotencatl, not in his current state. There was only one thing left to do. Cuauhtemoc straightened and threw his *macuahuitl* to the ground.

Xicotencatl furrowed his brow and cocked his head at him. "Why are you yielding?"

Cuauhtemoc let out a deep breath. "Because we should not be fighting."

Xicotencatl stared at him askance.

"The hornless stags have decimated the army," Cuauhtemoc said. "Our battle standard has fallen, and we have nothing to show for all our fighting. How did the Tlaxcalteca army fare against those hornless stags?"

Xicotencatl stiffened. "Those horrid beasts killed more Tlaxcalteca warriors than I can count."

Cuauhtemoc's heart quickened. Perhaps they could find common cause. "You must wish to see the *teteo* brought low as much as I do. Tlaxcala and Tenochtitlan must fight under one banner—otherwise, we will never be able to stand against the hornless stags."

Xicotencatl shook his head. "No army can stand before the *teteo* weapons." Xicotencatl squeezed the hilt of his *macuahuitl* and took a step forward.

Cuauhtemoc gulped but did not retreat. "No one nation can defeat the *teteo*, but many nations can," Cuauhtemoc said. "How many *teteo* died trying to escape Tenochtitlan?" Anger flashed across Xicotencatl's face, but he stayed silent. "Your people almost defeated the *teteo*," Cuauhtemoc added. "A few nights ago, we almost defeated the *teteo*. Who is to say we could not triumph, if we worked together?"

Xicotencatl laughed. "My countrymen would never make a pact with your countrymen. We have been enemies for too long to make common cause now."

"We were not always enemies," Cuauhtemoc said, desperation coloring his voice. "My people once called the Great North home. So, too, did your people. We have both won great acclaim throughout the One World but everything we have built, everything we have preserved, will be destroyed if we do not kill the *teteo*."

Xicotencatl snorted. "You urge me to look ahead, but am I to forget all the hurt and suffering your people have inflicted upon Tlaxcala? The sanctions, the wars, the tribute demands?"

Cuauhtemoc sighed. "I cannot tell you what to do. But you know as well as I that the *teteo* will never look upon us as equals. I am told they have taken Tlaxcalteca *pilli* for wives. I hear your own daughter was given to the fire-haired *teotl*."

Xicotencatl's face hardened. "Do not speak of my daughter."

Cuauhtemoc hid a smile. Every warrior, even one hard as glass, had a vulnerability. "It seems the rumors are true, then," Cuauhtemoc said. "Tell me, how much longer until she brings a half-breed into the world? Could you call such a thing your grand-child?"

Xicotencatl raised his *macuahuitl*, and Cuauhtemoc froze in place. He closed his eyes and waited for Xicotencatl to strike him down. To his surprise, Xicotencatl did not oblige. Cuauhtemoc opened his eyes and stared at the Tlaxcalteca general. His shoulders rose and fell with every breath he took, and he quavered like a star-mountain on the verge of eruption. After a long pause, Xicotencatl sighed and wiped sweat away from his brow. He lowered his *macuahuitl* and fixed his gaze on Cuauhtemoc.

"Get back to your countrymen," Xicotencatl ordered. "If you really mean to make a pact, you will come to Tlaxcala with an official delegation. We will discuss terms, then."

Cuauhtemoc let out his breath. He kneeled so he could pick up the knife that Xicotencatl had thrown at him. Xicotencatl narrowed his eyes and lowered himself into a fighting position. Cuauhtemoc shook his head and reached for the braid tucked behind his ear. He stretched it taught and cut off the tail end. Still kneeling, he threw the severed honorific to Xicotencatl.

"It took many years of fighting to earn that braid," Cuauhtemoc said. "Return it to me when I am in Tlaxcala."

Xicotencatl nodded and tied the braid around the hilt of his *macuahuitl*. Cuauhtemoc stood and made his way back to the Mexica army. His people had lost today's battle, but there was still a chance they could win the war.

Tlaxcala Province

Malintze wrapped her hands around the warm clay cup and took a sip of the frothy drink. Plain hot chocolate was much too bitter for her taste, and she had been pleased to learn the villagers had flavored the drink with honey. She licked her lips and let out a small sigh.

In a few days, the army would reach the capital of Tlaxcala and when they did, she would once again be expected to act as an intermediary. Perhaps some of the Tlaxcalteca dignitaries would question Cortés about the Sad Night, but she suspected that most of them would ask only about the Otampan battle. Distinguished statesmen always fixated on the great victories, never the shameful defeats. She understood the impulse all too well—almost a week had passed since the battle, but her thoughts often drifted back to the terror and jubilation of that day, like a moth to an open flame.

Malintze took another sip of her drink. She had seen little of the sun today and wondered if it might be better to stay under cover. The gray overcast sky did not portend warm weather, and the return of the rains meant a downpour could happen at any time. She sucked in a deep breath and closed her eyes. Perhaps later she would go inside. For now, she wanted to enjoy the feel of the cool breeze and take in the sight of the distant mountains. Besides, sitting outside let her listen in on the camp squabbles, and she had little else for entertainment these days.

Per usual, the Christians were arguing about gold. Cortés had asked the survivors to pool their resources so the company could purchase new supplies and new men in Cuba. So far as she could tell, none of the *teteo* objected to his plan. Rather, they objected to paying for it.

Seldom one to be dissuaded by vociferous protest, Cortés ordered the men to relinquish their gold and dedicated all his morning to collection efforts. With Pedro ever at his side, even the most disgruntled dissidents could do little besides grumble as they handed over their ugly ingots to Cortés.

Malintze traced the contours of the cup with her calloused thumb. Cortés had found a new group of men to cajole, and she could hear snatches of conversation if she concentrated. Then again, she could have followed the conversation even if her ears were stuffed with cotton.

Simply looking at Cortés, seeing that his bruised face still radiated warmth and friendliness, was enough to know they had not been conversing long. Cortés had a habit of offering compliments before commands, but his charm was like a morning mist: it did not last long and left little trace.

Once he concluded his blandishments were not producing the desired effect, his expression would turn cold and predatory. Any pretense of friendship would be abandoned, all honeyed words forgotten; veiled threats and curt orders would be given. And if all else failed, Cortés would fall back on violence, a thing as familiar to him as the word of his Holy book.

Cortés raised his maimed hand as if he were getting ready to strike the recalcitrant soldier. To her surprise, he clapped his hand down on the man's shoulder. She furrowed her brow. It was unlike Cortés to initiate physical intimacy so early in conversation. Malintze stared at his hand. Two of the fingers were bent at an odd angle. He had received the injury during the battle at Otampan, but she assumed he was on the mend.

344

Her eyes drifted upward. A visor hid most of his face from view, but she could spot drops of blood in his beard. Her stomach tightened as he tried and failed to make words. His eyes went wide, then stark white as they rolled backward. Before anyone could even try to catch him, Cortés collapsed to the ground.

Malintze jumped to her feet, spilling her drink. The hot contents of the cup singed her skin, but she did not pay the pain any mind and ran to Cortés. His men gathered around him, and the holdouts slunk away while the others were distracted. Malintze squeezed past the guards and stopped a pace from Cortés.

One of Cortés' guards dropped to a knee and removed Cortés helmet. The sight made her sick to her stomach. Weals and bruises covered his face, and his hair was matted with dried blood. The guard laid a hand on Cortés' forehead.

"He's hot to the touch," the guard whispered. "He has fever."

Malintze's breath caught. Soldiers gathered nearby shot each other worried looks. The *teteo* had lost over a hundred men to fever since the beginning of the campaign, and many considered it a death sentence.

Cortés muttered something unintelligible. The guard tilted his head and placed his ear above Cortés' mouth.

"I think he's saying water," the guard said.

Malintze snatched a water skin from a nearby man and handed it to the guard. The guard eased Cortés' lips open and dripped water into his mouth. Cortés lay still as a corpse as he did so, and the guards muttered amongst each other. Panic welled in her breast, and she swayed on her feet. The world was spinning too fast. It needed to slow down. Everything needed to slow down.

"Go fetch a physician," Pedro mumbled to no one in particular. He sighed and cocked his head to study Cortés' supine figure. "Bring a priest also." Some inner voice told

345

Malintze she should listen to Pedro, but her body refused to comply. She stood rooted to the spot, ensconced in a cocoon of denial and delusion, sure that she was dreaming. In a louder voice, Pedro said, "I am the captain-general now, and I will not be ignored."

Malintze blinked. The breath rushed from her lungs as if she had been kicked in the stomach. She could think of no worse man to lead the expedition. Cortés was not without his faults, but at least he had some ability to curb his violent impulses, some concept of honor. Pedro was little more than a violent brute, a coward who lied about abandoning his own men during the flight from Tenochtitlan.

She tore her eyes away from Cortés and locked eyes with Pedro. "You are the captain-general until Cortés wakes up."

Pedro's face soured, and he shot her a withering glare. Her insides chilled and she turned away. Unsure what to say or do, she made for a nearby hut. She disappeared behind it and her composure broke.

She brought a trembling hand to her mouth to stifle the sobs. Pedro would try to use her as she had been used before. He had no interest in her linguistic talents or her intellect; his interest in her had always been carnal. The taste of bile filled her mouth. If Pedro tried to lay a hand on her, he would regret it until the end of his days.

But what if a knife was not enough to stop him? In that case, she would have no choice but to seek refuge with the Tlaxcalteca. If they would have her. The *pilli* of Tlaxcala had extended her great respect in her duties as translator, but she had no idea how they would treat her if she came to them as something else.

Malintze took a deep breath to steel herself. She thought back to her final conversation with Motecuhzoma. He had warned her. He told her not to make assumptions about what lay beyond the bend, but she had ignored him. Freedom, independence, and status were at hand then—there had been no need to heed his warning. She cursed herself for being a fruitless tree and thought about what she needed to do next.

Cortés still had breath in his body and could soon recover. There was no need to panic or seek out refuge yet. If the worst came to pass, she would make her own way, same as always. The campaign would carry on regardless of Cortés. It had too much forward momentum to be stopped now—too much blood had been spilled to go back to peace and amity.

Malintze fixed her gaze on the distant horizon. Towering mountains dominated the landscape, obstacles she had overcome before, and the great sea lay somewhere beyond that. She had no idea what tomorrow would bring, or the day after, but she had no intention of meekly accepting whatever life threw at her. Regardless of what lay beyond the next bend, she would confront it with bravery and strength.

No matter what, she would survive and the fight would continue.

Historical note

Historical fiction is a tough genre. In almost every other genre of literature, authors can invent their own rules and color outside the lines because they have created the world. In historical fiction, we are working to recreate a world which means we have to hew much closer to the established facts.

So how do we discover the facts? We consult the sources. Unfortunately, not every source can be trusted. Cortés' letters make for interesting reading, but there's no reason we should consider his account the unfiltered truth. After all, Cortés admits to deceit in his own retelling and even remarks in one letter that "I had not slept for sixty days." I am no expert when it comes to matters of sleep, but I have some doubts about that statement. Cortés also wrote that he persuaded Motecuhzoma to surrender with an eloquent speech and a few armed men, but modern-day historians are extremely skeptical of this claim.

In the interest of realism, I have offered an alternative explanation as to why Motecuhzoma surrendered himself to Spanish captivity and used the mass poisoning storyline to help explain why Motecuhzoma tolerated Cortés and company for so long. To be fair, my alternative explanation does have some drawbacks. While the Mexica were very knowledgeable about local poisons, there's nothing I can point to in the historical record that makes it clear that Motecuhzoma was definitely planning a mass poisoning. Similarly, I cannot point to anything that indicates the Spanish and the Tlaxcalteca raided any palaces prior to the Flaying Festival Massacre, but it's not as if either of them were opposed to taking high-born people captive. On the subject of raiding, it is worth noting that Cortés and company probably took dozens of *pilli* hostage during their time in Tenochtitlan. I opted to not mention those other hostages for the sake of narrative clarity. I am reminded all the time that I ask readers to keep track of lots of names and peoples, so I try to make things easier when appropriate.

As for Motecuhzoma's death and the speech he gave upon Cortés' arrival in Tenochtitlan, I did my best to combine the popular theories in academia, but it's worth nothing that both matters are still hotly debated in historical circles. I should also note that I left many well-documented events out of The Bend of the River. I did so primarily for narrative reasons. To recount all the battles in the Tlaxcala campaign, or all the sorties that took place during the siege of Axayacatl's Palace, would have significantly lengthened the book and weakened the novel's narrative energy.

In some cases, I inserted characters into situations they probably would not have been part of. For example, Chichimecatecle very likely stayed in Tlaxcala during the march on Tenochtitlan but I included him in the raid scene because he will be an important character in the final installment of the Tenochtitlan Trilogy.

My aim with my writing is to put forward a narrative that is both plausible and compelling, and I consulted numerous resources to this end. Having said that, I do not intend for my work to be taken as the definitive account of the Spanish-Mexica war. Readers who want to learn more about this event ought to reference the resources mentioned below.

When it comes to secondary sources, Matthew Restall's "When Montezuma Met Cortés" is the book I leaned on the most. Nonetheless, The Bend of the River is an amalgam of many secondary sources and I also consulted "Inga Clendinnen's Aztecs: An Interpretation," Matthew Wills "The Mexica Didn't Believe the Conquistadors Were Gods," and Thelma D. Sullivan's

English translation of "Nahuatl Proverbs, Conundrums, and Metaphors, Collected By Sahagun," Marcy Norton's "Tasting Empire: Chocolate and the European Internalization of Mesoamerican Aesthetics," Manuel Aguilar-Moreno's "Aztec Architecture - Part 1," Restall's "The Murder of Moctezuma," Thelma D. Sullivan's "The Arms and Insignia of the Mexica," Gonzalo M. Sanchez's "Did Emperor Moctezuma II's Head Injury and Subsequent Death Hasten the Fall of the Aztec Nation?," Agustín Palacios' "(Dis)Claiming Mestizofilia: Chicana/os Disarticulating Euromestizaje," Michael Lopez's "A History of the Women of Mexico and Their Agency: Goddesses, Queens, Translators, and Nuns," Frederick A. Ober's "Hernando Cortés, The Conqueror of Mexico," and Kathleen Ann Myers' "In the Shadow of Cortés, Conversations Along the Route of Conquest."

When it comes to primary sources, I found the "Lienzo de Tlaxcala," "Codex Cozcatzin," "Codex Fejérváry-Mayer," the "Tovar Codex," Casas' "A Brief Account of the Destruction of the Indies," Thomas Nicolas' English translation of "The Pleasant Historie of the Conquest of the Weast India, Now Called New Spayne," and "The Conquistadors: First-Person Accounts of the Conquest of Mexico" the most helpful when it came to writing The Bend of the River.

When it comes to podcasts, articles, and videos, Flashpoint's History "Reconquista Podcast," Our Fake History's "Did the Aztecs Think Cortés Was a God, Part Two," "Weapon Masters - Atlatl vs Steel Armor," BBC's "Mexico City's Underground World", NPR's Aztec 'Tower Of Skulls' Reveals Women, Children Were Sacrificed, Reuter's "Gold bar found beneath Mexico City street was part of Moctezuma's treasure," NPR's "500 Years Later, The Spanish Conquest Of Mexico Is Still Being Debated," Science Magazine's "It wasn't just

350

Greece: Archaeologists Find Early Democratic Societies in the Americas," and Erin Facer's "Food fight: How a community in Mexico used food to resist the Aztec empire" the most helpful when it came to writing The Bend of the River.

Eagle-eyed readers may notice that I omitted mention of the sources that I referenced in The Serpent and the Eagle. This is a deliberate omission on my part. I still referenced many of the sources when writing The Bend of the River but in the interest of avoiding redundancy, I have only listed unique mentions here.

As for spelling, I should mention there is considerable disagreement amongst sources. In some cases, I use the Spanish spelling for an indigenous word. The Nahuatl way to write out Cholula would be Chollolan. I opted to use the Spanish spelling because that's how it shows up on most maps, and I always enjoy it when readers can connect places from my series to real-life locations. Tetzcoco is often spelled Texcoco, but I went with Tetzcoco to make it less likely that readers could confuse the word with Tlaxcala.

When it comes to the drawings, please keep in mind they are artistic renderings. The ruins at Cempoala are intact, so those can be recreated with a fair degree of accuracy. However, the pyramid at Cholula has been buried under grass and dirt for centuries now so that sketch is a bit more imagined.

Last but not least, I want to mention that little is known about Juan Garrido's early life. Some historians claim he was royalty, others contend that he came from a humble background and was a servant at one point. I chose to give him a royal background because I figured it would be a good way to impart information to readers about African politics at the onset of the Trans-Atlantic slave trade.

Note to readers

In the interests of accuracy, I should note which names I changed. Cotton Flower is an English translation of Tecuichpotzin. Some scholars contend the translation should be lord's daughter or princess, but I went with Cotton Flower to avoid confusion. I should also mention that Milintica is referred to as Tlacotzin in most historical sources. While the spelling changes depending upon the source, a part of me does wonder if I should have just used the name Tlacotzin for Milintica.

For those wondering why I went with the latter, I did so for reasons related to pronunciation and translation. In some cases, I shortened difficult names to make them easier for readers. For example, Ixtli should be Ixtlilxochitl and Catzin should be Maxixcatzin. Whenever possible, I like to use English translations for the difficult Nahuatl words but sometimes the English translations are just as distracting. In the case of Maxixcatzin, I think the English translation would have been especially distracting. With some of the very minor characters, I opted to leave their names unchanged. I figure it is alright to ask readers to manage with a very unfamiliar name three or four times, but asking readers to do so many times over is a bit much.

If I had to start the Tenochtitlan Trilogy from scratch, I would probably give Tezoc and Chimalli different names. After all, these are characters I could not find names for in the historical sources so my main concern was picking something that was either linguistically appropriate or symbolically meaningful. As a reader, I can sometimes get confused when I am reading a scene where an Alex interacts with an Anna so I can understand if some readers may have been confused by scenes where Chimalli interacted with Cuauhtemoc or Cuitlahuac or both. My sincere apologies to readers who I confused.

I chose the name Chimalli on account of the English translation but his story arc took a different direction than I expected so I may have been better off choosing a different name. In fiction, characters don't always cooperate the way we want them to. In any case, I encourage readers to consult dictionaries for name translations. Whenever I have the chance to give a character a name, I strive to give them a name that is meaningful in some way and astute readers may notice that the Tenochtitlan Trilogy contains quite a few Easter Eggs.

Whether or not you enjoyed these Easter Eggs, I enjoy hearing from readers and humbly ask you to post a review online. Leaving a review helps a great deal with finding the proper audience and every review, good or bad, helps.

Acknowledgments

The Bend of the River, like The Serpent and the Eagle, is not something I would have been able to write on my own. My friends and my family have been extraordinarily supportive of my writing ambitions, and I owe a special debt of gratitude to many.

First and foremost, I would like to thank my mother. Despite my many entreaties not to, she keeps buying my books. I also owe thanks to my godparents and to my sister, Mona, and my cousins Santi and Sylvie. Additionally, I would like to thank my Casey, Cailin, Armand, Jake, Lilly, Helen Hollick, Chris, Tom, Charles, Sam, Adrienne Terblanche, Gina, Herman, Beverly, Katie, Dannie, Pat, Brittany, Alex, Maria, Aditya, Aaron, Mary, James, George, Joe, Arthur, Laura, Devante, Paul, Alura, and Martha. The social media mentions and reviews really do help.

I also owe thanks to the authors who were kind enough to provide me advanced reviews for my work. Established authors have good reason to be wary of attaching their names to new authors, and I cannot say enough how much I appreciate the good will that Kathleen O'Neal Gear, Zoe Saadia, Matthew Restall, Ronald Wright, Andrew Rowen, K.M. Pohlkamp, and N.D. Jones have extended me. The visual arts community has been very kind to me as well, and I owe a great thanks to Anna McKinsey for the sketchings and thanks to Alamtwaha for the cover art. The painting featured on the cover of my work, The Battle at Otumba, comes from the Kislak collection.

Last but not least, I would like to thank Ms. Patterson. I have been coming to her for writing advice since fifth grade, and I am incredibly grateful for all the help she has given me. Public education works because of great teachers like her.